CREEK COUNTRY SAGA
Book 4

Bitter Eyes No More

Drawn by the Frost Moon

APRIL W GARDNER

BigSpringPress

Drawn by the Frost Moon: Bitter Eyes No More
©2017 by April W Gardner

Cover design: Roseanna White Designs
Cover model: Karina Infante
Model's attire: Therese Williams
Big Spring Press logo: Karen Gardner

Scripture quotations taken from the King James Version.

Library of Congress Control Number: 2017902609
ISBN-13: 978-1-945831-03-4
ISBN-10: 1-945831-03-0

Published by Big Spring Press
San Antonio, Texas

Printed in the United States of America.

To Morgan, the sunshine in my life.

Thus, speaketh the LORD of hosts, saying, Execute true judgment, and shew mercy and compassions every man to his brother. (Zechariah 7:9)

The Lord hath appeared of old unto me, saying, Yea, I have loved thee with an everlasting love: therefore, with lovingkindness have I drawn thee. (Jeremiah 31:3)

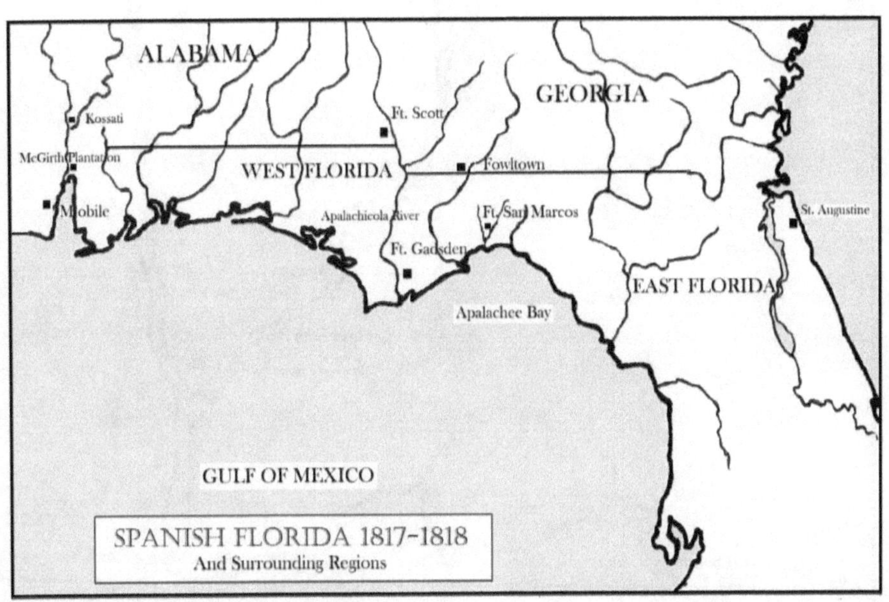
ALABAMA
GEORGIA
Kossati
Ft. Scott
McGirth Plantation
WEST FLORIDA
Fowltown
Mobile
Apalachicola River
Ft. San Marcos
St. Augustine
Ft. Gadsden
EAST FLORIDA
Apalachee Bay
GULF OF MEXICO
SPANISH FLORIDA 1817–1818
And Surrounding Regions

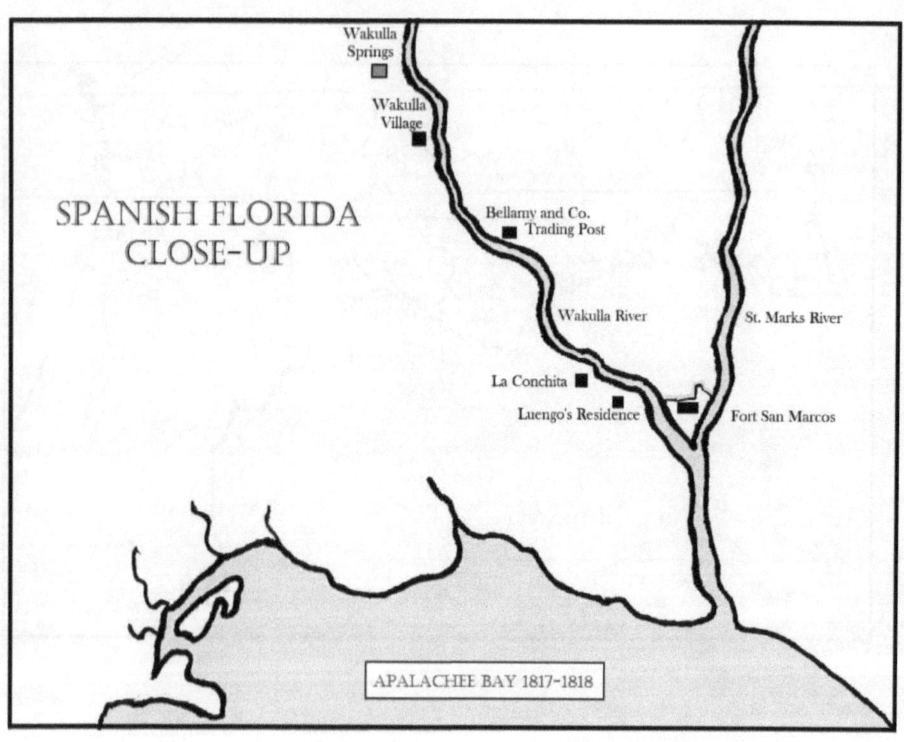

SPANISH FLORIDA CLOSE-UP
Wakulla Springs
Wakulla Village
Bellamy and Co. Trading Post
Wakulla River
St. Marks River
La Conchita
Luengo's Residence
Fort San Marcos
APALACHEE BAY 1817-1818

Cast of Characters

The Americans
Miss Lillian McGirth (Liana)
Captain Marcus Buck, Surgeon
Maria del Sol López (Marisol/Mari), Lillian's daughter
Brevet Major Dalton Ainsworth
Lieutenant Aaron Fanning
Private Clive Petit

The Spaniards
Don Diego López de Aragón, Viscount of Apalachee, patron of La
    Conchita
Barbury (Barb), Marisol's nurse, servant in Diego's household
Capitán Antonio Luengo (Toño), commandant of Fort San Marcos
Suni, nanny
Jose Espina, horse master
Fray Emilio Sanchez, Dominican friar
Cabo Javier Varela (corporal)
Teniente Prieto (lieutenant), garrison's commander
Cabo Barros (corporal)

The British
Robert Maxwell Bellamy, trader

The Natives
Tall Bull, Red Stick chief of Wakulla Village
Senior Warrior Fierce Mink, war woman, body guard
War Chief Water Moccasin, head of security
Pretty Wolf (aka Polly Francis), daughter to Prophet Josiah Francis
    (Hillis Hadjo)
Strong Bear (previously, True Seeker)
Big Warrior Totka Hadjo, brother-by-marriage to Lillian

Chapter I

In the autumn of 1817, Spain's control of Florida was gasping its last breaths, and strife on the frontier was stoking the embers that would ignite the First Seminole War…

Fowltown Village, Georgia
Big Chestnut Month (October) 1817

Captain Marcus Buck dropped to one knee beside an Indian's crumpled form and swept a hand down her face, lowering her lids over sightless eyes. He untangled her red, threadbare skirt from around her thighs and swabbed a spray of blood from the tawny skin at her jaw.

She was young, perhaps twenty. Cheekbones, arching and delicate. Lashes, thick as lovegrass. A lock of hair had been wrested from its knot at her nape and stirred like inky satin in the cool breeze. It was a gut-ripping pity she was dead and more so that her abdomen was softly mounded with child.

Shoulders slumped, he rested a limp hand on his sword's eagle-head pommel. Named Justice, the weapon had remained in the scabbard during the brief exchange of lead.

As skirmishes with hostile Red Sticks went, this one had been a sweep. One volley from each opposing side. Then, the Natives had fled into the surrounding wetlands, abandoning Fowltown, their village. This woman alone remained, victim of an errant musket ball.

American casualties, nil.

None of the two hundred-plus soldiers who'd crept in under the cover of darkness could rejoice more than Marcus, surgeon in the Fourth Infantry. And yet, a sense of foreboding settled in the pit of his stomach like a fever-borne malady. Nothing was ever simple with the Red Sticks, that fanatical remnant of Indians who'd refused to surrender at war's end. Instead of signing the accord along with the other Creeks, they'd fled to the wilds of Spanish Florida where, if suspicions were correct, they were being aided in their warfare by the British—a violation of treaty that kindled Marcus's marrow.

Footfalls neared from behind and slowed to a scuffling stop. "So much for no bloodshed." Lieutenant Aaron Fanning released a protracted exhale. "Someone's going to be chasing revenge."

"I would, too, if she were mine."

The placement of the scalp wound suggested a severed artery. Poor soul, she'd dropped unnoticed. While her people fled and Marcus's advanced, she'd lain unconscious and spilled her lifeblood. Marcus might have saved her, had he found her earlier, halted the bleed. Failing that, he would have broadened his experimentation and attempted a blood exchange. His own. Anything to avoid the ripple of retaliation these deaths would provoke.

Marcus looked out across the village to the smattering of thatched lodges: the chickens squawking before blue-coated soldiers, the council house being set aflame, and finally, beyond to the thickets leading into the swamp.

This was American land. The late Red Stick War had won it, but Chief Neamathla disagreed. That morning, he'd been wise to retreat before his enemy, but no Florida Red Stick, however weak or ill-prepared, ever surrendered. This meager battle, if it could be called that, was only the beginning of sorrows.

"Sergeant Garrigus found another in the chief's lodge," Fanning announced.

Taking up his medical bag, Marcus rose and swiveled to his friend. "Dead?"

Fanning barked a laugh, dislodging a thatch of rusty brown hair from beneath his bicorn. "Not by a long shot."

It wasn't hard to find Neamathla's lodge. Apart from being the largest, it was gathering an audience. Men stood outside to catch what they might of the action unfolding in the dim interior.

"Make way." Marcus ducked through the doorway.

Warmth enveloped him, created by the fire smoldering inside a ring of stones at the floor's center. Beside it, a tipped soup bowl and a discarded ceremonial pipe. Smoke still curled from the pipe's chamber, commanding the lodge with its acrid scent.

Two walls supported a set of bunks; on the third were a row of cane shelves that displayed various household goods; and backed into a corner, a small figure stared down three soldiers who held weapons in loose defensive positions.

"What's going on, Sergeant Garrigus?" Marcus moved through the men, assessing the prospective patient as he went—the woolen blanket encasing her, the bulge at abdomen level, her blood-wet temple, and cold, steady black eyes.

Garrigus, a good soldier who'd been with the Fourth as long as Marcus, jabbed a thumb at the captive. "It's a woman, sir."

Marcus looked askance at him. "You don't say."

Garrigus leaned close, speaking in a mock hush. "Thought to save you the embarrassment, sir. I never seen you with a woman. Wasn't sure you'd recognize one if—"

"Magnanimous of you, Sergeant." Marcus unfastened his bag's buckle. Though it had been a while, a long, lonely while, he knew women plenty.

"You're mighty welcome, Doc." Garrigus broke into a grin. "Not sure how you manage when I ain't here."

"Typically, I resort to what I picked up at medical school."

Four years of it. Harvard. Another four in the field, wearing the black coat of an army surgeon. And between the two periods, ten months press-ganged on a British frigate, as close to Satan's lair as Marcus cared to come and all the motivation he needed to propel every last redcoat from American shores.

Keen to stem the blood oozing from her brow, Marcus removed wadding from his bag while the woman glared at each man in turn. The hand she hid beneath the blanket sent a prickle up Marcus's neck and made his palm itch for Justice.

"That fancy school teach you anything about creatures that fall somewhere in the middle?" Quiet awe roughened Private Petit's typically raspy voice. "Look at that sour face. And the tattoos on that arm…" He said nothing of the limb's lean brawn that, given a chance, might put half of them to shame at the wrestling table.

Although the square cut of her jaw spoke of masculinity, her stature said otherwise, as did the feminine lips and the gently curving neck, the line of which led the eye to an arm clothed only in geometric patterns of ink.

"Was she struck?" Marcus halted his advance when the woman growled what could be nothing less than an oath to rip his heart out.

"Not by any here," someone said from behind.

"Is she a lunatic?" Petit asked.

"My current diagnosis—she's hell-fire angry." Marcus's low, soothing tone did nothing to extinguish that fire from the woman's eyes.

Lifting the compress, he demonstrated by touching the side of his own head before extending it to her.

She eyed the offering a moment before sneering and pulling the blanket tighter about her.

"Angry and cooking up a way to scalp us all," Petit said on a shiver.

"A little thing like her won't get too far." Garrigus slung his weapon over his shoulder by its strap. "Leveret, get one of the friendlies to translate. Petit, store that musket before you scare the baby clean out of her."

Marcus scrutinized the awkward swell of her body. Baby? Maybe,

maybe not. "Sergeant Garrigus, any idea why she didn't run into the swamp with the rest?"

"Not a clue. I came up on her rummaging around. She tried to shove past me, so I drew on her. She backed up quick-like and won't let no one near. I saw blood and thought maybe she's dazed."

Her eyes were clear, focused. Marcus shook his head. "Not likely."

At the sound of voices and hurried tread, she flung off the blanket. Her body was sleek and bare of all but a strap of leather binding her breasts and a breechcloth that exposed the full length of her legs plus one buttock.

On impulse, Marcus began to look away, an irrational apology on his lips. Then his stunned brain registered weapons attached to a belt. The gleam of metal kicked another set of instincts into play.

She lunged.

His hand whipped to Justice's hilt, and his feet skipped into an ingrained traverse retreat that kept him beyond the tip of her jabbing knife. Blue steel hissed as it exited the scabbard, its flicking tip meeting her forearm in a long, shallow slice meant to startle.

She gasped, eyes wide, and stumbled over his bag. Though she retained her weapon, a bundle fell from her grasp. In pursuit of it, her knees folded, her hand reaching downward, but Justice was quicker.

Marcus flipped his wrist, placing the blade's point at her throat one inch from her throbbing vein. "Hold right there."

She froze in a half-crouch, gaze leaping to the soldiers rushing into the lodge, an Indian at their fore, firing off a commanding set of Muskogee phrases. Three different weapons cocked as men fanned out behind Marcus. Despite the odds against her, she registered not a hint of defeat.

"Blazes, Doc. Never seen a sword come out so hair-trigger fast." Garrigus lowered his musket, even as the Indian straightened her posture, solidifying her stance.

"Have a care, Sergeant Garrigus," Marcus murmured. "She's quick with that iron and just as tough, I'll wager."

Curious as to what she'd considered so precious, he glimpsed downward to the blanketed parcel. Protruding from the partially opened bundle was a snatch of lobster-red fabric with several gold tassels. His pulse skittered as his mind leaped several years into the past and became ensnared on the phantom *crack* of a cat o' nine tails slicing the air.

His screams, his blinding pain. Rope digging into his wrists, plaited cording into his back. The stench of a corrupt navy drowning every one of his senses.

For justice—the vow that propelled his hunt for Iron Wood, covert British agent to the Red Sticks.

The woman's sly hand moved toward the tomahawk on her belt.

Justice reciprocated, lifting a notch, pricking a circular tattoo on her neck. Elbow high, Marcus jutted his chin at her. "Back up. Back!"

The interpreter bit out a couple of words, and acidly, she complied.

"It'll pain me to do it," Marcus said, eyes slitting, "but if you try another such move, I'll sever your jugular as payment."

"Sir?" Garrigus awaited orders.

"Disarm her. Carefully." Palms sweating, Marcus secured his hold on the sword's bone grip.

The translator filled her in, and as Garrigus obeyed, one side of her mouth hooked upward in an arrogant quarter-smile.

Holding her glare, Marcus snapped his fingers at Petit. "Tell me what she dropped there."

What did she deem equal to the value of her life?

"Sure thing, Captain."

When Petit, glancing up nervously, bent to grab at the blanket, the woman's gaze lowered to him, hand jerking. Marcus cocked his head and rotated the sword's tip until it drew a trickle of blood that pattered over her clavicle. And still, she didn't so much as wince.

Petit yanked at the bundle, spilling a calumet, a beaded pouch, and a brass plate. With them, a scarlet red British officer's coat complete with gold epaulettes.

At the sight of it, Marcus's blood spiked and his back tightened until his old wounds ached. Eyes affixed to the regimentals, his sword arm descended to skewer the red fabric with a spiteful twist.

Unarmed now, the woman squatted and, ignoring the coat, snatched the articles to her heart and lifted a silent plea to him.

All this for a few sacred objects?

A weighty sigh left his lungs. He sheathed Justice and crouched before her, then picked up the discarded wad of cotton and mopped at her rigid neck. "My apologies, miss. Next we meet, let's try to behave more civilly, shall we?" He lifted a terse smile, grabbed a handful of the coat, and basked in this small victory.

"Go on, then." He indicated the doorway.

As she rose, the distinct sound of manipulated parchment caught his ear. He shot to his feet and seized her forearm. A thorough review of her person revealed a bit of foolscap wedged between her belly and her breechcloth. "With your permission." He whisked the folded paper from concealment.

He returned a grin for her scowl, but it vanished at the sight of the correspondence. Flowing script marked the top edge, and center front stood a wax seal, broken but clearly distinguishable.

Heart lurching, he released the woman's arm and turned to his sergeant. "Let her go, Garrigus. I have what I need." His spinning mind barely registered the trace of her fleeing bare feet.

Bring me evidence, Major Ainsworth had said in answer to Marcus's request to personally investigate the army's suspicions. General Andrew Jackson, commander of the Fourth Military District, didn't care whether he had substantiation or a pile of dung, but Major Ainsworth conducted business by the book. He would have unequivocal proof, or he wouldn't sail. Marcus had no quarrel with the major's clean-cut methods. In fact, he lauded them.

"And what would that be, sir?" Garrigus asked.

"Proof, Sergeant Garrigus. Proof."

And the fair wind that would blow him to Fort San Marcos, Iron Wood, and God-willing, the errant Miss Lillian McGirth.

San Marcos, Spanish Florida

Frost Month (November, six weeks later)

The flagstone cutting into Lillian McGirth's knees wasn't painful enough to counteract the effects of a pair of sleepless nights, their endless hours split between rocking her ailing child and beseeching two things of God—forgiveness for herself, mercy for her child.

Lillian's lids drooped then jerked open to land again upon Santa Teresa in *La Conchita's* most sacred corner. Housed in an arched niche in the hacienda's inner wall and flanked by candles, the saint was frozen in white marble piety. At Lillian's back, the sun was slipping into the evening hours, its rays far too cool for the season.

Exhaustion was an unbearable weight, but Lillian obligingly muttered through. "I firmly resolve with the help of thy grace to confess my sins, to do penance, and to amend my life. Amen. Santa…Teresa de…" The clatter of beads against stone lurched Lillian from stupor. She collected the rosary, warm from her palms' embrace, and continued her recitations. "Santa Teresa de Jesús, reject not my petitions, but in your mercy—"

Marisol's sharp, pitiful cry from the upper story compelled Lillian to her feet. Stiff with cold, she employed the sign of the cross and finished the routine by leaving a kiss on the saint's worn sandal. She hastened to the plaza's open-tread spiral staircase and ascended to the loggia—the covered balcony that rimmed three of the four inner walls of the square compound.

Fully awake now, she scurried along the loggia and threw open the double doors to her room, sending their lace curtains whooshing to the sides.

Barbury, the baby's wet nurse, walked a tight circle in the center of the room, coaxing the baby with her bared breast. "She woke up fussier than ever, Missy Lillian. Won't take me. Not so much as a swallow."

Marisol, six months the following day, batted at Barbury's attempts. At the sight of Lillian, she gurgled a pathetic half-cry that wrenched Lillian's insides. "Oh, baby girl, you break my heart. Come here, sunshine."

Her full name was Maria del Sol, Mary of the Sun. And she was. A pure ray of light, straight from Heaven, the only light in Lillian's shadows-and-fear world.

Barbury, a runaway turned servant, released Marisol to her. "I's sorry, missy. Been tryin' hard." She tucked herself back into the bodice of her no-frills cotton gown.

Lillian brushed wispy umber hair across Marisol's damp brow. The baby had Diego's dark Spanish beauty and her Auntie Adela's lovable disposition, but no matter how hard Lillian searched, she could see none of herself in her own child. And she thanked God for it every day.

"I know, Barb. You always do." Lillian wouldn't trust Marisol's care to any other but Barbury.

Once Marisol's fever-warm body was molded to Lillian's chest, she hiccupped twice and calmed. She shoved her seed necklace into her mouth and lifted eyes as wet and glossy brown as the beads she gnawed.

Lillian smiled down at her. "Teething. We can hope that's all it is."

"We can hope." Doubt subdued Barbury's voice as she scrubbed flat hands over her lanky hips. "Two days now and hardly a drop. Cain't keep on this way. She gotta drink."

"Why are you not dressed?" Diego López de Aragón, *patrón* of La Conchita, viscount of Apalache, and her employer, entered without invitation or preamble.

The scarlet cape buttoned at his throat covered all but his white stockings, gold-buckled shoes, and the last six inches of his embossed leather scabbard. The silk netting that pouched his long hair marked his noble station. He whisked off his black three-cornered hat and beat his thigh with it. "It is the smallest of tasks to be ready when I say. Yet you cannot complete it!"

Loathing burbled in Lillian's gut, heating her from the inside out and radiating from her in waves she didn't bother to conceal. "Cannot and *will* not are beasts of a different color," she replied in Castilian worthy of any *Madrileña*.

"The officers are due to arrive within the hour. This is not the time to exercise your rampant wit. You will give Mari to her nurse, and you will make yourself presentable. Now—*ahora mismo!*" he said, rolling his *r* with flair.

"Shout all you want. Our daughter still suffers *la gripe*. I won't leave her for a single afternoon much less three days, or five, or only God knows how many you will demand!"

Cabo Javier Varela appeared behind Diego and propped against the door jam, his lusty eye in the process of undressing her.

While Diego silently reddened and built steam, Marisol rubbed her sweaty face against Lillian's bodice and fussed, scrunching up her body in discomfort and strengthening Lillian's resolve. "Max Bellamy translates as well as I. Best send your cabo for him." She refused to voice the corporal's slimy name.

"I will do no such thing! And you, señorita, will abide by our agreement or suffer the severest of regrets." Voice a growl, he neared, tromping like a bull, like the *toro bravo* he was.

Proud and bitter she might be, but Lillian McGirth was no fool. She unlatched Marisol's little fingers and passed her to Barbury who then moved to the patio door. There, the nurse quickly distracted Marisol with an impressive flock of white pelicans and the noisy beat of their wings.

Wishing she could fly south with them, Lillian turned back to Diego only to be stalked and prodded backward until her rear end found an obstacle. He slammed a forearm on the armoire behind her, rocking it and filling her nose with his spicy cologne, transporting her to their more intimate seasons and leaving her there with an uncomfortable mixture of longing and regret.

The pleasure of those months had been sweet. Unsanctioned indulgence, however, always came with a price. Hers was varied and so steep she might be in debt an eternity.

"I've grown rather weary of your defiance, Liana dearest," he said, using the Spanish version of her name.

"Keep your distance, *mi señor*." Perhaps the formality would remind him of their proper relationship: grand viscount and lowly clerk.

Or perhaps not, for when she laid a restraining hand against the blue sash at his midriff, the heat in his eyes shifted from anger to something else. His hand went softly to her throat where it stroked the place her blood pulsed. "I am wearier yet of the prudish lock on your door."

Cabo Valera sniggered, and while Diego looked over his shoulder to scowl the man into silence, Lillian lowered her hand in search of the knife strapped to her calf. Diego would get nothing more from her.

Never one for violence—at least, not by his own hand—he instead applied manipulation, using promises and her own natural and oft unquenchable desires against her. Of late, prompted by desperation, he'd discovered that fear had its own power. In Lillian, it was a crippling thing.

He noticed her clumsy attempt to access the weapon and clucked his tongue. "By the time you get that dagger in your hand, our guests will have come and gone. But I like that you try." He leaned in and spoke seductively against her ear. "Continue to defy and humiliate me, and penance and prayers be hanged, you will find me back in your bed for good. And I promise you will get not a wink of sleep."

That, her soul could not afford. Neither could Marisol, who was paying for her mother's sins.

Scrambling for confidence she hadn't felt in months, she wielded her most haughty glare. "Sleep *would* be scarce, because I would be keeping vigil for the moment you would least expect my blade in your back."

Diego chuckled and waggled her chin. "I do love your pluck. Now, bring it to San Marcos, along with your manners and your most polished *Americano*."

"Americano? The officers are Americanos?" Her arm slackened, and Diego put on that self-satisfied look that used to send her girlish heart racing.

Barbury spun back from the window, fear widening her eyes. For Lillian, American intrusion meant freedom. For Barbury, a reminder of slavery and, should the United States decide it wanted to own this land, the potential to be sent back to it.

Diego pushed off the armoire, giving Lillian a breath of space. "Did I fail to mention it? I beg your pardon."

This had been an intentional omission. If she'd had more than a tick on the clock to prepare, she would have devised a way to throw up a red flag, marking Diego as a target for American wrath. As it was, she would barely have enough time to brush her hair and buff her smile. Anger welled. "You don't care one scrap for me or my pardon! You manipulative—"

Diego nabbed her jaw and kissed her with such gusto his closely trimmed goatee burned her skin.

Treacherous thing that it was, her body sparked to life and answered him, as it did every time this man broke through what little reserves she scrounged together. Her back was arching toward him when she caught herself and broke away. Snorting, she swiped the back of her hand over her mouth. Oh, but she hated herself!

He peered down at her, seeming gratified by his own prowess and its heating effects on her. "Do you want to meet your countrymen or not?"

As she stood there, nodding, feeling dizzy and ill, her heart and hope skittering all over the place, he opened the wardrobe and rifled through it.

"How many have come?" Her spirits soared despite her child's afflictive whimper. This afternoon, Marisol would best be served by Lillian finding a way to get them out of there.

"A frigate full, anchored in the bay at dawn."

A frigate! Plenty of room for a woman and a baby. Plenty of room for cannons that could blow San Marcos off the Spanish shoreline. Diego's distemper and demands were beginning to make sense.

"They're claiming a stout gale at sea," he continued, squinting into the depths of her wardrobe, knocking things about. "A cracked mast and ripped topsail, a host of other troublesome repairs only a seaman would understand. But of those men lodging in *Capitán* Luengo's home, only three. Two coming now, another later this evening." His commentary degraded into curses surrounding Capitán Luengo's ferocious honor-driven hospitality.

"Since you aren't ready, I'll ride ahead." He shoved a mound of fabric into her arms. "Put this on and follow. You are to be there when their boots hit soil. Thirty minutes. No more. And find that maddeningly distracting allure of yours. You will need it. There is much to distract them from."

Much indeed. And there was much more she hadn't dared investigate.

Suddenly, the room began to slide across her vision. Lillian shook it clear and grabbed the post of the canopy bed. These episodes were growing more frequent, more disturbing.

"Entertain them." He threw petticoats onto the foot of the bed. "See to their every need. Deny them nothing. If they ask after our secondary trade, deny everything. La Conchita negotiates in crops and cattle, leather and furs. Nothing more. Understood?"

"Of course. You wish me to mislead them."

"Precisely."

"Lie to them."

"If that is what it takes."

"Commit treason."

"Ah, but you already have, my little *pistola*. All the more reason to lie." He grinned roguishly, then barreled on, giving no space for the protest building within her. "If you are convincing enough, when they leave, you may go with them. And"—he plopped a pair of slippers onto the rumpled gown in her arms—"I'll even pay your passage."

The air caught in her lungs along with any revolt she'd considered. "You would let me leave? And Marisol?"

At the mention of their treasure, his face softened; his gaze traveled to the child and caressed her affectionately, but after a moment, he stated bluntly, "A girl should be with her mother." As Lillian's throat seized and knotted, he strode to Barbury and rested his lips on Marisol's forehead. "It is only a little fever, eh? You will soon be well, *mi sol sin sombra.*"

"Mi señor, the hour," the cabo reminded him.

In a snap, Diego's tenderness vanished. When his line of sight collided with Lillian, who stood dumbstruck, his arms flew up. "Ay, woman, get dressed!" With that, he pounded out of the room, cape billowing. "Pepe," he shouted over the loggia's wrought-iron banister. "Saddle a horse!"

Cabo Varela slammed the doors shut, rattling panes and making the baby burst out in tears. Taffeta and muslin dangling from her arms, Lillian went to Marisol and placed her lips where Diego's had been, repeating his term of endearment. "My sun without shadow."

"Think he mean what he say, Missy Lillian? 'Bout lettin' you both get on that warship?"

Even as Lillian clung to the gown and all the hopes it embodied, disquiet budded within. To protect his holdings and his felon king, he would promise the world. But when it came time to follow through, he wouldn't risk letting her go. She knew too much.

And Marisol, his little sun? She was his only child. The evidence he was a true man and not impotent after all. For months, Diego had threatened to take Marisol, and only Marisol, back to Spain with him to be raised at court—a ludicrous idea since an illegitimate child born of a protestant mother would never be accepted into Spain's rigid, inquisitional arms. Residing in New Spain cushioned Diego somewhat from the Church's control, but entering Spain with such boldness would bring even a viscount under the sharp eye of the Holy Office, which Lillian knew from experience, needed little excuse to purge even the faintest trace of immorality and heresy.

But Diego *would* have his way. He always did. No American frigate would prevent it.

Lillian shook out the garment, gave it a long, hard look, then glanced at the clock on the mantel. Twenty-eight minutes and counting. "He meant not a word of it, Barb. Not a word."

Beneath a red-fog sky, Lillian's barouche came to a jerky stop. She pressed a hand to her forehead and sat perfectly still in the hopes the spell would pass before Diego reached her.

With the cocky strut of a conquistador, he strode the broad, dusty lane that marked the boundary of the villa, which sprawled out to his left, and *Fuerte San Marcos de Apalache*, which stood to his right.

What she wouldn't give for a few hours out from under his thumb, preferably basking with Mari in unadulterated sunshine. The world hadn't seen a clear sky since before the child was born. Aftereffects of a volcanic eruption in the Indies, some said. Whatever the cause, it had deprived even the Floridas of warmth, leaving many hungry, cold, and ill.

"Señorita." The Andalusian driver, Pepe Espina, drew out the word in exaggerated fashion. "I have business to see to before the Americanos arrive. Will you sit there all day?"

"If I wish to, *sí*." She wouldn't place a single foot in this unwelcoming villa unless she was on Diego's arm.

Her gaze stumbled past him and fell on the mission. The humble wattle-and-daub building stood center of the row of establishments that faced the fort, its roughly hewn wooden cross rising from the peak of its thatched roof. *Fray* Emilio, the region's only clergy and a Dominican friar, would be nearby, hounding some hapless wretch about his soul.

Abhorrence suffused Lillian's skin with a damp chill. Blessedly, her next scheduled confession was still two days out. Ten remained in her imposed canonical penance — long hours in prayer and a fast meant to purge her of fleshly desires.

Her sins had become a miserable, public affair, and the subsequent reconciliation with God seemed cruel. The consequences of breaking penance were crueler yet, but that was only part of what kept her to this method of spiritual renewal. The rest came from the constant bite of guilt over wrongs committed and her insatiable hunger for a man's touch. Neither of which she had the power to change on her own.

She'd tried.

For the benefit of her wicked soul, she was resolved to adhere to the penance.

"My affairs cannot wait." Pepe's finely tailored horseman's outfit would be handsome if not for the dullard wearing it.

"Pepe, you whine exceptionally well for a grown man, and since your affairs likely include an indiscriminate tart and a bottomless tankard, I'll conclude that they *can* wait."

At that, Pepe twisted back to sneer at her. "You have found me out, but fetch me a bottle of rum, and I'll have everything I need right here."

Lillian ground her teeth. She should have seen that coming. Did the languor have her so far off her game? Keeping silent, she let the man think he'd bested her.

A long shout came from the Wakulla River, which flowed no more than two yards from the base of the stone fort's western bulwark. A skiff was nearing the pier that jutted into the sluggish water. Holding a wobbling stance at the boat's helm, a soldier wearing the red-trimmed, blue regimentals of Spain hollered instructions to those awaiting the vessel at the quay.

Diego met her at the barouche's door and stopped, making himself as erect as his trim, five-foot-seven allowed. His brown and green-flecked eyes brought Marisol to mind. Barbury had promised to send word should there be any change in the baby's condition, but that didn't squelch the pang of worry that created a nauseous stew in her gut.

"You're flushed and unkempt." Diego had never been one for polite greetings. "Half the villa will think you've come from a romp in the hay."

"There's no getting anything past the good people of San Marcos, but when he sees beauty, every man stumbles." She leaned toward the driver's bench and touched Pepe's elbow. "Is that not so, Pepe?"

The Andalusian contorted back so fast, his hat caught the wind, lifting shadows from his startled expression.

Diego's thorny look settled on him. "Look me in the eye and swear you've not touched the señorita, or may the Holy Mother help me, I'll have the teeth behind those lying lips sent straight to the back of your throat."

Lillian might regret the provocation if the groom hadn't gone out of his way to find every rut in the lane between La Conchita and the fort.

Pepe paled. "No, for pity, no! I've touched no woman. Least of all your—the señorita." A careful study was made in the villa to never reference the impropriety of their relationship. Diego wouldn't abide it, to say nothing of the friar.

"There is no time for this. Later, we will speak." He turned to her, his oiled goatee glistening. "*La mano, maja?* Your hand?" His tone was cool with tension; his smile, stiff.

The term *maja*, used to describe the cheeky lower classes of Madrid, was typically a compliment. On Diego's tongue, it was a reminder of Lillian's true place in society, and it crackled inside her like water droplets in hot oil. Not that he would get the reward of seeing her spit and spew. "Grácias, mi señor." With her silkiest smile, Lillian took her time straightening the fringes of the silk *mantón* that draped her shoulders.

Lips pursing hard, he remained as he was, hand extended, palm up.

The moment she took it and lowered a foot to the barouche's step, Pepe shifted the reins, and the matched blacks stepped forward. She grabbed the swinging door and swayed with a bout of wooziness. The earth blurred, and she worked to refocus her eyes, heart pattering an ailing rhythm.

"Hold them steady, Espina," Diego snipped, hooking Lillian under the arms and swinging her off. "I need her in one piece."

"A thousand pardons, mi señor," the man replied in a tone that held not a hint of apology.

Affixing her hand to his arm, Diego guided her toward the pier and called an abrupt greeting to the fort's commander, Capitán Antonio Luengo, whom she affectionately called Toño. The man hurried across the drawbridge to meet them partway to the Americans disembarking the skiff.

The sight of the gentleman's friendly face eased the knot in Lillian's gut. If only a little.

"Toño, dear friend." Lillian increased her pace, detaching from Diego and reaching Toño with a broad smile that came easily.

Taking her by the shoulders, he steadied her for the traditional Spanish greeting—a press of their right cheeks, then swiftly, their left. "*¿Cómo está, bonita?*" He pushed her to arms' length to better see her and frowned. His unstrapped blue shako had been knocked off kilter, its crimson cockade tipping left.

As she straightened it for him, her smile faltered. It was hard to maintain pretenses around him. "I am well enough. But I've heard your afternoon has grown dreary, and I am sorry for it."

"Dreary? Ba! Not with you about." Toño snugged the shako's strap under his plump chin. "You gladden my day. As always." He smiled brightly to prove it.

Diego busied himself straightening his hairnet, ascertaining that all locks were properly stowed. He addressed Toño. "Have the *Indios* been notified?"

A tremor traveled Lillian's shoulders at the reminder of Wakulla, the Red Stick village not three miles upstream. The Red Sticks were a barbarous people, burning with the flame of hatred toward whites. It was that flame that lit the fires of Fort Mims and shot an arrow through her eldest sister, Beth—painful facts Lillian worked tirelessly to avoid pondering. Never far, however, was the promise to Beth to fight them tooth and nail. She'd been faithful to it, unlike their middle sister who'd married one.

Toño released her and turned to Diego, all business now. "Notified and warned. And your *soldados*?"

Along with endless acres of fertile land, the king had supplied Diego with his own squad of Royal Infantry to garrison the hacienda and surrounding ranch and farmland.

"Threatened with the skin on their backs, every last one."

"Mi señor, that is hardly necessary. We all understand the ramifications should our neighbors' sojourn on our shores go poorly."

"The rational among us, sí. Then we have Cabo Varela, who was seen on the parapet, shouting out to sea, demanding the Americanos not bother docking unless they are bringing Jamaican rum, sporting girls, and a good fight."

Toño fouled the air with vulgar comments on Cabo Varela's origins of birth. Remembering Lillian, he blushed and bowed deeply. "Forgive me, Señorita Liana. I forgot I was in the presence of a lady."

"Forgiven, Toño. And don't fret. You have created quite the illusion." She nodded toward the row of cannons on display at the top of the walls and the troop of handsomely clad soldados standing in formation. Impressive. Until one learned there wasn't enough powder in the bombproof to blow that skiff out of the water. "Your visitors will be duly awed by the might of San Marcos."

Diego didn't look as confident. "And if they are not, my capable assistant will help them along. She knows her duty."

Lillian sniffed at the assertion. "My true duty is to our sick daughter whose miserable cries still ring in my ear. If they do not in yours, Diego, then—"

"Enough! This development is larger than any ten daughters, as much as they might be cherished." Then, as he voraciously reminded her of their arrangement, she blocked him out to appraise her fellow citizens stepping onto the dock.

The one leading was a major, if she was reading the insignia correctly. He possessed an angular face and wore a stern expression. His motions were purposeful and commanding. The other, a lieutenant, followed and was a mere shadow in the presence of his senior officer.

In a protective air, Toño sidled left, partially blocking Diego from Lillian's view. "Have you threatened the skin on *her* back as well? If I see one mark on her—"

"But, Capitán!" Diego bowed back over his heels, both arms wide. "Your meager opinion of me is a great wound."

"Is it? A shame." Toño spoke through the broad smile he directed at their approaching guests. He closed the distance to the Americans and, hands going before him, made himself into the consummate host.

Lillian hurried to catch him in time to translate. "On behalf of His Catholic Majesty, King Ferdinand the Seventh," Lillian said, speaking to the foremost gentleman, whose brows hiked at her, "of the mighty and ancient Spanish Empire, I, Captain Antonio Luengo, commandant of Fort San Marcos of Apalache and surrounding regions, greet you in the name of our sovereign Lord and His Holy Mother. With the hopes for a fast and enduring friendship, I welcome you into my home and to East Florida of New Spain. Viva Fernando Séptimo!"

While Toño made a pretty bow, flourishing his hand to the side, the subordinate officer came to stand alongside his superior. He was a gentleman with an agreeable face, notwithstanding the leavings of a scourge of boyhood blemishes. He caught her eye and winked. Forward of him, but there was no condemning. Not with that affable smile he flashed.

"An American?" he ventured, not deterred by their lack of introduction.

Lillian bobbed a knee.

"Fancy that." The major bunched his lips.

Neatly bypassing the man's comment, she motioned for Toño to continue.

He did. "With me, Don Diego López, viscount of Apalache and royal merchant to our illustrious king. His assistant and serving as our interpreter, Miss Lillian McGirth. Myself," she added with as pleasant a smile as she could muster, considering the major's intense stare.

The major cleared his throat and granted Toño and Diego a single tight nod. "Brevet Major Dalton Ainsworth of the Fourth United States Infantry, your humble guest." He plunged ahead, so she slipped closer to Toño and quietly translated.

"Captain Buck, our surgeon, has been detained by a sailor who took a tumble from the mizzen during the squall. He intends to join us this evening."

Captain Buck? Lillian knew that name. It was attached to a nebulous thought she couldn't quite solidify. The list of names she'd accrued from soldiers passing through Mobile and Tensaw was extensive. She'd batted eyes at half of them. There was no telling which of them this Buck might be, but at least the aura around his memory was an agreeable one.

Major Ainsworth turned to the lieutenant. "Beside me is an indispensable officer of the highest caliber, Lieutenant Aaron Fanning, commander of artillery and able helmsman should the need arise, as our recent peril can attest. He will be assuming responsibilities at Fort Gadsden."

Lillian faltered at the mention of the fort, but Toño and Diego did little more than smile and nod. Either this was not new information to them, or they were not intimidated by the United States increasing its military presence a short trek to the west.

Lieutenant Fanning bent in brief obeisance. "My deepest gratitude, gentleman, for allowing our struggling vessel refuge in your harbor, and for your hospitality to my fellow officers and myself while the *Gallant Lady* undergoes repairs."

Toño gave a merry laugh. "We are neighbors and allies. San Marcos de Apalache opens her arms to you all." After instructing a set of floppy-hatted peasants as to the transport of the Americans' baggage, he escorted them all to the barouche, stating he was entrusting them to Lillian's care and looking forward to sharing his dinner table.

Once their guests had boarded, Diego aided Lillian into the carriage. She chose the forward-facing bench, smiling politely at the officers as they arranged themselves on the one opposite.

Before the brake was released, Diego leaned over the rear wheel and the joint of the collapsed hood to address Lillian privately. "You're enchanting, Liana. As I knew you would be. But to curb any temptation you might have to exercise your patriotic leanings, I have set certain countermeasures in place."

"What in the name of heaven are you talking about?"

His whiskers undulated with the arrogant slide of his mouth. "Trust me when I say you would be grieved beyond repair. Have a care, maja. If La Conchita comes to ruin, you will crumble with her."

Incredulous, she found not a word of reply. He would threaten her? Did he not think the prospect of leaving San Marcos with Marisol to be incentive enough to play her role? Apart from livid, she was baffled. Was this about the accusation of treason? The things she knew could certainly cause a stir, but she'd *done* nothing but translate and transcribe.

Before she could find her tongue, he stepped back, dismissed himself to join Toño, and instructed Pepe to roll out. The barouche eased into a comfortable speed while trepidation tingled a trail from her slippered feet to the tip of her frosty nose. As Lieutenant Fanning blithely commented on passing scenery, her mind stayed on Diego, her heart becoming a quivering shamble.

Lightheaded, she closed her eyes and willed strength and courage into her blood. With it, came a fierce determination. Whether her odious lover reneged on his end of the deal or not, she and Marisol *would* be on that ship when it hoisted anchors.

Regrouping with effort, she chiseled a smile into her features and focused on the men. "That gale must have been fierce. You both look done in. Captain Luengo's estate is small but peaceful. The ideal place to recuperate."

Major Ainsworth remained aloof, his posture severely erect. "And you, miss? Will we have the pleasure of your company again?"

"I'll be lodging at Captain Luengo's for the duration of your stay to see to any needs you might have."

"Excellent!" The lieutenant gleamed. "I look forward to it. We'll sit down over a cup of your strongest Spanish coffee and do a little strategizing."

"Certainly. I'll ask the cook if she has any puffed pastries. They're excellent. You'll surely dream about them tonight. But I'm curious…what could we possibly have to strategize?" She affected a laugh that she feared betrayed her unease.

"Miss McGirth," Major Ainsworth inserted, sitting forward. "All pretenses dropped, we're thrilled to find you here. I trust your presence will make our stay more tolerable and, quite frankly, shorten it. Your willingness to lend aid is gratefully noted. We are men accustomed to getting by with little in the way of comforts, so you'll find our needs to be few. But there *is* one who would be most appreciative of your service."

At last, a genial remark from the stoic major. She relaxed into a gracious smile. "Say the word, Major. I'm here to serve. Who can I help? One of your men? The soldier who's injured perhaps?"

He reclined again, crossed his arms, and probed her eyes. "Why, your country, miss. The United States."

"I'm only a clerk, sir. I know little, and I would make a woeful agent. You're asking a difficult thing of me." Lillian flattened her mouth at Major Ainsworth and leaned into the curve that carried the barouche onto the mile-long lane that would end at Toño's two-story coquina home.

These men, these *men*! Diego and his precious wealth. Major Ainsworth and his precious cause. Neither faction in this quasi-battle cared for those they trampled in the pursuit of their ambitions, only their deplorable struggle for power!

"Loyalty isn't always easy," the major said. "It is in times such as these that true patriots, and their counterparts, are revealed."

He would question her loyalty? Lillian's rested firmly on the side of the Americans, but there was Diego and his threats to consider. And all that he had with which to crush her.

She raked the fringes of her shawl across her thigh, but when it brought undue attention to her shaking fingers, she crumpled the silk within her fist and forced herself to meet the major's trenchant eyes. "My livelihood is dependent on my good standing with Señor López. Violating his trust would put me in an uncomfortably precarious position."

He flipped a dismissive wrist. "Twaddle. The citizens along our southern border are the ones in a precarious position. The war whoop has been heard repeatedly of late as the belligerents resume their war dances. They are ravaging plantations as far north as Brunswick. We suspect your Wakulla Red Sticks of those particularly cunning deeds. Lives have been lost, miss. Brutally taken. Scalped. Left for carrion."

"They are not *my* Red Sticks, Major. And I need no descriptions, thank you. I had my fill at Fort Mims." She closed her eyes to combat the disturbing images he'd conjured as well as the malaise exacerbated by the carriage's motion.

So, the Red Sticks were at it again. That changed things. How many lives had been ravaged as hers had been?

"Are you unwell?" Lieutenant Fanning asked.

Eyes still resting, she settled her head in her palm and held up a hand. "A moment, please."

A high-pitched whistle rang in her ear while her heart tripped out a frantic beat and sweat chilled her nose. This wasn't the usual debility. Something was amiss.

The men carried on dialog between themselves, but their voices were a buzzing mumble until her head jerked and her eyelids launched open. Had she fallen asleep, blacked out?

Mute, the officers stared at her, Lieutenant Fanning's brows pinching. Major Ainsworth eyed her skeptically and picked up precisely where he'd left off. "I'm familiar with your story, Miss McGirth, and you have my condolences on your tragic loss. But the war that was begun on that unholy ground continues to this day. You of all people should understand that we must *end* it."

"Major," the lieutenant said, "might we postpone this until the lady is feeling—?"

A sidelong, commanding glare from the major silenced him.

Lips pressed pale, Lieutenant Fanning retrieved a kerchief from his pocket and passed it to her. "Here you are, miss."

She accepted and smiled her gratitude as Toño's home came in view.

The dwelling was situated in the center of an expansive, well-manicured lawn and shaded by ancient oaks whose thick, sprawling arms dipped low to the ground. Its whitewashed exterior and red-tiled roof were a welcome sight and couldn't shelter Lillian quickly enough. Maybe she could plead exhaustion and retreat to her room. This talk of Red Sticks wasn't helping her head.

Major Ainsworth released a hefty, almost apologetic breath, then embraced Lillian's hand with his own two. "Agreements exist between our nation and those of Spain and Britain. Neither country shall lend aid to the Natives by means of weaponry nor shall they encourage war against us. We have recently come into evidence that Britain is in violation; however, all we have on Spain is our suspicion of foul play. If you care at all for your nation's women and children, you will help us flush out the culprits who are building the red man's arsenal."

She dabbed the square of cotton over her nose and began to wonder whether the *Gallant Lady* was truly in need of repair. "There is no love lost between the Red Sticks and myself. And I heartily agree that it's time they're stopped."

"Then you'll help?" Lieutenant Fanning's pitch swung upward with hope.

The carriage finally rolled to a stop before Toño's house, and Lillian sagged with relief.

While Pepe secured the brake and reins, she addressed Major Ainsworth's inquisitive stare. "Natives come and go regularly through La Conchita, but as you can imagine, I make a study of avoidance. Since Diego speaks Muskogee, he can deal with them directly. That leaves me virtually ignorant to their goings-on, but there are ledgers I've barely touched that might house the information you're seeking. I'll have a look, if that pleases you."

Pepe unlatched the door and kicked the hinged mounting step into position. While the lieutenant descended, the major stretched his mouth into what might have been intended as a smile but more closely resembled a grimace. "It's a start."

What more did he want? Her blood?

She placed her hand in the lieutenant's, taking firm hold in case her fickle knees betrayed her. "We'll have that coffee, Lieutenant, then I'll see that you're both made comfortable in your quarters. During your rest, I'll find an excuse to visit La Conchita before dinner."

"Can it not wait until tomorrow, Major?" Sensitive to her condition, Lieutenant Fanning solidly clutched her elbow. "If the doc were here, he'd insist on it."

Lillian arranged her mantón to block the wind from her throat, liking the young man immensely. "Thank you, Lieutenant, but I'd prefer to have done with it."

An hour later, after the men partook of refreshments and settled into their rooms, Lillian wrapped herself in silk and made her way across the lawn. Dinner was a late affair in Spanish territory; the sun would be fast asleep before the bell was rung for aperitifs. Plenty of time to make it to the hacienda and back.

Diego was out for the afternoon, but if he happened to return early and catch her, he would drape her in red and serve her to the bulls. For the next few days, she'd have to be shrewd in how she negotiated the game board.

Her trail took her within view of the posterior upper-story window that framed the lieutenant and his study of the landscape. She lifted a smile to him, then set upon the lane that had carried them onto the estate. A short distance down it, there was a forgotten, almost overgrown, path that paralleled the Wakulla River and passed La Conchita, which was a mile or so upriver.

Once the Luengo grounds were at her back, she began mentally shuffling through data for something, something useful the absence of which wouldn't draw Diego's attention—a near-impossible task. As was attempting this jaunt in her poor condition.

When she reached the path's opening, she left the lane and collapsed against the first trunk she came to. Panting through the din in her ears, she grumbled about exerting herself for men who thought her no more than a pawn to be shuffled about and sacrificed to a greater cause.

The rhythmic clop of riders coming from the direction of San Marcos coaxed her sweaty back from the tree. If she didn't move in a bit deeper, there would be questions to elude. As she pulled her skirt tight about her legs to keep clear of the winter-naked brambles, she beseeched God for cover, guidance, wisdom, a beguiling demeanor, a deceptive tongue.

She'd take anything He was willing to dole out to an unworthy child such as herself, so long as it satisfied Major Ainsworth, contented Diego with her performance, and ferried her and Marisol out of San Marcos.

Chapter 2

*M*arcus firmed his seat in the saddle as his mount, a blue-roan Arabian, grunted through its nostrils and tested control of the reins.

"Easy there, big boy. Not much can be done about it." He administered several smacks to the stallion's neck, pitying the hot-blooded animal for being kept at such a maddening gait. If not for their surly guide setting pace on a placid sorrel ahead—and if Marcus had any clue as to their destination—he would have kneed the horse into a mane-whistling gallop.

He had his own energy to expend, having been stowed in a ship's cockpit the last week, holding a slop bucket for a host of seasick soldiers. Then there was the knotted, scar tissue blanketing his back— the destroyed flesh that made him woman-shy and never ceased burning and tugging deep into the muscle beneath; its only relief, laudanum or stringent exercise. The first, he outright refused. The second, he partook of as often as possible.

While Marcus hankered for action, Pepe—if Marcus had understood the introduction correctly—was asleep on the job. The man lolled in the saddle, chin scraping his chest.

The rush of water arrested Marcus's attention, as did a stone bridge coming into view. A grin seized him as he freed the top button of his coat. Rapid-fire, he released the other nine in delighted anticipation of the river's freezing embrace. His back was in a fit of rage, and it had been nigh a week since his last full bath. Perhaps that was the reason for the roan's agitation.

Laughing, Marcus reined in, swung off, and began untying his satchel from the saddle strings. "Pepe, my friend, whatever you have in store for the next hour can wait. I've prescribed myself a stout mile of river."

Pepe snorted the sleep from his airways. He turned his horse back, a question hiking his foreign babble.

"Going for a swim." Marcus made a motion like pushing through water and pointed over the bridge.

Comical in his skewed hat, Pepe gestured ahead to a Spanish-style dwelling visible now through a coppice of swamp bay and myrtle.

"Join me," Marcus enthused, inviting the man with a wave. "It'll cure that sour disposition of yours, I promise."

Flapping an indignant arm, Pepe spouted a few bitter phrases, stole the reins from Marcus, and resumed his plodding course.

Enchanted by the crystalline water, Marcus skittered down the short, sloping bank and trudged through a good stretch of boggy grassland to reach a solid shore. There, he dumped his satchel and weapons, then dug out his lye soap, stripped to the waist, and abandoned his clothes in a heap. Wearing only his trousers, he stretched his arms wide, bringing them around to the back to touch thumbs.

He continued his stretches, soaking in the lush view, loving the Floridas as much as he ever had. His first visit, back in sixteen, had been about as pleasant as any blood-bathed mission could be, but that hadn't stopped him from becoming smitten with the land. Even in the harshest of winters, it exploded with life.

Where else might one find palmettos that dwarfed seven-foot azaleas? This shore was lined with them, a solid wall of green. The Floridas' only flaw, that odious red haze. He'd hoped to escape it here in Spanish territory, but there was no avoiding it, not even on the continent's southernmost edge.

Properly limbered, he raced through the shallows and dove arms first into the tranquil current. As expected, the water was gelid, instantly numbing, but he'd been weaned on the bracing Atlantic, and as a university student, he'd competed in the icy Massachusetts Bay. To Marcus, the cold was invigorating.

Marveling at the water's purity, he scrubbed himself pink, then dug in with zesty strokes, ignoring the web of pain that pursued him. For a distraction, he analyzed the details of his arrival: those who'd milled about the dock, those crossing the mote, the distinct lack of Indians.

A tattooed woman had bartered with a Spanish vendor. Several scantly clothed, cinnamon-skinned children had herded three scrawny sows down the main thoroughfare. But of men? Elders, warriors— none. Either San Marcos wasn't the hotbed of Red Stick activity it was reported to be, or they'd all scattered upon sight of U.S. colors flying above the *Gallant Lady*.

The fort was smaller than he'd anticipated, but it had a history of successfully defending this position with ease. It looked ready to do the same now, should duty require it, but he had little interest in the garrison apart from those who came and went through its gate—their nationalities, affiliations, objectives—and how he might unmask their illicit commerce.

For justice.

He brushed the bastion from his thoughts and, elated to be in San Marcos at last, strengthened his kicks, noting his warmed muscles had earned him a reprieve from the scorch spanning his shoulders.

A good half mile down, he tucked and turned back, laboring in the current until his lungs reprimanded him for having neglected his training. When at last his feet planted on the rocky bottom, his legs were threatening to cramp.

Streaming with water, he emerged and was bending to open his satchel for his spare uniform when voices reached him from beyond a stand of azaleas. The conversation was two-sided, male and female, the woman's syllables bitten out in frightened tones.

Obeying the prickle of wariness, he rammed his pistol into the waist of his sodden trousers, collected his sword, and peered discretely through the evergreen shrubs.

A slip of a woman wearing a Spanish shawl and a large, decorative hair comb stood in a challenging posture before an Indian. She was a pretty creature with a plunging neckline that was an inviting, heady brew.

Against his will, Marcus's froward eye took a hearty swig that, accompanied by a series of spluttering heartbeats, reminded him he'd been born a red-blooded males—a favorable sensation that burned away the river's chill and overran every argument for propriety.

The Indian canted toward her. Perhaps his desires ran a similar course? The notion slew the illicit kindling of Marcus's body, as did his notice of the small knife the lady held tucked inside the folds of her gown.

Alarm titillated every nerve, urged him to rush the field. Prudence, however, took it in hand. Creeping nearer the shrub's edge, he primed himself for intervention, while following the instinct to observe a moment more, to glean.

The red feather fluttering against the Indian's hair named him a Red Stick. And where there was one, there was bound to be a swarm of others.

Excellent.

Decked in typical Native-style, he wore an animal-hide breechcloth, leggings bound by thongs, ankle-high moccasins, a long-shirt beneath a woolen vest. His belt hung limp, having been depleted of arms, and he carried no musket. But Indians were deadly with or without weapons. Never to be taken lightly.

The Spanish lady seemed to agree. She snapped a command at him—in his own language, surprisingly enough—backing up as she did.

Despite her brandished weapon, the towering warrior reached for her. It was a casual motion, but the fact he did so despite her near hysteria sent Marcus's pulse into a seizure.

He rounded the bushes at an intolerant march. Sheathed and swinging at his left side, Justice made demands for freedom. He shushed it even while shouting a command understood in any dialect. "That's close enough!"

Both sets of eyes swung his way, the woman's huge and luminescent with unshed tears. The warrior halted, arm extended toward her. An instant later, he produced a long knife from his legging.

Hadn't Marcus known?

The next fuming tick of his heart unveiled gleaming steel. Maintaining scant purchase on equanimity, he released the scabbard to the grass and held the sword down and to the side. He slowed his approach. "No need to get testy, now," he said, forcing his tenor into that of a cool gentleman, as he might for an obtuse patient in need of taming. "The lady isn't fond of you. That's what her knife is saying. So, put it into retreat there, chief, and we'll all breathe a little easier."

The Indian's dark eyes flicked to her. Tiny though she was, she'd make a nice shield.

Dare try, sir! Sword tip flicking upward, Marcus drafted a nervy glare.

A wise fellow, the Native made no move of any sort but shot her through with an inquiry. She startled and gave it right back to him, punctuating her thought with a flash of her blade before sidling closer to Marcus, who could not risk taking his eye off the Red Stick to assess her state.

"Major Ainsworth said a Captain Buck was due to arrive," she said. "Is that you?"

Her speech, precise yet lacking the hauteur of the British, was decidedly American and spawned a hasty mental calculation. *An American woman, wearing Spanish garb, speaking Muskogee.* Most notably, she panicked in the presence of an Indian.

If Marcus had tried to predict whom he might meet here in the shrubs by the Wakulla River, he never, in a fortnight of guesses, would have happened upon the name Lillian McGirth.

That she was here at all had, up to this moment, been unsubstantiated intelligence. With it, had come the rumor that her patron kept her cloistered. Yet there she stood, in his own shadow, shaking him with her presence, for hadn't he just enjoyed a robust perusal of her?

What a kettle he'd boiled for himself! And beneath it, a lively blaze stoked by a vow he would be hard-pressed to keep. The realization swapped his black look for a wry smile. "Captain Marcus Buck, at your service, miss." And he would be—from this hour, until he completed his task by seeing that she was delivered safely to her father. Untouched.

There should be an illegitimate child about somewhere as well. Miss McGirth had taken, soul and body, to her role as prodigal, leaving no erring stone unturned. Marcus's sworn duty was to right them.

"Your timing is...spot on." Her voice, suddenly weak and breathless, perked his medical ear.

To Marcus's great relief, the warrior slowly stowed his knife, cocking a brow at Justice. With a courteous incline of his head, Marcus reciprocated by sheathing his blade. The Indian resumed his discourse with Miss McGirth, and because it was of a less quarrelsome nature, Marcus used the opportunity to assess his charge.

This closer view confirmed his initial sentiment: the woman was an exquisite representation of her sex, and his masculine eye would, unfortunately, have no complaints carrying out its protective vigil.

The surgeon in him commandeered that eye and was promptly disturbed. Those comely lips were drained of blood; her clavicles, though a siren to the mouth, were a shade too prominent; and there was an unnatural element to her breathing. If he laid an ear against that décolletage, he was sure to hear a pounding, erratic pattern.

And she was trembling like a fawn on untried legs. From fear, most would say. Her eyes told another story. They were dilated and marginally sluggish. There was no doubt about it—Miss McGirth was ill. Had been for some time. Marcus was fast following her trail, heartsick over her sad condition, disgusted at the viscount for allowing her to be up and about.

As the Red Stick spoke, she replied in his tongue but shifted focus to Marcus. He thrust a smile into place but feared it was tellingly grim.

Insecurity rumpled her forehead, nudging a fat tear over her lashes. It fell from her chin, and Marcus locked his knees to keep from tucking her under his arm and whisking her into a safe cabin on the ship where he could use whatever means necessary to untrouble her. This mission was larger than his nettlesome attraction to a misplaced woman, lovely though she was.

Even ill, she was finely beautiful, regal in her pearls and silks and in the highborn lift of her chin. The comb rose like a tortoiseshell crown from her glossy cocoa hair, painting her into the essence of nobility. Or a fitting consort for one…

Marcus doubted there was much he didn't know about her. Her father, Zachariah McGirth, had kept Marcus into the candle-consuming hours of several nights, filling his mind with happy visions of her childhood, then detailing the pitiable events of their greatest pain, including the death of her Spanish mother. McGirth had emptied himself like a man long deprived of a listening ear. He'd been desperate and grieving as though his daughter had died. Brokenhearted yet teeming with unremitting love.

Before he'd let Marcus step foot outside his home, he'd begged a promise of him—to care for her as tenderly as he himself would, to nurture her broken spirit, to regard her as virtuous, and as a father might, guard that very thing from pilfering.

Seeing no great difficulty in it and having absorbed a measure of the man's vision, Marcus had readily given his word. A mistake, for McGirth's terms were unattainable; his ideals were flawed. Marcus was flawed.

Miss McGirth was no springtide virgin, and Marcus was waist deep in desire.

He was also her sworn guardian. Rooting that fact into his mind, he opened his arm to encourage her to edge closer. As she did, lifting grateful yet unsteady eyes, his heart broke out of his chest and crept toward her.

God, salvage that crumbling pledge! A level head was needed for what lie before them, and Marcus wouldn't have it with his body sparking at every transient thought and his heart traipsing about like the impoverished vagabond it was.

Once he'd wrestled himself into submission and was satisfied Miss McGirth was calming, he took a hard, protracted look at the Indian's features, the fine, straight nose, the long lashes framing black orbs. Though his hair was cropped to his shoulders and suffering neglect, it was unshaven, and there was not one jot of ink on him anywhere—both characteristics a rare occurrence in Creek warriors.

Pleased at this second windfall, he chuckled and looked straight into the Red Stick's impenetrable eyes. "You are none other than the infamous Tall Bull of the Upper Creeks."

"How could you know that, sir?" Miss McGirth said. "You've only just arrived."

Marcus directed his reply to the chief. "I recognize you from the sketches General Jackson passed through the ranks. The authorities have cast you in a rather poor light, I'm afraid." He shook his head mournfully. "Tall Bull, you are man wanted by the United States government, and I am a man sworn to bring you in. If you'll relinquish your weapon, I'll take you in peacefully. No need to sully ourselves with blood."

Miss McGirth gaped at him and darted a glance into the trees. "Captain, you do realize there's a good chance you have any number of Indian trade muskets pointed at your heart?"

"I do," he said, putting on a cheerful tone. "Makes for a capital tale during bivouac, don't you agree?"

Her returning smile warbled, then faded altogether. "If you persist with your demand, you'll have a bald skull to back it up."

"Have a little faith, duchess. Will you tell him what I said?"

She did, and it earned Marcus a contemptuous glare and a wad of spittle on his boot. After several statements delivered harshly enough to jostle his earbobs, Tall Bull spun to leave.

He thought he'd walk away, did he? Marcus tossed the sword to his left hand and drew his pistol, leveled it at the chief's back. "Halt there!"

Remarkably, Tall Bull complied, turning back. Lips tight and veins straining against his skin, he was a tower of copper menace, but it was the arrow whizzing past Marcus's ear that roused his pulse. He flinched but didn't lower his weapon. It had been an intentional miss. Perhaps the Red Sticks didn't wish to add offenses to their charge.

"Captain!" Miss McGirth's cry was languid and wobbly.

He would attend her, but a warrior — no, a warrior woman — was rushing from the trees, bow fully drawn.

"Devil take her, it's the woman from Fowltown."

Miss McGirth swayed, shawl slithering down, eyes rolling. "C-cap…"

With a gnarl, he dropped the sword to catch her around the waist as she wilted. In the seconds it took him to ease her to the ground, upper body propped on his raised knee, the war woman had interjected herself between his pistol and the chief.

Heedless of the flinted shaft staring him down, Marcus trained his pistol on the naked belly visible between her parted wolf-fur cloak.

Behind her, Tall Bull crossed his arms, amusement illuminating his eyes.

Marcus scowled disdainfully; he wouldn't have taken the chief for a man who sheltered behind a woman's bow.

Her lips shifted sideways into a boastful curl that said she remembered their last encounter and was ever so pleased the tables had turned. Then she adjusted her own aim, lowering the projectile to align with Miss McGirth, the jut of her jaw leaving no doubt as to her resolve.

With the release of the pistol's cock and a single, snarled word, "Checkmate," Marcus dropped his weapon.

At a command from Tall Bull, the woman stowed her arrow. He bypassed her, stood over Miss McGirth, and conducted a too-thorough review of her person.

The nerve.

Marcus drew her closer and administered a censuring squint, which went unheeded. Though irritated, he sensed the threat had passed, so he snubbed the chief in favor of the lady. He arranged her lolling head in the crook of his arm and patted her cheek. "Miss? Can you hear me?"

Lids partially open, she followed his movements with erratic eyes, while a noise of frightened helplessness eked from her throat. Had she been drugged?

Marcus looked to Tall Bull whose expression had transformed to unmistakable concern. How very strange. "Do you have any spirits? Whisky? Tafia?" Marcus added, remembering the cheap rum traded to the Creeks.

Tall Bull removed a flask strung to the war woman's belt, popped its corncob stopper, and handed it over. The action incited a prickly exchange between them.

Marcus ignored the spat, praying it had nothing to do with the current value of his life, and poured the liquor over Miss McGirth's teeth.

She sputtered into full consciousness, choking and wrinkling her nose. "Foul stuff."

"Bucks like a green horse all the way down, but it does the trick." He gave it back to Tall Bull and pressed two fingers into the bend of her throat. As suspected, her pulse was brisk, irregular. "Anything hurt? Head? Stomach?"

She licked her lips and grimaced. "Everything is movement and confusion. It's making me queasy."

Tall Bull darkened her with his shadow. He dangled a small, leather pouch before Marcus and spoke a few words.

"Eat," the war woman offered, surprising Marcus with her English. "He says she would be wise to eat."

He accepted the purse with a thanking nod.

Without another word, they left. Miss McGirth tracked their retreat with a wary eye until they blended into the forest. Then she relaxed back into his hold with a thinly stretched release of air. "Please, don't make me move, or I might be sick."

"There's no great hurry. Take your time." Marcus loosened the pouch's tie. "Roasted pecans. Some of these in your stomach might help. Your admirer seems to think so."

"If that Red Stick was admiring anything, it was the thought of watching my white blood drain from a dozen wounds."

"That's quite a gory imagination you have there."

"Experience speaking."

Maybe, but Marcus wasn't about to let her wallow in it. Her emotional state was already shaky. "The only thing I hear speaking, besides your befuddled tongue, is that belly of yours. It's protesting neglect rather adamantly." He shook the open pouch in front her, but she looked off into the trees.

"No, thank you."

For ten seconds, Marcus let it go, then he recalled having been advised to use a firm hand at the start. She tended to resist male authority, trying it for weakness and taking advantage when she found it, but in all truth, she was simply in search of a man stronger than herself. A man who could parry her quick tongue when she was strong, and talk her down from unbridled fears when she wasn't. McGirth confessed he hadn't been that man for her, and she'd suffered for his ineptitude.

Marcus wouldn't make the same mistake. "The chief was right. You're a scrawny thing in need of a good fattening up." He waved the fragrant nuts beneath her nose.

She inhaled, moistened her lips, and feebly pushed it away. "He didn't say that."

"A man's eyes can say a great deal. Eat."

"I can't."

Why was she fighting this when she was clearly hungry? "Is that the trouble? You can't? Easily remedied. But let's get comfortable first, shall we?"

He'd rather she be tucked into a warm bed in that home he'd noted earlier but not at the risk of making her ill. She needed to put food in not spew it out, so he settled onto his rump, bent a knee as a brace, reminded himself he was a physician, and pulled her gently onto his lap.

Like a ragdoll, she let him, lids crammed shut and forehead wrinkling with discomfort.

Brimming with empathy, his heart lurched and fought its tether. Not good. Not good at all. The doctor speech was failing him.

He glanced behind to the shrubs that hid his belongings. Sensibility would put her flat on the ground and go for his shirt, but that would mean exposing his back to her, and the feel of her eyes raking his scars wouldn't be nearly as pleasant as the feel of her hair caressing his skin.

At the thought, shame swept in. This was an abuse of his role. What had gotten into him? He'd been warned she could suck the common sense right out of a perfectly reasonable man. It had taken all of five minutes to prove that statement true.

McGirth had told of local boys who'd foolishly vied for her affection. He was unclear whether she'd intentionally led them on or whether it was simply her beauty and bewitching nature that drew them like flies to a pitcher plant. That question now stood incontestably answered.

Her father's final message had been clear. *Don't look too deep into her eyes, guard your heart, stay on task. Above all, bring her home.* To the best of his ability, Marcus would.

Here was a mood-rectifying thought: he could imagine her virtuous all day long, but in the end, she was still a loose woman, though no worse a sinner than he. Feeling more his old, rational self, he shifted his position to put a respectable bumper of space between their bodies, then waited a mite longer to let her world stop rolling. When her lashes fluttered open, he tapped her lower lip with a nut. "Give the food a go. I warrant you'll feel better."

She hitched a tight-lipped smile and angled away.

Was that how it was going to be? All right then. Nothing he hadn't dealt with before.

He popped a few nuts into his mouth and chewed lazily. "A soldier defied me once. Refused to eat for two weeks. A protest to latrine duty or some such," he said around a mouthful of mushy nutmeat. "I told him if he didn't eat, I'd sit on him and feed him like a mama bird. Worked like a charm." He tossed in another pecan and, cocking a brow right back at her, dramatically worked the food around in his mouth.

"You wouldn't."

Getting a firm hold of her jaw, he leaned in. "Are you quite certain?"

The line of her lips solidified.

Marcus loathed playing the bully, but she'd never reach Tensaw in this condition. On that stark fact, he swooped down.

A little gasp opened her mouth.

He stopped several inches shy and hastily wedged a pecan between her teeth. Clapping strong fingers over her mouth, he swallowed and nodded. "Go on."

Without further complaint, not even an odious glare, she obeyed. He was about to inwardly trumpet when the seams of her eyes sprouted tears. "That wasn't nice," she mumbled around his hand.

Confound it all!

Resolved to his objective, he disregarded the awful remorse prodding his gut, as well as the tears pooling at his fingers. "Maybe not. But it worked. You're eating, and right now that's more important than your feelings on the matter. Now, finish them up." He filled her unsteady hand and praised God when she munched as instructed.

Tears continued their silent drip, reminding him he was a cad, but she couldn't be trusted to make prudent decisions. Not in this poor of health.

She shivered, and Marcus became aware of the drop in temperature, as well as the gooseflesh that coated her. He stretched for the shawl that lay nearby, forgotten and tucked it about her.

Eyes still closed, she lifted her chin to free it of wayward silken tassels. "You're a saint, Doctor Buck."

"How do you know? I could be a charlatan trying to woo you into sin with tender doctorly concern."

"Because threatening to force nut pulp down a woman's gullet is so alluring."

He laughed aloud. "I should have tried it years ago. Maybe I'd be married by now."

She smiled and eased her eyes open, taking a moment to blink and focus on him. "I've met enough men to know of what I speak."

He shook his head, unwilling to entertain her misconception for even a moment. His hands were stained with blood, drenched in it. And it had nothing to do with surgery. He deserved no praise. "Whatever golden pedestal you have in mind to put me on wouldn't hold up under my shameful past. Best save it for another."

Her lids drifted down again. She let out a long sigh and settled in, turning slightly into him, resting her temple on his chest.

His skin registered the sensation with delight and reprimanded him for having deprived it for so long. An age had passed since he'd been touched by anyone. Not since he'd escaped the British Royal Navy. Not since the sight of his mauled back had frightened his own mother, sent her weeping from the room.

He wouldn't soon do that to another woman. Especially not one in as infirm a state as this one. "Is the world still dancing?"

"Yes, but it's switched from flamenco to a cotillion."

"Were those flamenco steps then? I'd always wondered about the dance."

"Not very impressive, is it?" She chuckled richly.

"Miss, if you don't mind my asking, what ails you? Are you recovering from an infection or the grippe? A fall or blow to the head?"

"Nothing like that. I'm perfectly healthy."

"Could be vertigo," he continued, speaking more to himself than to her. "It's accompanied by dizziness, nausea, and emesis. Poor circulation is another possibility. Are your digits overly cold, numb, tingly?"

"My circulation is fine, Doctor. Truly. I'm well. Just…tired."

She sounded it. Exhausted. Physically, emotionally. And were her pupils unequally dilated?

"Close your eyes." He angled her face into the sun setting over his shoulder and used a flat hand to shade her from its red glow. After a few seconds, he told her to open, dropped his hand, and watched with dismay as her eyes went into a spasm that crossed them for an instant. She was probably seeing two of him. And yes, her pupils were unequal.

"Are you trying to pester me back to health?" She looked drowsier.

"How could I, when you are already in possession of perfect health?"

"Oh, you're a…clever one." Her lids drooped low; she would be asleep in moments.

"I try." He gave her a confident smile, using years of practice to mask his concern. "Rest another minute more, miss." He needed time to think, to run through the list of possibilities: bleeding inside the skull, aneurysm, tumor. Toxins and glaucoma were among the milder options.

"My name…is Lillian McGirth." She released a heavy, open-mouthed sigh, as though forming words cost her the last of her reserves.

"Pleased to meet you, Miss McGirth." Ever so.

The evening had trekked along quite smoothly. He'd bumped into both branches of the mission his first day in San Marcos—Miss Lillian McGirth and Tall Bull, the chief suspected of dealing directly with Iron Wood. But now, unease stabbed at him like the cold did his shirtless back. Her eyes had shown only a slight variation in reaction to light. Fatigue might have been the cause. But he knew better.

Just as he knew the Spanish were breaking treaty right alongside the British. Just as he knew that if he couldn't convince Miss McGirth to prove her loyalty by paving the way for invasion, General Jackson would drag her through the mud. Then, if she was fortunate, he would merely toss her into a cell for the rest of her life.

She stirred and mumbled. "My little Marisol could use a clever physician. You should…pay her a…visit…" Then she exhaled, and sleep overcame her.

Marisol. Her child? No name had been passed to him. That Marisol was also ill dispirited him. It would appear he had not one patient but two.

In the throes of an impressively deep sleep, Miss McGirth's eyes jumped beneath their closed lids. She wouldn't be waking any time soon.

The ache in his back flared, and the evening's chill deepened, but he sensed she needed sleep like a medicine, so as any good doctor might, he gave it to her.

The clamor of laughing gulls extricated Lillian from a dream-infested sleep. Her body convulsed, bringing her torpid mind back from Diego's chains to the riverside and the gentleman who cradled her.

Captain Marcus Buck, surgeon. The American. The saint. The stranger. Despite the familiarity of his name, his face rang not a single bell.

She blinked into his bare chest and wiped at moisture that had seeped from the corner of her mouth. It might be embarrassing to be caught drooling, if she felt he were the type to mind.

What had possessed her to fall asleep in the first place? The tug had been fierce, as it often was, but it had been the sense of absolute security — the first in an age — that had allowed her to succumb to it. If only she could indulge a bit longer, but, no, she mustn't. She'd already presumed too much.

To steady herself, she laid a hand flat against him, noting his crisp, clean scent of lye and appreciating he was solid, unmoving. As was the rest of the world, thank God. Reluctant to set it all to spinning again, she eased upright and remained motionless.

Senses sharper than they'd been in a while, she absorbed her surroundings with renewed awareness. All that remained of the day was a glow that billowed up from behind the trees on the opposite bank. It stained the Wakulla's ripples with fluctuating tones of orange and red while blackening palms and moss-encumbered cypresses in the first dark shades of the night. Pecan husks scattered the nearby ground, engorging the air with the sweet, musty scent of their decay, and beneath her fingers, warm flesh of the masculine variety.

The man was a rock. He exuded fortitude and security, and she felt as though she could sit exactly so until week's end, absorbing his strength, and not be ready to give him up.

"How do you feel?" He considered her with wide, vigilant eyes. One of his hands rested lightly on her back, the other on her arm as if he expected her to teeter and intended to perform a rescue.

Dear God, he was an admirable soul.

She smiled, relieved to find the lightheadedness had mostly abated. "My head is a little clearer, thank you." And she had more energy than she'd enjoyed in a week.

He'd been correct about the nuts; they'd helped. Their buttery flavor remained on her tongue, and she wanted more. The doctor had been too smart for her, manipulating her into breaking penance, but now that she'd trespassed, she saw the wisdom in eating. She would need strength to flee this place.

"Was I asleep long?"

"Not long enough. I suspect you could sleep the day away and wake up needing more."

"I haven't slept much lately." In addition to the recent vigils for Marisol, she'd spent a month of nights at the altar in attrition and begging God to provide a way of escape. The hours she did spend in bed, she was always on edge, expecting every tiny noise to be Diego coming for his dues.

Or Cabo Varela. When Diego was away, the cabo was assigned as her guard. He'd never touched her, but his eyes said he was waiting for the right opportunity.

Doctor Buck nodded, while performing a close-range examination. Earlier, she'd detected shades of desire in those gray eyes, then a flash of concern, but now, his expression was unreadable.

"Let me guess. I'm dying," she teased, suspecting she was simply over-tired and underfed. There was little he could do about either.

To defy the Church was to call down trouble. Fray Emilio's power was extensive and awe-inspiring. He was the only man in San Marcos whom Diego cowed to, which left Lillian vulnerable to him.

Doctor Buck's focus shifted, even though his eyes didn't move. He was seeing *her* now, not a patient. It was a kind look, compassionate. Not a hint of seduction, but that didn't stop Lillian's heart from sighing. Apart from Toño, who was a father figure, and Max Bellamy, whose heart belonged to another, men hadn't been so kind of late.

"We're all dying, Miss McGirth." His mouth bent in a smile of the more serious sort.

Marcus Buck… His name, it said something to her. But those dark eyes and that straight nose…the slender mouth… It was set above a strong chin and framed by a jaw soft enough to lend a certain boyishness. The hint of a full, dark beard on his shaven cheeks, however, rescinded any notion he was anything but a man. An attractive one, at that.

She let those details wander the stores of her memory. No, no recollection whatsoever.

He tipped her head into what was left of the sun. Could he read the desperation in her? The longing, the need she had to be gently touched, to be protected from Diego, from herself? To be cherished? The last, a fool's wish.

"If not impending death, then what do you see?" she asked.

For a lengthy, unblinking time, he scrutinized her, his expression far too intense, his thumb absentmindedly tracing a line on her jaw, entrancing her and enflaming her need.

Of a sudden, he dropped his hand and set her on the ground away from him. He stretched his legs. "I see a woman who should be indoors, sitting down to a steaming bowl of soup. But as alluring as it is, I *refuse* to regurgitate it for you, so don't bother asking." He wore as straight a face as any she'd seen.

At her outright laughter, he broke into a grin and stood, bringing her up with him. The abrupt firming of his lips and splaying of his nostrils hinted at poorly disguised pain, but he banished it in a trice. "Steady on. You're leaning. Take a moment or someone might mistake you for a tippler."

She'd been called worse. "Let them think what they will," she said, taking note of his form.

Extraordinarily broad shoulders tapered in a sharp V to his lean waist. Muscle bulked his arms; it thickened his neck and defined his chest and stomach in a way she'd never seen. Great strength must accompany such an unusual body.

Unusual, yes, but not unappealing.

Though indisposed, she removed her gaze to his face and took a stab at his age. He surpassed her twenty years by a half dozen or so, each one visible in the hairline creases at the corners of his mouth and in the experience wizening his eyes.

A shiver rocked him.

She *tsk*ed and whipped off her mantón and threw it around him. "You're chilled to the bone." There he stood half naked and frozen stiff, all because of her, and she hadn't even thought to offer him her shawl until he was shivering.

Draped in silk, with blue tassels catching on his chest hairs, he threw back his shoulders, appearing affronted and knowing full well he looked more than a little ridiculous. He started to shrug out of it, but she gave his arm a little slap. "You're dangerously cold, and you know it. Wear the thing. Besides, it's just desserts for the momma bird performance. Take it on the chin, Doctor." With a yank, she tugged it closed in the front.

He donned a conciliatory smirk. "All right, but let it be known, you throw a far meaner punch than I."

"Proudly noted."

"There's a clean set of regimentals in my haversack. I left it there, beyond those shrubs." He offered his arm, and she gladly accepted. As they made their way to where he'd indicated, he said, "Who is Marisol?"

"Did I mention her?"

"You said she could use a clever physician."

"I did?"

"Mm-hmm."

What else had she said? This inability to hold her thoughts together or keep up with conversation was taxing and worrisome.

"What's wrong with her?" he asked.

She chose her words carefully, avoiding the truth. "A fever's plagued her for two days. The vomiting started this morning. She's a tiny thing. Six months tomorrow. Señor López sent a report earlier saying she's no worse than this afternoon. No better either."

"She's your daughter, I take it. And the father would be Señor López?"

Lillian stopped dead, effectively removing herself from him. She must have said more than she realized. There was no use denying it, but now he would judge her, like all the rest.

Well, she thought with a stubborn cock of her jaw, she wouldn't apologize or bow her head in shame. Not about Marisol. No matter how she'd come into the world, she was the best thing to ever happen to Lillian, who would welcome a lifetime of rejection to be assured one more day with her little sunshine.

"Is that a problem?" she said loftily.

"I won't deny you've created an unsavory stew for yourself, but I'm an impartial doctor not a judge." His smile was kind, a lance to her defensive posture. "Take me to her. I'll do whatever I can to help." He pointed to the densely shadowed forest, its palms crackling in the breeze. "Mind turning that way so I can dress?"

When she did, he put the shawl about her and, some minutes later, rejoined her again fully dressed—black short-tailed coat and knee-high gaiters; white neck kerchief, buttons, and binding; gray trousers; and a bicorn that labeled him an officer.

She'd always been partial to a man in uniform, but this one, whose coat barely contained his breadth, had just spoiled her to all others.

He was delectable. And unwed. However, in the brief period she'd spent in his company, she'd come to respect him too much to entertain fanciful notions of romance. He deserved better than her.

That fact didn't stop her from enjoying their riverside stroll or feeling a tad smug to be seen on his arm as they neared the estate.

The grounds opened before them, the whitewashed house setting off Toño's plump figure as he trotted his new Arabian before his guests. Another man was with them, but Lillian couldn't identify him until his bright laughter rang across the yard.

Max.

For no reason at all, Lillian laughed with him. The Englishman's perpetually good humor was always contagious no matter the distance.

"You must be feeling better," Doctor Buck observed.

"I am, but Maxwell Bellamy is the sort who could make the Devil smile on Easter."

"Bellamy…he's French?"

"British. Leftovers from the conflict. Former Royal Navy, actually. You might appreciate that, being an army man yourself."

His stride hitched as a dark cloud passed behind his eyes in the first look of displeasure she'd seen on the man. Maybe he didn't appreciate it? But he would fall in well with Max, same as everyone.

Eager to help him along that way, she continued. "He's an adventurer of the truest sort. Couldn't get enough of our *untamed land*, as he calls it. At war's end, he shucked his uniform and came back. He works in trade now. Out of the Bahamas. He has a store a couple miles up the Wakulla. You'll like him. He gets on with everyone."

"Including the Devil." The doctor's eyes went tight in their long-distance focus. "I'm intrigued."

"Your name is eerily familiar, but I'm certain if we'd met, I would have remembered you." If nothing else, those stunning shoulders.

"I *am* rather unforgettable." He flashed a mischievous grin that had probably melted the hearts of a dozen young ladies, hers included.

"What you did today certainly was. Thank you for stepping in. I…wasn't handling it so well myself."

He studied the ground passing beneath their feet. "I wouldn't trust a loathsome goat with that warrior woman, but the chief… He gave me a start at the first, but before it was done, he'd proved sensible. In fact, when you fainted, he became concerned."

An abrupt, disbelieving laugh rattled her chest. "You're mistaken. There are a few exceptions, to be sure, but on the whole, Creek warriors are incapable of showing concern toward white women. Not even children earn their pity. That tip is also given from a well of experience." Her volume was increasing, but it couldn't be helped.

The subject invariably made her unreasonable. It made her blood spike and her breath come fast. She should shut it down before she ruined whatever good the doctor might see in her, but she couldn't ignore such an ignorant statement. "Would you like to know the last thing that Red Stick said before he stalked off? He told you to keep me alive because he isn't *through* with me yet. I read that as a threat. To my life, perhaps. How do *you* interpret it, Doctor?" Sarcasm lathered her words.

"I can't be sure, but his bearing was mild," he said, maintaining a polite, conversational tone. "He didn't seem the type to snuff out a woman's life, no matter the color of her skin."

Out of respect, she gave thought to his perspective by considering her own memories of those frightening moments. Tall Bull had barely resembled the man she'd known in Kossati. His flowing hair had been replaced by a shortened, poorly managed mane, taking with it the vanity that had always characterized him. In addition, he'd been more solid, stately, and it was true he hadn't done or said anything outright menacing. He might have even looked concerned, as the doctor stated.

She shrugged it off, unwilling to excuse the Indian. "As they say, looks can be deceiving. He's a wanted man for a reason."

"Because he refuses to abide by the treaty. General Jackson might disagree, but I've read every report on the man. To my knowledge, he's but a marauding thief and a relentless, deluded visionary. The army intends to bring him to heel, but he's not a killer of innocents."

Wrong. Tall Bull's tomahawk had been put to good use at the massacre of Fort Mims. For all she knew, it could have been his arrow that killed Beth. His presence there was enough to earn him a noose. "Then your reports, and thus your knowledge, are lacking!" Her heart was pounding now, making her head buzz.

"Whatever you may think, I feel certain he has no designs on your life."

Fists balling, she pulled up short. Tears stung the backs of her lids, but she barely noticed for the pricks of light sparking in her periphery. "I won't have you defending that man to me!"

"Defending him? No! I'm attempting to relieve your distress!" He shoved fingers through his hair, knocking off his bicorn.

She blinked hard to clear her vision and jolted when the doctor grabbed her by the arm to straighten her. Had she been about to topple?

He sighed and bent to retrieve his hat. "Instead, I'm adding to it. Forgive me, Miss McGirth. I underestimated your sensitivity to the matter." The hat went back on along with his straight-backed composure.

If she hadn't known it before, she did now: the man was a dear. And she was an edgy cat, back arched, claws extended.

She lowered her head with a shake. "You couldn't have known I would come apart. It's the Red Sticks, you see. They affect me." The sour taste of their name thrust her gaze into a skittish rake of her surroundings. "Compliments of Fort Mims. And one lovely year as a captive." Bitterness underscored her tone—the unveiling of her truest heart.

And this fine gentleman was getting a full view. Shame should accompany her knowledge of it; determination did instead. Major Ainsworth had presented her a convenient, if frightening, opportunity to thwart the rebels, and Tall Bull's statement had reminded her of its dire need.

Doctor Buck's countenance was shifting toward compassion, but before he could employ it, she rushed to speak, hands knotting before her. "Your Major Ainsworth rattled me earlier with talk of your *true* mission."

His compassion gave way to nostril-flaring vexation. "Allow me to apologize for my superior. He is known for being somewhat abrupt and single-minded. I hope he didn't upset you too severely."

"He did that." Her short laugh faltered, betraying her nerves. "But he's right. The Red Sticks are a scourge. If I can help in any way, I *should*." The emphasis was for herself.

The innocents along the frontier shouldn't have to live in fear or suffer the fate of her neighbors and friends.

Lillian's own fear, that of Diego catching her, should be dwarfed by the import of the mission, but she knew what Diego was capable of, how he could make her suffer. But if she succeeded… How delightful it would be to ruin him!

A smug smile crooked her mouth. "Diego López is long overdue a good humbling. Happily, doing so will also hamper the Red Sticks."

"So, he *is* aiding them?"

"Oh my, yes. Where else would they get their weapons, their supplies, their everything? I understand you need intelligence proving that. I might be able to help."

"Truly?" Doctor Buck's glow of delight was instant. "You are a gift, Miss McGirth, and I'm beyond thrilled to have you join me — us. It's an important assignment. Important to *me*."

"So I see." It was in every crinkle of his smile, and she was gratified to have put that very thing in place. With luck, it would stay. Resolving to ruin the don didn't make it any easier of a feat to accomplish. The likelihood of failure was — No, she would not consider it.

Max's laughter floated across the field, but even *it* could not assuage the needles of anxiety prodding her stomach. "You understand there is great risk involved for me?"

Smile jelling, eyes sobering, he looked to where her hands had renewed their twisting. Cautiously, he reached, hovering above them.

He thought she might protest? Absurd.

She latched onto him, but he unhooked her and began kneading away rigidity. Its effect was immediate and far-reaching, working even the kink in her middle.

"I do, miss. And that risk plagues me. Your safety is of prime importance, and I will do everything in my power to ensure it. Just the same, please use the utmost caution. I wouldn't abide you coming to harm. No matter the mission."

Was it a comfort he intended to ensure her safety or a worry that he so strongly felt the need for it? There would be less reason for concern if he would promise passage on his ship.

The request budded on her tongue, but remembering the major's insinuation of disloyalty, she snipped it off. Major Ainsworth's doubt in her, coupled with Diego's accusation of treason, confused her, but mostly, it struck terror in her bones.

Before broaching the subject of flight from San Marcos, she would prove the major wrong. Then, she would lay bare her personal trouble. Surely, out of gratitude, he wouldn't deny her refuge. She was an American after all, and she *was* on his side.

The pressure on her hand increased, drawing her back to the doctor's charitable eyes.

She straightened, trying to match his reassuring manner. "Thank you for your concern. I share it, but the don is no heartless Red Stick. I survived them; I'll survive him too."

That calming smile of his wavered. "Your trials during the war grieve me. Perhaps you'll consider me an understanding friend. I'm no stranger to the shadows of a difficult past and the turmoil they can inflict."

His eyes lost focus, drifted beyond her. To that very past, she reckoned. He released her, exchanging her hand for his sword's pommel.

"Doctor Buck." She knew what it was to become ensnared in those uncomfortable places. When he returned to her, blinking, she provided a sympathetic smile. "Those shadows, they darken you. Even now."

"Do they? No surprise, I suppose." He tucked his chin, thoughtful.

"Was it the war for you as well?"

He regarded her before giving a great exhalation. Even after he seemed resigned to speaking, his mouth opened and closed twice before finding purchase. "At the start of it, a British frigate seized my father's sloop. We were off the coast of Massachusetts. They pressed me into service. I was…enslaved. For almost a year. I've spent the intervening time overcoming the impact of it." The smile he afforded was likely meant to offset the gravity of such a statement, but it was too labored to be effective.

"Doctor, that's…" She destroyed the lump forming in her throat; few men valued pity. "It's an atrocity. All of it. War, enslavement, man's capacity for great evil. I'm truly sorry." Peculiar, though, that they'd each spent a year in captivity. Different enemies, different settings. Same war, same sorrow. "Thank you for telling me, sir. Not easy to speak of, I know. But it *is* uplifting to find an understanding friend."

She affectionately pressed into his hand. He firmed the connection, clinging as though to salvation until, of a sudden, he let go and swept his arms behind him.

When his face finally rose, it carried none of the angst she would have expected; its previous warmth was restored and deepening with his study of her. "Quite agree." He leaned into a polite bow. "And now you know *my* motivation for expelling foreign influence from our shores."

A noble one and every bit as solid as her own. "I'm glad for it and shall add yours to my own. For wrongs done against us both. For justice," she asserted, coming alive with the charge.

Surprise registered on him. It remained while he pondered her, brow lowering. "Indeed… For justice."

Without prelude, he drew his sword and held it before her, blade flat against his palms. "Please, have a look."

Uncertain, she bent to examine the weapon, which appeared to be standard issue. She knew little of swords, having picked up her sparse knowledge from Phillip Bailey, a childhood friend and former infantry officer. His sword had been almost identical, down to the brass eagle head crowning the handle.

The doctor's blade was straight with one finely sharpened edge; its motif, a gilt shield bearing an infantryman. Nothing else stood out to her apart from its pristine condition, but he clearly expected her to make note of something. "It's beautiful. The steel is exceptionally blue.

The blade is unmarred and the—" What was there, between the motif and the guard?

Eyes still refusing proper focus, she neared, squinting, and slid a finger across an etched scripture reference.

When she opened her mouth to ask after it, he preempted her. "Thus speaketh the Lord of hosts, saying, 'Execute true justice and shew mercy.'"

Her eyes jumped to his. "Justice?"

Chin dropping in a slow nod, he penetrated her with his gaze. Scouring for…what? "And so I've named her," he said, voice low, intense, "Justice."

"Señorita!"

Lillian turned.

One of Toño's sergeants jogged across the green. "*El capitán os busca!*"

"Tell Toño I am coming," she called back in Spanish, "and ask Ines to put out a bowl of broth, then come back and show the doctor to his room." If she could find a solitary moment away from those with feet quick to run to the friar with a report, she would eat a little for strength.

When she turned back, Justice was stowed. He smiled and extended his arm.

She accepted and, while they completed the walk, explained his sleeping arrangements and her role in his stay. As he was shown to his quarters, Lillian freshened up and went to the servant's table situated in a small room next to the kitchen. Pleased to find it empty, she sat down to a bowl of chicken broth heartened with rice and partook a bit of it before setting the bowl in front of Toño's dog.

Rapid hoof beats carried in from the yard. When she went to the side door to see who'd arrived, the doctor rushed in, bumping past her, face rigid.

"Pardon me, miss. I'll be back." He was already halfway down the hall, coattails flapping, before she could ask what troubled him.

"Miss McGirth." Max's voice turned her back to the open door. He stood in the yard, hat in hand, as dashing as always in his tan breeches, gray frock coat, and spotless-white, ruffled shirt.

With a strengthening meal in her stomach, she skipped down the porch steps and opened her arms to him. "Max, how are you? Scaring off the Americans already?"

"I've sent the doctor for your woolen wrap. You're needed at La Conchita." He angled in for two kisses but lingered on the first, turning it into a dread-filled embrace. "Lillian, dearest, Marisol has taken a foul turn."

Chapter 3

Skirt in hand, Lillian stormed the spiral staircase of La Conchita's courtyard, Doctor Buck behind her. She'd expected to be greeted with her infant's wailing, but the silence terrified her.

Above, Barbury leaned over the loggia's rail. "You brung a doc? Jesus be praised."

"What's wrong, Barb?" she called up. "Pepe wouldn't say."

"She ain't right, Missy Lillian, just ain't right. And Suni, that old biddy, won't hear nothin' I say!"

Lillian blew past Barbury and burst into her stifling suite. The fire was ablaze; the windows were closed.

Suni, Diego's mulish childhood nanny, held the swaddled baby tight against her chest. Tears coursing the myriad seams on her cheeks, she paced before the poster bed but stopped upon sight of Lillian. "*¡La nena no se despierta!*"

"She isn't waking," Lillian explained to the doctor as she dashed in. "Give her to me!"

Mari was limp, and an angry red rash peppered the lower half of her face. Heat penetrated the swaddling—Suni's antiquated remedy for any illness.

"God have mercy, she's burning up!" Lillian said.

"Get her out of that wrap." Doctor Buck crossed to the window, threw back the drapes, and flung wide the balcony door, allowing the cold air to sweep in.

"This is your doing. *Yours!*" Suni accused with a fierce jab of her finger. "God's wrath has caught up to your wickedness." She clutched the ivory crucifix atop her black taffeta widow's garb, as though to protect against Lillian's iniquity.

No time for a hopeless defense, Lillian hurriedly unwound the linen but went motionless when Marisol contorted in a wave that ended in a spew of bile.

With her next breath, she gurgled and choked.

"Doctor!"

"She's aspirating!" He snatched the baby away and flipped her onto her side, laying her side along his arm. As her body convulsed and retched, he dispensed firm pats to her back and spoke in low, soothing tones. "It'll be all right. A cough will not end her. Give it some time." His smile was closed and small but no less a mainstay.

Unsteady and terrified, Lillian fixed her eyes to him.

His own rose and probed her. "Stay with me, miss. It would grieve me to let you fall."

Long minutes passed, and all the while, Barbury wiped up the splatter, and Suni sobbed through the decades on her rosary. At last, Mari's wheezing ceased, and Lillian sank onto the bed.

"That's the way, sweetheart." Doctor Buck laid her on her back beside Lillian. "Big, deep breaths. No more frightening your mother, hear?" His voice was far too calm for the situation.

Lillian was screaming inside her head, but he moved at a confident, steady pace, unpeeling layers of clothing.

"This fever has wrung you out, little lady, but I have a mind to put an end to it" He pressed his middle finger to the inside of her upper arm, then glanced up at Lillian and offered her a smile that, should it be bottled, would be the cure to any number of illnesses.

The vice on Lillian's mind eased, so she went to the bureau drawer for fresh diapering. "Barb, make sure that basin has plenty of fresh water."

While Barbury took the pitcher and hurried out, Lillian hoisted the basin and went to the window and flung the stagnant water into the night. "What happened, Suni?"

Still clasping her rosary, Suni emerged from the corner, the fan in her apron pocket thumping her stout middle. "My Diego was called to Tallahassee, and that cabo of his refused to get off his loafing backside to fetch either of you!"

"Worthless man!" Lillian plunked the basin onto its stand and began collecting the damp clothing the doctor was removing from the baby. "Did he go, or do I need to whip the worm into action?"

If Diego wasn't summoned, more than one back would feel his wrath.

"*Pues, ¡nó!* The cabo sent Pepe for you and another soldado for my Diego. I heard someone ride out hard for Tallahassee. And well he should!"

The journey would take the messenger into the early hours, and Diego wouldn't be back before midmorning the following day.

"What is this?" Doctor Buck stood at the edge of the bed, looking down at the baby who was naked but for the teething necklace. Her ribs protruded in sharp angles, contrasting severely with her sunken belly. That awful rash on her face extended down onto her chest in tiny, broken blisters.

Lillian grasped her throat. "That rash! It's the first I've seen—"

"The necklace, miss. Where did she get it?"

Why? Had the seeds caused the irritation?

"Where?" he repeated, more insistent.

"I-I made it for her. From the shrub in the plaza below. The tall one. She's teething, and—"

"Do you know what species of plant it is?"

Panic began a slow crush of her lungs. "No, I'd seen the Indians do it, so—"

"Not with these they didn't." He captured the candle off the bedside table and went to the fireplace to light the wick. "Find me a knife."

Had she given her baby those awful hives? The dirty clothes tumbled from her grasp. Afraid of the truth, she withdrew the knife at her ankle.

He returned the burning candle to its place, severed the necklace string, and scooped the unconscious child off the bed and away from the offense. "Ah, doesn't that feel better?" Hastening to the basin, he cradled Marisol's floppy body and caught Barbury's eye as she came back in, water sloshing over the brim of her pitcher. "A cup, please."

She swiped the water glass from the nightstand, and as the doctor used it to ladle water from the basin, self-loathing rose in Lillian's throat so thick it cut off her wind.

The contents of the glass poured over Marisol, but she didn't react, not even a flinch. "Barb," he said, "set up another basin here beside this one. We'll rotate them and rinse a full ten minutes."

Afraid to do more harm, Lillian wept and stared at her motionless child. What sort of mother did this? The type who rightly deserved every tragic consequence that came her way. Unwittingly, or otherwise, she was proficient at destroying those she loved.

"Diego." His name came out on a strangled whisper. He would rage. Fear compounded upon fear, smothering all thoughts but two: Lillian had harmed their child, and Diego would have his vengeance.

Barbury returned, bearing a second basin, and took in Lillian's storm of tears. "Why, missy, it gonna be all right."

But it *wasn't* all right! Marisol looked near death's door. The seeds had unnecessarily complicated an already dangerous fever.

Doctor Buck stepped to the new basin and put Marisol under the fresh, running water. The pitcher went dry, so Barb hurried out to refill it. Tears dripped from Lillian's chin, and she gasped in frenzied little puffs.

"Look at me, Miss McGirth," he said, repeatedly bathing Marisol's neck and chest.

She shook her head, unable to release Marisol from her sight for fear she would miss her child's last breath.

"You will look at me and listen, or you will remove yourself from the room until you are fit to do so," he said calmly, firmly. "I understand your distress, but this display of grief is no help to anyone.

Dry your face"—he nodded at the towel on the stand's rack—"and take over here."

She choked on a persistent sob, but he was right. With a cleansing breath, she nodded and did as told.

Marisol's head rolled over Lillian's arm, and her toothless jaw hung loose. Heart in knots, Lillian resisted pulling her against her chest where her clothing might irritate Mari's tortured skin.

Using his handkerchief, Doctor Buck picked up a seed and examined it beneath the candlelight. He nodded somberly. "Castor seed. It's known to cause a reaction with generous contact. If the seed's skin is broken…" He resumed his diligent inspection.

Reaction… Generous contact…

Nausea festered. Once again, faintness came on like the plague. She propped against the basin's stand and watched with escalating anxiety as he threw the seeds into the fire, handkerchief and all. He spun and began stripping the bed as Barbury entered. "I want the baby's clothes boiled, and ask the lady there"—he gestured to Suni—"if she'd be willing to help me put fresh linens on the bed."

As Barbury hastened to his bidding, he went to the armoire, but Suni ordered him with signals to return to Marisol. At the basin adjacent to Lillian's, he scrubbed his hands with enough ferocity to remove skin.

She squeezed her eyes shut, both to block the sight and to rectify her vision. "Tell me everything. I can handle it."

His hands came to a standstill in the water. Slowly, he turned to her, looking first at her shaking arms then her swimming eyes. His own filled with doubt as his lips went taut. "They're bad enough, but she couldn't have ingested much." He picked up the towel and dried his hands. "The best we can do is begin pushing fluids right away. Until we know more, let me do the worrying. Agreed?"

"You expect a mother not to worry?"

He heaved a sigh, his gaze falling to Marisol and lingering. Was he counting the times her chest wall retracted under her ribs? Did he note the cracks in her thirsty lips, the way her eyes were rolling erratically behind their lids? What did these things mean to a learned man like Doctor Buck, a man who knew the seed's potential?

In one afternoon, he certainly knew enough about the child's mother and her cursed nerves to be frugal with his truest thoughts. That fact spoke louder than any verbalized death sentence.

Death. Could it truly come to that? Her baby's hot, dry skin said it could. As the full potential for disaster settled in, her breathing accelerated. Desperate, she resumed rinsing. Lillian's lungs spasmed with a series of sharp intakes, her need for air not being met quickly enough despite her lungs sucking faithfully at the air. *Weak, always weak!*

Doctor Buck gripped her elbow. "Slow your breathing, miss, or you'll go into distress."

She couldn't. A violent tremble sprang to life in her middle, shaking its way out, propelled by a question she was too afraid to ask for fear the answer was *no*.

"Let's get you both into bed." He set the glass down, and took her around the shoulders and under the knees.

She gratefully released her weight to him, absorbing his mind-soothing strength, tucking Marisol against her, willing God to forgive, forget, restore. Though she doubted He would, within the brace of the doctor's arms, she regained her breath.

With unexpected generosity of spirit, Suni slipped a pillow in place an instant before Lillian's back met the headboard.

The doctor began a retreat, but Lillian stopped him with a grip on his wrist. She lifted her eyes to him, took a stab at hope, and gave the question life. "Can you save my daughter?"

⁂

Marcus tugged, but Miss McGirth's hold was unexpectedly firm. Even the frailest of patients could conjure strength. Evidence of desperation. Not a word had been spoken of death, yet she knew. Mothers always knew.

He ached for her. Pity the woman for having unwittingly poisoned her child.

"Can you save her?" The shake she gave to his wrist affixed his attention to those walnut-brown eyes.

How was he to defend against them? They were awash in tears, luminous in the candlelight, pupils inordinately large, lashes thick and wet. A rift tore across the wall of his careful reserve, letting the urge to cosset away her anguish seep through.

Could he do it with a father's mindset as the vow dictated? A brief inner review snuffed that possibility. The remedy might be the same — a warm embrace, a softly spoken word — but McGirth's requisite father figure would not be dispensing it.

Unnerved, he rent his gaze from hers, relieved at the sight of Barb standing by the foot of the bed. Brows arching in silent inquiry, she straightened, ready to serve.

"Barb, we'll need cool water in a tin for Marisol and a small serving spoon. For her mother, a dry gown and warm wrapper. And see about having dinner brought up. It promises to be a long night."

The woman slipped out, and finding no other excuse for distraction, he returned his focus to Miss McGirth. With equal diligence, he looked away again — to the black-clad woman crying in the corner, to the open patio door and the gibbous moon scraping against the balustrade, to the baby whose tiny organs valiantly fought the toxins — anyplace but to the mother where impulses would goad him to stroke her hair and lie.

Whatever Marcus did or said in the next minutes, it would *not* include the ugly facts — that a single seed could drop a man in a day, that the only antidote was a hope in God's mercy.

"I've lost so many already, if I lose her — Doctor, I *mustn't* lose her. Please."

"If you're asking a promise of me, I cannot give it." By delicate coaxing, he removed her fingers and turned for the hearthside and its sad scattering of glowing embers.

Using the poker, he organized them into a productive mound that balanced the freeze he'd produced in the room. While he worked, he focused his ears on the old widow pattering about behind him — a preferable sound to that of Miss McGirth begging her child in subdued, heartrending tones to forgive her.

He propped his forearm on the mantel and, let the growing heat singe his cheeks and airways—a hiemal frost compared to what Miss McGirth had endured in the flames of Fort Mims.

Because of that very battle, Marcus believed her to be worthy of respect, regardless of her recent poor choices. Major Ainsworth didn't agree. Guilty until proven innocent was his personal motto, and innocence could be proven only through absolute cooperation with their mission. Anything short of that would label her a traitor.

Marcus drank in the searing heat until his lungs burned with it. McGirth had sworn she was a true citizen wrapped in an inextricable web of intrigue. For justice, she'd said with fiery intent, proving her father correct and herself a beautifully kindred soul. It also affirmed his belief that this was God's assignment, not his.

Major Ainsworth should be mollified now regarding her loyalty, but Marcus was far from comfortable with the jeopardy she placed herself in. What exactly would it cost her, and would Marcus be able to live with the product of her sacrifice?

The old woman closed the window with gusto, causing Marcus to yank his head up and bringing him eye-to-eye with a sight that sent him skipping back a full pace, heart pounding a ferocious beat.

On the mantel before him sat an expertly crafted model ship, her rosewood glossy in the firelight. She was a fifty-gun, spar-decked frigate and fourth-rate ship of the line. Attached to the mizzen course, frozen in a proud wave of her colors, was a tiny Royal Navy ensign. That hideous flag.

Her rigging, portholes, anchors, dials, wheels—all accurate to the detail. And he should know. He'd spent an agonizing eleven months and three days enslaved to her life-sized twin.

Ire glowed within him. At the brazen nerve of the Royal Navy; at the endless backbreaking labor, the scorching sun, and blistering cold; at the injustice of slavery and being forced to fight his countrymen; at the upwelling of grief that didn't need to *be* except for Britain's greed and lust for war. But the fuel that made his blood burn hottest was the fact the British frigate was displayed on a Spanish mantle in his dependent's quarters.

Reflexively, his hand sought the comfort of Justice's hilt. Finding his hip empty, it struck out and wrenched the frigate from its stand. He ripped away the Union Jack and tossed it into the fire. Thinking better of it, he hurled the frigate in too. The flames sparked and licked, hungry for the silken sails and bubbling varnish, and as the miniature vessel settled into the embers, he grinned at its smoking, upturned hull.

Many nights he'd dreamt of the *HMS Scourge* tinting the night in oranges and blacks, and if he happened to be tied to the mainmast awaiting his next encounter with the cat when it went down, it wouldn't have made a lick of difference. So long as the accursed warship met the ocean floor.

This scant holocaust would have to do for now, but he *would* demand atonement. For himself, for justice, and yes, for Miss McGirth who'd bravely taken up his banner. Currently, she had eyes only for her child and had, thankfully, missed his coarse behavior.

Empowered, he returned to them, determined to make a difference. It was time something went right for this woman, and he was proud to have been given the responsibility. Whether her child reached Tensaw with her, only God could say, but Marcus would hang by the neck from a bowsprit before he let the British and their covert allies ruin her life. She needed a protector and healer, and by God's leave, he needed to be that man.

It was an irrepressible calling, and he wasn't one to shirk his duty. Duty and desire, however, were often muddled. Care would have to be taken to keep them in their proper order. A vow was a vow.

He leaned over the baby, tuning into her serrated breaths, each one agony to his ears. "You asked if I can save her." Locking eyes with Miss McGirth, he willed courage into her. "It's the habit of some in my profession to hide painful truth, but I strive to be forthcoming," he said, pulling the sheet up to the baby's chest. "The seeds can be deadly, and Marisol's constitution is considerably weakened, but I'll remain at her side and yours until we see this through."

"Deadly." Torment distorted Miss McGirth's lovely features, and for the first time in his vocation, Marcus wished he were one to lie. At least, she would be better prepared should the child pass into the hands of Jesus. Filled with an awful dread, he sank his head into his palm and prayed until her voice opened his eyes.

"Is her fever down?" She was testing the baby's forehead, hope livening her.

His lips found Marisol's temple and measured her temperature. "Cooler, yes." He couldn't bring himself to point out that simply removing the baby's swaddling had achieved most of that improvement.

A shadow of a smile wobbled at her lips. "I'll consider it a positive turn."

Stymying the urge to correct, he curved his mouth into the smile he knew put patients at ease. There was no accounting for what God could do. He hunkered down at the bedside and prayed truth into the hope he'd given her. At his murmured amen, he stroked the baby's silken arm from elbow to wrist, forefinger dragging her curled fingers open. He left it there in her hot palm, sad for having never known her.

"She's a pretty little thing," he said, admiring her dark brows and hair, thicker and longer than expected in one so tiny. "You must be proud."

"Sometimes," Miss McGirth said, her voice a hush, "when I look at her, my heart swells so full of love, it pains me to breathe. Have you ever felt such a thing, Doctor?"

The query drew his eyes to hers, regrettably, for in their sheen, the memory of her hand against his skin came back full force, and he nearly lost himself. Through a skittering pulse, he scrambled to remember what it was she'd asked. "No, I can't say that I have." The greatest love he'd experienced was toward his mother, and while strong, it hadn't come close to producing what Miss McGirth described.

"Poverty comes in all shapes. I'm sorry for you, sir." She laid a kiss on the baby's cheek, the love she'd spoken of radiating from her face, her voice, the trace of her fingertip across the baby's brow.

Marisol's hand twitched and tightened, clasping reflexively onto him.

His gaze flew to Miss McGirth, but she was focused on her child's little mouth puckering into a frown.

"Doctor!" She clawed the shirt at his shoulder. "Do you see? Is she waking?"

Shock launched Marcus to a standing position while apprehension bound his tongue. He wouldn't be too hasty to put the danger behind them.

When Marisol emitted a squeak and began working her jaw in a sucking motion, Marcus offered her searching mouth a bent knuckle. She took it readily.

He sprouted a smile. "Well, good evening, little beauty. You sleep as hard as your mother."

Miss McGirth laughed outright, then directed her voice to the bedchamber's door. "Barb, we need you up here! Quick!"

Half an hour later, the baby was at Barbury's breast, intermittently fussing and suckling. Marisol's fever still raged and unless the candlelight deceived him, her skin was jaundicing, but this desire to put something into her belly, while not exactly a new lease on life, was the very thing he'd prayed for — a positive turn.

Miss McGirth emerged from behind a rattan screen, wearing a calf-length bed shift and wrap-stays that accentuated her too-spare frame. Disease? Digestive complications? Whatever the cause, this leanness had little to do with the toxin.

She held the screen for support while blinking almost imperceptibly sluggish lids, and Marcus frowned. He couldn't take her home this unwell. McGirth didn't need the additional worry.

After spending a moment orienting herself, she sent a devoted look her child's direction and came to Marcus. He startled when she cupped a hand behind his neck and pulled him down to press her cheek to his.

It staggered him, sent one foot to the side to affect a more solid stance. His heart, treacherous thing, jabbed his ribs in a rise of manly heat that sent his hands to her waist to steady her. *Your oath, man!* He disengaged, arms falling to his sides.

She kissed the air at his right ear and repeated with his left. Going up on tiptoes, she embraced him and uttered quiet thanks that set him ill at ease and cooled his blood.

He'd earned no thanks. Not yet.

Shuffling footsteps announced the impending arrival of the widow — Suni, she'd been called earlier. He set Miss McGirth away in time for the old woman to turn the corner. She bore a tray topped with a stick of bread, boiled eggs, and sardines.

Marcus jumped to relieve her of it. "*Por favor*, let me help."

She grinned, rattling off something in Spanish. He looked to Miss McGirth.

"She says you're a true *caballero*, a gentleman. And a good doctor besides."

"Gracias, señora." He set the tray on a writing desk and paired a modest smile with a generous bow. "Miss McGirth, I—"

"Lillian," she cut in. "Please. If we haven't arrived at our Christian names by now, we never will." Her smile was wholesome but did strange things to him all the same. Better they never arrived.

"Forgive me, miss, I wouldn't have you thinking we've made it to the shallows yet. Miss Marisol will require a close eye for several days. There is her liver to consider, whether it was damaged, and her kidneys."

"Oh…" Her expression fell.

"But she's well beyond what I expected for her at this point. Take heart, miss. God hasn't forgotten her."

Sorrow crept back into her weary eyes. "I should have known." As though considering flight, she looked furtively to the door.

"Have a seat. We'll put something in your stomach." He broke off a hunk of bread, but she moved toward the door, gaze lingering on Marisol.

"Not hungry, thank you. I had soup at Toño's."

"Where are you going?"

"To pray. In the courtyard."

"Stay here where it's warm. God's ears work in this room too."

"It's my habit to go before Him at the shrine, and I'll thank you for not asking me to break it."

There was no arguing with prayer. "All right. So long as you put on slippers and a bed jacket. The night is growing frigid. And Miss McGirth," he said as she teetered and grasped for the bedpost, solidifying the matter in his mind. When she finally pulled her lethargic eyes to his, he continued. "You have fifteen minutes, then you're going to bed. If my suspicions are correct, your blood is tainted with toxins as well."

Chapter 4

*M*id-morning of the following day, Marcus stepped noiselessly from Miss McGirth's apartment so as not to wake her. He eased shut the door's latch and turned with a spurious smile for the guard sitting on the loggia banister—Marcus's guard, a blue-coated, short-legged Spanish soldier who smelled of old sweat and two-bit cologne.

Marcus hadn't had a moment alone all morning. The man had even jogged the riverbank, keeping pace with Marcus's swift strokes. Either the Spanish were alert to his covert mission, or the guard took his job too seriously. A laughable notion, based on his grumbling and dour looks.

Marcus, who'd gotten little sleep in the night, felt no pity for his unwelcome shadow. Marisol's sad mewling had kept him on edge all night, but by dawn, he'd felt confident enough with her condition to seek out the river. He'd pushed hard through the exercise, releasing tension, until he'd crashed on the bank, spent.

Back at La Conchita again, he'd been escorted to a new room. His haversack had been brought over from Captain Luengo's, and laid out on the bed was yesterday's uniform, laundered and pressed.

After making himself presentable, he'd had a look-in on his patients and found both to be enjoying a deep, healing sleep. Satisfied, Marcus began down the stairs.

The soldier followed.

According to Barb, Don Diego had visited his child while Marcus swam. After, he left for the day, presenting Marcus the perfect opportunity to nose around the place for leads. Except he couldn't because of the guard's perpetual presence. But better here and monitored than not here at all.

He bounded down the last three stairs, delighted the baby's temperature was gradually coming down. The olive tone of her skin made it difficult to assess her liver, but he would know more when he could examine her eyes. He was almost ready to say she was past the worst of it, but there was a long way to go, and he needed her at full health. Both of them. It would be difficult transporting them in their weakened states. All that, not considering the don and the power he wielded.

Marcus stopped in the corner of the courtyard where pavers gave way to a patch of black earth cultivated with palms, yucca, and castor, the last of which rose so high its topmost leaves hung over the upper banister. The season's bitter temperatures hadn't sat well with it; frost-shriveled leaves littered the slate. Just as well. It needed to die.

He circumvented the winterized fountain and chose a café table with a solid view of the upstairs room. Yawning, the guard slouched against one of the numerous columns that supported the second-story arcade. Marcus disregarded the man's lazy-lidded stare and withdrew his pocket notebook and pencil. To the *jeer-jeer* of a blue jay presiding over the birdbath, he began jotting about last night's intervention.

Miss McGirth's full diagnosis was as baffling as her daughter's was straightforward. The toxin showed itself plain in her dilated eyes, but what condition imbalanced her humors to make her so thin? He fervently hoped she wasn't dying of a waste.

The scuffle of tired feet lifted Marcus's pencil from his log.

Suni appeared from a servant's corridor, so he set down his notebook and stood. She greeted him with exuberance and a plate of bread, thinly sliced salt pork, and several orange wedges. Beside it on the table, she set a creamy cup of coffee. She clapped his cheeks between her palms and with an exaggerated smacking sound, planted a kiss center target, then fired terse words at the guard.

The man rolled his eyes and stood erect, but after she left, he slumped again, withdrawing a deck of cards and shuffling them noisily.

Marcus was putting the coffee to his lips when one of Miss McGirth's double doors creaked open. The blue jay shushed, the coffee steamed Marcus's nose, and the cards in the soldier's hands went still.

She emerged, wearing the clothes she'd slept in—white linen cap and bed jacket that tied in front—but her hair was down and everywhere. It was in complete disarray but stopped his heart midbeat. A few pounds would complement her frame; a touch of health, her complexion, but God forgive him the libertine thought, he'd take her precisely as she was.

When Lillian began down the stairs, Doctor Buck set his cup down, stood, and placed his hands behind his back, accentuating his striking figure. A lovely scene to wake to: the doctor, his water-darkened hair falling in shining segments over his forehead, his lavish smile, the unmistakable attraction coloring his cheeks.

The picture would be faultless but for Cabo Varela who shoved off a column and watched her descend. Was he playing sentry? What a pest he made of himself, spoiling the morning.

On the way down, as she breathed in the toasty overtones of roasting coffee beans, she gave the rail a good portion of her weight. A full night's sleep had her feeling a sight better, but her legs were feckless and untrustworthy. She looked to Santa Teresa and prayed first, that she wouldn't stumble and make a fool of herself and second, that her missed terce recitations would go unnoticed.

"Good morning." Doctor Buck's eyes moved over her in a neutral manner, judging her condition.

"Why yes, it is. A very good morning." Sensing he wouldn't be content until he'd finished his examination, she stood patiently for him.

He finished with a study of her eyes and a brief touch to her forehead that added a touch of heat to her own cheeks. The minuscule wrinkles at the corners of his eyes expanded with his smile. "I concur. Disorientated at all?"

"It's much improved."

"Your exposure to the toxin must have been minimal." He pulled out another chair for her. "And the little miss?"

Cabo Varela sat on the fountain's rim, arms supported by his splayed knees. While he fanned and collapsed a deck of cards, he carried out a bold perusal of her.

She shuddered.

Diego would have told the cabo to be vigilant because he trusted no one. He also made fast enemies of those who betrayed him. Barbury wouldn't breathe a word about the cause of Mari's illness, but Suni might have caught on. Lillian fended off another shiver, nixing the thought of Diego's wrath. There was no room in her frazzled spirit for such fears.

She snubbed the cabo and accepted the chair, lifting slightly so Doctor Buck could push it in beneath her. "She's much improved. Would you agree she's over the worst?"

"My thoughts have been traveling that same path." He took his own seat. "We'll need to wake her soon. It's important we replenish her fluids to flush the toxins from her body."

"Actually, Barb is feeding her now."

Diego had denied Lillian the privilege, insisting she act like a noblewoman, though he had no intention of making her one.

He nodded to something behind her. "Suni is here with your coffee."

Stunned, Lillian took it gratefully and switched to Spanish. "Grácias, Suni. Have you seen the gardener? There's a job I have for him."

"There she goes again, thinking she's *la doña*." Suni scowled and wagged a finger at Lillian. "Her ladyship is gold. You are but painted tin. Bought for a pittance and useful for only one thing."

A degrading comparison. But how else was a mistress to liken to the wife?

While fever flared up Lillian's neck, Cabo Varela snickered at her. "What would that useful thing be, señorita? Come over here and show me, eh?"

"Bah!" Suni turned on him, sending her crucifix in a violent slide across her chest. "You're not man enough to handle this one. Look at you. Can't even stand straight, slouching like a drunk. Missing a few cards in that deck of yours, if I had a guess," she said, rapping her forehead. "My Diego is a beautified saint to put up with you. With *both* of you!"

She came full circle to a wide-eyed Doctor Buck, noticed his full plate, and transformed into a doting grandmother, complete with a pinch of his cheek. "But eat, eat! That perfect coffee will crust over with ice before you get it to your lips." Muttering about handsome doctors and bossy wenches, she stalked off toward the kitchen.

Cabo Varela renewed his shuffling with extra vigor, eyes narrowed on Lillian until Doctor Buck stood, faced the man, and laid a casual hand on the sword fixed to his hip.

Cabo Varela stood as well, chin angled high.

She sipped her coffee, amused at the showdown. "A Spaniard will die before he loses honor by backing down, so unless you're willing to oblige, you may as well sit."

"He's trouble, that one," Doctor Buck said, while bending at the waist in gallant concession. "Aren't you eating? I'll share." He sat and slid his plate across the table, then broke the bread in half and held out a piece.

With a skittering glance at the cabo, she took it. She was allowed bread. After savoring a few divine bites, she set it down and dusted the crumbs from her fingers, wishing for her cloak.

The doctor frowned. "Is your stomach troubled?"

"No." She scooted the plate back toward him and bent one corner of her mouth. "Has anyone ever told you how unmannerly your prodding is?"

"Actually, you've been spared my usual approach to interrogations." He affected a grin that was at once charming and peevish. "Since it isn't appreciated, I'll forgo the manners. Lillian McGirth, you're a scrawny little thing, and if you don't eat more, you'll shrivel up and slip through the seams in the slate, never to be seen again."

Peevish be hanged; she laughed wholesale. "What a pity that would be, for the world to be deprived of my sublime presence. Suni, in particular, would be bereft."

"Don't fret. I'll be here to offer my cheeks for a good pinch. That seems to bring her strange pleasure."

"I'm sure you would. You're too good not to. If you were Catholic, your confessor would have already petitioned the Holy See for your eventual sainthood."

His fingers went to his unshaven chin in thoughtful poise. "Don't saints get new names? I rather like mine as it is."

"You're thinking of nuns and monks, but saints do get different titles. Let's see…" She traced the rim of her cup with a fingertip. "How about Venerable Servant of God Marcus Buck of— Where are you from?"

"South Carolina, but with that mouthful of a name, I'd expire before I finished introducing myself."

She loosed another laugh, feeling lighter than she had in a month. "You'd already be dead! It's a prerequisite for sainthood."

His eyes flared open for an instant before he swiped a negating hand. "Then I'll be the exception. Sainthood premortem."

"Now *there's* a challenge for you. Oh, I've got it. The Eminently Good Marcus Buck. Has a nice solid feel to it. Don't you think?"

Gaiety shone from his eyes a short while before fading with spirit-sapping retrospection. "Perhaps on another man."

Recalling his impressment? No, this was regret and seemed directed at himself. A tragedy.

She placed her hand beside his on the table, grazing their pinkies and warming her voice. "Burdens aren't meant to be carried alone, Doctor."

Breathing deeply, he dragged his hand away. She couldn't recall any instance where an unattached man displaying signs of attraction had ever rebuffed her, no matter how piddling the flirtation.

Confused and a little abashed, she dropped her hand to her lap.

What had she intended with it anyway? To feel appreciated, as usual. How many times had Papa said her value wasn't found in a man's attention? So many her brain replayed his exact inflection. As a younger woman, she'd brushed off his advice, but the wisdom in it had eventually become apparent. Though too late to save her virtue, Lillian had adjusted her thinking as well as her behavior.

Until Doctor Buck. Of all men to lose her fledgling propriety with, the saint.

He sat forward, concern budding in his softening eyes. "Have you any burden I might relieve you of?"

"Me? I, that is…" She choked on the backfire and lied. "Very kind, but no, thank you."

Though his eyes flickered skepticism, his smile was gracious. "I understand, but do remember the offer." He moved the plate back toward her. "Now, eat. Doctor's orders."

"Later." When she wasn't the focus of Cabo Varela's scrutiny.

Doctor Buck slanted his head. "For a girl who grew up on the edge of civilization, I'd think you'd have learned to be less choosy."

"How do you know I grew up here?"

"You didn't. You grew up in Tensaw."

"Did Barb tell you that?"

"Your father. I spent a weekend with him last month." His face was straight and his tone matter-of-fact. He was as self-assured as ever, gaze unwavering, while *she* groped to find footing.

"My…father?"

He nodded, spoke deliberately. "He told me I might find you here."

"He did?" she said, eyes sprouting dew, sight wandering the courtyard as she absorbed the revelation.

How could Papa have known where she was? She had yet to write from San Marcos to tell him they'd left *El Retiro*, Diego's plantation in

Pass Christian. That was where Papa had last seen her. He'd searched for two months before arriving, worn through but so relieved he'd wept on her shoulder.

He'd stayed a week but hadn't been able to convince her to come home. At the time, the work had been good, simple. Diego had been a dream, promising her marriage. Seven months later, babe in arms, she'd learned he'd never meant to make a respectable woman of her.

She'd written Papa faithfully, filling him in on the details of her life. All, except Maria del Sol and how once the child had arrived, Diego had revealed himself for who he truly was—a cunning, son of an alligator who would grin to earn an escudo, then snap the head off the man who'd paid him.

Even so, Lillian had remained in Florida to avoid Totka Hadjo and the shame returning home would bring, but she hadn't fared much better with Diego López or the Church.

Papa would be appalled if he knew the half of it.

She straightened, and as her tongue ran a slow trail between her lips, a sudden, vicious longing for her father took her by the heart. "How is he?"

"He's rather…" Doctor Buck seemed to choose his words carefully, abandoning one thought for another. "He misses you fiercely."

Papa had said that many times before, but if she went home, she would take her sins and her reputation with her. Both would destroy him. Tears swamped her, but at the sound of male voices entering the plaza from the outer yard, she scrubbed them away.

Miss McGirth was handling the news better than Marcus had anticipated. She recuperated her genteel comportment as she rose to welcome the men striding through the plaza gates.

They were Lieutenant Fanning and that English seadog, Bell something or other. Marcus couldn't recall. The previous day, he hadn't heard much beyond *former Royal Navy*. The bosun's flogging count had been too loud in his ear. Even now, his back twitched at the remembrance.

Miss McGirth's velveteen voice brought him out of it. "Mr. Bellamy, Lieutenant Fanning." She curtsied prettily, seeming not the least concerned with her state of undress.

There was something entrancingly wild about this woman—an intriguing blend of cultured debutant, unkempt settler, and artful coquette—and it nearly did him in at every casual graze of their bodies. Or not so casual. He rubbed his tingling pinky as she continued the greeting.

"Gentlemen, to what do we owe the pleasure?" Lillian asked.

Fanning nodded to Marcus and turned to the lady. "Good morning, Miss McGirth. We've come to see about the patient."

"How is our little gem?" Maxwell Bellamy's decisively English accent was a grating noise. He brushed cheeks with her, having taken irritatingly well to the Spanish greeting.

Another mark against him.

"A sight better than last night. Max, I—" Her throat bobbed with a swallow. "I thought I'd lost her."

Bellamy wrapped an arm around her shoulders and aligned her to his side. "There, there, dear girl. The fact remains you did *not* lose her. Do we have the gent here to thank for that?"

"Indeed, we do. Have you met the good doctor?"

"I haven't, not formally. A pleasure, sir." The Englishman doffed his feathered tricorne.

Marcus allowed a tight smile, his thoughts on all the reasons the man might be found here, now. "Mr. Bellamy."

Bellamy wore the practical, well-kept rigging of a successful trader, but that was no trifle feather pinned to his hat. It belonged to a red-tailed hawk, and according to Totka Hadjo, in any Native region, only lauded, deserving warriors were allowed them. So, what skullduggery had earned Mr. Bellamy warrior status?

Royal Navy, handsy with the lady, chummy with the Red Sticks. The man was accruing quite the collection of tallies.

"Let's dispense with formalities, shall we?" the Englishman said. "You saved Mari, so I intend us to be fast friends. Please, do call me

Max."

Marcus's blood began a rush. He barely restrained a scoffing snort. Friends! He'd neither extend nor accept goodwill with any English seaman, much less one living among the Spanish—and the Red Sticks, if that feather could be trusted. For all he knew, Bellamy was Iron Wood himself, that slippery British operative.

Feeling contentious, he smirked. "Formalities are my dearest friends. I like to keep them around me."

Bellamy's smile broadened. "Is that how it's to be, then? No *Marcus*? No *old chap*?"

"If by *it* you mean an as-of-yet unmerited casual rapport, then yes, Mr. Bellamy, that is how *it* is to be. Not Marcus, and certainly not *chap*. Captain Buck will suit."

Bellamy studied Marcus before nodding considerately. "I respect a cautious man." He responded with such amicability, Marcus felt a twinge of regret.

The other twinge—the one that occurred with every bend and twist of his back—far outweighed it. "The English might have a little sense after all." A smattering of disdain slipped into his tone.

"Do forgive him, Max," Fanning said on an edgy laugh. "He's harmless. So long as you don't provoke that sword of his."

If the Englishman's responding laughter wasn't genuinely congenial, then Marcus didn't bleed red, white, and blue. "It wouldn't be my first experience with the business end of an American sword. Generally speaking, they're of poor make, and I have yet to meet one that can best even my deficient skills. I've no great fear of them, especially when wielded by *good* doctors."

The man's antler-handled bowie knife was positively leering at Marcus, boasting of its Indian construction. "Then perhaps you've never been properly acquainted. Care for a little sparring? I'd be pleased to change your opinion." Marcus reached for Justice and exposed a half foot of her steel.

In an impressive instant, Bellamy drew the bowie in a saber grip, his left foot skipping back into a strong-side-forward stance.

All right, then. The man had training.

"Good gracious, Marcus, remember your manners." Fanning shoved Marcus's sword hand downward to re-sheath the weapon. "If you don't start behaving, the gentleman will think you're a backward colonial."

Miss McGirth stepped in with a light, diffusing laugh. "Put away your swagger, Captain Buck, and Max, if you touch that knife again, you may take yourself back to that wretch of a Spanish corporal and the card game you're losing."

"Losing, she says." Bellamy barked a laugh. "Never! I let the lesser man win."

Miss McGirth lavished them with gorgeous feminine laughter. "Because you're so gallant and generous."

"How well you know me, love."

"Well enough to know you're as much the cad as you are the cavalier."

A smile plucked at Marcus's mouth. What else did she know about the barnacle-back?

Bellamy looked to Fanning. "That, Fanning my man, is our cue to be gone." To Marcus he said, "I'll leave you to the perils of Miss McGirth's nimble tongue and bid you good day. Until tomorrow then, old chap." He slapped Marcus on the shoulder and backed away, grinning as he went, eyes alight with merriment once again.

Marcus failed to smile back.

Lillian waited until the gates had closed behind the men before she turned to Doctor Buck.

Scarlet patched his cheeks, and his knuckles were still white about his sword's handle. He took several profound breaths, but as he scrutinized Max and Lieutenant Fanning's exit, the hostility lingered. It appeared the man could be ruffled. And poor perplexed Max had been both the cause and the target.

Since the doctor appeared unable to extract himself from his eclipsing fog, she said, "Tell me why you were in Tensaw."

He blasted air through tight lips and came back to her with a wan smile. "I was in Mobile for training. Took the weekend to visit a friend, Phillip Bailey."

"Ah, Phillip Bailey." She led a stroll through the courtyard. "There's a fine man for you. Tensaw's most eligible for an outrageous number of years. Good neighbor of ours. He used to swim under me in the lake and pinch my toes. Scared profanity out of me every time. Which was, of course, why he did it. If my mother was around, all the better."

The admission brought back Doctor Buck's laughter. "I can see him now."

"How do you know Phillip? No, wait…" That nebulous memory took form at last. "He spoke of you! How could I forget?"

"Did he?" Doctor Buck said. "I shudder to think what he might've said."

She smiled. "All good, rest assured. Have you heard from him lately?"

"Turns out he recently moved north. Took his half-negro wife to Creek country. Imagine that." He rubbed the back of his neck and went pensive.

Half-negro? Creek country? "Are you certain?" Highly unlikely.

"Seems mixed-raced marriages aren't illegal in the tribes."

Yes, she knew that. As a chill came over her, she stopped before the birdbath and stared at the odious castor mirrored in its watery surface. A fitting visual to compliment the topic of Creek country.

No one could pay her enough to return there. She'd believed Phillip to share her sentiments. In fact, they'd spoken of it liberally — of their abhorrence of the savages and deep resentment for crimes they'd committed. How ironic that Phillip would resort to living among them.

Lillian's own eyes blazed with fear of them, or so she'd been told. Totka, her precious brother-by-marriage, had pronounced her eyes bitter. And he'd done it so often, the ugly name had stuck.

Bitter Eyes.

Yes, they were. Thanks to him and five hundred bloody Red Sticks just like him. And heaven help her if she shed a tear over it. My, but that Indian hated her tears!

Angrily, she swiped at the birdbath water, spraying droplets clear to the table where Cabo Varela was pinching an orange slice from the doctor's plate.

"Anything is possible, I suppose. I'm glad for him. For them both." She meant it but couldn't help the sting of betrayal.

"Miss McGirth, while I was there…in Tensaw…" Doctor Buck struggled for words, terrifying her as to where this conversation was leading.

She'd believed them to be strangers, but if he'd been a recent visitor in Tensaw, what might he have learned?

"Hester spruced up the loft for me," he said. "It hadn't been touched since you left. Your bed is lumpy."

"You slept in my bed?"

"Does that bother you?" The ribbing twist of his lip was surely more seductive than the man intended.

It fired up her cheeks and made her chest swell with a robust intake that became fixed.

Ever diligent, his eye honed into the movement, then flitted off, fluidly taking the angle of his body with it, putting her in his shadow to allow her a moment's composure. A most reprehensible need.

She released her lungs in a forced rush and looked down to pat her wet hands against her nightgown. The reminder of her undress exacerbated her body's fever.

"I, er, I…" Had he asked her a question?

Oh, for goodness' sake! Men and beds and nightclothes—no decent woman would get her blood in a tizzy over them! For shame. She loosened the tie on her jacket to allow a breeze, finishing as he turned back.

"Rather, it *was* lumpy," he went on smoothly, as if he weren't perfectly aware of her reaction to the topic. "I put new ticking in it for you. Strung it with new ropes. And I repaired the chinking along the west wall. It was crumbling onto your bureau."

"Oh? That's…thank you."

"It was my pleasure." His voice was too warm. He needed to stop.

She didn't want to hear more. Not about how he'd slept in her bed, or how he'd readied it for her, or how she shouldn't have left it in the first place, which was where this speech was surely leading.

Resuming their trail around the plaza, she put zest into her steps. The wind funneled through the arched entry, bringing in his soapy scent and blowing her hair across her blazing face. She left it as cover.

"As I was leaving, your father sent Hester to town for the makings of new bedclothes. He's hopeful you'll be home soon."

An acidic laugh cut from her. "He'd think different if he knew I was—" She bit her tongue before calling herself a hussy.

"An unwed mother?" He dropped his voice. "He knows."

That stopped her in her tracks, splashed cold water on her wanton thoughts. Papa couldn't know. She'd filled her letters with lies.

She spun to Doctor Buck and swiped the hair from her eyes to read him, prepared to rail at him for lying or condemning. But his soft-eyed demeanor was so open, so sincerely poignant that her animosity fizzled into a slump of her shoulders.

"He's had eyes on you, miss. Who, he didn't say, but he knows. Everything."

Max had to be the source. He'd met Papa in Pass Christian, and it was like him to go out of his way for her.

With his usual hesitation, Doctor Buck took her hand and stroked its back with his thumb.

She riveted her attention to his golden touch, to its warmth and tenderness, to its steady back and forth, but though she tried to hide in the delicious feel of him, his difficult, quietly spoken words still found her. "He'd like you home as soon as it can be arranged. There's Miss Marisol to consider. He wants to know her."

How many times had her quill been poised to share in the joy of Mari's birth only to retreat? Pricked by the laying bare of her sins, she withdrew from him, turning. "Marisol…I should check on—"

"Stay." He grabbed her wrist. "We should address this. Now. Before the don arrives."

"Another time. Let me go." She contorted her arm to no effect, raising her voice. "Let me *go*, Doctor Buck."

"Your pardon, miss, I cannot oblige. Listen to me."

Cabo Varela meandered toward them, smirking around the orange peel he gnawed, happy as a monk at mass to watch her struggle. He wasn't the only one. Servants materialized in doorways, sentries at the gate. They were probably, each one of them, inwardly gloating.

Burning tears surfaced, but she refused them liberty, tucking her chin against whatever it was Doctor Buck purposed to say.

"You are an unwed mother under duress with no prospects to speak of outside of a tenuous relationship with a disreputable lover." His hushed, stolid manner eased the delivery. A bit. "You are nearly three hundred miles from the shelter of any proper benefactor, which is wholly unnecessary considering your father's substantial means and willing forgiveness. To top it off, your loyalty to your country has recently come into question. It is imperative you quit this place at once. There is no *another time*."

She winced. His unabashed candor blistered, but she had no means to defend herself because he was right. Diego was a scoundrel, she was his mistress, and Papa would forgive her. But who would forgive *him* for welcoming a tramp into his home? Who would forgive little Charlie for being reared by a sister with too loose a hold on her virtue? What prospects would he have as a businessman?

None, none, and none.

Then there was Totka. Lillian was convinced there was no such word as "forgiveness" in the Creek vocabulary. Not of the sort she would need from him. But Doctor Marcus Buck—knight errant, Don Quixote come to life—was blind to those facts.

Weary of it all, she rubbed her temple and longed for her room, her bed. "Forgiveness is a beautiful ideal, but no matter your quixotic ventures in saving the distraught damsel, it isn't applicable here. Forgiveness will not be had. Not for me."

"Forget that then." He leaned in, speaking in private tones. "All that matters is that your father has put you in my care. Given me complete authority over you, along with instructions to return you to Tensaw straightaway."

Her foot fell back a step. "You're—? Authority? My father did *what*? I don't believe he'd do such a thing."

Papa had never been a weak man, but somehow, she'd always been just a little stronger. And what was this about Doctor Buck, the *stranger* she'd happened upon yesterday, being her guardian?

"I have it in writing if you doubt. He is serious about this and intends to have you home. Begin your goodbyes, Miss McGirth," he confided urgently. "To the Floridas, the Spanish, and most especially the don. Forgiveness or not, you are quite finished with this place. When I leave, duchess, I intend for you to be at my side."

Chapter 5

$\mathcal{L}$illian's first instinct was to balk at Doctor Buck's assertiveness.

From one breath to the next, he'd gone from kindly doctor to commanding soldier, and her prideful nature objected. But what he offered was exactly what she wanted: to be sheltered, tenderly cared for, whisked away to a safe place. She wanted—no, needed—to have her worries fall on shoulders stronger than her own. And Doctor Buck's seemed more than capable.

She'd expected to have to wheedle help out of him, yet here he was insisting it would be—as though by some Divine order. Had Lillian's sacrifices moved God's heart, opened His mercies to her? It was a bewitching thought and terrifying in its high likelihood of disappointment.

"Do you hear me? I'm getting you and Marisol out of here. Miss McGirth?" He gave her wrist a little shake that brought her around. "What I need from you is implicit trust. Can you give me that?"

"Easily." Her nod was instant and firm. "And I hope you'll trust *me* when I say I can't go home. Anywhere but home." A glance at their surly guard elicited a long sigh. "Then there's Diego. He won't let Marisol go. He'll fight you for her, and he'll win. There's also his garrison to contend with. Eighteen soldiers plus four Indians in his employ. They have orders to keep Marisol in the hacienda. I've tried leaving before." She shook her head, grimacing at the memory. After being caught, Lillian had spent the next three days locked in the servants' quarters.

Doctor Buck's smile eased wide with challenge. "A little pressure in the right places, and he'll let her go. Leave it to me," he said with such confidence she was tempted to believe him. "Besides, we haven't any choice but to make it happen. This place is corrupt. Soon, it will be much worse, especially for you."

Unease crept in about her toes and twined up her spine. Wind blustered, ruffling her hair and scampering under her chemise. She hugged herself against its chill. "All right. I'll leave it to you."

"Excellent." His eyes wrinkled with a smile, then fell to her mouth. He lifted a finger as if intending to unhook the strands lodged in its corner. Stopping shy of it, he made a fist, pulled back, and glanced toward the gate. "From what I understand, the don will be arriving soon. He shouldn't see you this way, looking at loose ends. Why don't you go up and dress. Hurry back, duchess. We still have much to discuss."

"Duchess?"

He fashioned a sheepish half-grin and hefted a muscled shoulder. "It fits."

How he figured her for a duchess was beyond her, but he could name her a horned toad, and she'd be just as likely to worship him. How could a woman not? He'd saved Mari, and now, he was going to save them both. A fervency to help him welled within her. She would get that intelligence for him if it cost her the skin on her back to do it.

When he raised his eyebrows and pointed to the upper story, she wondered for one tick how long she'd been gazing up at him adoringly.

Blushing, she ascended, swept Marisol out of Barbury's arms, and twirled until her bed jacket opened like an umbrella and she felt faint. She snuggled the baby close and breathed in her delicate, milky scent.

"Why you so giddy, Missy Lillian?" Barbury took Mari back and prodded Lillian into a chair. "That fool Varela fall on his sword?"

"Better." Ignoring a tipping sensation, Lillian popped back up, rushed to the armoire, and grabbed the first day dress she laid eyes on.

A wisteria-print calico with a ribboned waist, a smocked cuff, and a cleavage-baring neckline—the only variety Diego allowed on her hangers.

She tossed off her jacket and slipped behind the dressing screen. "The doctor is getting us out of here. Both of us. Isn't it wonderful? Oh, and he knows my father! They've been conspiring, those two, working out a way to get me home, but you know how I feel about *that*." Her nightclothes were on the floor before she noticed the silence on the other side. "Barb?" She peeked around the screen.

With Mari fast against her, Barbury rocked on her toes, bleeding tears.

"Barb, whatever's the matter?"

"Gonna miss you both, is all."

Then the awful truth hit her. Barbury wouldn't be coming. She was a free woman, but only in Spanish Florida.

In her chemise, Lillian stepped out from behind the screen, anger curling her fingers around its frame. Diego, that conniving fop! Yet again, his oppressive thumb came down, controlling her, crushing her. From the start, he'd not allowed her to nurse her own child, shackling her to Barbury and thus, San Marcos.

The last time she'd tried to leave, Barbury had agreed to go with her as far as the border, but they'd never made it past the first off-shoot of the Wakulla River. That hound Varela had sniffed them out.

Diego had all but lost his mind on her. Poor, darling Barbury never told Lillian the penalty she'd endured, and Lillian never found the courage to ask. Knowing a little something of bondage, her friend hadn't blamed her for any of it, but she'd been clear she wouldn't be party to another escape attempt.

In her eagerness, Lillian had forgotten all this. "Won't you consider coming—?"

"No, missy."

Lillian began to plot a solution. "When we arrive, my father will pay you well for your time and service. He did it before with Charlie. If you come—"

"No! I ain't steppin' foot outside Spanish country. Not for you, not for this sweet baby, not for sweet baby Jesus hisself. I *ain't* goin' back to Brunswick."

Regulating a rise of panic, or trying to, Lillian held out both hands, palms down. "It's all right. Doctor Buck has probably already thought it through and come up with something. He's nothing if not confident."

She'd learned during the Negro Fort disaster that it was the duty of every United States officer to confiscate any runaways they encountered. No Spanish official would be fool enough to impede them.

In a perfect world, he would stay ignorant of Barbury's status. But if he found out? She couldn't conceive of Marcus Buck, the quondam British slave, putting Barbury in irons, but what might Marcus Buck, the army officer, do?

Heart in her throat, Lillian went to Barbury and hugged her close, Marisol wedged between them. "I'll miss you too, dear friend." She pulled back, not missing the doubt and fear swimming in the other woman's eyes. "Pack me a satchel? I'd like to be ready to leave at a moment's notice."

Barbury wiped her nose with the back of her wrist. "Sure thing, Missy Lillian."

Lillian finished dressing, wound her hair, scrubbed her face, and tied her cloak at the throat.

When she reached the plaza, she put the gate in her sights and kept going, motioning for Doctor Buck to join her.

He stowed his notebook and followed. "Taking the air?"

"Not exactly. I'm going to the gardener's shed out back."

The guards swung open the gates for them, giving access to the outer yard. A ten-foot coquina wall enclosed the two acres of land that housed the hacienda, stables, barracks, warehouses, and various other outbuildings.

Marcus let her pass through first, turned to the cabo, and swept his arm before him. "After you, señor."

Cabo Varela flicked his shako's brim. *"Muy amable."*

"He says you're very kind," Lillian informed, "but I wouldn't take it as a sincere compliment. The man is incapable of good in any form."

"Under the right influence" — Buck pointed heavenward — "even the most wicked is capable of astounding change for the better." His unexpectedly serious reply directed that stinging truth straight at her. He thought she was wicked.

Hands clasped at the small of his back, he twisted toward her as they walked, mouth opening to speak then hanging silent through the glazing of his eyes and the wooden angling of his neck. Pain, if ever she saw it.

"Doctor?"

He blinked, met her eyes, blinked again, and slung his gaze forward.

Lillian was never one to release a prying question, but the sharpish click of his teeth and the bunching of the muscle in his jaw did it for her.

Allowing a respectful silence, she rounded the naked hibiscus bushes that rimmed the hacienda's west wall. The barracks lay off to the left, and a short distance beyond them was the gardener's shed.

As they neared the stables, a soldado stepped from its shadowy interior. "Varela! You're needed. Get in here."

The cabo wasted no time abandoning his post. Holding his musket strap in place on his shoulder, he padded off.

They were at the shed before she found the gumption to address the concern churning her stomach. "Have you thought of what we'll do for a wet nurse? Barb won't be coming."

His fingers closed around the door's handle and stilled as he looked back at her, all evidence of his earlier discomfort quite gone. "Your father sent me off with a full purse. I'll offer generous wages."

"It won't make a difference. She'll refuse."

"What reason does she give?"

Lillian lifted a silent, straight-lipped smile.

His erect posture went lax. "She's a runaway."

The man was sharp.

Dread tumbled into her stomach. "I'd hoped you wouldn't learn of it, and I'd never forgive myself if she were sent back because of me."

"Nor I." He yanked on the stubborn door, shaking the entire building to get it open. "Slavery is a detestable practice. I won't be party to returning her to it."

She smiled and laid a grateful hand on his arm. "I should've known not to worry."

His arm swung down, shedding her touch. "In such matters, caution is never in poor judgment." He opened the door wide.

Coughing on the dust they'd raised, she squinted and scanned the space, looking for something to hack down the castor. A sheaf of long-handled tools—shovel, spade, rake—stood against a tower of stacked crates. "I offered to pay for her services and see her discreetly returned, but she refused."

Behind her, Doctor Buck muttered tersely under his breath. "Miss McGirth."

"Yes?" Shovel in hand, she turned.

Tension stiffening his moves, Doctor Buck stepped aside.

Awash in daylight, Diego stood outside, a storm seething in his eyes. "Well, maja? Where are my two kisses?" Sarcasm oiled his voice. "Are you not glad to see me?"

God have mercy, this was not good.

In the confined space, Lillian shimmied past Doctor Buck. When she brushed against him, he took refraining hold of her elbow. Their gazes connected for a flash, his teeming with warning.

It was endearing of him to care, but where Diego was concerned, it was a futile effort. She rotated her arm free and exited the shed.

The don's toggery was rather dramatic: pink velvet breeches, double-woof sleeves, and gold vest. A green cravat and matching sash at his waist completed the ensemble, making him the archetypal rich *majo*. Bold, conceited, defiant of conventions.

"Always," she said dryly. "Your virility makes my woman's heart sigh at every glimpse of you."

He snagged her arm where the doctor's touch still lingered. Fingers clamping and pinching, he pulled her to him. Cooperatively, she went, shovel scraping the ground behind her. While she gave the obligatory kisses, he stood stock-still, not returning the gesture, like a king collecting tribute from a vassal.

He removed the shovel from her. "If you put your back into it, you can be done digging my daughter's grave before siesta. What then? An escape with the heroic *médico*?" He tossed the tool against the shed with a clack.

She'd been a fool to think he wouldn't find out. He owned San Marcos and every eye and ear in it. Beside her, Doctor Buck tensed, the cords of his neck beginning to protrude. To diffuse both men, she rendered a light laugh. "Don't be ridiculous, Diego."

His rejoining laughter was low and caustic. "That is all—*do not be ridiculous, Diego*? On you, my sweet, nothing says *guilt* better than a stunted tongue."

"Guilty of what, exactly? Loving my child until it is an ache in my chest? Guilty of weeping over her for endless hours? Of cutting my knees in prayer before God? Sí y sí! I am guilty. And only I, for you know *nothing* of these things."

The vice on her arm tightened. "Take care with your accusations, señorita. You are only her mother."

"Is everything all right?" Doctor Buck stepped closer.

"Everything is perfectly divine," she returned in English.

Drawing on her extensive skill at dissembling, she relaxed her posture and donned a buoyant smile, determined to throw the doctor off his drive to intercede. It would do neither of them any favors. "He's in a mood to bellyache, but he's harmless."

She continued the charade with Diego, wielding her most fluid Castilian. "If you were half the gentleman you feign to be, you would express your indebtedness to the médico instead of attacking me."

"Am I in debt? I was not aware."

"Ay, come out of yourself for once. The doctor is responsible for breaking our daughter's fever. When we arrived, she was a furnace.

As of a short while ago, she was nursing greedily and was a great deal cooler to the touch."

"You should have said." Diego extended his hand to Doctor Buck, who considered it one instant short of offense before accepting. After a curt bow over the joined hands, the don gripped him by the shoulder and laid a hand over his own heart. "A thousand thanks, *amigo*. Maria del Sol is the light in my eyes, the pride in my walk. She is the very beat of my heart. I will cut down any who harm her and reward any who show her favor."

He released Doctor Buck and, wiping his hands down his front, turned to Lillian. "One of Luengo's dimwit *soldados* fell from atop a bull and cracked his head. I want this Americano to visit him. My sergeant, there, will guide him. While he is away, you will give me a full report. Now make him understand. Then I want him gone."

Lillian hedged, pretenses of aplomb slipping. Doctor Buck, gone?

Fear stripped her throat of moisture. Her legs begged her to flee, but there was no way around this. It was her problem. Hers alone. She was the dolt who'd sold her soul to the Spanish devil, and she was the dolt who'd almost killed their baby. In truth, Diego was allowed his anger, and she deserved whatever consequences came of it.

Slaying her dread, she turned to Doctor Buck with a blithesome spirit. "Don Diego has been agonizingly poetic in his gratitude for your assistance. He speaks of reward but fails to elaborate on what or when. He's generally all bluster. Oh, and he wants you to see about a man who took a fall. The soldier standing there with the horses will be your escort."

He glimpsed that direction. "What of their own surgeon?"

"He didn't say."

"You'll be coming along, will you not?"

"The don has other plans for my afternoon. Besides, I wouldn't want to leave the baby."

His frown held nothing back. "I won't abandon you to this man's angry whim."

"Pft! He's never laid a violent hand to me. Truly, I'll be fine." It was becoming increasingly difficult to repulse Doctor Buck's concern.

Everything within her demanded she beg him to stay, to inundate him with how very cruel Diego could be. But if there was one thing she'd learned in the last year and a half, it was that every foolish decision came with repercussions. Running from them got her nowhere but deeper into the pit.

She slipped her arm through Diego's and put on her cheeriest expression. "Run along, sir. Set a bone, hack a limb. I'll see you at dinner, and for every stitch you secure to that man's head, I'll eat a bite of bread just for you."

Her stab at playfulness did nothing to relax the hard set of his shoulders. But after a moment, he leveled a stony look at Diego—the subtlest of threats—then trotted off to the horses.

Playing the well-bred noble, Diego clasped the hand tucked into his arm and began back toward the front of the hacienda. "Before we sit down to that report, I have some business of my own to see about."

The shouts and jeers of a spirited card game led them to the barracks door. When Diego opened it, the men inside—five in all—launched to their feet. A chair fell backward, several cards floated to the ground, a flagon tipped. Cabo Varela snatched it up, and as he shook red liquid from his boots, his pillaging eyes wandered her figure. While a leer climbed the cabo's face, Diego nudged her indoors.

The garrison's senior officer, a lieutenant by the name of Jaime Prieto, stepped forward. His coloring favored those of the northern regions—green eyes, sandy hair with hints of auburn—but it was his genuine kindness that had always made him shine.

The weight of his juniper eyes falling softly on her slackened the vice on her airways. "Señor López, señorita, *bienvenidos*. To what do we owe the honor?"

"Gracias, *Teniente* Prieto," Diego said. "There's a little matter I wish to discuss with you. But first"—he patted the hand Lillian used to clutch his arm—"the señorita, well, it's rather unusual, but she has been asking after you very fine caballeros." At her sharp intake, he locked down hard on her arm. "She's heard of your lively games and has expressed a healthy desire to play. Since I was coming anyway, I thought to myself, what better opportunity to show the señorita what good times can be had here among my most *vigorous* soldados."

They stared at Diego, mouths agape, none making a move to pull an extra chair to the table. At last, Teniente Prieto spoke. "She wishes to…*play*? With us?"

"No, I do not wish—" she began, but Diego gave her such a jerk that she yelped in pain. "You've had your laugh, now stop this at once!"

"Actually," Diego said to the men, ignoring her clawing fingers, "and I hate to disappoint, but she asked after Cabo Varela, specifically."

Concern contracted Teniente Prieto's pale brow, but the cabo began toward her, his sneer growing. "All the ladies do."

Several chuckled, but with a snap of his fingers, Teniente Prieto shut them up.

"Cabo Varela, you were senior officer while Prieto and I were away, no? I believe I owe you." Diego shoved Lillian forward. With a cry, she landed against him, the wool of his uniform burning her cheek. Before she could gather her balance, he had a lock on her.

"Diego!" She pivoted back and flung herself at him but was stopped short by the vice on her arm. "If you turn your back to me, Diego López, you had better guard it well!"

"Maja," he said, drawing out the word, spreading his hands wide. "Such animosity over a game?" He looked to Teniente Prieto. "Shall we speak outdoors?"

"I see your godless thoughts, Varela. Release me!" She beat at his chest, and he cursed and hooked an unbending arm about her waist.

Her heart beat a crazy, disturbing rhythm, and her limbs trembled violently. Once the true fight began, she would have none left in her and, of all the things to endure, not being able to fight for her dignity was the most terrifying. "I hate you, Diego López de Aragón, *hate* you!"

"Caballeros," he said, as he opened the door. "Beware of an *amante* with so much spirit. She'll satisfy you at night but spit in your wine at breakfast." He grinned maliciously.

Only Cabo Varela laughed. It was hot and sour against her neck.

"Teniente Prieto!" Lillian caught the man's eye. "You know this is wrong!"

The man had the decency to flush pink and lower his eyes before muttering something to the man beside him and marching past Diego out the door.

Before Diego shut it behind him, he looked to Cabo Varela. "Take good care of her for me, eh?"

"You have my word on it, mi señor. With pleasure."

"Diego. Diego!" Terror scratched at her insides. She ripped at her captor's sleeve, shouting with all her throat would give. "You cannot leave me with him!"

"Come now, señorita," Cabo Varela said, getting a better handhold. "I am not *all* bad."

"You are the Diablo's own henchman!" She swiveled and spat in his face.

Calmly, he wiped it off and spoke over his shoulder. "Get out. All of you."

"If any man of you has a shred of decency, you will not abandon me to him!"

The scuffle of boots was the sound of their betrayal.

When the back door slammed shut, Cabo Varela set her away from him and took a gander down the front of her. "Not much to you these days, beautiful. Hardly more than a bite. And this cloak"—he flicked the tie under her chin—"does nothing for your figure. But I can work around it."

She smacked his hand away from the opening. "Let me be, Javier," she said, using his given name to remind him he was a christened child of God. "What of your girl in the villa? Think of what your mother would say of this behavior!"

He yanked her close, giving her a prime view of his nose. "What of *yours*? I daresay you are a disgrace to her."

A rumbling laugh came from the table. "The swine lectures on disgrace."

Cabo Varela wrenched his neck for a glance behind him to where a lone soldado twirled a glass of wine. He sent up a rank curse. "I told you to get out, Barros."

"And Teniente Prieto told me to stay. Come, you were winning. Set her down and get back to the game." He gave the table a couple of inviting smacks. "This is your only warning."

"Or what? You'll play the hero and save the whore?"

"Boots on Florida soil a week and already I know better than to get within a meter of that nymph."

An instant of worry flashed across Cabo Varela's face. His sight skipped to the door, then down to her as though assessing whether she was worth whatever he planned to steal.

"Listen to him," Lillian rasped through her lacerated throat.

On a rising smirk, Cabo Varela shook his head. "He made me instructor of a lesson I have yet to give."

"He'll have your liver for pâté," Barros said lazily over the rim of his glass, "and I will be the one spreading it on his toast."

Why did he sit there!

Resigned to fighting her own battle, she kicked at Cabo Varela's shin as a pathetic cry squeezed through her cinching throat.

Diego's genial laughter could be heard just the other side of the door where he stood in conference with his garrison's commander. She shoved against the cabo's shoulder with her free hand, dragged a full breath, and put agony into her cry. "Diego, for the love of God, forgive me!"

Cabo Varela jolted at her broken plea. The alarm in his eyes said he knew the game had been lost, but he wasn't quick enough to withdraw. The door swung open, catching him elbow deep inside her cloak.

"What is this?" Diego demanded, boots thudding across the planked floor, cape billowing out around him, flashing its sin-black lining. "Get your hands off her, you savage!"

The cabo released her with such eagerness he sent her stumbling into the bunk behind. She bumped her head on the lofted bed and landed onto the lower one.

"But mi señor, you said—"

Lillian regretted being too disoriented to see Cabo Varela fly across the room, but when she got her bearings, the sight of him, legs over his head and arms tangled with a chair, made up for it. He unscrambled himself as Diego stalked him.

"What, *what* did I say? Eh? That you could touch her? I have no memory of that. None!" He turned to Barros. "Did I say he could touch her?"

"No, mi señor. You said she wanted to play." Barros motioned to the card table. "And you told Cabo Varela to take good care of her."

"*Así es.* I did." His eyes shifted to the backtracking cabo and became slits. "And the wriggling maggot gave me his word that he would."

Shakily, Lillian climbed to her feet, and using the beds along the wall as support, moved behind Diego and toward the exit.

Cabo Varela was erect now, flinging blood from the corner of his mouth. "You said you owed me!"

"A mere observation. I said nothing of payment."

"You threw her at me, you manipulative dog!" Cabo Varela hurled himself at Diego, but Teniente Prieto was ready and snatched him short.

Lillian made it to the door's edge but clung to the post, fearful of letting go and falling.

"Shut him up, Prieto," Diego growled, "before I draw my sword in front of the lady."

"Hold your temper, soldado, or I will have it flogged from you!" Prieto said.

"You'll soon see who has the final say, López!" Cabo Varela spewed hate and promises of vengeance as Diego helped her manage the step.

The door slammed shut, but the sounds of grappling men pursued them.

"What in the name of every mother's son took you so long!" he snapped, half dragging her across the yard. The hook of his fingers in the pit of her arm strained the shoulder he'd already bruised. "You poisoned our daughter, Liana. Poisoned her! And you didn't have the decency to ask forgiveness. A shame it took Varela's filthy paws to wring it out of you, but I cannot say I regret stripping you of your will!"

As if to prove him right, her knees gave out. In a humiliating display of weakness, she slithered down the front of him, grasping for a handhold on his clothing.

Arms limp at his sides, he watched, letting her reach the ground. "I don't even know you anymore. Get up, maja."

Sobbing, she tried, but her legs refused to function. "P-por favor, D-diego. *Piedad!*"

Was that *her* miserable voice begging for pity? She didn't know herself anymore either.

"Enough sniffling. You have only yourself to blame." With a snort of disgust, he got an awkward hold of her through the bulk of her cloak and, with a grunt, lifted her off her feet. "What does she do while I am away securing the roof over her head? She cavorts with the Americano, telling him who knows what about La Conchita." He panted and puffed all the way around the back of the hacienda, veering toward the row of servants' quarters.

"I swear t-to you, I've told him n-nothing, nothing," she stuttered through her sobs, shaking her head in a slow wag, wishing it were a lie, wishing La Conchita would go up in flames.

"You've already proven I cannot trust you. Not for one moment! Your very breath is a liability to me. In your prayers, be sure to thank God above you are my child's mother, for if you were not…" A rising growl ended with the kick of his boot against the door to one of the servants' quarters. As did everything else, it yielded to his command.

The room was empty. He dumped her on the bed and began pacing the small confines as she lay on her back exactly as she'd fallen, hair strewn across her face, and awaited his judgment.

As hard as he'd been, he wasn't finished with her.

At last, he stopped before the crucifix on the wall above a table in the back. When the rise and fall of his shoulders evened out, he came and scrutinized her so long she was nearly overcome with the urge to squirm away.

Gradually, anger slid from his features, taking with it the *diablo* she'd cursed. He stepped closer, swept the hair from her face, and laid fingers against her jaw. "There was a day I thought I loved you. Do you recall?" His voice was tender, as it had been at the first.

Oh, yes, there had been a day, once.

Like a bullfighter performing an elegant *pase*, he swerved his cape off his body and onto a chair. His hat followed, then his net, freeing his hair to tumble down his back. While she silently cried, he studied her, eyes flaring with a familiar burn. He lowered himself to the edge of the bed and collected her tears with his knuckle. "Shhh, maja. We are done with that unsightly business. Now, we can speak of more pleasant things."

He bent, planting his hands on either side of her. His frame was lean, but powerful, well-formed, and bronzed. Her fingertips could quote every inch of it.

"I was thinking of our dance in the moonlight. Your irresistible duende. Remember how you swayed in my arms? And the strawberry patch. We shared a kiss there. Ah, but you tasted like spring and ripened youth." He traced her lips, and she loathed herself for closing her eyes and fondly recalling how cherished she'd felt.

And for allowing him to caress her now. She should spit on him, beat at him, call him the son of a hound he was. She might if her will weren't in pieces, if her spirit weren't in such dire need of forgiveness.

"It was beautiful, no?" He brushed his mouth against hers, speaking softly, loosening the ties at her throat, laying open her cloak. "*Bruja de mujer.* Bewitching woman."

He moved impossibly closer. "Remind me of how it once was. How you stirred me. Why I took you in. Help me forget my anger, Liana." He pressed the flat of her hand against his chest.

At the feel of him, Suni's accusation whipped her conscience: *you are but painted tin, bought for a pittance and useful for only one thing!*

Lillian's fingers coiled. She angled her face away. "Varela is right. You are a manipulative dog."

With a speed born of swordplay, he snatched her by the chin, yanking her back, giving voice to the *toro bravo* he carried in his blood. "Perhaps I touch tenderly now, but I am not above returning you to his bunk. If you hope for a shred of mercy, you will make me forget the awful thing you've done! Do we have an understanding, *maja*?"

She deserved whatever he dished out, but by God, she wanted mercy! His grip strengthened until she found words. "We do," she whispered, broken.

Triumphant, he rose.

To the metallic clink of his sword belt coming unbuckled, she curled away, buried her face in a rank blanket, and flinched at the *clunk-clunk* of a door's crossbar falling into place.

Chapter 6

Beneath an evasive moon, Marcus leaned against the balustrade of Miss McGirth's terrace, hands flat on its stone coping. Its icy surface numbed his palms and made his knuckles ache, but he barely noticed for the insane bird sharing his solitude.

He was no naturalist, but he knew a falcon when he saw one. What little light the stingy heavens offered caught in the bird's mottled white underparts and yellow eye-ring.

Marcus had been scanning the enclosure for Miss McGirth when the raptor descended like a spirit from the midnight sky, having forgotten it wasn't a bird of the night and men weren't to be trusted.

Marisol's fussing seeped through the door.

He glanced back through the glass and sheers. The hearth projected light that bathed Barb in quivering amber as she wearily paced the floor. The baby squirmed against her, whipping the air with a tiny arm. Hours had passed since the woman had lost the energy to hum. Like Marcus, she'd been worn to a nub.

Five times Marisol had lain in her basinet, sweating through a fever only to waken a while later, crying. Marcus hadn't known a baby's cries could be sweet, but somehow this little jewel managed it. From adorable downturned lips, she gave intermittent chest-stuttering sobs. They stretched Marcus's heart, bent it in an arc that attached solidly to her frail body.

The longer this excruciating night went, the more worried he became. She hadn't wet but one napkin in eight hours. In that period, he'd twice listened to her eager, gulping meals. For the amount she was consuming, she should have gone through several napkins by now. He'd applied gentle pressure to her kidneys with no response of discomfort. Perhaps she was simply storing and replenishing lost fluids. But the fussing and the perpetual fever…

"God, help her." Marcus certainly couldn't.

She needed her mother. Refusing himself another stomach-wringing look at Miss McGirth's empty bed, he turned back to the night.

The falcon was gone. In its place, a feather teetered on the rail's edge. As it took flight on a draft, Marcus snatched it, then ran his fingers down its ten-inch silken vane.

It was a relaxing exercise that he continued as he raked the arena spreading before him — the stately loblollies to the right, the row of servant's quarters to the left, the perimeter wall beyond them both.

No Miss McGirth.

That evening, when he'd gotten back from seeing to the soldier — who hadn't had more than a knot on the head — he'd been surprised to find she hadn't returned from whatever errand the don had sent her on. She was still gone, and it sat very wrong with him.

Marcus hadn't seen the lord of the house yet either. After dinner in the room, he'd sent Barb down to ask again after her mistress. She'd turned somber. *No one's tellin' me nothin'*, she'd insisted, but something was wrong, and that something was Diego López. Marcus would lay stakes on Justice, he was so certain.

A host of degrading names queued up on his tongue, ready and willing to be used on the don. In the meantime, he'd use them on himself for being as useful to Miss McGirth as an empty scabbard.

More than once he'd been at the top of the stairs, sword at his hip, determined to spend the rest of the night combing San Marcos. Each time, her daughter's mewling had brought him back. Miss McGirth would want him here, and who was to say the second he turned his back, Marisol wouldn't disappear too? He'd be a pox-crusted redcoat before he lost them both.

The clouds shuffled about, exposing the moon. Marcus lifted his eyes to it and the sliver of gray rimming its left side. Three nights from full, it was a clock ticking down the hours until the *Gallant Lady* sailed for Fort Gadsden. *Five days*, Major Ainsworth had said when they'd cast anchor. *If we don't have what we need by then, we never will.* Marcus from two days ago had agreed, but *this* Marcus repented of it.

This Marcus wanted Miss McGirth and Marisol gone yesterday, but he would stay as long as necessary, do whatever necessary to root out Iron Wood and uncover evidence that would set the agent up for destruction.

For justice.

At the sound of a male voice, Marcus spun.

The don cradled his daughter, bouncing her lightly.

"High time," Marcus muttered. He flung the balcony door wide and swept the billowing sheers from before him.

López wore only his breeches. His feet were unshod, and his hair was loose about his face. A jerk of his chin cleared it to allow for the message he sent Marcus's way. The one-sided pluck of his lips, the ruddiness staining his cheek, the stench of toil exuding from him, the sated look about his wine-dulled eyes—they were words unspoken.

Marcus looked to Barb. "I fear the lady can be found in this man's bed."

She slumped. "I 'spect you's right."

"Would she have gone there willingly?"

The question cinched her upright again. "Law, no. The don always hankerin' fierce-like, but the missy, she sworn him off sometime after I first knowed her. Summer's heat it was. Guilt come buzzin' by, see, and she got bit good. But the don be powerful persuasive, and ain't much a momma won't do for her child. She—"

Marcus, having heard enough, kicked the door with an angry heel. It slammed, rattling the bottles on the vanity. Barb backed into the space between the desk and the armoire.

He tossed the feather on the desktop, eyes darting to Justice where she hung from her belt on the back of the chair. Breaking into a sweat, he relished the message *she* would send. His fingers spasmed and, in that disturbingly familiar way, begged for her bone hilt.

The don tapered his eyes, daring, but Marcus was no fool. Though he carried the protection of the United States Army, he knew Don Diego López was arrogant enough to disregard it on a caprice. Deliberately, he contracted every muscle to keep his body in check. He and López would have their fight, but this wasn't it.

Marisol needed his care more than the don needed his steel. And Marcus refused to repeat his mistakes.

López lowered his sight to his whimpering daughter and spoke in the smooth, lisping tones of the Spanish — surprisingly gentle for one with eyes as wintry as his.

"Where is she?" Marcus demanded. "What have you done to her? Ask him, Barb."

"No, suh. Not me." She retreated farther.

Languidly, López settled his attention on Marcus. "*Buenas tardes, Doctór* Buck."

"He tellin' you good evening, suh," Barb supplied faintly.

"Is he? Perhaps he's been too distracted to notice, but we're several hours into the new day." Marcus took deliberate strides toward the don, appreciative of his advantage in both height and brawn. "Tell me the child has a hope of seeing her mother tomorrow."

This, Barb stammeringly translated. The don's glance at the clock on the mantel said he'd understood. A query on his brow, he went to it, ran a slow hand over the marble where the frigate had once stood. He was looking to Barb as though to question her, when Marisol arched her back and let out the first substantial howl of the night.

"It's the heat." Marcus went to them, speaking to the baby in consoling tones. "You're feverish, and your clod of a father brings you to the fire. Of all the blockheaded things to do." He held out his arms and pegged the don with a no-nonsense eye. "Give her to me," he said, using the cool command that worked best with stubborn patients.

Upper lip twitching, López gave him such a look of disdain,

Marcus was sure he'd be dismissed from the room, the house, the country. But at the beat of Marisol's fist, López kissed her forehead, buzzed a few words, and relinquished her.

If nothing else could be said of the man, he was at least a doting father.

He left without further comment, and Marcus was so relieved to still have possession of his young charge, he'd begun dabbing ointment into her weeping rash before he realized he hadn't gotten an answer about her mother.

A growl erupted in the back of his throat.

"You askin' for it, doc, flappin' at the gums like you done. He ain't the featherbrain you think he is." Barb used a sleeve to scrub her sweaty forehead.

Marcus moved to the cool air squeezing through the cracked window and plucked a tear from Marisol's chin. "He's featherbrained enough to hand this little jewel over to me and walk away without a backward glance."

"Cain't argue that." Her voice cracked with fatigue.

"Go to bed, Barb. I'll see her through the night."

"But, doc, you ain't slept—"

"It's not up for discussion. No sense both of us being awake, and your milk won't hold out if you fail your rest."

She made her way to the adjoining room and spoke around a massive yawn. "Wake me if you need me."

"She'll require a feeding bottle. Three nights from now." He'd see to it Fanning procured a goat.

A long silence followed until at last she nodded. "I'll see what I can do."

Her door clicked shut as Marcus strolled to the balcony door and slipped between the curtains and the glass. As he swayed and watched the moon march in and out of patches of clouds, he reclaimed his composure, and Marisol quieted. "Three days, my lady. Then I'll take you to meet your grandfather. When your mother gets back, we'll tie her to that chair right there and tickle her toes until she promises not to disappear again. How is that for a plan?"

Marisol let out a sigh, her body going limp.

His innards tightened with affection. How blessed he was to be assigned her keeper, to do this for McGirth.

That wasn't the full truth of it anymore, now was it? He was doing it for her, for their well-being. Evil resided here. Marcus felt it like the Florida sun on the back of his neck, an inescapable scorch. Oppressive. Wearying.

That aside, Marcus was growing attached.

The clock's hands slid into the next hour as he patted Marisol's bone-dry napkin. He dreaded putting her down and having her wake again, but he'd barely completed the thought when his own lids were dragged earthward.

Sluggishly, he went to the bed and, not bothering to remove so much as a boot, stretched out on the mattress, arm still cupping Marisol. She stirred and murmured, then flopped a leg onto his chest and gave an impressive snore.

Trapping a snicker, he marveled at the strange pinch inside him. A little taste maybe of that ache Miss McGirth described?

Feeling somewhat featherbrained himself for not having tried this earlier, he adjusted the pillow and let a prayer for the woman carry him into a numbing sleep.

The morning was dark and crisp, its air clean. Lillian pulled it deep into her lungs and let it out in a puff of white, sad that it would do nothing to purify her.

Diego's lively pace led her to the stables. Pepe scratched the forehead of her readied horse. Seeing them, he removed his hat and bowed his head. "*Buenos dias*, mi señor."

Neglecting the servant's greeting, Diego took Lillian by the waist to lift her into the saddle, but when she reached for the cantle, she noticed her bare wrist. "My prayer beads!" At Diego's look of impatience, she added, "Fray Emilio will be suspicious if —"

"I know, I know." The friar could stretch a suspicion into Divine

Truth in less time than it took to light a votive, and Lillian could ill afford another violation. "Go get them. And don't linger over the baby. I want you to the mission and back before breakfast."

As was Diego's pattern, he wouldn't be able to swallow a bite until he knew the friar hadn't chosen this week's confession to shift the Church's holy burning wrath to him.

Lillian seethed over his unfounded worry. Fray Emilio's role as inquisitor in this region of New Spain held full, unquestioned authority over the *pueblerinos*. However, his power was somewhat limited regarding nobles, even one of middling rank such as Diego. There would be no mind-numbing interrogation, no putting him to *the question*, or torture. Not without the approval of the inquisitor-general of the Holy Office of the Inquisition.

The one power the friar did have was that of *vergüenza pública*, that shuddersome public shaming. A man's honor was everything, and from Diego's own lips, he'd spent a lifetime cultivating his. *Honor without ships is worth more than ships without honor*, he was known to say, reiterating that he possessed both and intended to keep them.

Of course, holding up the public banner of honor and living by its conventions were completely unrelated. The former was rigid, meant to be unquestioned. The latter, to be bent and broken as often as lust and greed and every other mortal sin demanded.

"I'll hurry," Lillian said. She was eager for a whiff of her baby's skin, but Diego wasn't alone in his aversion to the weekly ordeal.

She lifted the hem of her cloak, slippers kicking up dust in her long strides toward the hacienda's gate. By the time she reached the staircase, she was winded and faint and had no recourse but to pause or stumble. As she lingered on the rail, she hugged her laboring ribs, revolted by the ache of Diego's morning exercise lingering in her bones. He'd kept her occupied until not fifteen minutes earlier when he'd ordered her into the modest, unassuming gown he'd had the laundress fetch and left to command that her horse be readied for her jaunt to San Marcos.

Her skin was tacky with his sweat, and her hair was sloppily pinned with arms too weak to hold up for more than a short period. But there was no time to amend her attire. Fray Emilio, who viewed sloth and murder on equal plane, expected her knees on the ground before the altar at the strike of six.

To that end, she drove herself up the stairs and around the loggia. Quietly, she slipped into her suite.

The drapes were pulled to, not a wisp of light allowed entry. But there was no missing the familiar sound of her child's brisk, grunty intakes, the pattern Lillian had come to know and love. It was serene. Healthful.

She let out a mighty breath. Sometimes, where Mari was concerned, God listened.

There came the sound of another presence, this one deeper, stronger, a man's. Doctor Buck, had to be.

Curious to see him, she peeled back the edge of the window hangings and waited a beat for her eyes to adjust.

The chair he'd occupied was empty, as was the divan Barb used for nursing. But the bed, its curtains yawning wide, nestled a figure that populated half its space.

Doctor Buck wasn't a tall man, not by Creek standards, but he had three inches on Diego. His shoulders alone dwarfed the diminutive Spanish mattress, their distinctive breadth recognizable even now.

Lillian padded across the room, easing between the bedside and the basinet, squinting into the predawn murk. Her breath caught.

Fully clothed, Doctor Buck lay on his side, feet crammed against the footboard, one arm under his head, one stretched over Lillian's child in a loose protective embrace. And Marisol, that greedy little ray of sun, had stretched out beside him, every inch of her smashed against his chest, head tucked beneath his chin, fist attached to his coat's lapel in the exact manner Lillian would were she ever given the invitation.

Smart baby. Beautiful man.

Had Diego ever cuddled Marisol in such a way? He'd certainly never shared his sleeping space with her. That, he reserved for her mother. A fact made more heinous by the angelic vision before her.

This, *this* was right and good, if fleeting, and everything she longed for but was too faithless to believe would come about.

While Lillian had lain under Diego's febrile weight, praying God would turn a blind eye, begging Him to save her child from this nightmare, Marisol had been safe in Marcus Buck's arms. Tentatively, peace crept around the edges of Lillian's heart, seeking entry, but she held it at bay while gripping herself to keep from crawling into the idyllic scene. This canvas held no place for her, not even a petty corner. But Marisol, she deserved this security and tenderness, given unconditionally despite her unholy entry into the world.

Ah, that Doctor Buck was a splendid, covetable gentleman. She would stitch him into her pocket never to let him free were she certain the filth inside wouldn't desecrate his upstanding reputation.

From the bedside table, the rosary's silver crucifix winked, depositing Lillian back at the impending confession. She snatched the bracelet, splashed lemon water on her wrists, and hurried out the door.

She went to the friary's chapel in the same manner as always, riding sidesaddle with a mounted guard on either side and breathing a prayer, "Freedom from this place, please God. And a bit of mercy."

"We must move faster, Señorita Liana." Teniente Prieto was with her today as well as Barros—as Varela had called him. They treated her with careful deference yet urged a swift clip.

Hood up, she trotted her mare into San Marcos, grateful she'd made it without sliding from the beast's side. *Calle Principal* boasted the same shops as every other main street on the peninsula: haberdasher and fishmonger, among others. Each keeper came to his shop's entrance to welcome her with a colorful array of foul names. Back rigid, she fashioned a charming smile and nodded politely to each in turn, praying down judgment on their heads.

The fort reared up on her left. Three figures, two male and one female, began across the mote. The day's first blush was upon the sky, so under the penumbral trees, they were mere silhouettes, their turbans, feathers, and fringed leggings identifying their race, their bows and fierce strides shrinking Lillian in her saddle.

"Teniente," she asked in a discrete tone, "didn't Toño command the Indios to stay away until the *Gallant Lady* sailed?"

In that instant, the tallest looked back. The movement coincided with his emergence from the trees, dispelling the worst of the shadows. *Tall Bull.* No mistaking that striking face. And beside him, the warrior woman. Her scowl shone through the dusky light, directed one second at Lillian, the next at her chief who'd stopped to follow Lillian's progress. Body halted at mid-march, he locked onto her with an intense inquisitiveness that shook her breath.

"No one commands that one," Teniente Prieto replied.

"I would imagine not."

The little war woman's lips moved, and Tall Bull flinched and went back to his business. Perhaps someone did command him.

"Olé, the pretty lady! See how she comes to me?" Cabo Valero slumped against the open doorway of the *taberna*, a glass sloshing wine over his hand. "*Así es*, that's right. Come this way, you glorious darling, and we will finish what we started."

"*Idiota!*" A chesty barmaid shoved him back into the dim interior, slamming the door behind them.

The friary bell drowned Cabo Varela's shouted response as it began to toll the hour. Lillian's every muscle stood at attention.

May God smite that bell! Lightning, fire, ash. And a stout wind to blow it all to sea!

She imagined Fray Emilio's sweaty hands wrapped around the rope, pulling, releasing, hoping to next grip the length of cane that had ushered her into San Marcos. Seven stinging blows—the number it had taken her to admit she was a godless harlot with a mal-conceived child.

That horrible day, she'd been carried from San Marcos shattered and facing forty days of penance. In gratitude to her for bearing the blame and salvaging his honor, Diego had requested permission to keep her on as his assistant. Since her services benefited the Spanish Crown, the friar had granted it on the condition she confess weekly until her sins had been expunged.

Thirty long and hungry days had transpired with nothing more than bread and broth passing her lips. No, there had been one exception: a pouch of nuts from a man who hadn't required fasting or prayer to disregard her sins.

In addition, he'd nourished her body and spirit, both of which longed for him now, his gracious touch and affronted sword. In his place, she received a dusty road leading to a lonely altar and a man of the cloth whose love of power exceeded his love of God.

"*Deprisa*, señorita, hurry!" Reaching from his mount, Teniente Prieto took her mare by the bridle and urged them on for the last stretch. The wind flung back her hood and whipped water from her eyes.

Though squat and crumbling, the whitewashed mission loomed large and brought bile to her throat. Her mare skidded to a stop before its doors, then the teniente was hauling her down. He shoved her all the way to the altar where she collapsed, hands smacking the cold dirt floor as the bell's last *dong* faded out. Her hair tumbled over her face like a veil.

To the coniferous aroma of frankincense, she hastily made the sign of the cross.

"My prayers are with you," Teniente Prieto murmured and tramped out the way he'd come.

Breathing thickly, she sucked hair into her mouth. "Receive my confession, Lord Jesus Christ. Grant to me true contrition, so that I may by penance make satisfaction for my abundant sins. O, sweet Jesus—" The rustle of robes coming from the sacristy behind the altar hit her like a cattail.

She raised her voice in false confidence. "O, sweet Jesus give me true sorrow for my wrongs and a genuine purpose to never again commit them."

"Prostrate before the Lord, my child? *Bien, bien*, good." The friar knelt beside her. "Corporal humility is a sign of the truly penitent. Are you repentant?"

Hands splayed in the dirt, she swallowed, seeking moisture for her dry tongue and finding none. "Sí, *Hermano* Sanchez," she said, using his Dominican title of *brother*.

"Hmm, we shall see."

The simple line sent a chill into her soul.

"Hail, purest Mary," he said, launching them into the rites of confession.

Her response came out on a sheepish whisper. "Without sin conceived."

"I invite you to confess, keeping the truth and the Lord's Holy Name always on your lips."

Lillian recited the list of sins she'd prepared. A good list, it contained several venial sins and ended with a more impressive one that would satisfy the friar as to her thoroughness. "The doctor pressured me, hermano, and seeing I could not walk for the debility of my penance, I took the nuts he prescribed."

"And?"

What else did he want from her? Diego had warned her to keep him out of the confessional, and he'd assured her their hours together had been kept secret.

"And-and later, at his insistence, I took a few mouthfuls of broth with rice. As you know, my will is weak, but to compensate, I doubled my time at the altar despite my ailing child."

Her arms shook; her elbows threatened to fold. *God have mercy, God grant me undeserved mercy!*

"Ah, yes, the progeny of lust. She is God's reproach to an iniquitous woman. Would He had spared her a life of shame and sent her to Abram's bosom."

Lillian's arms popped straight, elbows locking. Her nails gouged the earth as anger lapped at her blood. He could insult Lillian, belittle and humiliate her, beat her until her bones cracked, but he could not disparage God's sweetest creation! And to wish death upon her? What sort of man was this? He was no man at all! He was a-a—

Jaw shaking, she bit down hard on her lips, the vilest of names hammering the backs of her teeth, demanding freedom.

"Have you no other misdeeds to account for?"

Dirt wedged beneath her nails, she dragged fists up her thighs as she straightened. Chin tucked, hair obscuring her view, she saw nothing but the legs of the wooden altar table and the white lace frontal dangling between them. She beat back hot virulence before opening her mouth. "Not that I recall. For all these, I seek forgiveness in the blessed name of Jesus Christ. Absolve me, hermano, I plead."

He stood, dusted the knees of his black habit, and rounded to the front of her, hands clasped beneath his scapular. "And why should I when you harbor like a treasure the greatest of all sins?"

She looked up sharply. "*Perdón?* I…what sin do you mean?"

Imperiously, he peered down at her from a face too bulbous to be in any way handsome. "What other, but that which perpetually hisses desire into your wicked ear, driving you to reckless abandon of the faith! The sin I speak of, señorita, is the pleasure of the flesh," he said, hissing out the last syllable.

"No, I would not—!"

"You would add deceit to the charge against you?" He bent over her so abruptly, so closely, the crucifix of his rosary smacked her in the chin. "You are a vile enchantress! Yes, with those very eyes that look upon me now, you lure men to their spiritual doom. They flutter and tease, using the powers of darkness to strip a virtuous man of his will."

Her heart was a bird, flapping wildly; her throat, a cinching belt. "Where have you heard such lunacy? I am a true daughter of the faith!"

"Your actions tell me otherwise."

He couldn't know what she'd allowed in the night! Diego had been so certain. Fray Emilio was merely testing her. "What actions? Who are my accusers? Show them to me!"

"Ay, *pero hija*, you accuse yourself," he said in a ragged undertone as he dragged a hot finger down her neck. Putting it to his nose, he inhaled. "I smell iniquity on you, beneath a fragrance of lemon that is not quite cunning enough. Your soul reeks of carnality." At her gasp, he pulled away. "With whom have you been? Tell me now, and your affliction will be lightened."

She shot to her feet, wishing for a handful of dung to throw into his sanctimonious face. "I will tell you nothing, and I am *not* your daughter!" To involve Diego would be to hang herself.

Fray Emilio grinned, revealing teeth more belonging to wolf than man. "An apt confession, *hija de Satán*. But I will not give up. There is hope for you yet." He looked to the back of the nave. Lifted a finger in command. Brought his haughty gaze back to her. "Prepare to have your soul exorcised of darkness."

She spun to flee, but Teniente Prieto blocked the only exit, a splotchy flush on his throat, a rod of green cane in his hand.

Defeat crumpled her lungs. What child of God had ever hidden from His wrath? Not her.

Barros stood beside the teniente, choler whitening his mouth. Diego would be livid, and these men would feel the brunt of it. But no man defied the inquisitor.

Fray Emilio washed his hands in a basin on the altar table. "Take her to the *picota* in the market." The pillory, her old friend. "Strip her and lay the cane to her back until she proves herself purged by professing illicit relations and divulging the name of her amante."

Behind Lillian's gown, her knees threatened to double. *Sweet Christ in Heaven, have mercy!*

Teniente Prieto approached, his unhesitant footsteps contradicting the apology in his eyes. He took her by the arm and spoke low and close. "Keep the pride in your backbone, *bonita*, and thank a pitying God it is me who holds the rod."

"He removed it from Varela." Trepidation lowered Barros's tone.

Cabo Varela. What delight he would have had tearing the skin off her back! And what a horrifying task for his substitute.

Teniente Prieto was a decent man and soldado besides. At first sign of trouble, he would have sent runners for Toño and Diego. The first would delay the carrying out, giving time for the second to arrive and put a stop to it.

On that comforting thought, she lifted a tight smile. "Grácias, Teniente. May God remember your kindness. Do what you must."

A thump to Marcus's cheekbone yanked him from sleep. His eyes opened to five pudgy toes. He sat up, blinking away dreamless slumber.

Marisol lay perpendicular to him, having rotated in the night. Morning light, dulled by that constant haze, entered from a gap in the drapes and revealed a vast improvement in the baby's rash, as well as a dark circle of wet beneath her.

"Good morning, happy little miss." Marcus took her under the arms and picked her up out of the stain. When her soggy napkin fell to the mattress, he laughed. "No more worrying about *you*."

She squealed through a toothless grin, and in her brown eyes, Marcus saw her mother.

At the thought of her, the night came back to him in a horrifying rush. Not a dreamless sleep after all.

Miss McGirth had come to him in a fog, browbeaten, beseeching. She'd shoved her daughter into his arms, and as he'd drawn Marisol close, he'd made promises about her safety that had no bearing on reality.

Then the woman was sinking into murky, fathomless water, and Marcus was abandoning the child for the mother. He'd pursued her hard, trailing her tangy scent and the blood that streamed from her broken body. The chase dissolved into a dream-world mist, and he was left wondering and disturbed, unable to shake it.

So vivid! The smell of her was still thick in his nose. The sight of her, mangled and bleeding... He shivered.

Gnawing a finger, Marisol cooed at him and instantly dispelled the gloom.

"What a charmer you are." There was no help for it but to land a noisy kiss on her cheek.

The door half opened, and Barb stepped in, smiling broadly. "If you wasn't awake, I was gonna have to pry them eyes open."

"This naughty pipsqueak did it for you." Avoiding the soiled spot on the mattress, he swung his legs over the edge and passed Marisol to her nurse. "Any news of Miss McGirth?"

"Yes, suh. Come and gone at sunup."

"Why? Where?"

"Goin' to the church. Like she do every Friday."

He wasn't sure whether to rejoice or discharge a brittle oath. His charge had been by, and where was he? Snoozing away the morning. Incompetence at its finest. He stretched for the boots he'd kicked free. "Was she well?"

Baby on hip, she gathered diapering supplies from the chest of drawers. "She was halfway down the lane, 'fore I saw her, but she looked right enough to me."

Frustrated, he yanked at the boot's laces. "How long will she be gone?"

"Should be back soon now, so you sit tight. Go on down and have you a bite of somethin'. Oh, and while you eatin', read this." She handed over a crumpled note. "Pepe brung it."

Marcus smoothed out the scrap of paper. The tight script belonged to Fanning.

Come at once. Be advised: commander refusing transport of cargo.

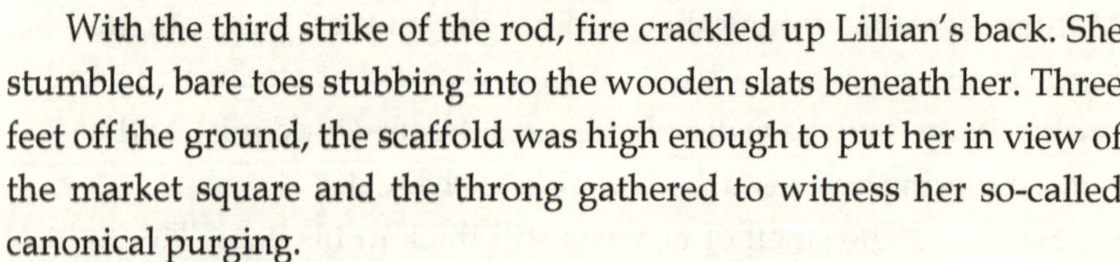

With the third strike of the rod, fire crackled up Lillian's back. She stumbled, bare toes stubbing into the wooden slats beneath her. Three feet off the ground, the scaffold was high enough to put her in view of the market square and the throng gathered to witness her so-called canonical purging.

Pain whitened her vision, but it was not the half of what it could be. Teniente Prieto applied a lighter rod than the last man. God bless him for bearing Diego's inevitable vengeance for her sake. The other soldado to beat her had hidden under the friar's habit a week before Toño arranged a new assignment for him. St. Augustine, though, hadn't been quite far enough.

Through watery eyes, she scoured the crowd for Toño but saw only a sea of spiteful pueblerinos and a barrage of mud and refuse.

Christ, show an ounce of favor!

The fourth blow was lightning. It wrenched muscle and knocked her feet out from under her. With the next, her backbone would surely fracture.

Tears overflowed her cheeks and drained from her nose. Salt coated her lips. Sweat burst from every pore, and her flimsy chemise stuck to every damp curve. La vergüenza pública was a cruel trial on par with the cane's.

Diego wasn't so coldhearted that he would abandon her to this crucible…was he?

To relieve her arms and regain a bit of dignity, she shoved her feet back under her. She was bracing for the next slap when the friar's voice penetrated the clangor between her ears.

"The Church demands a name as evidence of your liberation from evil." He'd positioned himself on the dais out of sight to her left. "Are you ready to make known your amante? Lillian McGirth, what pious man have you beguiled?" He butchered her English name.

She sneered, then closed her eyes to find a moment of respite before it began again. The friar knew perfectly well whose scent she wore, and she wouldn't give him the pleasure of hearing her voice it.

While the friar awaited her response and the crowd murmured impatiently, Barros moved in to wipe sweat from her forehead. "Make it stop, señorita," he implored in her ear. "Provide a name. Any name!"

It was understood she should not speak the rightful name. For the moment, Fray Emilio held the power, but he would be stripped of it the second Diego entered the square. She had only to hold out. Diego would come. Surely, he would come. And where in the sweet name of Our Lady of Mercy was Toño!

"Say it," Barros urged. "Say his name!"

"What innocent man," she said through gritted teeth, "would you have me ruin?"

"Varela! Who else?" he whispered harshly. "The man hasn't been innocent a day in his life. If the don had not stopped him yesterday, he would have—"

"But he didn't."

Cabo Varela was scum, but Lillian knew what it was to be

manipulated and used. She would take no part in it.

"He has no honor to lose! Liana, the friar is determined. You will not survive *the question*." His words tumbled out in a desperate race. "And if you do not survive, the teniente and I won't either!"

"*Basta!*" Fray Emilio's command sliced the air. "Enough. If she were going to talk, she would have already. Teniente, resume."

Under his breath, Barros released a blaspheming oath on the friar, wrinkled a commiserative brow at her, and backed away.

The crowd hushed, and Lillian grappled the iron ring on the post above her head, determined to stay upright.

Exclamations of surprise and annoyance rose from the crowd. Feminine squeals of fear moved in like a wave, growing in volume. The platform pulsed with the rush of feet.

"Teniente, behind you!" Barros leaped from view.

A grunt and *thud-thud-thump* followed. The rod whistled, and Lillian stiffened in anticipation. But the blow never arrived. A clatter preceded the cane's flight as it skittered past her across the scaffold and flew into the masses below.

"What are you—? Someone stop that *salvaje!*" Fray Emilio shouted.

Savage? Lillian twisted to see.

Tall Bull was four strides distant and closing, reaching for her. The sight of him—war in his eyes, knife in his hand—sucked the life from her knees. She sank with another shock to her joints. Through its burn, her feet frantically scraped wood, swiveling her away from him. But where was there to go?

His hard-as-cordage arm clamped about her midriff and propelled her back toward him. "Would you like to complete the beating, then?" he said in Muskogee, his breath suffusing her with the sweet aroma of holly tea. "I would be happy to tell your bluecoat medicine man you died honorably."

Lillian tilted for a view of his face to confirm he was gloating in her pain. Instead, she found undercurrents of sympathy. Tension rippled the muscles of his jaw as, with consideration to her wounds, he lifted her and shelved her derriere on his upper thigh.

At the weight coming off her wrists, she gave a little cry of relief and slumped over his arm, confused and physically disoriented. As he focused on knifing through the rope, she found nothing inside her but gratitude. Loathsome, mind-boggling gratitude.

"You cannot—! Someone, stop that-that—!" Fray Emilio's sputtering protest was lost in the pueblerinos' indignant voices.

"Who does he think he is?"

"The Indios have *complete* disregard for the laws of civilization."

"Where is Capitán Luengo? He would not stand for this!"

"Teach him a lesson, Teniente!"

But no one would because no one dared. Lillian knew it, the soldados knew it, and the audacious chief beside her knew it.

The Red Sticks were a sovereign people, not bound by the laws of San Marcos's Most Catholic King or the Holy Church. Not only were they powerful, they were powerful allies. Their chief would not be regulated. He stood head and shoulders over every Spaniard present, and if any man doubted Tall Bull would not use his skills in battle to stay his chosen course, he was a fool.

That Tall Bull had chosen to use his sway to spare her the remains of this ordeal was-was-was— She didn't know. Couldn't grasp it, couldn't think. Could barely breathe for the pain.

A final, furious slice of his blade freed her. He threw the frayed rope at the friar's sandaled feet and turned his back, and hers, on the man's fuming.

"Can you stand?" At her nod, he lowered her feet to the slatted dais, and then, the villa's perfect silence, he flicked debris from her hair and used the tail of his long-shirt to wipe her face dry of mucus and filth.

Barros stood off to the side, watching the procedure from a blackening eye.

Tall Bull paused to fling a word at him. "*Capa.*"

It was an order at once rebuffed by Fray Emilio who invoked damnation down on them both, but it was the Indian whom Barros jumped to obey, stumbling over himself to bat aside her corset for the cloak underneath. He tossed it across the platform to Tall Bull who caught it and with deft fingers secured the ties at her neck.

She scraped a dry tongue across dry lips. "*Estometv ceme?*"

"What does it look like I am doing? Fastening the capa to better hide your nakedness." He picked straw from the wool, mouth finally tipping into a hint of the cocky smirk she'd known in Kossati. "I can carry you, but your dignity would be better served by walking."

God knew her dignity could use a boost. In answer, Lillian began across the stage, each step a question of endurance. "Barros, my horse?"

"Sí, Señorita Liana." The man marched to do as asked, scattering gawkers before him.

At the steps leading off the scaffold, Teniente Prieto stepped aside, head lowered. As she passed, she brushed his arm with grateful fingers. "I will…speak to him," she assured, out of breath.

By a power not her own, she traversed the parted crowd, Tall Bull silently dogging her steps.

Barros held the horse steady for her. "Can you even ride?"

"Just…give me a minute." Sweating profusely, she gripped the cantle in one hand, the pommel in the other, and leaned heavily against the horse's flank. She felt the villa behind her like a wall of judging eyes, inwardly cheering for her collapse. If she didn't get moving, she wouldn't disappoint them.

Resolved not to faint, she lifted her cloak to search out the stirrup, but the effort shot flickers of black across her vision.

"Liana!" Toño was suddenly beside her, gingerly supporting her. "What has been done to you? No, no, you will not ride alone. Here" — he swiveled her away from the mare — "the chief will take you home."

Tall Bull was already seated kingly astride Barros's horse, looking down at her, arm extended, palm up.

Fear shot through her middle, as in an instant, she was transported to Singing Grass's courtyard where this very man had sat just so. Only that time, it had been her sister he'd hauled up and carried away.

Three days later, Adela had returned so disturbed she hadn't found herself for a week. Ever the protector, she never told Lillian what all had transpired, but if Adela, the rock, had been so affected…

Lillian turned into Toño's chest and fastened to his coat, face buried against his neck stock. "Find another," she said hoarsely. "Take me yourself. I cannot ride with him!"

"Why not, *chica*?" He stroked the hair from the side of her face. "What has he done but spare the skin on your back? Take the Indio's hand. I cannot do more."

Of course. As it was, the inquisitor would likely have words with Toño for interfering, and not five minutes ago, Tall Bull *had* proved himself…what? *Trustworthy* was the first word that came to mind, but she killed it. No Red Stick was that. *Sensible*. He'd been sensible. Abundantly so, considering his red skin. It would have to suffice.

"*Bueno*." She let go of Toño's clothing, and before creeping fear could alter her course, she faced the Indian, placed her hand in his, and let herself be lifted.

Chapter 7

"Grácias, Pepe." Marcus chucked the reins to the groom. Rounding the horse for his bag, he ducked its swiveling head and received several splats of hay-scented sweat on his cheek. He'd spurred the animal hard. Too hard, by the scowl crooking Pepe's mouth and the heated Spanish phrase that left it.

Marcus jerked at the saddle strings until they released his kit. "Has Miss McGirth returned?" The man merely hoisted an indifferent shoulder, so Marcus waved off the question, already quick-timing it out of the stables, the new guard close at his rear.

She had to be here, he told himself. Simply because the day couldn't go any fouler.

Major Ainsworth's summons had ended in nothing shy of disaster. He'd stalked Captain Luengo's parlor, fuming, indignant about not being apprised of Miss McGirth's "nefarious circumstances," as he'd coined it, but the previous month, in the brief Marcus had submitted, he'd been utterly forthcoming about her amoral situation. Clearly, the man hadn't fully read it.

When she'd merely been in a questionable situation with the Spanish, the major had been diffident about coming to her aid. But now that she was in bed with the blackguard López? Had borne a child of him? The major was scandalized, compelled to wash his hands of her. All in the name of decency and patriotism.

The only chance she had of avoiding a traitor's noose was to shell out substantial intelligence before the general's invasion clock struck midnight. There was little there with which to defend her, but Marcus had wielded it ardently. It hadn't made a whiff of difference.

Fear for her hurtled him toward the hacienda gates. Before he reached them, practicality slowed his stride. Miss McGirth shouldn't see him this way. Constructing a placid demeanor, he entered the compound.

The soldier trailing him grunted with relief.

The upper room drew Marcus toward the staircase, but movement through the study's partly open door veered his line of sight to a seated woman. He knew that crushed silk. Air vacated his lungs in a whoosh, his instinct being to charge to her in a flurry of questions. Checking the chaotic beating of his heart, he changed course.

The tobacco-scented chamber resembled that of any highbred gentleman's—walls lined with the spines of a thousand dusty books, stuffed birds on display in glass cases, a boulder of a desk presiding over it all—except for three elements: the black bull's head mounted over the fireplace; the twelve-sword rack beside it, fully stocked; and the beautiful woman sitting erect before the window, framed perfectly by its arched vault and made an angel by its glow.

Miss McGirth perched on the edge of a cushioned bench on the opposite side of the room, torso angled away. She was a wisp of a thing, a house of cards on a shaky table.

Every fiber of Marcus's makeup screamed, *intervene!* But how? Sailing was the ideal route, the quickest, safest. But it wasn't the only one. To a bottomless bog with Ainsworth! Marcus would find another way.

When he stepped into the library, he took care to create a noisy stir, but neither the hinges' groaning nor the muted fall of his heels distracted from her obsession with whatever lay beyond the bars that crisscrossed the window's exterior.

"May I join you, miss?"

"Do, please, come in." Though she held a book open at chest level, her attention remained fixed on the outdoors.

He stopped an arm's reach away, and still, she didn't turn. Foreboding rippled his insides. What was she hiding? If there were bruises on her, even a single smudge, he would hunt López down and— *No rash vengeance.* Miss McGirth needed him to keep a clear, judicious head.

"Thank you for tending Marisol in my absence," she said.

"She's a joy, but it was no easy feat setting aside the drive to tear up the countryside in search of you."

"I feared you would be anxious."

"What's kept you away?" In her silence, he urged, "Where did he take you?" No response. "Miss McGirth?" He laid a hand on her shoulder, but like a touch-me-not, she shied away.

He retreated a half step. Her pattern was to warm upon contact, never flinch. Heart impatiently marking time, he clasped his hands at his lower back and settled into a relaxed stance. Like that delicate shrinking plant, she would unfold again in time.

An inch of air separated the open pane from its wooden case. A breath of wind slipped through and fondled the edges of the letter in her lap. It swept over Marcus next, entering him with a lemon-fresh scent that took his eyes to the place a woman typically applied perfume—the hollow at the base of her throat, its exaggerated depth, and the too-rapid pulse tapping at it. Her upswept hair was damp from a recent washing, but that didn't account for the bead of moisture that followed the curve of her neck and disappeared behind her shawl. The air held a chill too deep to allow for perspiration. Fever?

She closed and lowered the book. "What do you make of that sky, Doctor?"

Marcus bent to see the world from her perspective. A strip of hazy, cloudless gray stretched between the top of the window's casement and the red clay tiles that roofed the perimeter wall.

"Nothing extraordinary. Except that it's looked the same for a twelvemonth. Drab and hazy."

"I miss the blue." Haltingly, she turned and offered him a closed-lip smile.

In a thorough sweep, he checked each feature, hairline to chin. Perfectly untarnished.

A coil released in his chest, caving it with an exhale. But as he registered the strain distending her nostrils and the wound in her eyes, the coil rewound.

He'd entered San Marcos aware of her emotional fragility. Evidence of it was already annotated in his log. It had presented at the riverside as well as over Marisol's unconscious form. He was tempted to excuse those instances as rational, but her responses fell just the other side of healthy. It was likely her current distress was also exaggerated.

He repaid her meager smile with interest, but when he got no return on it, he sobered. "We'll have our blue skies again. It cannot go on like this forever."

"That's what I've told myself every hour of every day. All things, even the dreadful, *especially* the dreadful, must end sometime or other." She was no longer speaking of the thin layer of atmospheric ash, and it ached. "For me, you *are* that end, Doctor Buck. An answer to my prayers."

He forced a smile. Thanks to Major Ainsworth, the borders of New Spain were still well beyond her reach, and every moment Marcus spent under the don's roof, they grew more distant. None of this information, however, was privileged to Miss McGirth.

No, he must tread lightly where she was concerned. There was also the hope she would come through for them in a large enough way to move Major Ainsworth's heart regarding her plight.

She tucked her skirt under her leg to clear the other half of the bench. "Sit with me?"

He accepted. The soldier made himself comfortable in a neighboring wingback chair.

She tapped a nail against the cover of the book on her knee. "Have you read Saint Teresa's autobiography?"

Marcus tilted his head to better see, but its Spanish title was lost on him. "Can't say that I have. Are you an admirer of hers?"

"It's required reading, but I've found I like her. She was of excellent character, always endeavoring to be blameless before our Lord. She strove for a life of absolute purity. Imagine being the woman unfortunate enough to fall in line behind her at Heaven's gates."

Marcus chuckled, but the questioning flash of her eyes said she hadn't meant it in jest. He cleared his throat and tried again. "It would only be unfortunate if her worthiness were to be measured against the saint's instead of the standard Jesus established, which of course, is Himself. If the woman was as upright as you say, she wouldn't abide being exalted to the level of Christ."

"Quite true." Miss McGirth's smile was tight as she laid the book on the table to her left. She breathed deeply, lips firming. Air left her in a jagged trail.

"Has the malaise returned? May I check for fever?" He lifted a hand, but she slanted away.

"There's a ship arrived in the bay, flying the Union Jack. You've heard?"

A deliberate diversion, but a most welcome subject. Marcus sat forward. "I have not."

"You will soon enough, but what you won't hear is that before it came in sight of your own frigate, a skiff was lowered and sent up a small tributary. To the tribes."

Intriguing. "And its cargo? Provisions, weapons?"

She shook her head. "I can't be sure."

"But you have an idea."

"The Red Sticks have been anticipating the arrival of a certain chief."

Blood hastened through his veins. "Do you mean—?" The mention of an ignominious name, such as that of Josiah Francis, was sure to secure the guard's unwanted attention. "The founder of Holy Town?" Marcus finished.

It was reported Francis had left from Negro Fort on Prospect Bluff to beg support and generosity of the British Crown. That was nigh on two years ago.

"Your guess is the same as mine."

"How do you not *know*?"

"I've consistently refused to deal with or even speak of the Indians. But all the same, I have ears, and information tends to trickle my way whether I like it or not. Is this at all helpful to our cause?"

"It is, along with hard evidence."

"I'll see what I can do about that. Be sure to tell Major Ainsworth it came from me. He seems to believe I am in debt to America and in dire need of settling it." A derisive puff blew from her nose. "I'm happy to help; no need to hurl unfounded threats at me."

"You would be mistaken to take the situation lightly, miss. And they aren't unfounded."

"I'm no traitor, Marcus Buck." Prickles marked every word.

"You needn't convince me. Unfortunately, your employ in the Spanish government says otherwise. Should La Conchita be found to be actively supplying the belligerent Natives, the lord of the estate as well as his king will be required to answer for the breach, but you…" He couldn't bring himself to speak of execution.

"What about me? I've done nothing wrong."

He released air from tight lips, resigned. Better to instill an action-prompting fear than to shelter her all the way to the gallows. "Your passion for this cause is heartening, but I've just been informed that your circumstances are so suspect, your dalliance with the don so damaging, that your attempt to help will not be enough to prove your loyalty; you must *produce*. Only you can protect yourself from the law. And do not doubt, Miss McGirth, that if the general deems you a traitor, he will make an example of you, even if he has to hunt you down to do it."

"Please, Doctor Buck, call me Benedict." She gave an abrupt chortle, all but rolling her eyes in the process.

Why was she not taking this seriously? Very well, he could speak more bluntly. He faced her squarely. "My aim is to get you out of this place, but my power goes only so far. I am a man owned by the United States, every word and action chained to its whim." He let his fear for her bleed into his timbre, and as his voice rose, so did the guard. Marcus ignored him. "You will leave this place by the good graces of my superior, not mine. And he has already assured me that if you cannot remove the stain on your name, you will regret it. If you hope to return to your father without a price on your head, we must clear your name and fast."

The guard questioned her, but she dismissed his concern as effortlessly as she dismissed Marcus's. After the man plopped back down, she turned to Marcus, chin tipped, lashes sweeping low over commanding eyes—the duchess unveiled. "This conversation baffles me. I cannot imagine any decent officer condemning me for what little I've done for the don, dalliance or not, especially after my pledge of support, which I *will* prove today. For justice, remember?"

Her cold hand capped his where it sat in a fist on his thigh. "You're a dear to worry so about me, Doctor. But you needn't. I shiver to think of it, but worst case, I fail and am forced to start afresh with a new identity." Eyes misting, she shrugged. "My name isn't worth keeping anyway."

"Rubbish!" To keep from shaking sense into her, he stood abruptly. "Your father would give everything he owns to have you home again. Every head of cattle, every withered tobacco plant. God bless him, he'd give every breath in his body!"

Her eyes shuttered. "My father doesn't understand how I'd ruin him."

Heaven help him, this woman was forcing his hand! He firmed his posture and his resolve, already regretting how his next move would break her. "He's dying."

Shock registered on her like a blow. Her body jolted; her throat loosed a hacked choke.

Prompt remorse sluiced over him in a sickening wave that pushed him back down to the bench. "I hadn't intended to tell you yet, or in such a way. It was—"

"He's dying?" she squeaked out, all vestiges of the duchess obliterated. "Of-of what? How long does he have?"

Marisol's faint squeals floated down from the upper floor, and Miss McGirth looked longingly toward it.

A troubled sigh left Marcus as he reconciled himself to completing one of the ugliest aspects of his profession. "Abdominal tumor. He has another two months, three at most. Assuming I'm correct on the extent of its spread."

As he spoke, she stood and backed away from him, arms limp before her, eyes wide and glassing over with whatever unpalatable vision was alive behind them.

He rose and reached out, intending to lend a comforting touch, but he arrested it, knowing better than to unfurl that sail. Not with this woman.

If she noticed his withdrawal, she didn't care. The pain clouding her eyes had carried her elsewhere. To Tensaw, he hoped.

"I was to tell you only as a last resort. He'd trusted…"

His hesitation pulled her from inside herself. "What?"

"That you wouldn't have to be dragged home by the threat of death, but that you'd come willingly, for the love of him."

"It is because I love him that I stay away!" Her voice broke on a sob that wrenched his heart. When she covered her face with her hands, Marcus waffled. She should be crying on the shoulder of a friend, not into her hands. He would offer, but he dared not presume she wanted his comfort. After all, he was the one who'd crushed her world.

"Of course, you love him. He knows that." He came alongside her, patted her back.

With a heightened cry, she recoiled, and he berated himself for not heeding his instincts. "Please, miss, forgive my bungling."

"Don't trouble yourself. I'm well." The flats of her fingers swiped brusquely at her cheeks. "And I'll see about getting what we need."

She eased onto the bench and opened the volume. "Our friend here seems eager to be rid of my display of emotions. If you'll check on the baby, he'll follow and leave me to do a little digging in the lord's files. I know precisely where to look."

"With pleasure." Sketching a generous bow, Marcus left to climb the stairs, a smile coming over him.

With a little luck, before sundown, the first branch of his assignment might be on its way to completion. And that would prayerfully lead to the security of the second.

Upon reaching Marisol in her room, he laughed at her slobber bubbles and blew a lungful of air against her naked belly. She cackled and pumped her legs until he couldn't take it anymore and plucked her off the bed for a squeezing embrace. "Your mother is a gem, did you know?"

"What she done that made you so gone-to-blazes jolly?" Barb worked around Marcus's arms to straighten the baby's layers of flannel and linen.

Beyond the open double doors, the soldier leaned over the loggia railing chatting lazily with a fellow in the courtyard below.

"Nothing yet," Marcus said. "It is the hope of what may be that makes me act the fool."

"You gonna offer her your good name? She ain't much to look at now, but you wait 'til she start eatin' again. Once she put a little padding back on those pretty hips, you'll see."

"Miss McGirth is lovely regardless, but she's—"

"Taken?" Barb gave a sassy smirk. "You gonna fix that though. Gonna slap *Buck* onto her name and thank her for it."

He was?

You are. The Spirit's voice, precise as a church bell.

Marcus could only blink. Tacking *Buck* to the end of her name would fix more than one problem. Logic reminded him she was a mistress. No longer of her own choosing, but a mistress nonetheless. A very pretty one whose company he happened to adore, whose mind polished his own, and whose pain so mirrored his it could be called design.

But marry her? Lord, have I misunderstood?

No answer came, so he began doubting he'd heard anything at all. Besides, he was under oath. God honored oaths, as did Marcus.

"'Til you do," Barb went on, oblivious to Marcus's dialog with

Divinity, "better watch yourself around that diablo stud of hers. He'll clip your angel wings quicker than you can say pompous Spanish jackass."

Impressive sword rack or not, the don didn't frighten him. "I'll keep that in mind."

"You bettuh." One brow arching, she settled onto the divan with the baby, so Marcus moved the screen to give her privacy, happy to set that awkward subject aside.

Suddenly exhausted, he dropped into the chair at the writing desk and landed an elbow on its surface. A sheet of foolscap slipped and began a fluttering trail to the ground.

He caught it and became hooked on a familiar name gracing the top left corner.

Adela.

It was the beginnings of a letter to Miss McGirth's elder sister.

She'd written little more than a greeting, and every word of it had been scratched out with several harsh strokes of the quill. But below it, across the middle of the page, laid down in an unsteady hand was a single paragraph.

Is not this the fast that I choose: to loose the bonds of wickedness, to undo the straps of the yoke, to let the oppressed go free, and to break every yoke? Yet even now, declares the LORD, return to me with all your heart, with fasting, with weeping, and with —

The scripture ended there with a splat of ink that had been smeared to the page's edge.

Marcus's eyes circled back over the text, once, twice, pausing on each pass at two locations. "Is that what this has been about?"

"You say somethin', Doc?"

"I most certainly did." He skipped around the privacy screen, letter held before him like condemning evidence. "She's *fasting*?"

A blanket covered Barb, shoulder to waist. Vigorous suckling noises came from beneath. She patted the baby through the blanket and *tsk-tsk*ed at Marcus. "That ain't my business, no suh, so I been keepin' my tongue. But now you know, I gotta say, this penance be the ugliest piece of business I ever saw. She say not to tell 'cause it between her and Jesus and that unholy friar. But you probably the last man in San Marcos to hear tell."

"To hear what exactly? What penance?"

"She makin' her heart right with Heaven. Got to, that friar say, for sweet-talking the don into her bed. And birthin' this little beauty here. Missy Lillian, she been prayin' and fastin'. Forty days, like the Lord Jesus Hisself. With not more than a scrap of bread to hit her belly 'tween suns. Eight days to go."

Forty days? *Forty?* Insanity! A death sentence for a woman of as slight a build as hers.

Did no one care? López had her gallivanting the countryside, playing interpreter and escort. Suni hadn't brought her breakfast, not even that scrap of bread she was allowed. Barb hadn't uttered a sound until Marcus had confronted her.

But the Red Stick, Tall Bull... He'd disapproved, acted, advised. An unlikely source of help, but Marcus would take it and thank God.

He would like to accuse himself of not pinpointing her trouble, but there was comfort in having finagled food down her throat at every opportunity.

The friar, though, and the don? Inexcusable behavior! Even a man unlearned in medicine should be familiar with the results of an extreme fast. Or was that their intent, to slowly kill her?

Marcus marched to the armoire. "Find me a satchel, Barb, and gather a few items for the baby. I'm getting her out of here. This very minute."

"There be a bag under the bed, already packed," she called.

Perfect. He knelt in search of it.

"But she won't be leavin', suh." Barb appeared from behind the screen; beneath the cover, Marisol snorted through her meal. "There's no walkin' outta here with this child."

"You just watch me." He dragged the leather satchel from the dusty shadows. "And Miss McGirth, she's gone along with the atonement? No protest?" Satchel in hand, he stalked toward his medical bag by the vanity.

"Ain't had much choice. Soon as she step outta line, she know it. Doc, suh…" The sudden trepidation in her voice stopped him short.

"What is it?"

She licked her lips, snagging a nervous glimpse of the guard still in relaxed conversation in the loggia. "The way you come up here all cheerful-like, I expect you don't know what been done to her, but you should."

What had been *done* to her? Marcus's innards clenched. "I'm listening." He crossed his arms, wishing he were barreling out of the hacienda gates, Miss McGirth under his wing.

"I cain't say the don give his go-ahead for it. No, he likely as spittin' mad as you gonna be. He was the first time it happen. Don't imagine much has changed 'tween last month and this. But, uh, she been beat, suh. In the square at the pillory. Before God and every soul who care to see."

"Beat? As in…flogged?" His arm went behind him, seeking support from the bedpost, the flesh of his back screaming in empathy.

Barb nodded, her throat convulsing with a swallow.

His mind whirled back to his recent exchange with Miss McGirth. The tension about her, the stiff posture, the withdrawal at his touch — each an affirmation of what Barb said. She'd been molested and flogged. On his watch. Could he have failed her more?

"She come back smellin' like a privy, the poor woman," Barb continued. "Could barely stand up. That Indian chief brung her home. Carried her clear up them stairs to where you be now. Took me three washes to get the stink off her."

Anger mounted inside him, spawning sweat and tumbling out in an oath to send La Conchita's unlicensed dealings up in a swirl of flame. He put its master through the same treatment. Bags in hand, he strode toward Barb, arm extended. "Give her to me. I'm leaving."

After a halfhearted resistance, Barb relinquished her.

Babe in arms, Marcus was leaping from the second-to-last stair to the plaza slate by the time the soldier began shouting an alarm. The gate guards had their swords drawn before Marcus reached the fountain. He smirked at their idiocy. Did they intend to slice at him with López's baby in his arms?

"Miss McGirth!" At his shout, Marisol squealed in fright.

The study doors flew open, but it wasn't the lady who emerged. Maxwell Bellamy, with his icy eyes, was genuine trouble.

As defeat approached, Marcus slowed, rounding the fountain at a panting stroll that was brought to a halt by the trio of sword points glimmering before him.

"Marcus, old chap, where are you off to this fine afternoon? Not attempting a rash and poorly thought-out kidnapping, I hope."

Actually, he was.

Bellamy stood eye-to-eye with him and, though not stoutly muscled, carried himself with the swagger of a man who'd battled his way through a great number of scrapes and come out the victor. A sword sat on his thigh, but its lack of a second strap to keep it from swinging, told Marcus he didn't often wear it and thus wasn't a proficient.

That bowie, however, and the occasionally vicious glint in Bellamy's eye… If the man ever got past the length of Justice's steel, Marcus might be in trouble.

Marisol whimpered at his ear.

"Sh-sh-shhh," Marcus consoled, then looked to Bellamy. "Just bringing the child to her mother. Where is she?" He peered beyond Bellamy into the study but saw little. "Miss McGirth?"

"Your concern is laudable but quite unnecessary. Don Diego sent me to make certain she's comfortable and safe. I've seen to both." Bellamy reached for Marisol, but Marcus used his shoulder to block the move.

"And I should believe that's true because she was taken such excellent care of this morning?"

"Your anger is justified." Bellamy nodded, eyes grim. "The don is outraged as well. He loves fiercely, but his revenge is a thing to behold. He'll see justice exacted."

The firm statement eased Marcus's mind a degree, but he shivered to think what a man like Diego López might call *justice*. He doubted it bore any resemblance to his own concept of it. "And how would he feel to learn his daughter and guest were treated to a clear view of his soldiers' swords?"

"Right, except for one detail. You're no longer a guest." Bellamy neared, voicing a command that sent the guards, minus one, back to their posts.

The original guard took the satchel from Marcus and lobbed it across the plaza to land at the base of the stairs. Then, he broadened his stance, daring Marcus to make another move.

The smile Bellamy offered was practiced, unreadable. "Don Diego thanks you for your excellent service, and I thank you for your intriguing loyalty to Miss McGirth. Few care to mine beyond her position to reach the gold hidden beneath."

So, they were evicting him. Taking mother and child and resealing the vault on the hacienda. If Marcus walked out now, would he get back in? He could give Justice a taste of English blood. If he worked the courtyard correctly, he could impair these four quickly enough to make it through that gate, but the outer wall would do him in. The odds would whip him, and if they didn't, Major Ainsworth would. For spoiling their mission because of a "treasonous wench."

No, Marcus would have to wait, pray, draft a new battle plan.

"I'd love to say it's been a pleasure." Bellamy shook his head in feigned heartache.

Marcus glared at him, unable to hear anything but that imperious British inflection.

"Why so hateful, old boy? Miss McGirth calls me her friend. And this one…" Bellamy beamed at Marisol and tried for her again.

Embittered, Marcus let him wriggle her from his grasp.

"This one adores her Uncle Max and doesn't understand why her fine doctor cannot do the same." Bellamy bounced her on his hip and chortled at the drool that flung off her lower lip. "Mari, tell Doctor Buck goodbye, then." He extended his hand to Marcus. "Thank you for everything. Caselas will see you to the gate."

Ignoring the gesture, Marcus choked the handle of his sword and told himself to behave, to bide his time. The *Gallant Lady* wasn't due to sail for three days, plus what remained of this one. This wasn't over.

"A word before I go," he said.

Bellamy cocked a brow. "Let's have it."

"If you truly do care, as you seem intent on making me believe, you'll see to it that Miss McGirth eats. Swear to me she'll be fed properly, starting immediately. Slowly at first. Mild foods. Anything rich will make her violently ill."

"Blow me, but you're rather intense. Is it so dreadful?"

"Her bodily systems will begin shutting down soon, if they haven't already."

Bellamy's parted jaw wiped away his arrogant demeanor. "I'll speak to His Lordship at once. But I don't foresee him defying the friar. He would spill his blood to protect the Church and her rulings."

"Try reminding His Lordship that this is not the Judean Desert, and Miss McGirth is *not* the Lord Jesus Christ." Marcus's voice lowered to a near growl. "If he insists on starving her, he should be made aware that he is putting his child's mother at serious risk of heart failure."

"Then Diego be hanged. I'll feed her myself." Bellamy nodded firmly. "You have my word as a gentleman and as a man who cares a great deal for Miss McGirth's health and happiness."

Marcus wanted to be snide and disdainful. He wanted to accuse the man of manipulation or deceit. But for all his plundering of Bellamy's mien, he found only sincerity. Working against everything within him, Marcus lowered his chin for a quick, silent recognition of their accord.

"I sense an exceptional concern in you for the lady. In fact, it mirrors my own." Bellamy finger-combed Marisol's hair off her forehead. "Diego has been a loyal friend to me these many years, but his approach to handling the gentler sex, mistress or otherwise, is rather confused. His possessiveness is exaggerated, at times to the point of harm. Little would make me happier than to see Miss McGirth hied away to the *Gallant Lady* and the Port of…wherever it is your journey takes you. So long as it is not here."

A pretty speech. Too pretty not to be a trap.

"Your distrust is plain to see," Bellamy carried on. "While I cannot imagine what I've done to merit it, I'm willing to set aside my offense for the hope that, where Miss McGirth is concerned, you will consider me an ally."

An ally? The idea of it was laughable at best. Marcus caught that very thing before it filled his mouth and set him on an irreversible path. He ran his tongue over his teeth to buy him a moment to puzzle the matter. If there was even a small chance Bellamy might help Miss McGirth leave La Conchita, Marcus had to consider it.

"What sort of an ally?"

"The sort who would partner with you to get her out of here. In an organized, more discrete fashion than whatever barmy thing it was you were attempting here."

Condescension aside, Bellamy's offer was attractive, if perilous. More than perilous, it was downright idiotic. Marcus would be sure to regret it, Fanning would be sure to ask after Marcus's sanity, and Major Ainsworth would be sure to give him an ear-bleeding dressing-down. But if it got Miss McGirth out of San Marcos?

Lord, shouldn't I be the one to guide her to health and home?

No, child, I should. The Spirit's moving within him was instant, the peal of another church bell. The feel of it against his pride was that of a sandspur under his heel.

To the tug and burn of every scar on his back, Marcus put down his pride and returned Bellamy's solid grip. "Ally, then. For Miss McGirth."

Chapter 8

*M*arcus shivered inside his shin-length cloak, more from nerves than the gusts swirling in off the river. In the shelter of a fragrant orange grove, he latched his gaze to La Conchita's perimeter wall. It was thin in the distance, its whitewash luminous even under the nebulous moon. Earlier, he'd noted a path leading from it to the dock that cut into the river some twenty paces ahead and to his left, but Miss McGirth would likely choose another, less obvious route.

The hard edges of crinkled paper bit into his curling fist—her missive. He should have burned it the minute Barb slipped it into his pocket, yet there it was, stuck fast to him, its three lines scrolling before his mind's eye: *Grove by the dock. Midnight. L.M.*

This had to be the dock she meant, though it was well past midnight. After the morning's abuse, she would be suffering too greatly to venture much farther afield. She shouldn't be venturing at all, but he wouldn't lie and say every fiber of him wasn't stark with readiness to see her and know she was well.

A spasm cinched his back muscles, and agony shot along his nerves. He seized the nearest branch and doubled, fighting the rise of gorge and terror for what lie in store for Miss McGirth should she scar.

He'd been ill since his dismissal earlier in the day. At dinner, he hadn't so much as lifted a fork. Then, Barb had arrived, seeking advice regarding Marisol's deteriorating condition, and his stomach had all but capsized. *Give her a yarrow tea bath,* he'd advised. *And cider vinegar wraps for her wrists and feet.*

Since, he'd cleaved to Miss McGirth's note and the stroke of twelve.

As he methodically breathed through the remnants of his back's heatless scorch, he stamped his boots to revive numb feet and release burgeoning anxiety.

They were mad to attempt this rendezvous. Her for arranging it, him for agreeing. He would be madder yet if she didn't show soon.

An amber flicker caught his eye; mid-stomp, his foot stilled.

Two swaying lights neared, blinking through pastureland that separated the grove from the wall. His heart thrummed a dithering beat. Miss McGirth? Or those in search of her.

He withdrew farther under the canopy, and although the unpruned trees provided excellent cover, he pulled the cloak about him to conceal the glint of his weapons.

The lights floated closer, and soon, two forms became well-defined: a shako-wearing, musketed soldier and a woman. They split near the river, the soldier moving away and the woman meandering toward Marcus's position.

Miss McGirth.

He could see her clearly now, as she bent over the brush that grew along the riverbank. Sweat sprung to his hairline and chilled the back of his neck. Strain in its basest form. But she was there, within sight, and moving agilely enough, thank God. If he were forced to walk away now, he might relax enough to catch an hour of sleep.

She dallied at a cluster of twiggy shoots, poking through them before moving on. Should he go to her? No, her light would give him away to the escort who was still too close for comfort. After a time, she looked behind her to the soldier's diminishing light, then ahead to the grove. Lantern lifted, she broke into an earnest march.

Marcus wove through the trees to intercept her, cloak whipping out behind him. He called to her as loudly as he dared. "I'm here!"

She perked at the sound, adjusted course. Stopping at the grove's edge, she hooked the lamp to a low branch and left it to hasten into the black coppice. "Doctor Buck? Where are you?"

"Here. Here!" In his race, a limb caught him in the chest. He ducked it and swung up in time to receive her embrace. Its enthusiasm pushed him back a step.

"Aren't you the dearest sight!" Burrowing into his cloak, she attached at his waist and went flush against him.

Exactly where he'd wanted her. Though he hadn't known it until she was filling his chest with her heat and his nose with her citrusy scent. His hands, though, where to put them?

Her hold of him loosened as she pulled back to speak. "But I shouldn't have sent for—" A sharp gasp cut her off.

Marcus flung his arms wide. He'd taken her by the shoulders, not the back. Was the damage so severe? He grimaced, beat back alarm, and replaced it with a physician's impassivity. "Barb told me. But there wasn't time to elaborate. How bad is it?"

Going rigid, she leaned away and looked off.

He cupped her elbows and peered at her obscured profile, wishing he could ignore his impulse to heal. "Forgive my prying, but humor the doctor. If I don't know the details, I can't help. How bad? How many strokes?"

Silence continued, but the shudder rolling over her spoke loudly enough.

Oranges thudded to the ground about them, and the wind filled with their tangy-sweet aroma. Still, she remained as she was, fingers tightening about the fabric of his coatee. Was she reliving the pillory? Watching the speck of light that marked the soldier's path?

It appeared through the trees, winking out as it passed behind thick foliage. What was the man doing out there? Searching for something? At least they could monitor his whereabouts. That said, he was probably thinking the same of her light.

"Four." The softly spoken number wrenched Marcus from his vigil.

It could be worse. Much. A flake of hope eased the harsh line of his shoulders. He squeezed the back of her elbow. "Now bear with me. One question more. Did he break the skin?" Whoever *he* was. Best if

Marcus never knew.

"Maybe, I don't think so. N-no, no blood."

"Good. Yes, good. Good to hear." His simpleton's response didn't even touch the relief parading through his soul. It weakened his legs and made his hands beg migration to her face. *Untouched, Marcus. Do not err!* The violence at the hands of others could not be undone, but for his part, he would remain true.

"You can rest easy then. If you scar, it will be minimal."

Her head pulled back around to him. "I hadn't thought to worry."

Right. She wouldn't have. "All the better." Smiling, he dug into his cloak's pocket for a small glass pot and pressed it into her palm. "Arnica ointment for the pain." The simple act made him feel a trifle less useless.

"Most kind, thank you. You have been—" Emotion axed her voice. She wrapped his hand in hers and hunched over it stiffly. Little noises, like bridled anguish, eked out of her. This pain, however, wasn't bodily, and it pierced him through, as well.

In miserable warfare between encouraging her to let it out and fearing that if she did, she might irrevocably shatter, he simply cradled the back of her neck and waited, one eye on that bead of light. Was it nearing?

Her tears splatted his wrist. "He-he stripped me. It was cold but"— a voiceless sob jolted her—"the sweat, I was sweating. Soaked. And my chemise, it— I was all but— Doctor, it was, it was, it was—" She sniffled spasmodically, snatching at breaths in between.

Her father wouldn't let her to cry unheld.

"Come here." A single tug had her against him, muffling her miserable cries. "I know. I understand, miss. I do." Although the nakedness, *that* he'd been spared.

Outrage quivered through his muscles. What follower of Christ would even think to do such a thing to a woman? Marcus might try to imagine the depths of her humiliation, if he were certain it wouldn't send Justice on another rampage.

Boldly, he stroked her trembling jaw, and for the first time, thanked

God for his own ordeal, for the insight it gave him and the comfort it might be to another. Next, he asked for strength to speak of it. "When I was with the English, I was flogged."

The announcement dammed her tears. She lifted her face and sniffed, listening.

"Pain aside, it's humiliating, dehumanizing. At some point, I...lost the contents of both my stomach and my bladder. Oddly, every time I think back on that day, those are the details that stand out: the degradation, the mockery." Even now, it enflamed his throat.

Her lack of response kindled regret. What must she think of him, a man who'd lost such complete control of himself? He'd exposed too much. "Forgive me. That's no subject for a lady."

"No," she was quick to say. "It helps, and I can see how that might happen. Truly."

"It pains me that you can identify." No woman should relate to such a horror. Then there was that selfish sliver of his heart that wept joy at having found someone who did. "Though it's distasteful, at least now you know to trust me when I say that after these contusions heal and you're far removed from this place, San Marcos will become but an ugly blotch in your memory. You *will* recover from this, miss. I'm sure of it."

These many years later, Marcus himself had yet to fully mend, but her circumstances were different. She had an unscarred back, and she had a kindred friend.

Restoration of spirit was equally important to that of the body, and until God removed her from his care, Marcus was committed to treating both.

Marry her... The idea lingered, peeked around corners of a back room in his mind. He shut the door, but it creaked open again of its own accord.

Nodding, she withdrew from him and seemed to regather composure. Wiping at her face, she looked to the pasture and the lantern that was indeed approaching. "I've wasted time, and now, it appears Barros has figured out that yarrow doesn't grow in November.

I convinced him that Mari might die if he didn't let me out to find it."

"And, how is she? Fever down at all?"

"It was never up. Sorry for the little fib."

He should be upset at her for making him worry. Instead, his throat rumbled with a chuckle. "Smart woman."

A groan slumped her posture. "Maybe not so smart. I called you here to give you a record of transactions with the Indians, but they're gone. The ledgers, he moved everything. All of them." Her voice graveled with defeat, but at least she was taking the charge seriously now.

"I'd planned to rip out a few sheets for you," she said, "and when I sent the note with Barb, I was positive it would be a simple thing to get, but then they weren't in the drawer. They weren't anywhere!"

Diego López certainly couldn't be accused of being brainless.

Marcus wrung the back of his neck. "Don't fret. We have time to find something else, but whether we do or not I *am* getting you out of here. Just you remember that. And, miss, no more unnecessary risk. You needn't have come."

"What, summon you, then abandon you to frost and worry? I think not."

"I wouldn't have waited long for—"

"You *would* have. All night. And don't you deny it."

His chest rocked with silent laughter. "I've been tried and convicted, and that without proper defense. What shall my sentence be?"

"¿Liana?" the soldier hollered as he traipsed a straight line through the grasses. The lamp went before him, high and bright. His features were becoming distinguishable, and they weren't of the congenial variety.

"*¡Ya voy!*" she responded, turning. "I should go."

Promptly, Marcus spoke in a hush. "What do you know of Iron Wood? An Englishman in deep with the rebel Creeks. Is it Bellamy?"

"Max?" She backed away, shaking her head. "He's too dear. It's unfair of you to ask. I'll give you Diego. Not Max."

"You're right. Not fair at all. But consider that uncovering his intrigues might be all the salvation you have."

At her acute intake, he freed her to ponder that unpleasant truth.

"Liana, *¿Dónde estás?*"

"*¡Voy!*" She collected her skirt and snaked through the covert for where she'd hung the lantern.

Marcus shadowed her, averse to relinquishing her to the Spaniard with the disgruntled voice. "Did Bellamy feed you?" he whispered closely.

"Yes." Her face pointed toward the soldier who walked the meadow just the other side of the wall of shrubby trees. He seemed to be trailing sound of their footfall.

"Follow his lead. No more fasting."

"I won't." She strode toward the light's cast, but Marcus stopped and backed into the obsidian shelter of low-lying limbs, enveloping himself in his cloak. When she stepped around a trunk, the lantern's deep orange glow revealed the moment she noticed him tucking away and the despair that crumpled her brow.

A branch snapped as Barros approached her lantern. "*¡Por los santos, mujer! ¿Dónde te has metido?*"

"*¡Un momento!*" she shot back. Before the man could catch sight of her, she slipped into Marcus's cove and pressed his hand to her cheek.

It was warm, silken, and far more darling than was good.

"Marcus Buck," she said on the slightest breath, fingertips gliding along his cheek. "I sentence you to a lifetime of loyalty. My own." Not a hint of coquetry. Only devotion, pure and right.

A lifetime of loyalty? She'd as much as pledged herself to him.

Did I not tell you? the Spirit uttered. *She's yours.*

The trail of her fingers ended on his mouth as though to levee a reply. It was just as well. Breath fleeting, mind reeling, he'd fallen into disrepair.

She made no other sound, no other move but to lay her lips in his palm and fill it with her shallow breaths.

Recklessly, he allowed her to linger and indulged his thumb by taking a long, slow brush of her skin. "Go." The word was but a wisp, given as he nudged her toward the light, the soldier, and a fate he feared like a scourge yet couldn't command.

Lillian swiped her upper arm across her sweaty forehead and scooted the old blanket she was using as a knee pad closer to the castor's stalk. Kneeling, she took up the pruning saw in her gloved hand and resumed work, gritting her teeth against the misery in her bruised back.

The arnica had been applied twice since her midnight tromp through the grove. It helped, but the stripes still pained her terribly. Regardless, she wouldn't let it slow her down. Papa was surely suffering more than she, but he'd never let discomfort take him off his feet. Neither would she. There was too much to do before leaving San Marcos behind forever.

Starting with this tree of a shrub.

The saw's teeth dug into one of its reddish stalks, bleeding juices down the stem into the rich black earth. A suckering shrub, the stalks were abundant. The smaller outlying ones gave way with relatively little effort, crashing into the courtyard with a rustling swoosh. Spiny seedpods and bits of dry, crumbled leaves littered the slate and clung to Lillian's hair and tacky skin.

She scratched a bit of something from her cheek, concerned about too much contact. Indignation shimmied through her and straight down her arms to the saw. Each tug of it strained her weak muscles and sore back, but never had work felt so good. Her heart pumped furiously but felt haler than it had in weeks, thanks to Doctor Buck.

And what had she been doing while the poor fellow was being ousted from the hacienda? Exactly as Max instructed. He'd been given an unsavory job, he'd said, and would appreciate her cooperation. Not wishing to direct Diego's wrath onto her friend, she'd placed herself on the bench at the window and cried silent tears while Doctor Buck called for her.

Shortly after, Max had sat her down to the most beautiful dish she'd had in a lifetime, assuring her Diego would allow it, and if not, Max would bear the rebuke himself.

There'd been no need.

Diego had come in — from where, she'd dared not ask — disheveled and smelling of exertion, but calm. Whatever pursuit had occupied him those hours had purged the hellion that she and Tall Bull had encountered on the lane between San Marcos and La Conchita.

After, he'd asked no question, not even whether she'd divulged his guilt in the matter. She suspected his sword had already supplied his answers. Of course, the crimson specks on his cuff *could* have been wine…

When he'd tenderly braced her head and locked his mouth with hers, he'd reminded her why she'd first followed him to his bedchamber that sultry September afternoon.

A girl had entered, virginal and trusting, starry-eyed. And, in all but the most intimate way, a girl had emerged. It had taken motherhood and La Conchita's slap across the cheek to bring out the woman in her.

Thoughts coming back to the task at hand, she dragged the serrated edge through the stalk's dense flesh one last time before tossing the tool aside. She stood and kicked at the stubborn plant, raising a tirade in three languages as she recalled how Diego had made her drunk on him. Over the weeks, he'd left her so blissfully replete she'd had little room for remorse.

Until her courses stopped and her stomach revolted.

She'd cried until her throat ached, but when he'd come upon her flung out on the bed and bemoaning her state, he'd danced her round the room, laughing and calling himself twelve forms of a man — all of them robust and potent and possessing a finely honed aim.

He'd lavished her with affection, which had vanished upon first sight of his daughter. Lillian had gotten not a scent of it since. Not until the previous night, when he'd invaded her room, smothered her with a kiss, and left her with promises of a wholesome breakfast.

In the interim, she'd lied to Barros, tromped through the grove, and lied again. Couldn't a woman relieve herself in peace? She snickered at the memory of Barros's embarrassment, then touched her cheek where Doctor Buck had. The man hadn't left her thoughts since she'd left her kiss in his palm.

One of those being the harrowing realization that to lose bodily functions in the way he described, a man had to be quite severely beaten. She never would have guessed he'd experienced such an ordeal. He was so…so *capable*. A bulwark. Unflappable.

Whereas she… Shame enveloped her, flooded her chest with heat.

They'd spent the same months as prisoners, but when put into perspective, Lillian's trial—the worst of it—had lasted but a day and was but a leisurely stroll compared to what he'd endured.

Yet he'd been understanding of her anxiety. Compassionate, patient. A saint.

He was every woman's dream, but not every woman could relate to him on such an intimate level. That privilege was hers and hers alone. Might he feel the bond as keenly as she? She'd spent the night wondering but had gotten nowhere.

Deciphering the guarded doctor was a challenge. At her touch, he'd weakened with desire. Ever so slightly, but she had a practiced eye to these things. She knew. Still, he'd remained the most stolid of gentlemen, and at her vow of loyalty, he'd not so much as jarred a breath. He simply didn't respond to her in the usual way of men. Intimate connection aside, it was wise of him. For so very many reasons.

The trouble with it? It mushroomed her admiration.

Above her, a towering trunk resisted its demise. Replicating the sound of a hundred rattlesnake buttons, it rained debris with brazen effrontery. She let her foot fly into it and grinned at its quaking.

Over that morning's milk-thinned porridge, she'd eaten as told and was now benefiting from the added strength. She felt it in the clarity of her mind.

The world was sharper, more colorful, less frightening, and she was raring to conquer it. At least this cursed patch of Spanish soil. She was hauling back for another solid plant of her heel when a hand clamped her elbow, making her jump.

"*Hvtec.* Hold." Tall Bull, regal in his silver headband and chieftain's poise, directed mild censure down on her from his lofty height. "Why are you destroying it?" The severity scoring a ditch between his eyes struck a twanging chord of fear.

Blinking up at him, she breathed hard through her unhinged jaw and lectured herself into retaining composure. He'd not harmed her before. He wouldn't now.

She moistened her lips with a darting tongue and found her Muskogee. "Its seeds are deadly. A small taste nearly took my child on the journey."

The creases around his mouth smoothed. His fingers relaxed but didn't let her go. "I heard of her sickness but was not told the cause." With an understanding dip of his chin, he hooked his fingers under the beak of his tomahawk and pulled it from where it rested on his left hip and used it to indicate a wooden bench. "Rest. I will finish."

Having no objection to the man's help and, strangely, only a little to his presence, she sat, keeping a cushion of air between her screaming back and the bench's.

Compelled by his great stature, Tall Bull squatted to complete the task, lips moving in what she knew to be a prayer. Was he blessing the vile thing? Asking forgiveness for her brutality toward it? Seeking permission to end its odious life?

While pondering Indian beliefs she would never understand, she studied his perfectly balanced profile and recalled the village chatter for her captivity days. The whisperers said he would soon divorce his wife, and the unwed maidens, lashes fluttering, had held their hopes high.

In the safety of her thoughts, she harrumphed. Her heart had fluttered aplenty when he'd ridden from Singing Grass's courtyard, a stoic Adela inside the jail of his arms. Lillian hadn't been certain she would see her sister again.

Lillian looked away, annoyed that she had rid herself of Totka's dark intentions only to be presented at every turn with his even darker cousin.

A twinge of conscience drifted her lids shut. It would be easier to hate the man if he would keep to his pattern of arrogant rogue instead of playing her champion. With a jerk of her arm, she whisked a stray lock from her face and inwardly yielded to the duty of being civil toward him.

More than civil, she must be gracious. He'd saved her from untold pain and further humiliation. Maybe even, as Teniente Prieto had asserted, from death.

Tall Bull hacked low on the shafts, severing them with precision and speed until he'd made a carpet of branches and half-shriveled foliage. He straightened and rammed the tomahawk handle back under his belt.

Uttering quiet thanks, she rose, filled her arms with fodder, and informed him she intended to burn it. The load she carried dragged behind her with a noisy scratch as she made her way through the plaza and yard. At the perimeter gate, she was prepared to argue her cause, but the guard opened without question, raising a sloppy salute to Tall Bull, whose lengthened stride overtook her. The mountainous burden he carried must have cleared the courtyard of brush.

They followed the sounds of the river until the earth began to slope toward the water. She glanced left to the orange-laden grove and the secret place where Doctor Buck had exposed the tender regions of his heart. When might she see him again? Not soon enough.

In a spot barren of all but sand and burs, Tall Bull dumped the branches and turned toward a stand of palms that bowed over the water.

Her own smaller load landed on his before she trailed him. "The Spaniard is away for the afternoon." She referred to Diego in the manner of the Indians. As if he were the only Spaniard worth noting. To them, perhaps he was. "Why have you come? Have you no plantations to raid? Slaves to capture?" The wry twist of her lips contrasted her intentionally buoyant tone.

He slowed so she might catch up. When she did, his eyes, shadowed by dark lashes and thoughts she was happily not privy to, leisurely took in the length of her.

"No slaves today. Unless you are offering yourself?"

She resounded a dry laugh. "Those days are done. I am slave to no man."

"Are you certain?"

Her mouth went flat. "Do not presume to know me or my situation."

"I know that your preening snakebird of a Spaniard keeps you and your child under guard in his home. But perhaps his actions are meant to protect since your holy man, the Black Robe, is fiercely loyal to his role as keeper of the law."

Tall Bull began scavenging for dried palm fronds, plucking fragments off the ground with a sweep of his arm. "You would have fared far worse had the Spaniard been Muscogee. Clan law would have been carried out swiftly, before I could have arrived. Better an injured back than a severed nose." He shrugged. "Such is the risk taken by she who lies with another woman's man."

"You show yourself a fool if you believe any woman has power against the Spaniard's will. And I had no knowledge of his wife! Not until shortly before we arrived at La Conchita. Not two moons past." Why was she explaining herself to this Red Stick?

His arm stopped mid-reach; his back, mid-bend. "He deceived you?"

"Marriage is *nak-vcake*." Sacred. To be revered, protected. "I would never have knowingly violated it. It angers me that you think I would." In a tiff, she scooped up a few scraps of dried fronds and stalked back to their rubbish pile.

Having filled his arms with tinder, he joined her where she was crouched and arranging the fronds to best catch flame. He shredded a leaf to make a nest for the first sparks. "You were right," he said after a time. "I presumed too much. *Em merretv v'ne*."

Lillian's gaze snapped to him. He wanted forgiveness?

He was focused on the task at hand, but his features, like his voice, held no sign of mockery. Speechless, she handed him a length of fibrous petiole.

"The man is a flesh-eating maggot," he continued, bitterly now. "The wife should have divorced him before putting the Great Water between them."

"She is a faithful *Católica* and will never divorce."

"Foolishness." He shoved the dried stalk into the stack. "At least she was wise enough to abandon him. You, too, should leave. Bind yourself to a good man. One who will treat you well."

"I am an unwed mother, a woman forever marked by disgrace. No good man will have me." Which was likely the reason for Doctor Buck's practiced discretion. Her father though, he would have her.

And Totka, he would have her blood...

Terror at the thought of returning constricted her chest. But there was no help for it. Tensaw had summoned, and it was time she answered. No matter the night's failure, she would find evidence. She would clear her name. She *would* go home.

Grief washed over her eyes, but she set it aside. There would be time to mourn. Later.

"How soon you forget you are adopted Muscogee." Tall Bull fished flint and steel from his pouch and worked them over the stringy ball he'd created. "In Wakulla, a child is always a gift from Creator, and a woman's pleasure before marriage is never wrong. Under my protection and that of Beaver, you may have the unwed warrior of your choosing. Without shame or judgment. You are no disgrace, Bitter Eyes."

She flinched at her Muskogee name, then stared at him a moment before a brief, incredulous laugh rocked her shoulders. "Do you not know why it is my eyes are *bitter*, Tall Bull? Because a swarm of blood-lusting Red Sticks made them so! After what I have endured, how could you think I would lay that aside and open my blanket to any of them?"

"Easily. Muscogee women are respected and cherished by their men and protected by clan law. You have seen the power they hold. In their wombs, their lodges, and in their keen wisdom. Their counsel is highly sought after. By even the *miccos*," he said, tapping his chest, referring to chiefs. "For your resentment and pride, you would choose the heartless Spaniard over such a life?"

If he knew what she'd done—to his cousin, to *him*—he would retract that invitation, cut out her tongue, and call it just. And, God help her, he would be right.

"That happiness is beyond me. I am far too ugly a creature to hope for it. The bones have been cast. I will take my chances here."

For three days, at any rate. Until she sailed for Mobile. Diego was due to travel to St. Augustine after the evening meal. His two-day absence would make leaving San Marcos a tad easier.

Tall Bull reached out and, with the pad of his middle finger, grazed her jawline, earlobe to chin, and tipped her face toward him. "Woman, your beauty tilts a man's world, and your sharp mind is a challenge he craves. Any warrior would be honored to call you his own."

She smacked away his hand, straightened her legs, and looked down on him with brass. "Diego will remove that finger, joint by joint, for its audacity. And if he does not, I will."

Tall Bull prodded the fuel with a stick, a smirk climbing his lips. "If he wishes, he may wrestle me for the chance to try."

He rose, regaining the upper ground. And upper it was. At this close of quarters, she was forced to bend her neck considerably to retain eye contact.

Refusing intimidation, she lifted her chin in as haughty an air as she could. "Respect women, do you? How? By leering at one as if she were a honey-glazed morsel of meat?"

The lateral swing of his gaze said she'd not imagined a thing; its swift return said he wasn't a man easily deterred. "Am I not a man? I too enjoy a challenge."

She moved off a distance under the pretense of tossing a stray limb into the fire. "Thank you for your help. Now go away."

"I cannot."

"Very well. *You* may tend the fire." When she turned to leave, his voice stopped her.

"Did your lover not tell you? He requested my presence. Here. For the days he is away at Augustine. I am to use any means necessary to protect Muscogee and Spanish interests."

She looked back. "Protection from…what?"

"Play the ignorant child if you will, Bitter Eyes, but the Spaniard knows you went out in the night. And it was not for herbs." A dry smile touched his lips. "I would like to hope you would never direct the bluecoats' ire at my village. But a warrior will not survive on hope alone, so I will do as the Spaniard asks and shadow your every move."

Chapter 9

"I suppose Varela, here, won't be making it to your féte tonight," Bellamy said as he and Marcus worked over the soldier's bloody, unconscious form.

Marcus hadn't a clue how his guard had ended up in such a deadly state. He'd simply arrived on the scene, and as always, set to work with all diligence. Although, the passing seconds were proving his efforts to be tragically insufficient.

Focused on reading the man's thready pulse, he almost missed Bellamy's strange statement. "My what?"

"Dinner. At La Conchita. Served in your honor." At Marcus's blank look, Bellamy, the callous ox, grinned. "Don't tell me you haven't been invited to your own party."

Five hours and one funeral later, Marcus entered the hacienda alone and to the sound of a single Spanish guitar plucking a tune rife with Arabic influence. Its melancholy character fit his mood perfectly.

This pattern of failings must stop. In his line of work, each was a burden one carried beyond the change of blood-spattered clothes. At times, he wondered if he should try his hand at something less costly to the heart, such as instructing. No doubt his father could get him into Harvard.

A liveried porter was stationed at the open gate. He tapped his hat and extended his hand, palm up. Marcus relinquished his bicorn, but when the porter tried the same with his medical bag and sword, he chuckled low and wagged his finger. "I think not."

The entreaty to relinquish his weapons continued, but he paid the servant no heed and, shoving Varela to the recesses of his mind, scanned the courtyard for a face he knew would make the day more bearable.

La Conchita under torchlight was a strikingly exotic world. It teemed with color: vivid green in the potted banana plants, red and yellow in the streamers scalloping the upper banister, soft white in the water spraying up from the triple-tiered fountain.

The water's gurgle-and-splash mingled with the conversations of the twenty or so people milling about—servants and soldiers, including Captain Luengo and Marcus's own comrades in arms, Lieutenant Fanning and Major Ainsworth. Marcus's eye gravitated to Miss McGirth who faced away from him on the opposite side of the fountain.

Chief Tall Bull stood to her left, so near that his unbound hair brushed her neck. He was slightly bent at the waist so that his words fell neatly on her ear. Arms clasped behind him, he was loose and relaxed.

What was the Red Stick doing here, and what reason could he have for crowding the woman? "Only one," Marcus grumbled on a chafing breath.

Miss McGirth had claimed the man intended to kill her. If so, it was to eat her alive, bit by scrumptious bit. Perhaps she was right to feel uncomfortable around him.

In the face of his boldness, she moved not a muscle, but her shoulders were set stiff.

Marcus began that way; however, before he made it three steps, Bellamy moved in from the right.

"Doctor Buck!" Sporting a broad smile, he stole Marcus's hand and gave it a fierce pump. One would think they'd been friends an age.

Marcus tugged free. "Mr. Bellamy."

The Englishman looked his usual sharp self. Brushed tricorne with preened hawk feather. Ruffed sleeves protruding in perfect folds from his frock coat. Leggings, spotless. Spatterdashes, the same.

Next to him, Marcus, in his rumpled uniform and a damp head of hair, was an unkempt vagrant fresh from a night in a gutter.

To complete the stark contrast, an elegant woman stood beside him. She was beautiful, Cleopatra reborn with her straight posture and even straighter free-flowing black hair. The courtyard was too dark to know the color of her eyes, but their thick lids named her an Indian, despite her lighter skin.

He was trying to make sense of a Native dressed in a costly European gown when Bellamy spoke. "Good of you to make it. It occurred to me we might be starting the festivities without the guest of honor." He laughed.

"Yes, well." Marcus stole a glance at Miss McGirth who'd begun touching her hair in self-conscious fashion. A smile slid up the chief's cheek, and Marcus grew antsy to be done with the Englishman. "Alma was heavy on my mind, so I decided to swing by and check on her."

After the hasty burial, Varela's grieving woman hadn't had the power to keep herself upright because Marcus had transferred her blood into a corpse-to-be. Needle in arm, he'd argued his case until Alma yanked the tube out, spritzing blood and crying that if anyone's humors mixed with her lover's it would be hers.

Marcus had relented, and it had ended in yet another blood transfer gone tragically awry. Death would have absconded with Varela regardless, but that didn't lessen the stab of failure.

Spitting out the dregs of remorse, he fixed eyes on someone he *could* help. "Mr. Bellamy" — he pointed his chin across the courtyard — "does Miss McGirth seem perturbed to you?"

Cleopatra released a burble of laughter. "My uncle has that effect on women," she said, her accent negligible. "But don't worry. Bitter Eyes is safe."

"Bitter Eyes?"

"Her Muskogee name."

Not a flattering one. "I see. And you are?" Marcus perked one brow at Bellamy.

"How forgetful of me," he responded. "Captain Marcus Buck, I'd have you meet Pretty Wolf of Wakulla, chieftain's daughter and niece to Chief Tall Bull. She is the heart of her people and its greatest treasure." A besotted mooncalf, he beamed at her.

She rewarded his compliments with a comparatively dim smile.

"An honor, miss." Marcus bowed.

"Likewise. I have heard many great things about you."

"Don't tell me Mr. Bellamy has been secretly singing my praises."

"Oh, but he has." At Marcus's skeptical look, she amended. "That is, when he is not calling you a backward colonial." She winked at Marcus, and Bellamy hacked on a poorly concealed chortle.

"Pretty Wolf is learning the finer points of winking," he explained.

Marcus smiled at her. "A beautifully executed wink, miss."

"*Maddo*, thank you."

A single, clear *ding* of a bell came from the far side of the plaza.

"Dinner is served." Bellamy took Pretty Wolf's hand into his elbow. "May I escort you, milady?"

She laughed, but her words were lost on Marcus. He was already making a path to Miss McGirth, whose eyes were busily sweeping the compound. For him?

Before their gazes could connect, López led her inside, Tall Bull close behind. The guests queued at the door while the don extended a personal welcome to each. Marcus was almost the last to enter, and when he did, López stepped aside and clapped his hands to call the buzzing hall to attention.

Marcus set his bag on the floor against a wall and took in the place.

The chamber radiated opulence. Buffed parquet flooring glistened in the light of a hundred candles. Twenty red brocade chairs rimmed the lace-trimmed table, and crystal sparkled the length of its surface. A flagrant display of wealth.

Grinning, López hooked onto Marcus's shoulder and jerked him close. He launched into a monologue, using an entire arm to accompany the ebb and flow of his volume. He went on for a time before Miss McGirth's zesty scent washed over Marcus, carrying him back to their appointment in the grove. His fingers curled, trapping the remembered sensation of her lips.

What had spawned such forwardness? Gratitude, to be sure. Then too, it might've been a recognition of their uncommon bond or a stamp on her vow of loyalty. Whatever the cause, it had touched on a longstanding need. A mortifying number of years had transpired since a woman laid tender lips to any part of him. Miss McGirth's were, disastrously, quite welcome.

Her hushed voice came at him from behind. "I'll translate as soon as the merry-andrew says something worth hearing. So far, it's all flowery bilge and rot."

A snort of laughter seized him, but he coughed it back.

López smacked him on the back and squeezed the top of his shoulder as Miss McGirth drew so close that some part of her brushed the back of his arm.

During a moment of hush, the rapid, nosey breath of an infant skimmed Marcus's ear. She was holding Marisol? At the reminder of a life he *had* saved, a smile warmed his chest. He hadn't known until that moment how much he'd missed the little lady.

"He has yet to speak a single heartfelt thought," Miss McGirth went on, "such as an appreciation of your keen perception and vast medical knowledge. As well as your readiness to act on both. Or how fine a man you are with Marisol."

López's droning faded as Miss McGirth's rich tone swept over Marcus's world like a tide, caressing his sore heart and washing away debris from the afternoon's storm.

"Or how you sacrificed endless hours of sleep in exchange for genuine worry over us both. Or how you've not held my stupidity against me. Instead, you've resolved to see us both freed from this nightmare."

The don finished and released him, but as the assembly gave a polite pit-a-pat of applause, Miss McGirth continued. "There is not space enough in my heart to hold my gratitude. Thank you, Marcus," she intimated urgently, clasping his hand where it dangled at his side.

She wore no gloves, imprinting him with the feel of her. Cool, smooth skin over delicate bones that oozed desperation. The last being the most detrimental to his floundering objectivity. A fine thing, her touch did unusual things to his pulse, dampened his shirt, and made him crave more.

And it scrambled his thoughts. López was saying something, unwrapping an item from black velvet, but Marcus could focus on nothing but the woman attached to him.

Distance. He needed distance.

The don withdrew a miniature sword from the cloth and presented it to Marcus, giving him the perfect excuse to disengage.

"As a show of appreciation, the vermin presents you with a letter opener." Miss McGirth interpreted at normal volume. "Instead of the gold-plated sword of a king you deserve."

Fanning choked and, pounding his chest with a fist, excused himself to the plaza. Bellamy, who stood not three strides away, zipped a look of alarm from Miss McGirth to López. Did she trust the Englishman so implicitly? That couldn't be wise.

Marcus took the gift with a deep, protracted nod of his head. He slid the six-inch steel blade from its tiny embossed-leather sheath and studied the intricate patterns on the hand guard as well as the meticulously wrapped silver wire on its pommel. Miniature it may be, but it was no trinket.

"It's a beautiful example of Spanish craftsmanship. You honor me." He gave López a sweeping bow and, letting his mind fill with Marisol's endearing babble, had no trouble speaking from his heart. "Thank you for the privilege of treating your child through her illness. I've found nothing but joy in watching her come to full health. She's a jewel, señor, of the rarest kind, and if hers were the only life God ever used me to save, my calling into the medical field, and every toil and heartache that accompanies it, would have served its purpose."

While a servant took back the gift to rewrap it, Miss McGirth stepped around him and with tears in her eyes relayed his message. To the embarrassing eruption of applause, Marcus got his first full look at her. It was an eyeful, yet he doubted it would be enough to avoid an evening of ill-bred fixation.

Her eyes were unclouded; her posture, steady. Health was already improving her coloration. That was where his medical eye closed and in its place opened the eye he'd like to claim belonged to a vigilant guardian but, in all brutal honesty, was simply a man's.

The perfect disorder of her hair was coiled high with a profusion of spirals cascading around woven pearls and a large comb that added the illusion of height and royalty. The tendrils about her neck led his eye downward to a décolletage that was accentuated by a sash bound snug about her ribs.

The trail of his gaze continued the length of her gown's gossamer fabric, which had no defense against the firelight behind her. It outlined her figure with startling clarity. The attire could hardly be appropriate to the weather, and it certainly wasn't to a gentleman's thoughts.

She was stunning, but a prick came to his conscience, and with the diverting of his eyes, he became aware that other men's attention likely replicated his own. It worked under his skin like a festering splinter. Then McGirth's image was before him, wielding his rugged Scotsman's glower and calling upon that cumbersome vow. Obedient to it, Marcus followed her closely to protect her from visual plundering.

She guided him to a place at the far end of the table and to the right of the master's chair, rounded the table, and took a place opposite him. Tall Bull stationed himself to her immediate left. By the peevish look she gave the Indian and the curt word she gave the don, Marcus surmised the chief didn't belong there. But López made no move to correct the situation. In fact, he invited Pretty Wolf to join her uncle.

The leech that he was, Bellamy followed.

"We're an eclectic group, to be sure," Major Ainsworth said as he took up residence at Marcus's right with Fanning beyond him. The rest of the party filled in the long table as their stations dictated. "Look at us. Three upstanding officers feasting with an insurgent, an Indian princess, and a Spanish don accompanied by his high-rent trollop."

The chatter in the room kept the major's remarks inside their small circle, but Marcus, biting his tongue to keep from reprimanding his commander, glanced at Miss McGirth to be sure she hadn't heard.

Her focus was on Marisol, the nipping kisses she was applying to her neck rolls, and the belly laugh she was drawing out. Now there was an agreeable sight. More so than any translucent gown. Their effects, nevertheless, were strangely similar, pinching and tugging at his need in such a trying manner, he was compelled to look away or make a fool of himself by joining them.

Barb waited behind the lady. At the dismissing twitch of the don's fingers, she held out her arms. "Bedtime for the little miss."

Reluctantly, Miss McGirth surrendered Marisol and watched her leave with her nurse. Her chest plunged with a sigh that, though silent, was felt clear to Marcus's gut. It made him fidget inside with a twinge that approximated possessiveness.

It was an ambiguous feeling and unknown territory, but one thing was certain—the child more rightly belonged to Marcus than she did the don. Miss McGirth and all that pertained to her was under Marcus's authority. His argument would never survive the don's court of reason, but if necessary, sword in hand, he would stand by it until he'd won his case.

"It's refreshing," Fanning was saying, "the foot soldier dining with his lord."

"More like fleas dining off a dog," Major Ainsworth muttered, grating Marcus like a dull blade.

He could barely keep a cool head with the man whose every word echoed back with *nefarious, nefarious, nefarious…*

"A very wealthy dog who happens to be our host," Marcus said. "Patience, gentleman. Shortly, we'll have what we need and be on our way."

Major Ainsworth took an impatient gander at Miss McGirth. "I'm beginning to doubt that."

In truth, Marcus was too. He was fumbling both missions quite expertly.

Eyes closed, Don Diego spouted off a few lines, crossed himself, and invited everyone to be seated. The first course, chilled prawns, was served. Conversation around the table was full and agreeable, except for the one taking place directly in front of Marcus. It seemed a shade beyond pleasant, at least for one of its participants.

Tall Bull's body leaned into Miss McGirth's space, his forearms uncouthly flat on the table, his elbow a hair's breadth from her plate.

Doing a first-rate job of appearing unperturbed, she ate around him, keeping pace with whatever lively banter they exchanged in his tongue. However, the occasional flit of her eyes to Marcus gave glimpses into her discomfiture.

If the table weren't so broad, Marcus would kick the chief's shin. Perhaps Justice would reach?

The don casually plucked the pink legs off a prawn, one brow raised to the pair, amusement curling his lips. Did he have no objection to the chief's open study? Marcus was about to interrupt, but López beat him to it, settling back and embarking on what promised to be a lengthy discourse.

Eyes on her plate, Miss McGirth listened, then lifted her lashes to Marcus. "Doctor, His Lordship was recounting what he knows of your surgical exploits from this afternoon, but he'd like to hear it from you. He considers himself a man of science and is fascinated by the idea of transferring blood from one person to another."

"Oh, it's fascinating all right," Bellamy muttered, squeezing a prawn tail to extract the meat. The Englishman had been present to assist but had spent more time behind the shack, green and retching, than he had in actual attendance.

"Barbaric, if you ask me," Major Ainsworth said.

Fanning leaned over his plate, enthusiastic. "I couldn't disagree more. Captain Buck's experiments are bold, innovative, progressive! He's a true pioneer. If ever I'm stuck through and bleeding out, do please, give me another man's blood."

Miss McGirth susurrated an interpretation for the don, while

Pretty Wolf appeared to be doing the same for her uncle.

"Perhaps it's a topic for another time?" Bellamy pitched a crustacean shell onto his plate, pallor touching the edges of his mouth. "We have the ladies to consider."

Marcus wrung the head off a prawn. "So very chivalrous of you, Mr. Bellamy, to think of the ladies' delicate natures. But this is the don's table, and if he wishes to hear about cauterizing nicked arteries, I have no choice but to oblige." He directed his dialog to López. "A sea urchin's needle, sir, is hollow, strong, and sharp. The perfect instrument for puncturing veins and transporting blood from a donor's arm directly into a recipient's."

Adam's apple working furiously, Bellamy rolled his eyes closed. Marcus repressed a grin, and Pretty Wolf sent them both a curious glance. Tall Bull spoke, consternation characterizing his statement.

"My uncle is stunned," Pretty Wolf said, "that any person would allow his spirit to enter the body of such an unworthy man."

Marcus shook his head at the chief. "Not the spirit. Only the blood. A woman's actually, which might have been the cause of failure."

"I beg to differ." Miss McGirth paused with a gracious smile for the footman who removed her plate. "It failed because God chose to spare the rest of us one more day of that man's odious presence."

Marcus gaped at her. "Your fervor surprises me, miss."

"Only because you didn't know the man."

"I know enough. He was attacked from behind, thigh sliced to the bone. He was then left to die in a swamp. Unfortunately for him, he was resilient and dragged himself on his belly for half a mile before he came upon help."

"Is that a prompt for pity? Because I'll find *none*." The dark gems dangling from her earlobes twinkled against her caramel skin, beautifully framing her eyes, her vast and achingly bitter eyes.

"A shame," Marcus said.

"You're disappointed in me." She employed her footman's smile, sans warmth. "I had a most disturbing discourse with the don this afternoon after which I deemed Varela's end to be fitting for any who would molest a woman and out of spite arrange for her to be publicly beaten, while she in ignorance protects his name. No, he gets no pity at all from me." The acid in her words was clear in any language yet foreign to the sweetness they'd so recently shared.

The table fell into awkward silence. Then, her report sank in.

Varela had molested her? How extensively? Any degree of invasion merited the law, but if the dastard had ravished her…

God, what am I doing here? I'm a waste of a man if You won't use me!

Well, that was the end of useless. One way or another, before the night was through, Miss McGirth and her child would be under *his* control.

"Nicely done, boyo." Bellamy's derision broke the hush before he leaned to address Miss McGirth down the table. "Hear, hear, love. You have my full support. The rogue got more than enough pity from Doctor Buck. He gives every patient thorough and impartial treatment. Is that not so, Doctor?" he said, regurgitating Marcus's reasoning for working so hard to save the man.

Through the roil of nausea, Marcus worked a firm reply. "It is indeed. I swore an oath to it."

As a physician, he'd sworn to apply all required measures for the benefit of the sick. But as a soldier? He couldn't say that if he'd caught the man in the act, he wouldn't have let Justice have a sampling of him. The pity in that situation would have been the moral obligation to piece him back together.

He waited for heartsease from Miss McGirth but none came, not so much as an understanding nod. Surely, she knew he had no choice in such matters.

The door to the plaza flew open, and the porter, looking harried, rushed to speak in the lord's ear. Within moments, Miss McGirth was rising, her plate in one hand, her glass in the other.

Every American at the table leapt to his feet, followed swiftly by Bellamy and more slowly by their host.

"I believe I hear the baby crying," Miss McGirth said, her voice tight. "Please excuse me, Doctor Buck, for quitting your party so early."

Mere heartbeats after she slipped through the side door, the porter admitted a sour-faced, black-robed friar.

"Thorough and equal treatment, my dainty little foot." Clutching the hem of her gown, Lillian charged up the staircase.

If that brute had received equal treatment, he'd have been held down and molested by someone twice his size. Marcus Buck's abundant mercy might have a defect after all.

But Diego! He'd been delusional to think news of her broken fast wouldn't reach the tonsured devil, and *she'd* been delusional to think Diego would defend her. She hadn't needed him to tell her to leave and take all evidence of dinner with her; he couldn't have paid her to stay. An overdose of reason-numbing fear had sent her scurrying into the kitchen where she'd shoved her dishes at the first footman she'd encountered.

Backbone raising a hearty protest, she rounded the loggia's west corner at a gown-twisting speed but drew a swift halt when she reached her chambers, entering as only a mother could — softly, ears tuned to signs of wakefulness, eyes straining for a glimpse of her baby.

The room was dark and empty, but the door to the adjoining room stood open. From it, Barb hummed around Marisol's sleepy gibberish. Best not disturb them. Lillian was too riled anyway.

The balcony and its solitude beckoned. She plucked her bed jacket from where it draped the dressing screen and slipped outside. The moon was large behind the curtain of gloom hanging above her, and she longed for a glimpse of it. She stood a while, taking calming breaths, listening to the soughing pines, while the moon's distorted glow trekked across the landscape and her spirit found a measure of peace.

The moon was emerging from behind a swaying palm when voices and horse tread sounded in the yard and moved beyond the wall. It was Pretty Wolf, riding at her usual gallop, petticoat glowing pink in the strange moonlight. Leaving already?

A man trailed her on his own mount. Max's laughter rang across the marshy plain, and Lillian smiled. The lovable rogue was smitten.

Their hoof beats faded and quiet descended until it was shattered by the faint, yet distinct, clashing of swords coming from within. Lillian hurried indoors, almost colliding with Barbury.

"The don's fightin' him, Missy Lillian! Got 'im in the courtyard, backed against a wall!"

"Who? Who is he fighting?" *Blessed Teresa, not Marcus.*

"The doc, missy!"

Lillian had witnessed Diego at swordplay. Marcus would never survive.

She tore a path out the room and into the hook of Tall Bull's arresting arm. Her momentum doubled her over it, taking her feet out from under her and wrenching every bruise on her. For one endless second, she hung from him like a blanket on the line, but she was soon scratching to be freed.

"Be still, woman! You cannot stop them. They must finish it."

"Finish what? This is madness!" Legs kicking, she stretched for the loggia's railing and succeeded in attaining a handhold. He let her pull them both toward it, giving her a view of the match below.

Marcus's back was nowhere near the wall. In fact, he fought from atop the fountain, skipping along its rim with a panther's stability and grace. He matched Diego's speed and confidence, move for move, and when his next lunge caught Diego off guard, tipping him out of balance, Lillian began breathing again.

Maybe the doctor could hold his own. At the very least, it was a fair fight.

She went limp. Relieved and a little stunned. Who knew a physician could rival a Spanish nobleman at swords?

As her mind relaxed a degree, she finally noticed the dinner guests who encircled the plaza, including that hateable friar. Hanging on every thrust and parry, they made not a sound.

Diego and Marcus had stripped to trousers and shirts, and the area had been cleared of every moveable item. This was no precipitous fight of passion; although, to look at Diego's fiery eyes, to watch his ferocious cuts and hear his growls, one might disagree. Marcus, though dripping sweat, was silent, impassive, methodically crisp as he articulated in and out of drives and deflects.

"The meal was going well," Lillian said, not taking her eyes from Marcus's soaked back. "What went awry?" The battle moved beneath them, so she twisted to see.

In a bold move, Tall Bull hiked her up so her shoulders were level with his. He leaned against the railing to provide them both a better view, effectively putting his cheek within inches of hers.

She jerked away to widen the distance, little good it did, and bestowed him with a disapproving sidelong glance.

"Nothing. It is merely a wager."

Men and their ridiculous wagers! "The Spaniard never fights for a *mere* wager but to humiliate and defeat."

"If that is humiliation the medicine maker displays, I will take a measure of it myself."

The Red Stick had a point. Marcus was something to behold. He was supremely confident. Perhaps even cocksure. Anything but humbled.

"What are the stakes? What will he lose?" *Please God, not his life.*

Tall Bull clucked his tongue. "Pity the man for owning so little of your faith."

"The stakes, you irksome Red Stick, what are they?"

"There is only one thing they both want. The thing that I now have." Tall Bull's chuckle reverberated clean through her breast, its meaning-filled quality setting her on edge. "*Centat*, Bitter Eyes. You."

Marcus ducked under the flying chair, certain he was done for, but its leg only tapped his skull on its way past. Before its wind had settled, he leapt from the fountain's rim to the café table, boots sliding into a collection of half-empty wine glasses. They teetered and sloshed, but his next leap took him to the floor ahead of them. On descent, he kicked backwards against the table's edge, sending it into López.

He landed and kept going while, behind him, glass splintered on the slate. The clang of metal followed with López's heated protest topping it all off. By the jostle in his voice, he was tripping.

The trick bought Marcus time to put much-needed space between him and the too-swift, too-vicious Spaniard. It also repaid the wine splashed in his eyes their first minutes out, as well as the chair at his head.

Perhaps López was frustrated he hadn't cut Marcus already, that he had yet to even get close. Or perhaps he always fought dirty. It was likely a combination of the two, mixed with a healthy serving of desperation.

His child was on the line, her fate determined by the first to draw blood.

Diego had to be quite confident in his skills to wager her, or mentally deficient. Deficient, for his hot temper often powered his moves and reduced his skills, equalizing him to Marcus's less-skilled blade.

When Marcus had proposed the match, he'd reckoned his height would give him leverage and his greater strength and prime conditioning, a vital edge over López's superior ability. He'd been correct. If he could hold the man off until he'd worn him down, he had a half-decent chance at winning.

Still springing, Marcus reached center-courtyard, planted a foot and affected a full turn. It brought him into low guard with seconds to spare.

López was a fury, charging him, sword high and descending for a diagonal slice.

Marcus met him with an off-center advance and a deflecting blow that angled the attacking blade away. For two beats, López's gut was open for a downward slash, but the required reversal of Justice's blade and López's impetus stole the opportunity.

Sword lowering, López sailed past, but it was unlike the man to give up the attack so easily.

Propelled by a lurching pulse, Marcus spun, sending Justice

behind him ahead of the move. She caught López's backhanded cut as it was snipping the shirt at Marcus's kidney. The vibration of her steel had never felt so beautiful.

He completed the turn with finesse and seized his foe's imbalance to employ a strong thrust to the belly. López volted right and parried so nimbly, so powerfully, Marcus didn't see it coming.

Steel rang loud, resonating in Marcus's bones and forcing him out of line. He recovered in an instant, but the damage was done; he'd been rattled.

The warp of López's face said he'd noted the slip in confidence.

Going into this spar, Marcus had known it would be a challenge—the man was a Spaniard after all and had probably cut himself free of his mother's womb with Toledo steel—but all Marcus had to lose was his presence in the hacienda. What he gained? Miss McGirth and Marisol, that very night.

The lady stationed above him was a continual reminder of what he risked. That she was encaged in the chief's arms amplified it. She was a loadstone to men of every ilk and would never be safe on her own, unwed. He would rectify the latter if God spoke but once more, and if the lady and her father agreed. Maybe it was the heat of battle making him crazy in the head to entertain such a thought, but what did it matter when it empowered him?

Casting aside every doubt, Marcus reached for techniques he hadn't used since the fencing hall, then redoubled his efforts.

The smirk vanished from López's face about the time sweat burst from it. He jetted an acrimonious set of words that preceded a half-hearted lunge. His blade's tip prodded for an aperture at Marcus's lower leg, the third such attempt.

Easily deflected, they were questionable feints since he stepped with his strikes, his body following the attack. But the man was expert enough to feint naturally, using it to set up a trap.

After one more furious whirl around the plaza, López's endurance had noticeably dimmed. His thrusts lacked their usual authority; his blocks came a fraction slower. Sweat streamed into his eye. A series of blinks ferried him into a pass that targeted Marcus's calf. It was predictable, though more sluggish than usual.

Mechanically, Marcus lowered Justice into an easy, derailing swipe, but with a speed born of lightning, López broke time.

He transitioned to an upward rotation that flung Justice's tip to the ground. In one mind-numbing move, he flourished his blade, sliced, and spun to the crowd, arms raised in triumph.

Dazed, Marcus panted at the cheering audience. Then, pain registered.

Diego's blade moved faster than Lillian's eyes could manage. In the next instant, blood sprouted from Marcus's cheek.

She covered her mouth to restrain her cry, but Tall Bull grinned. "Well done!" He set her on her feet. "Buck makes a more formidable enemy than I had believed. I cannot recall ever having seen the Spaniard sweat."

As Diego's soldados crowded him with shouts and thumps of praise, Marcus stood in the center of the plaza, alone, chest heaving, Justice hanging defeated at his side. He lifted his head, eyes aligning with hers and, in a single heartbreaking look, begging her forgiveness.

She shoved past Tall Bull and took the staircase at a dash.

Lieutenant Fanning reached him first. "…the five minutes you agreed to," he was saying. "My advice? Make it four. And stow that sword before the fiend takes it as an invitation and comes back for more." He grinned and smacked Marcus's arm. "Beautifully played, sir. The major and I will meet you in the yard. Miss McGirth, all the best."

She might've curtsied; he might've bowed. She was too focused on Marcus, his wound, and their waning minutes to notice.

Sweat dripped from the hank of hair falling between his eyes; it plastered his wine-stained shirt to his body, bringing every quivering muscle into stark relief. Wafting off him were the scents of sacrifice and blood, the last streaming too steadily from that cruel cut. It spattered down his front and onto Justice.

The Kiss, Diego called it, a widely dreaded Spanish technique that targeted sensitive areas of the face. Meant to cripple in true battle, it infringed on the rules of a gentleman's spar. So typical! But Marcus had gotten off easy with a mid-cheek slit making a tear's path straight down.

"How deep is it? Let me see." Cupping his slick neck, she pulled him closer and uttered unblushing profanity. "Leave it to that conceited peacock to cut his opponent's face in a wager!"

Barbury hustled over, carrying a bundle of cloths. "The doc's too handsome. That the plain truth."

Too handsome, too respectable, too magnificently accomplished with that blade. Earlier, the dining hall's admiring response to his speech had sealed his fate. Lillian should have known the evening would end this way, should have been on alert and warned him.

As it was, he had yet to make a sound. Still breathing heavily through his mouth, he peered down at her pityingly, as though she'd been the one with her face laid open.

Worry encroached. Sloughing it, she held the rag against his wound. "It's two inches, easy. But I've seen him do worse to his closest friends. The man is positively mercenary and not to be trifled with!" She took another cloth and wiped at the crimson tract on his shirt.

Anger and the remnants of fear vied for the use of her tongue. She shot them down in favor of staggering gratitude. He'd done this for her. *Her*. A woman so corrupted by bitterness it seeped from her eyes.

Marcus stowed the sword and took over holding the bandage. Pinching the slit, he began to shed his fluster. "Upon my word, he was fast."

"But you were stunning. Positively brilliant, sir. I would lay coin on Justice every time." She caught Barb's eye. "His case, please. Check the dining hall."

"He struck with the speed of a viper," Marcus continued.

"Because he is one."

The snake's horde of kowtowing subordinates still encompassed him. They trumpeted and raised a toast with a spirited *salud!* that rankled to the bones. Only Teniente Prieto stood apart, glass untouched, mouth an intolerant slash.

Lillian riffled the crowd in search of Toño but found only the friar, his dark countenance and black robes blending into shadowy recesses near the shrine. How befitting the man. His body pointed her direction, and though his face was obscured, she had no doubt he watched her. A wolf stalking its prey.

"Miss McGirth." Marcus abandoned the compress and took her hands in his tacky grip. "Forgive me. I knew it was long odds, but I never actually thought I'd lose. It was arrogant of me. Now, I've locked myself into a promise to leave you be. I've failed you, miss. And Marisol, I—"

"Drivel. Utter nonsense." Wriggling a hand from his grasp, she replaced the bandage and put his own over it. "The ship repairs are on schedule, I hear. That gives us over a day until she sails. We'll think of something. Your own words, those."

Eyes closing, he shook his head, felling hair across the bridge of his nose.

He was taking this too hard. She brushed the hair aside. "The contest was admirably fought. All I can feel is gratitude that you're alive."

Diego broke from the crowd to regard them, his hair glossy and disheveled, his white shirt open to the naval in an arrogant boast of his chiseled torso, his hazel eyes a set of marbles, cold and hard. What had she ever seen in him?

"Listen, now. We don't have much time." Marcus's hold ground her knuckles. "The ship is slated to sail Monday morning at high tide. That's shortly before dawn. There's a man in place ready to secret you and the baby out of here the night before. You'll be brought to me and from there, taken to safety."

"By whom? What man?"

"Bellamy's arranged it, but he's refused me the details."

Max and Marcus? Colluding?

"When?"

"Tomorrow, near midnight, be ready." His thin smile opened that ghastly slit, and her heart bled. He would bear that mark forever.

When Diego moved toward them, impatience driving his strutted steps, so did Barbury, holding out the medical kit. Seeing it, Diego stopped.

Blood dripping, Marcus shoved the case under his arm. "Until tomorrow, Miss McGirth." He wavered in a hungry study of her, then swiveled to Diego.

Fearlessly, he drew his weapon, raised it in a swordsman's salute—cross guard brought horizontal beneath his eyes—and waited for Diego to return it. At its absence, he strode from the hacienda, medical bag in one hand, bared sword in the other.

Lillian's heart tripped, lost its footing, and fell after him. With a sharp intake, she scrambled after the treacherous thing, fumbling miserably. Even while she admonished herself to keep after her heart, to lock it back in place, she was forced to admit that there was nothing to do with a man like Marcus Buck.

Except lose her heart to him.

Chapter *10*

Lillian untied her sash and gingerly wormed the gown over her head. Sending Barb to bed ahead of her hadn't been the best idea. She flung the wisp-of-a-gown over the top of the dressing screen, glad to be done with it. Glad to be done with the day.

The bed's plush mattress beckoned. In her chemise, she picked her way across the dark room, massaging her scalp and unseating her coiffure. Hair tumbling, she stopped at the vanity to deposit the long-toothed *peineta*. As she dug hairpins and pearls from the mass of gnarly tresses, she smiled and let Marcus monopolize her. Marcus, those powerful shoulders, and that brilliant steel.

A hummed sigh left her before she even knew it was on its way up. Rolling her eyes, she yanked a comb through the underside of her mane. If she wasn't careful, the doctor would reduce her to a swooning flibbertigibbet en route to having her heart broken.

Marcus Buck was not eligible. Not to her. He was polished gold to her tarnished brass, and she had the birthing scars on her belly to prove it.

In addition, she owed him an insurmountable debt. Several, actually. Tomorrow, she'd begin repayment. She'd ravage the study. There had to be *something* there that would satisfy.

The bedroom's doors flew open behind her. She spun to face the intruder.

Tall Bull stood in the entry. On either side, the doors swung on their hinges, lace curtains dancing crazily. The plaza torches flickered behind him, making him a silhouette. A rather imposing one. His chest hauled wind, as though he'd made a mad dash up the stairs, not that she'd heard a single beat of his stealthy Indian feet.

"The Muscogees *do* consider it a courtesy to knock," she said dryly, hand on hip. "Or have you grown so wild in your flight from civilization that you've become no better than an *efv-somkv*?" A mangy dog. Although, Tall Bull could roll in the mud and crawl on all fours, and he wouldn't come close to resembling a dog. Not even with that unkempt hair of his.

He stared straight ahead at the balcony. "That door, did you close it just now?"

"It has not been touched since I arrived some time ago." She crossed her arms. "Why?"

"*¿Con quién habla usted?*" Suni came out of the adjoining room, feet shuffling and hair mussed. Spotting Tall Bull, she gasped. "*Madre santísima!*" Making a sloppy sign of the cross, she scurried from view.

Tall Bull accepted her interruption without a hitch. "I was outside and saw —" He went to the patio door. Tested the knob. When it held, he stood with his face inches from the sheers and became very still, except for his shoulders, which rose and fell with his heightening breaths. Slowly, as though dreading what he might see, he pushed aside the curtains and peered into the night.

"*Está rezando?*" Suni's brusque undertones originated from a black corner.

"Not praying, no. Thinking…I think." Whatever it was, it frightened her. "Was the patio door open before I came up?"

"In this cold? But the baby!" Suni gave an indignant snort. "What manner of nanny do you take me for? But of course it has been closed."

"Go back to your room. I'll speak with him." Not waiting to see if Suni did as told, Lillian took several chary steps toward Tall Bull and transitioned to Muskogee. "The old woman says the door has remained closed. What do you see?"

He made no move to recognize her but continued his surveillance.

"What is it?" she tried again, fighting to keep a steady voice. Staying clear of the glass, she came within arm's reach of him. "Are we in danger?

In the plaza, servants were putting out the torches, gradually dousing the room with darkness. Tall Bull's dusky complexion fused with the night, but his long-shirt, rolled to the elbows, glowed pale.

"Tall Bull?" She touched his bare forearm and quickly retracted.

He didn't move. Was he in a trance?

Growing bolder, she took light hold of his arm. It was cool and covered in chill bumps. She gave it a little shake and hissed, "Stop this!"

In the black, she didn't see his other hand until it covered hers. She startled, but his clamp on her wrist, while not threatening, held her in place. There was a slight tremor to him, and it wormed uncomfortably inside her.

"Let me go." She retreated.

"Wait," he said, fingers firming, still staring at nothingness. "Tell me what you see. There. In the pine."

Obediently, she looked to the tree and squinted. "The branches move in the wind. I see nothing unusual. It is too dark."

His muscles flexed beneath her, hardened. With a rapid release of breath, he flatted his hand to the glass, his breath creating a damp, foggy patch. "Grandfather Moon is uneasy." It was large behind the curtain of gloom and cast a massive ring of fuzzy, rust-tinged light that was both eerie and enchanting. "For many nights, he has hidden himself behind the screen of clouds. Only at times does he look down to see whether we have repaired our offenses and balanced our spirits with love."

"What offenses?"

"To know, each must turn his ear to Creator and listen, for soon, Grandfather will cover his face in darkness and remain behind his veil until all things have been set right."

"An eclipse?"

He nodded, tension petrifying his arm. "The time has come for us to mend wrongs."

Did he mean *them,* him and Lillian? If so, he was quite wrong. That time would never come.

He let the sheers fall back into place but stayed as he was. Long moments passed before he looked at her. Then, he reviewed her, head to foot, in as exhaustive an inspection as he'd given the pine. His face was masked by deep shadows that hid his intent. He could be thinking anything, and it frightened her. The uptick in her heart was surely evident in the abnormally broad movement of her chest.

"If I'd come across you in the wood," he said at last, his tone neutral, "I would've believed you a spirit, dressed as you are in white."

Her laugh was breathy, nervous. "No spirit. Only a simple woman."

"No woman is simple. You are each complex, deserving of thorough study."

Oh? He'd studied *her* long enough. She tested his hold, but it remained firm.

"*Kusvpetv*, please," he said. "Your touch, it grounds me. And it..." He glanced around as though to find the right words hidden in the obscurity. Then, he withdrew. "It has been a trying day. You should rest."

Cradling her hand, she backed away, not fully believing he wouldn't press his desires—whatever those were. But as he stretched out on the divan, she began to relax.

"He cannot sleep there!" Suni rasped from her blackened alcove. "Make him go! Make him go!"

Lillian took a long look at the Red Stick bedding down not ten feet away. Fear sprouted, probing her for weakness, reminding her of the things this man was capable of. Jaw clenching, she lectured herself on the stupidity of making herself vulnerable to him in this way. But looking at him now, at his powerful length draped over furniture that could barely contain him, she reasoned he would do whatever he wished no matter what she asked or said or did.

"No, Suni." The words came out strong, surprising her. "He senses a threat. I want him close. Lock your door if it makes you feel safer."

Grumbling about savages and interrupted sleep, the old woman did as advised, the scrape of her bolt a nervy herald.

Lillian threw back the heavy bed curtains and turned down the covers, but before climbing in, she let her hand linger on the down comforter. The night was cold, and Tall Bull had only his long-shirt. Impulsively, she dragged the comforter to him.

At her approach, he sat up. "You bring me a blanket?"

"Even the Bitter Eyes has a heart." She smirked into the gloom and tossed it over his legs.

He whisked them out from under it and stood. "I cannot."

"You would disdain my kindness?"

"I will not lie covered while there are children in my village who have only the arms of their loved ones to warm them."

Her foot withdrew a step, fingers landing on her throat. "They have no blankets? Does the Spaniard know?"

He must. It was his business to know. Why had he done nothing?

"I was town micco. It is my failing."

Was chief?

Tall Bull collected the blanket from the floor and pressed it into her. "Maddo, Bitter Eyes. Go hunt a dream." He resumed his awkward position on the couch.

Sleep didn't come easy. She lay like the dead, afraid to move and draw his attention, knowing full well he kept an ear pointed her direction. The night ended abruptly when Marisol woke before dawn, chattering happily from her cradle. Lillian groaned and prayed her child would go back to sleep, but a short while later, Suni left the room with Mari in her arms, allowing Lillian to finish her rest. When at last she'd gotten her fill of sleep, she opened her eyes to a beautiful stream of undiluted sunlight.

And no Tall Bull.

Not only was the room empty, but the hacienda was free of the master's oppressive presence. He was to have left for St. Augustine for whatever business drew him there. He'd never said, and she'd never asked. She felt almost giddy at the thought of an entire day without him. To top it off, tomorrow, she would be free of this place. Forever.

Stretching grandly, she smiled up at the blue velvet canopy until she got a whiff of chorizo. *Breakfast.* She could have breakfast!

Stomach rumbling, she flung aside the covers and greeted the frigid day with exuberance. When her bare feet hit the cold tile, a shudder snaked up her spine. She was gripping the bed curtain for support, poking a cold foot under the bed in search of her slippers, when an echo of Tall Bull's voice dashed away her smile.

The children.

Here she was lounging in luxury while they huddled for warmth — a familiar predicament. The winter she'd spent in the woodland, hungry and frozen, was far too recent a memory. Well, she refused to sit by and do nothing.

The bed curtains were halfway removed from their rail when Tall Bull walked in and caught her standing on the bed in her nightclothes, fighting the curtain rings. His hair was wet; his skin, fresh and vibrant in its bold color. "And to think," he said, "I almost took another swim and missed this fine view." An appreciative smile eased over him, and Lillian's balance faltered.

She snatched at the bedpost, unable to help her returning smile. "Stop your empty yammering and help me."

He did, reaching easily for the stubborn rings and eying her speculatively. "You are changed. Happier. Why?"

She pondered his assertion and decided he was right, for if she could smile in the presence of a Red Stick she *had* changed. "The sun is shining, the Spaniard is gone, and I am helping the children," she said, pleased to have come up with three very good reasons apart from the most prominent — Marcus was breaking them free.

"*Hopuetake estomet?*"

"*Your* children. Wakulla's. This fabric is for them. Those will go as well." She slid the last ring from the rod, then pointed to the stack of blankets she'd abducted from the trunks of various guest chambers.

Surprise abruptly curved his brows upward; misgiving inverted them again. "What will the Spaniard say about—?"

"The Spaniard can drown in his chest of escudos for all I care."

He laughed and reeled the drape about his arm. "Sunflower will hug your neck and brag that she was right about you. Get dressed. We go at once."

Right about her? Lillian dared not ask what that meant. "I have work to do here." Such as tear apart the don's study. "Sunflower, whomever that may be, must content herself with *your* neck."

"Show some respect, little woman. She is your clan mother."

Lillian would never remember she was Beaver. She leaned into the bedpost, reluctant to give up the higher ground. "How can that be? I've not even been to Wakulla."

"No need. Your plight here is known in the village. Beaver's anger is stirred at the Spaniard's callous handling. Since you have no other kin within a hundred sights, Sunflower claimed responsibility of you and your daughter. She is eager to meet you."

"Very kind, but—"

"But nothing." Without warning, he hooked an arm about her waist and, to her yelp of indignation, swiped her off the bed. He dropped her to her feet and swatted her on the rump, propelling her toward the armoire. "You are coming."

Lillian rode atop a mound of blankets in the two-wheeled, wicker-sided cart. A fine mist hung in the air, leftovers from the sudden afternoon shower that had drenched them. Suni had been right to insist they cover the blankets with tarpaulin.

Tall Bull walked at the front, guiding a mule that chattered with an obnoxious honk and blow at every odd opportunity. His tramping feet signaled the end of his patience was near.

Two and a half miles into the journey, Lillian's stomach protested the jouncing ride. Her nerves compounded the matter. This would be the first time she stepped foot in a Creek village since she'd fled captivity. That she was choosing to do it—and with gifts—at once made her proud and revoltingly ill.

"Stop," she shouted, gorge rising. "Stop, I need to—" She leapt the side of the cart, splashed through a puddle, and emptied her stomach into a stand of sedge.

"I told you the spiced pork would not settle well." Tall Bull loomed over her stooping form. "It is too soon since your fast."

"I miss Marcus," she groaned in English. Marcus would be stroking her back and rescuing her hair. With a flail, she shoved at Tall Bull's leg. "If you have nothing comforting to say, be gone."

Tall Bull snorted but didn't abandon her.

A water gourd appeared beside her, swinging from a strap, its sloshing insides a beautiful sound. She mumbled a "maddo" and rinsed her mouth with the sweet water. "I will walk. The trail is too rough."

Stomach aside, her tender back couldn't take one more rut. Walking would ruin her slippers and the hem of her dress, but she couldn't arrive in Wakulla hunched and pale and looking like easy pickings.

These were rebel Creeks, after all. The worst of the worst.

To give the appearance of indifference, she strode five paces ahead, fending off the bines of honeysuckle twining into the path. They'd not gone a hundred paces farther when three warriors materialized out of the thickets. Armed with muskets carried in loose readiness, muzzles trained downward, they crowded Lillian on the narrow path.

Panic clawing to the surface, she reversed her stride, snatching at her gown to keep it clear of her scrambling heels. She bumped first into the mule's oversized teeth, then into Tall Bull, stepping on his toes before ungracefully attaining a more secure position behind him.

He grunted at her, unlatched her fingers from his belt, and greeted the men. "Any activity at the perimeter?" They returned the shake of his arm with an interesting mixture of camaraderie and deference.

The eldest stepped forward. He was a man nearing his thirties whose forearm paraded a winding inked snake, a single drop of venom on its bared fangs. As with most warriors, his head was shaven but for a shorn strip running vertically forehead to nape. Attached at the crown was the usual red feather coupled with that of a hawk. A chipped front tooth characterized his grin as he jabbed a fist into Tall Bull's shoulder. "Only you, making enough noise to give away our position to the white man's Great Father in Washington."

"If his bluecoats attack in the night, we will know who to blame," another said, earning laughs all around. The mule joined in, which sent a chuckle up even Lillian's burning throat.

Snake Arm laid a telling hand on the head of his belted tomahawk. "The prophet will chafe at seeing you back so soon. How will he steal the people's hearts," he said, voice low, condescension thick, "if you give him only a day in which to do it?"

Ah, so the renegade prophet and chief, Josiah Francis, *was* back.

Tall Bull stood a little straighter, all humor gone. "Wield that tongue more carefully, brother. My loyalty to our micco remains true." With a triplet of clicks, he took the mule's bridle and spurred her back into a plodding walk.

Lillian debated the cart's more discrete interior but, feeling calmer for having been ignored by the men, turned it down to work out the kinks in her spine.

The younger warriors filtered back into the coppice, but Snake Arm, looking appropriately penitent, took up position on Tall Bull's left. "I will go with you a ways. How long do you stay?"

"We leave shortly," Lillian stated resolutely. The sooner the better.

Both men looked back, but Snake Arm spoke first. "You are the Spaniard's woman?"

"She is Bitter Eyes of Tensaw," Tall Bull answered for her, as his comrade fell back and matched his stride to hers.

After a moment's blunt perusal, he shook his head. "The name is an ill fit. Your eyes are as large and sweet as a doe's. And about as frightened. Whatever my brother has told you about me is not true. My bite is only a little venomous." He brandished that nicked tooth in a grin.

"Is this man a snake that I should be cautious of him?" Lillian directed the question ahead to Tall Bull who responded with only a muted laugh.

Snake Arm, however, let his mirth fly free. "She is a sharp one, micco."

They were nearing the village and news of their arrival was stirring the lanes. Pestered by uncomfortable memories, Lillian hugged the mule's dusty side. To disguise her anxiety, she worked in a jest. "Let me guess. Your war name is Rattler Buttons."

Tall Bull chuckled. "Close. He is called Water Moccasin. His rank is war leader to the tribe." Grimacing, he rubbed the heel of his hand against his seat. "And he is a dreadful pox on my—"

"Ho!" Water Moccasin chortled. "Do not listen to him, sweet doe. I have saved him a great heap of pain on the battlefield as well as off it. But if there is any to be found, it is in the stump of his right arm. It was ripped from him when he left for the Spaniard's lodge."

Tall Bull snagged a backward glance and kicked a stone with his heel. It pegged Water Moccasin in the shin. To the man's good-humored snarl, he said on a laugh, "I stand corrected. He is war leader to the tribe *and* my strong arm, bloody and torn though it may be."

Water Moccasin whipped an arrow from his quiver and bopped Tall Bull with it on the back of the head. "That was for Mink. *She* is your strong arm."

Tall Bull dodged another swing, forehead a map of surly wrinkles. "Save your disrespect for another time. There are children coming."

Sure enough, a passel of little ones, ten or so, wearing the scraps of long-shirts and blankets, rounded a bend to welcome them with cheerful abandon. "Orphans of the war," Tall Bull explained over their jabbering.

Several attached to his legs, while others scaled the cart and tumbled into it. One fearless girl, wearing shin-high moccasins and a trade-cloth shift, raised her arms at Lillian.

"This one is called Cricket," Tall Bull said, yanking the child's braid, "because she is naughty and chatters into the night."

There was no resisting the giggling sweetheart. Lillian hiked Cricket to her hip and buffed her chilly thigh to warm it. "We have brought them blankets," she announced to Water Moccasin over the girl's head.

The war chief threw back the tarpaulin and grinned. "So you have. I knew my resourceful brother would not be kept down."

Tall Bull swung a lad onto the mule's back, and Cricket abandoned her to do the same. To their delight, the molly pointed her muzzle at the dreary sky, curled back her lips, and sang like a raucous canary.

The cart continued forward, rolling toward Wakulla's outermost family compounds. Lillian expected they would enter the town's center, but Tall Bull took a sharp left and led them down a quiet bordering lane.

Water Moccasin drew alongside Tall Bull and lowered his voice. "Have you considered that the prophet will take sorely to this latest provision of yours? His pride will be stung. Are you prepared for it?"

"The blankets are my doing, not his," Lillian said. Was she protecting the Red Stick?

"Maddo, little sister," Water Moccasin said. "The children thank you, but Tall Bull is leading the cart. It is enough to earn him resentment."

Tall Bull frowned. "We will see."

"Whatever the outcome, I stand by you, brother. Always." In farewell, Water Moccasin took Tall Bull's arm in a grip that jerked him out of step. Then, with a nod for Lillian, he returned the way they'd come.

The warning damped Tall Bull's mood. He plucked every child from the beast, proclaimed them all a smelly herd of mules, and commanded them to the river to bathe. Once they'd cleared out, he picked up the pace and pointed his face straight ahead to the lodge at the end of the lane.

A black woman stood over the courtyard fire, stirring a pot of something fragrant. Slave? Servant? Clan? In Creek villages, it was impossible to know without asking.

Tall Bull lifted a friendly hand to the woman before directing his voice toward the shingled dwelling. "Sunflower, I've brought you kin!" When no one emerged, he turned to the black woman. "Where is Sunflower?"

Before she could reply, a single mounted warrior bore down the trail, chased by a surge of dust. He wore a Native's crimson turban, but his complexion was fair. The prophet Francis? His father was said to be Scots. Hence, the name.

Tall Bull's expression went dark in an instant, harking Lillian back to the younger version of him. The one Lillian had feared like the yellow jack.

"Take the blankets inside, Bitter Eyes. I will be only a moment." He set out to meet the man partway.

"Hurry," Lillian threw at his back.

The men's muted exchange rang hot. Despite Tall Bull's assertive tone, he kept a submissive posture. The elder's skin reddened, and when he turned his implacable eye on her, his voice rose.

Lillian began unloading, carting steep armloads, ditching them in a disorderly pile in the lodge. After the last load, she ducked from Sunflower's dwelling in time to see both men quitting the compound. Francis, galloping down the lane. Tall Bull, stalking into the woods, abandoning her to the whim of the village.

Lillian eyed the mule determinedly. Five minutes. She'd give the Red Stick five minutes, then she would make her own trail home.

"Won't be gone long," the black woman said, ladling her steaming concoction into a clay bowl. "Goin' to the council square or warrior's lodge, be my guess." She extended the dish, but Lillian didn't want to eat.

She wanted to leave. "Thank you, no."

"Suit yourself. Look to me like you could use a bellyful a somethin' though."

A scrawny smile tried for Lillian's mouth as she assayed the strange woman.

She was a willow branch, lean and lissome, lovely in her full lips and midnight skin, but she was misplaced in this Red Stick village.

"Are you a captive?"

"Why you askin'?" Suspicion thinned the woman's eyes.

"Because I've been one. Slavery isn't a pretty place to be, and if I can help you in some way—"

The woman grunted and dumped the stew back into the kettle. "I heard 'bout you, Lillian McGirth. That was a rotten thing they done at Mims' place, but you oughtn't to yap about what you ain't got a clue."

Lillian bristled. "I'd say a year as a slave gives me more than enough experience to speak on the matter."

"You go on to Brunswick. Spend a year in a tobacco field under sun and whip. Add in the foremen's fat gut pinnin' you down whenever, wherever. After, we'll talk about slavery like we's equals. Until then, you jest think on blessin' Jesus for makin' *your* mastuh a red man."

Jaw snapping open, Lillian sucked a breath to let fly the lash of her tongue but stopped. She found no rebuttal to such a distasteful argument.

"We got company," the woman said, eyes fixed to a spot behind Lillian, "but I don't think she here for me."

Lillian turned to find a woman standing beside the lodge.

The war woman. Same circular tattooed pattern. Same frosty eyes.

Except, now, instead of weapons and breechcloth, she wore a loose-fitting red shirt tucked into an indigo skirt that boasted three bands of yellow ribbons appliquéd to the hem. The feminine touches were little comfort in light of those heavy-lidded eyes.

Lillian stepped into Muskogee. "Are you…Sunflower?"

On a deliberate approach, the warrior shook her head.

Lillian swung back to the black woman, but she, having hefted her pot off the fire, only offered an apologetic smile and headed indoors.

Feigning mettle, Lillian lengthened her backbone, but there was little to be done about the tremble in her voice. "Then who are you?"

"I am Fierce Mink."

This tiny woman was Tall Bull's strong arm? The tattoos were intimidating, but Lillian, though quite short herself, had at least an inch on the woman.

"What is Tall Bull to you?" Mink said.

Lillian knew exactly what Mink asked but resented the woman's intimation—as well as her intimidation—and refused to give her the answer she wanted. "He is cousin to my sister's husband."

Mink sneered. "Do not let the skirt and ribbons mislead you—I am a senior warrior, assigned protector to Micco Tall Bull."

"And you must protect him from me?"

"He believes you will bind his broken spirit, but he is mistaken. Your beauty has fogged his eyes. Every look at you keeps him from the correct path. And the blood moon will *not* wait. Stay away from him, Bitter Eyes, or you will regret it."

"Take your threats elsewhere. I have no power over that man."

"Your beauty is your power! My life's purpose is his safety and well-being. I would gladly use my last breath to preserve them both. Not that subduing a noxious Spanish weed would require it."

"I do not take well to being bullied by savages." Lillian had barely finished speaking when she knew she'd made a grave mistake.

Reaching an instant boil, Mink stalked to her, fists clenched. "Take the mule and leave. *Now.*"

"Gladly," Lillian spat.

Battling horrifying tears, she set to work unbuckling the mule's breeching straps. The cart's shafts dropped, and following the children's example, Lillian hiked her skirt and climbed the animal's side.

Mink tossed her the halter rope, smacked the molly's rump, and sent them off at a brisk pace. An ungraceful exit, but Lillian didn't care so long as it carried her away from Mink, Wakulla, and her idiotic decision to leave La Conchita in the company of a Red Stick.

Tall Bull emerged from the woods to her left, bewilderment scrunching his face.

Well, let him wonder! She was through with this place. Her heel punched the mule's ribs, transitioning them into a lumbering gallop.

"Where are you going?" he shouted at her back, but she kept on. "Bitter Eyes!"

She didn't check the mule until she reached the picket guards a full mile from the village.

Water Moccasin took hold of the bridle. "Why the hurry, sweet doe?"

"Your war woman sent me on my way with a pretty threat that I dared not take lightly."

A muscle rippled in the war chief's jaw. "This is not the first time I find myself apologizing for her bad manners. How can I make it right?"

"You can let me pass."

He did but sent a warrior to accompany her. Tall Bull would be on her trail soon, but it might take him a while to get his hands on a horse. She knew from Diego that proper mounts were hard to come by for the Indians.

Back at the hacienda, she went straight to the study, closed the door, and upended every drawer and file, searching, desperate to find something, anything, evidence that would ensure she left this Red Stick-infested swamp and never came back.

Breathless, she stood in the middle of her mess and glared at the floor-to-ceiling bookcase, the only place she hadn't looked. The crumbling old books could hold a shipload of documents between their covers. They were never touched, rarely dusted.

Her eyes traveled every shelf, every spine, looking for inconsistencies, for signs of disturbance. She was growing discouraged when, at the second shelf from the top on the far left, she spotted a spine that protruded the tiniest bit from the others on either side. And was that a sliver of white between it and that green volume to its right?

Afraid to hope but giddy nonetheless, she slid the ladder over, hiked her gown to her knees and over her the crook of her elbow, and scaled the six rungs like a billy goat.

Cervantes' books of poetry ceded four pieces of fine quality parchment.

Right there, clinging to the top of Diego's library ladder, she unfolded the first in a flurry of clumsy fingers and hungry eyes. Time dissolved as she pored over the sheet. By the end, her heart soared.

This was it. Exactly what Marcus needed. Proof undeniable.

Bursting out in a triumphant laugh, she slapped the sheets against her heart and let herself believe she'd come upon something that might satisfy.

"Woman," Tall Bull's voice boomed across the room. "What have you done to this place?"

Chapter *II*

"Well, that settles it then." Major Ainsworth stood, scraping his chair along the fort's roughly laid stone floor.

Marcus and Lieutenant Fanning followed suit, while Captain Luengo's attention was split between them and Miss McGirth's flowing translation.

The chamber was cramped and cold, a dank cavern of stone with only an undersized chimenea to ward off the encroaching winter. A prescription for pneumonia, if ever there was one.

Captain Luengo rose from his desk and, from her seat at his side, Miss McGirth did as well, a shiver jostling her torso. The captain appeared snug in his navy blue, woolen regimentals, but the white lace shawl draped over Miss McGirth Spanish comb and shoulders couldn't offer much by way of warmth. It was certainly becoming on her, though, with its tasseled edges framing her face. A large silk rose nestled in her hair at the comb's base, its berry-red paralleling the chill-engendered blush on her cheeks. The appraisal stopped there, for any lower would provide Marcus's eyes with more than his imagination — or his conscience — could handle.

Scooping bodice aside, seeing her mollified his worry. It had been almost twenty-four hours since he'd left her in the hacienda's courtyard — an arduous spin of the clock's hands, to say the least. He'd felt every tick of its passing like the needle he'd driven through his cheek.

The sutures stung, but he smiled at Miss McGirth anyway. She needed it, considering she'd not formed one herself during the ten-minute farewell between themselves and Captain Luengo. Per usual, her translation had been faultless, a gorgeous breathy stream of Spanish alternating seamlessly with English.

But fear stirred behind her eyes. At the prospect of fleeing the region come midnight? Probably. And he had yet to break the news that she would not be traveling with him but taking an unknown trail with an unknown man. McGirth wouldn't be keen on this surrogate plan, but there was no choice save go along.

God seemed to have a different vision of how this must flow. Marcus had thought himself the sturdy bridge between her and safety. As it would happen, he was merely another twig tossed about in the current. The best he'd done was hold her head above water and pray the river dumped them into a tranquil bay, but even that was being ripped from him. Their current diverged here.

For a while, at any rate. Marcus's ear was still perked toward Heaven, waiting for that final, conclusive intimation.

Major Ainsworth jutted his hand toward Captain Luengo. "General Jackson will be pleased to know he has an ally in you."

The commandant came around the table and accepted the gesture with a beaming smile. "Rest assured," Miss McGirth interpreted, "that your generals will always have a friendly harbor in San Marcos." The very invitation Major Ainsworth had been hoping to wheedle out of the man.

"Gracias, señor. Muchas gracias," Major Ainsworth said, his accent so atrocious that even Marcus could appreciate the butchery. "I trust our gifts will be enjoyed by all. The rum, they say, is the finest to be had in the Caribbean."

Captain Luengo wrapped a hand around the brown bottle on his desk—one of a dozen in the crate they'd had delivered—and spoke around that perpetually generous smile.

"He'll distribute them to his officers this very evening," Miss McGirth supplied. "But the wait for the mangos to ripen is an unnecessary cruelty to which he must object."

The major released his usual unpracticed bark of a laugh. "Our stay here at San Marcos has been delightful, Captain Luengo. Sincerest appreciation for your lavish hospitality."

While Miss McGirth conveyed his sentiment, Marcus leaned to speak discretely to the major. "Permission, sir, to address Miss McGirth privately?"

"Very well, but first, I'd like a word with her myself." He formed a smile.

Might the man have changed his mind about allowing her passage? Hope lightened Marcus's steps as they exited to the inner ward.

To their backs, the fort rose in an imposing wall of stone, but before them, a ten-foot wooden palisade comprised the eastern wall. It swung a sharp left, creating the northern wall, and at the pickets' juncture, stood the gate leading to the moat, as well as Tall Bull, the sight of whom was beginning to grate.

He chatted amiably with four Spanish sentries, but the moment Marcus stepped from the captain's chamber, the chief's attention was instantly fixed on him. Or better put, on Miss McGirth, for when she crossed the ward ahead of the men, the swivel of his head tracked her progress.

Captain Luengo offered to show them to the wall walk so they might appreciate the fine view of the river and village. Regrettably, Miss McGirth would not be attending them, she informed, but she assented to the major's request for a private audience with her.

Fanning took it upon himself to bid Miss McGirth farewell with two Spanish kisses. She bestowed him a lovely string of laughter and converted the kisses into a rather long embrace. It chaffed like new boots, until her gaze sought Marcus over Fanning's shoulder. Not a lazy look nor a casual one, it lingered, entering him with the intensity of a patient facing a bloodletting. That might be a laugh on her lips, but the anxiety in her eyes eclipsed it.

An artful smile appropriated his mouth. *Father, what are You thinking ripping us apart?* He trusted her with no man half as well as with himself, and though it made him a boaster to believe it, in the care of any other, she would sink, choke on fear. *Keep her afloat, Lord.*

Once Captain Luengo and Lieutenant Fanning had left them for the wall walk, Major Ainsworth wasted no time about his business. "Miss McGirth, seeing that your father is absent, allow me to assume his role and speak with candor." His tenor was crisp, not a hint of warmth.

This did not have the sound of a man bearing good news.

Miss McGirth sensed it too. She pitched leery eyes at Marcus but only fleetingly. Hands folding before her, she formed that gracious, duchess poise. "Certainly, Major."

Marcus braced himself, then thought better of it and took the offensive. He stepped forward. "Sir, if you'll allow me—"

The major hoisted a silencing hand and an intolerant eye. He pressed on, undeterred. "Find your way out of San Marcos, miss. Soon. Build a respectable life. You are too fine a lady to prodigal your years in this uncomely manner."

The veneer of duchess fell away. Her clutched hands rose to grasp at the hem of her short-waisted spencer. "I...don't understand. I'm leaving with you. Tonight, I... Doctor, is that not so?"

Wrong, wrong, this was going terribly wrong! Air eked from Marcus's cinched throat. "Actually, Miss Mc—?"

"You've not told her yet?" Major Ainsworth swiveled to him.

"Told me what?" Her gaze bounced from Marcus to the major and back. "Marcus, er, Doctor Buck, has there been a complication?"

Her eyes, coming at Marcus with such desperation, formed in him a mouthful of belittlements perfectly suited to Ainsworth. Teeth clamping, he swallowed them down, while the man who'd earned them flushed with choler.

"Captain Buck, *what* is going on here? Why has this woman not been properly informed?"

"You precipitated me, sir." Marcus's tone rang one jot shy of disrespect. "I delayed, hoping to spare her, hoping you would have a change of heart about taking her." But he should've known. The man *had* no heart.

"What?" Miss McGirth said, her voice small and wounded. "You won't take me?"

"Confound you, Captain, for putting me in this position!" The major cursed liberally, and Miss McGirth startled.

The tears came next, followed swiftly by her trembling lower lip. In Marcus, they cued nausea. In Ainsworth, they cued a thrust of the chest. "Spare me the display. I will *not* have a change of heart."

Fingers tangling in her shawl, she dragged it off her head and bunched it two-handed under her throat, covering that indecent exposure of flesh. "Because I've provided no evidence? I tried. Truly, I did! Marcus, tell me it isn't true. We're going with you, Mari and me. Aren't we?"

Marcus locked eyes with her, willing her to trust him. "Remember what I told you in the hacienda? Nothing has changed."

"But *everything* has changed!"

Tall Bull split from the sentries and began toward them.

"Get a hold of yourself, miss," Major Ainsworth hissed. "You're drawing unwanted attention." He twisted to Marcus. "Take care of this, Captain. *Now.* You have one minute to break with this woman." Without so much as a fare-thee-well to Miss McGirth, he stalked toward the wall-walk stairway.

Tall Bull was thirty paces out and nearing, displeasure hardening that broad Indian brow.

"You're leaving us here?" she said, voice breaking, lace strangled between her fists.

"I have no choice. Our mission has run its course, and I have little power outside of what my commander allows. I'll speak with him again. Strongly."

Her chest rose sharply in her pursuit of breath. "Marcus, I cannot do this without you!"

"You'll have to! Be strong, miss." He wanted to comfort her, but there wasn't time for so much as an inward groan; that blasted Indian was bearing down on him.

"As I said, *nothing* has changed. The previous arrangement stands." Even though he wasn't at all sure of the details or if they would come together. "Trust me, and if you cannot manage that, trust Mr. Bellamy. He has connections and should be able to accomplish what I could not." *Lord God, tell me I've heard Your voice in this!* It certainly wasn't his own. To trust Mr. Bellamy was idiocy.

Despite Marcus's fervid assurances, she blinked at him, looking dumbfounded and lost, shawl now trailing the ground.

"Until tonight, miss." Afraid his touch would shatter her, he gave a curt bow, jerked a nod to the glowering Red Stick coming to a halt at her side, and left her for the parapet and his loathsome commander.

From a gap in the battlement, Marcus watched Miss McGirth cross the moat, Tall Bull steadying her faltering step. They arrived at a handsome roan tethered beside a trough. Tall Bull unwound the reins and lifted her face to him.

She angled her chin, pulling it free, but he wasn't deterred, moving his hand instead to the back of her bare neck and coaxing her into his chest. Her hands went up as a barrier between them even as her forehead fell against his shirtfront.

She'd resisted less than Marcus had expected, but then, she'd just had her world crushed. By him.

As the chief soothed her with deep strokes on her back, he tipped his head toward Marcus and gave him a long look, one meant to convey a message. He could have been glaring at Fanning or Major Ainsworth who stood to Marcus's left, but Marcus knew he wasn't. This was a jab, some sort of threat.

For one irrational moment, Marcus considered shouting a protest. Reason banished the urge. She should seek comfort wherever it was offered, seeing how Marcus wasn't available.

That reality was disturbing. More so than he would have expected. It coated his tongue in bitterness and crushed loose battlement mortar beneath his fingers.

Fanning cleared his throat. He observed Marcus from the side of his eye, a medley of concern and amusement poking one brow skyward. "I agree. He's rather liberal with his hands."

"By our standards," Major Ainsworth said, "but you must remember these people are uncouth, largely uncivilized."

Fanning quirked his lips. "I can't believe all Indians are *that* cheeky. Did you see the look he gave you, Buck?"

"Couldn't miss it." Marcus brushed grit from his fingers, attempting the appearance of mild interest. "The man is known for flouting rules and authority, even that of his own tribe. Now that he's been named chief, I suppose he makes his own rules."

Tall Bull swung up on the animal and reached for her outstretched arms. She would ride with him so readily? What of her fear? Her insistence the man might want her dead?

The audacious Indian cozied her between his legs, pulled her against him, and lifting a smirk to the parapet, spurred the animal into motion.

A low growl rolled from Marcus's throat. Enough! His spin toward the stairs was jerked to a stop.

Fanning held fast to his arm. "He's taunting you," he said under his breath. "To draw you away. Let him go."

"But Miss McGirth—"

"Is fine. Don't forget it was he who saved her from the pillory. He won't hurt her."

Hurt, no. The opposite. And Marcus wasn't sure which of the two tragedies would rip him deepest.

Be a father to her, I beg you, McGirth had appealed.

Ridiculous!

The only part of her Marcus might be interested in fathering was her child. True, their lives were diverging, but he was a man of means, and given leave, he could obliterate the miles easily enough. If she would have him.

She will, God intimated. *Marry her.*

Marcus's spirit seized. Then, it wobbled under a storm of emotions—elation, relief, uncertainty, its remedy.

In the eyes of society, nothing good would come of marrying a soiled woman accused of treason. In his...? A chance at contentment he'd lost hope of ever owning.

He didn't need a night of dalliance or even a single press of their lips to know their intimacy would more than satisfy. López, a man not limited in his pick of consorts, kept her under lock and key for a reason. Blessed day, she'd packed more seduction into the scrape of their little fingers than any scrupulous fellow should be asked to endure.

But all the seduction in Spanish Florida couldn't sway him unless it flowed from a woman who spoke his heart. And she did, every day more fluently. She'd seen through his veneer into his pain, his past, and his drive for justice. Having discovered it, she could have taken him as no more than a vengefully charged monster hiding inside the coat of an accomplished doctor, an object of horror and pity. But instead, she embraced it. All of it. He could search a lifetime and never find another like her.

Frankly, subjecting her to his unbecoming flesh frightened him cruelly — for her stability, for his own pride — and though his intuition said she would not shudder, he couldn't be sure. That said, when exposed to his stint with slavery, she'd bypassed degrading pity and gone straight for his torch. Carried it, burned with it. And so, she'd become the very companion he lacked but had been too unbelieving to seek; she was release for his secrets, hope for his future, shelter for his languid spirit. Simply put, she'd proven herself to be the understanding friend they'd proposed that first hour with such uncanny accuracy.

Yes, if she agreed, he'd marry her. First, he'd fulfill his promise; he'd usher her toward home, then call his pledge, God-be-thanked, complete. Once he'd brought Iron Wood to the law, he would invade Tensaw, tell McGirth his version of a decent vow had reeked, and propose a better one.

Releasing a burdensome breath, he glanced at the sun, a beautiful ball hung low in an azure sky. Only a few hours more until their meeting. It would kill him, but he would wait. In the meantime, *God, protect her from that Indian.*

"Let's not forget Miss McGirth's part in it," Ainsworth said, seeming to have missed the hushed interchange between Marcus and Fanning. "She's not exactly a lady, and think what you will, Captain Buck, the woman is in league with the devil."

"Oh, I wouldn't be so hasty to judge," Fanning said, a sly grin forming. "I happen to be in possession of a little something that might prove otherwise." From his cuff, he pulled a small square of folded paper and waggled it before his nose. "When she said goodbye, she left this in my hand." That explained the overlong embrace.

Heart leaping, Marcus arrested himself from snatching at the note.

"It's your name on the front, Major." Fanning handed it over.

Looking skeptical, Major Ainsworth unfolded it and read silently. At its end, he snorted. "The woman is next to useless. As expected, she gives us nothing."

Hard to believe. "Nothing at all?"

"A fine list of excuses and pleadings. She claims to have found evidence. A directive from King Ferdinand himself, if you can believe it."

"For whom?" Marcus asked.

"The don, she says. Instructions to collaborate with Iron Wood, whom she labels 'agent to the Red Sticks.' She doesn't, however, name the man. Negligence of the grossest sort."

"Could be she doesn't know," Fanning offered.

"Do you *truly* believe," Major Ainsworth said, "that she could live among them all this time and *not* know?"

"Just speculating, sir. Devil's advocate, benefit of the doubt and all that."

"And the document?" Marcus said. "Does she have it?"

"Handily confiscated just this afternoon." The major administered the note a disdainful flick of the finger. "She finishes with advice on how to manage that insane prophet, Francis. Imagine it, a wench advising *me* on my job. Dash that woman! Who does she think she is?"

"She's torn, sir." Marcus stiffened every muscle in the race to corral distemper. "Caught between two worlds and desperately afraid."

"Desperately foolish." Major Ainsworth doubled the paper and ripped it in two.

Marcus caught his breath and thrust out his hand before the major could rip it again. "May I read it?"

After a moment's hesitation, the major shrugged and passed it to him. "Burn it when you're done."

"Thank you, sir." He shoved the bits into his pocket before the man could change his mind. "Sir, if I may…" Unwilling to resign the dispute, he fired off another attempt. "I believe in my heart of hearts Miss McGirth is a true citizen, helplessly locked in a power play. For the love of pity, she's a Fort Mims' survivor! Hasn't she been through enough? A word from you, sir, and the commandant would insist on her release. Won't you reconsider?"

Incredibly, a hint of softness came into the major's eyes. As he silently considered the argument, Fanning perked hopeful brows at Marcus, but moments later, Major Ainsworth shook his head. "If she'd produced something of consequence, I might have changed my mind, but after this obvious withholding of information…"

He sighed dramatically as though the truth pained him. "I'm familiar enough with General Jackson's iron policies to know better than to give aid to any individual of questionable loyalty. That she's a loose woman, well…" He spread his hands. "That seals the matter. I have too much to lose, too many men to protect. No, Captain Buck, I'll not give that woman quarter. If you want her out of here, do it yourself. I'll not prevent it. You have nine hours. But if you make me shove off that dock without your hide onboard, I'll charge you with desertion." With that august threat, he spun and left them for the staircase leading down.

Fanning winced. "She could hang, you know, if the general gets his hands on her. I hope, for her sake, you've arranged a solid alternate plan."

Turning back to the wall and the village beyond, Marcus searched for the man and horse carrying off his charge, but it was useless. She was gone.

It was up to Bellamy now.

Marcus forced air from between pursed lips. "As solid a plan as one can arrange with an Englishman."

A snort rocked Fanning's entire frame. "Max Bellamy? You're relying on that Indian lover? *Now* who's toying with the devil? What's gotten into you, Buck? Do you know what will be said of you should anyone learn you're shaking hands with Iron Wood?"

"We don't know for certain that's who—"

"Don't play the dunce with me, Mr. Harvard! Maxwell Bellamy *is* Iron Wood. We both know it. You've gone too far bringing him into your confidence. McGirth would never expect you to consort with the enemy to—"

"Shame on you, Lieutenant Fanning!" Marcus stepped into Fanning's space, went rigid. "Shame on any gentleman who stands by idle while a man beats the life out of a woman. She's a slave to him, man! To his ledgers, his religion. His *bed*." He pounded his fist on the battlement's upper edge. "And one way or another, I intend to get her out of it!"

Mounted sidesaddle, Lillian's hips were narrow enough to wedge between Tall Bull's hard stomach and the high Spanish-style horn. That wouldn't have been possible a month ago, before she'd fasted and depleted every ounce of cushioning on her body. Before Marcus had brought his beautiful smile and his beautiful hope, then taken them both from her.

She clenched her throat to deny a fresh wave of tears and shook with the effort.

"Are you not warm enough?" Tall Bull angled an arm across her chest and down around her waist to pull her closer. It locked her against him, but she didn't have the presence of mind to do more than mourn that broken promise to fight tooth and nail.

Loneliness was a terrible thing, but she'd grown accustomed to it. Abandonment, however, was an agony that ground to a halt every thought but one—she'd earned it.

God never showed Himself more real than when the next tragedy struck. His name was written all over this disappointment. If it wasn't punishment for her sins, it was a protection for Marcus from her.

Marcus had said this fiasco wasn't his doing, that he would try again to win the major over, and no doubt he was truthful. But after introspection, he would realize God knew best—Marcus was better off without having to deal with her.

But that left her without *him.*

She brought her rosary bracelet to her lips as her eyes squeezed shut. *Lord Jesus, I beg mercy for myself, mercy for my child. I beg it, I demand it. Oh God, don't leave us here!* She hurled the prayer to the Almighty but could've sworn that a moment later it *tinged* against Heaven's door and fell back to Earth.

Hand dropping to her lap, she let the side of her head land against Tall Bull where it fitted to the crook of his chin. Even though the day was cold enough to turn his breath vaporous, he wore no outer clothing—only a loose woolen vest. Still, heat radiated from him.

His thighs jerked, setting the horse in motion. She took a handful of his vest and swayed with him to the rhythm of their mount, marveling at herself for having come to a place of trust with this Red Stick. It was a good feeling, this letting go of fear. Mending wrongs, though, was another matter altogether. It involved confession and forgiveness, neither of which he would likely be partial to.

As they passed the friary, her nostrils twitched, picking up phantom strains of frankincense. Fray Emilio stood outside its open doors, arms crossed and hidden inside the wide sleeves of his cowl. He watched them with rapt interest, sending her pulse helter-skelter through her veins.

Without the Red Stick, she was a hen on a butcher block.

He kept the horse at a smooth gait, and when they reached the turn for La Conchita, he veered left onto a road that paralleled the river.

"Where are we going?"

"The springs beyond my village. Grandfather Moon will rise full tonight, directly over the water. The sky is clear. It should be a vision."

Vision or not, she had an appointment. Max had been strangely absent since last night's soiree, but he would show. On the whole, he didn't care one whit for America or her army, but he'd enjoyed Lillian's friendship from the start. If he said he'd get her out, he would.

"I cannot go. The baby, she needs—"

"She is always well cared for, is she not?"

"Yes, but—"

"Wakulla Springs is a place of healing. There, you will feel Creator quite near. You need such a place." He rapped his knuckles on her knee and stated, "This, you will do."

She twisted her mouth but told herself his motive was pure. "Swear to me we will return soon."

She would *not* miss the rendezvous. If she did, there was no assurance she'd see Marcus again. Ever. Apart from this place and his duty to her father, which would soon be fulfilled, they had nothing— her one-sided romantic fancies not included.

"It is not far," Tall Bull replied, "and Grandfather has been rising early of late. He might be visible already, albeit pale in Grandmother's light. Trust that your spirit will thank me."

Tall Bull halted their mount at the top of a short ridge that overlooked the spring.

Before them, the river expanded into a teardrop-shaped cove encompassed by a dense forest. It was a mesmerizing sheet of turquoise, home to an abundance of riotous waterfowl and a bald eagle that screeched from the heights of a cypress. And at the cove's farthest point, hovering above a prodigious magnolia, the daytime moon, full and pale against a violet sky.

Her eyes drank it in as her lungs filled deeply with becalming air.

"Did I not tell you?" A knowing smile graced his voice.

"Mmm, you did." Abandoning reserve, she leaned back against him.

Here, in this paradise, it was easy to imagine they weren't enemies, there'd been no war, and the world was perfectly whole. Free of violence and revenge.

And bitterness.

She could even envision the possibility of a clean soul and a new beginning.

Impulsively, she snatched the mantilla, peineta, and flower from her head. She shook out her hair and scrubbed her scalp with all ten fingers. "Find them a home." She held up the items. "Pretty Wolf might think them useful." Lillian was done with them.

"She might." He tucked them into his saddle bag, then took her by the hand, left the horse, and descended the ridge. A treacherous path led to a flat span of stone whose craggy rim dropped into the crystal water.

Beneath the still, deep surface grazed a herd of manatees. Fifteen, perhaps twenty, plowed lazily through the vibrant green grasses that swayed in the currents.

"They're so close," Lillian exclaimed, toes hanging over the edge.

"The water is deceptively clear."

"How deep?"

"Do you see that large stone with the jagged edge?"

She studied the bottom but saw only a rippling prairie.

"Farther out." He scooted closer, pointing, but when she shook her head, he put his arm around her, lowered to align his sight with hers, and turned her face to the right. "*Vsv*. There."

Tension swamped her body as her perfect world shattered. Her mind darted to the knife strapped to her calf.

"Easy." He jostled her shoulders until she reminded herself she was protected by that intangible clan mother.

When she relaxed, he said, "Now look again. The rock with the teeth on the outmost edge. Do you see it? I dove there once, where the water turns a deeper blue. My ears felt as though they'd burst with the pressure, and yet, I never touched bottom."

He had yet to remove himself, so his clean, woodsy Indian scent enveloped her, followed by a whiff of sun-dried holly, the white-drink tea. Did he carry the leaves? She closed her eyes and in the next intake of air was in Singing Grass's lodge, balanced on a stool, standing on her toes to hang bundles of the shriveled leaves from the roof's cross-pole.

Adela was there… A vision came of her crouched and holding the stool steady. She was smiling up at her, always smiling. Probably still was, more so now with Lillian gone. But in those early days in Kossati, most of her smiles had been for Lillian, whom she'd loved more than anyone.

A murky image of Totka tried to materialize, but Lillian shoved him further into the shadows and focused on Singing Grass's children. Their laughter had been a constant around the place.

That summer three years ago had been hot and long but peaceful. Lillian's perpetual terror that she would be sold off to some lecherous warrior had, in the end, been unfounded.

The woman in Sunflower's yard was right. Being a Creek slave hadn't been *all* bad…

"Where are you, Bitter Eyes?" The pad of Tall Bull's finger drew her face back around for a close-up of those brown eyes.

And just that quickly he deposited her back into reality. She exhaled and spent the next minutes evading his questions about his Kossati family. Papa had kept her well informed of Totka's affairs, but telling Tall Bull was risky. It was time he knew the truth about his cousin's situation, but Lillian wasn't sure she had the courage to face his reaction. She supplied enough information to satisfy him and set off for the ridge.

"Where are you going? We've only now arrived."

"It has grown late. If I stay out with you after dark, the Black Robe will surely learn of it, and you will be looking for me again at the whipping post." She kept her tone light, but it could easily happen.

"You need only come with me to Wakulla. My people will protect you."

This again? "All except one. Your little body guard is frightful." She moved a stiff sassafras branch from her way, let it go, waited for the ensuing *smack,* and grinned.

Tall Bull grunted but didn't miss a beat. "That she is, but no matter Mink's personal likes, you are clan sisters, which makes you hers to protect."

They were clan? "Do clan sisters threaten one another?" she said on a blow, winded from scaling a mossy slab.

There came a pause before he responded. "I will speak with her, but Mink is a dutiful warrior. She would not break the nail on your little finger without my consent. Clan aside, it is her obligation to protect me, and those precious to me naturally fall under her shelter as well."

Lillian laughed at the ridiculous implication. "Now, you will say that I, the woman who looks upon the Muscogee with bitter eyes, am precious to you."

"You could become so. With time." He passed her on the path, leapt up to the next ledge, turned, and lowered his hand to her. The thick canopy and waning daylight bedimmed his face, but that haughty bearing shone through all the same.

She made her own way up. "What a storyteller you are."

At the top, he lifted a palm to stop her near him, saying nothing until she met his sober gaze. "I mean what I say. Consider it, Liana. We would make good mates for each other."

So *this* was his motive for bringing her to this place?

Flustered, she stormed past him and up the ridge, breaking branches and crumbling earth in her efforts. She took the last rock with all the dignity she could muster, considering her tender back, and set out toward the horse, scrambling for a change of subject. "Does it not wound your manhood that a *woman* is your protector?"

He came alongside her, traveling with ease, slowing his long stride to copy hers. "Why should it? Besides, Mink is no woman. She is a *war* woman, and I've felt the loss of her keenly these last days, like a hollow in my side."

A mist was creeping in through the dark labyrinth of oak. She plunged headlong through it, eyes fixed on the waiting roan. "I might say the feeling is mutual. Why not ask her?"

"Because she is a warrior." His reply was quick and hot, as though it weren't the first time he'd given it. They'd arrived at the horse, but he wasn't through. "She is…plain. And strong. Independent. I've no wish to sleep with a man, for she is that in all but breasts and-and—"

"And everything else."

A scowl overtook him, as well as whatever thought directed his blank expression to some nebulous point behind her.

She untethered the horse, smug for having distracted him from herself. "In fact, she is a woman in all but the arts of war."

"No, *you* are a woman." His tug on the reins snapped them from her. He tossed them aside and, before she could blink, got hold of her waist and the back of her neck. "Every curve of your body tells me so. Where she is hard and unbending, you are soft, delicate, in need of a man's strength." He spoke coolly, as though laying out the differences between a rifle and a musket.

So dispassionately, in fact, that he lulled the fists that throttled the fabric at his shoulders and sapped the starch from her knees.

But that thumb of his… It caressed the column of her neck. "Your skin is perfectly unblemished, not tarnished by markings and violence," he continued, stroking, hypnotizing, "and your gait is rhythmic, as a woman's should be. Mink is a warrior, but you… You are all woman."

With the casual manner of a man sampling corn mush from a spoon, he bent and tasted her. Her body jolted and produced a gasp and a distressed cry.

He released her like a red-hot stone, confusion recasting his expression, then regret.

Stumbling backward, she scrubbed her lips. "But not *your* woman."

Exhaling, he raked fingers over his forehead and into his hair, jutting his feathers to the side. "Why do you resist? Did you not say no one else will have you? You need me, Bitter Eyes. And I need reconciliation. Agree to be my wife. We will dance before the People and return to Conchita for the baby. We will teach that Spaniard he is no man to rule us."

"Have you lost your reason? Your wrongs against me and my sister are far too great to reconcile."

"I regret my actions from that time before…before…" He choked on his words, then mustered composure. "My plea beneath Grandfather's listening ear is to have my offenses undone. To have them blotted from all memory." His single driving stride brought her within range of his gusty breath. "Yours included."

She backed up, and her shoulder blades rammed the horse's haunch. The animal skittered a sidestep that opened a path of retreat.

But Tall Bull's hands were on her arms, drawing her close. "You *can* forgive me, if you wish it. Must I beg? Then I do!"

The angst contorting his features pricked Lillian's pity. For who better than she to understand the stab of remorse? Their offenses, however, were as far removed as a candle from the sun that sank fast behind him. Hers were a tongue of flame; his were a blazing, life-scorching menace she would never, *ever* forgive.

She hardened herself to his agony and reached for the tool surest to set him off her scent for good. "My sister lives," she divulged without preamble.

His countenance went slack, eyes searching hers. "Your sister… What did you say?"

"When you came for her that day, I told you the illness had taken her. It never did."

"Copper Woman is not…? But the grave I saw, freshly dug, it—"

"Her name is Adela." Lillian flat refused their Indian names. "And the grave belonged to a passing traveler. I scarcely knew him."

Brusquely, he set her away and backed off as though touching her polluted his war medicine.

Well done, she told herself, until the wrinkles of confusion above his nose redoubled into ridges of anger.

"You *deceived* me?"

Her heart lurch violently.

"Then I carried the deceit to Totka. After I swore I would do him no more harm. And he…he broke. Before my own eyes my cousin shattered and—" He reconquered the space he'd put between them, nostrils enlarged. "Why?"

Regret closed in, clogging her reasoning with dread. Knowing better than to let him smell it, she shot back her answer. "Why else? To keep them apart!"

"You used me, you miserable woman. He loved her. With a purer love than either you or I will ever know! And with the lash of your bitter tongue you struck it down! Why? Why!" His fury jostled his feathers, lifting the red one in a mocking wave, dredging up her promise to fight along with an ancient, long-suppressed rage.

It boiled out her mouth. "I have told you before, Red Stick! Yet you close your ears and continue with your unwanted advances. For his brutality, Totka Hadjo has no right to my sister! Just as you have no right to *me*. Can you not see? Your hands are bloodied with the slaughter of my people, and no matter your recent kindness, I cannot see past it!"

He sputtered, arms bent and stiff, fist a white-knuckled ball. Before she could find the good sense to scramble away, he stalked past her toward the horse, bumping her aside.

"*Now* tell me you want me," she spat, stupidly stalking him. "Tell me you will make love to me into the dawn. Tell me we can bind our lives and forget the sorrows of war!"

He spun back, halting her tirade. "Your selfishness makes my own into child's play," he ground out, "and I would sooner bind myself to a thorn bush than you."

They stood an arm's reach away, each glaring the other down with no success. But it granted time for fear to battle anger for dominance. When fear won out, it rode a wave that tore through her veins.

What had she done? Alienated an ally? Assured an enemy?

That piercing black gaze said yes, *yes*.

"S-say what you will. Let your anger run free, but consider this—you used my sister for vengeance. I used you for the same. Balance has been restored." Never was there more appropriate time to claim Creek clan law.

He snorted, eyes as cold as a brumal gale. "No, it has *not*." Reins in hand, he leapt upon the roan's back and looked on her with disdain. "But after tonight, Bitter Eyes, it will be." He wrenched the horse's head, presenting Lillian with its rump.

"What do you mean?"

He urged the animal into a trot.

"You are leaving me? Tall Bull!" She rushed after him, fear clogging her airways. "I must get back. Someone is waiting for me!"

Laughing, he drew rein. "Someone who? Do you mean the man charged with breaking you away from the Spaniard?"

"Did…Did Iron Wood tell you?"

He leaned over his thigh to put his stony eyes on her level. "I am that man," he ground out, "and I have done as he asked. Enjoy your freedom, Bitter Eyes."

"Freedom? No, you were to take me home. To Tensaw. Both of us! Marisol and I and—"

"Eh-yah!" His heels gouged the horse.

"Tall Bull," she screeched, running after him, desperation overcoming dignity. "Where are you going? Tall Bull!"

"To find a new path," he tossed over his shoulder. "A better one than you."

They were late. By a great deal.

Marcus paced the rickety porch of Bellamy's trading post two miles upriver from San Marcos. A pebble's kick away, the Wakulla coursed toward the *Gallant Lady*. Without him. If he didn't start paddling soon, he would be late as well.

"Whoever you hired wasn't worth my silver," he said. McGirth silver, actually.

"Wrong there. He's too good for it." On Marcus's next pass, Bellamy lobbed a clinking wad into his chest. "Almost forgot that."

Marcus hefted the leather pouch. "He refused it?"

"Wouldn't take a single coin. Said he owed her a debt anyway. I tell you, he'll come through." Though Bellamy sounded confident, the rapid tap of his knife's butt against a support beam said he shared Marcus's anxiety.

"That has yet to be seen." Marcus tied the bag to his belt and rubbed at kinks on the back of his neck. There was little to be done for the searing ache radiating from his spine. Maybe he should swim the river back…

"Ten minutes, then you should be on your way."

"I'm aware of that, thank you." Loose slats squeaked beneath Marcus's clomping tread, but the racket neglected to obscure the Indians' persistent drumming.

If Miss McGirth was hearing it too, she would be in a state.

Father, shelter her spirit. Free her of this place.

A rustling noise from the bushes hurried them both to the building's corner where a boar's snuffling greeted them. Aggravation mounting, Marcus scanned the clearing between the trading post and the wilds beyond, but his eyes strained uselessly against the dark.

Night under the swamp's impenetrable tree cover was always cave-black, but tonight it was oppressive, palpable. It pressed against Marcus's eyes, thickened the air, and made him uncomfortably mindful of every breath. He hadn't known they were due an eclipse. Under normal circumstances, he would appreciate its rarity, but this affair was leagues from normal.

From the store's interior, a clock chimed twice, each a stab to Marcus's tumultuous stomach and the swing of an ax to his plan. "This doesn't mean she won't make it out," he muttered to himself, resuming his patrol. Only that he would be forced to leave without knowing what became of her.

Not in the plan at all. None of it, curse that bigoted major of his!

Curse his own royal incompetence, too. He'd loused up both missions, failing on so many levels he grew dizzy contemplating them all, as well as their repercussions. Miss McGirth suffered direct consequences, and Marcus… How would he bring himself to tell a dying man his daughter was missing?

Acid climbed his throat, resisted his swallow.

And what of his martial efforts? All he had to show for this assignment was a shredded note from a suspected traitor and an unsubstantiated report that Francis had returned. The country's borderland citizens wouldn't thank him for not breaking down the sale of arms that was wreaking havoc on their lives.

Marcus's boots scraped to a halt. There *was* still time to build upon one aspect. If Bellamy was amenable…

Having stopped before the barred front door, Marcus pondered its cumbersome chain. What might be found on the other side of it? An armory? Audacious of Bellamy to bring him here where the scent of musket grease and gunpowder practically rode the wind.

He joined the man at the porch rail, clasped his hands over his tailbone, and let a minute pass before embarking. "I heard the prophet Francis is back on this side of the world. In Wakulla to be exact."

"Did you?" There was no falter in the rap of Bellamy's knife. "If that's true, he would make quite the haul for you Yanks."

"He's a slippery one to be sure, but we'll catch him eventually."

At the man's airy chuckle, Marcus frowned. "I've been curious about your profits, Mr. Bellamy. How much does a trader make off an Indian? Let's say, per musket. Are we talking shillings or sovereigns? Or perhaps…you're paid in slaves? Several are reported stolen from Georgia. The evidence leads to Florida and a crown-appointed agent to rebel Natives."

Bellamy's chummy laughter cut through the pitchy air. "What fanciful world do you live in, good man? Maybe you should read fewer books on medicine and more on history. The American Indian hasn't seen a British agent since you colonials whipped us at Yorktown. And I haven't sold a single firearm to the red man, per the treaty." Not a hint of bother reflected in his rebuttal.

Marcus might think it a mistake to believe he'd found Iron Wood, except that Miss McGirth had all but branded the man so.

"Not true by a league," Marcus continued, as flawlessly confident in accusation as Bellamy was in denial. "Unless you're engaging in wordplay? Donation *would* be more the British style. The supply of arms we came across at the Negro Fort was rather impressive. One hundred sixty-three barrels of black powder, if I remember correctly. Rather generous, you English."

Bellamy dismissed that with a snort. "A different situation entirely. That gift was pre-treaty, and need I remind you we were at war?"

Molars grating, Marcus planted his hands on the railing and focused on the burn nagging at the gap between his shoulder blades. "Not at all. I have my own personal reminders. Thirty-nine of them, to be exact."

A pause.

"The lash was it? The Royal Navy did away with it long ago and for good reason. You colonials always were barbaric."

Nice jab, but every thrust had its parry and counter, Marcus noted with a screw of his lips. "Are you certain? Because the cat was a favorite on the *HMS Scourge*; although, only those serving compulsory terms felt her bite. We *barbaric* colonials."

"Ah, so…press-ganged? And by my own navy. Hmm." The man had the decency to sound apologetic. "Bad luck, that. And now you're out for revenge."

"Revenge is for the lawless. Justice has always been my calling, and it will be had the day I track down Iron Wood."

"Iron Wood, eh?" Bellamy's silhouette affected a contemplative posture, head lowered, chin in hand. "Never heard of her. She must be a new build. Where does she make berth?" Prevaricating never came more naturally to a man, confound him!

Marcus bestowed a dry laugh. "In a clapboard trading post a couple miles up the Wakulla. Just now, she's well hidden in her mossy cove, surrounded by her fleet of Natives, but mark my words, Mr. Bellamy, she *will* sink. And I intend to be the one to rake her stern."

"Sounds like a bear of chore." Was that a grin in his voice? "You'll need an army for it, boy-o." Definitely a grin.

There came no temptation whatsoever to reciprocate. "As it would happen, I have one."

The swish and crackle of foliage spun Marcus toward the trees.

A young Indian emerged at a jog. Alone.

Marcus leapt the stairs to meet him in the barren yard, Bellamy on his heel. "Where is she? The American, Miss McGirth. Why isn't she with you?"

The brave responded in Creek.

Bellamy took over the exchange, each hasty line terser than the last. It was over before Marcus had an inkling as to what was going on, but Bellamy's concluding spew of colorful language was telling.

"Well?" Marcus demanded. "Where is she?"

Bellamy stared after the brave's retreating figure. "Miss McGirth won't be meeting us. She's…been detained."

"By whom? One of the hacienda guards?"

"No, she got out. But the baby didn't."

Marcus picked up swearing where Bellamy had left off. He stalked off several paces to find a washboard for his tongue, a halfway moderate tone, and a new plan. It took some moments, but bearing all three, he returned. "She'll be distraught. Where did he take her?"

"I'm not sure exactly." Frustration rang through Bellamy's huff. "Partway through the breakout, my man reconsidered. He's left her to find her own way."

"Find her own—? *What?* Didn't he owe her a debt or some such? Is this how he repays it! Forget that." He cut a banishing swipe. "Just tell me where he left her."

"Somewhere north of Wakulla Village. The brave didn't know or wouldn't say." His pitch dropped by several degrees. "Buck, she's alone."

"Are you telling me she's been left to fend for herself in-in *this*?" Arms wide, Marcus signaled the ebony swamp.

"Yes, *yes*, that's what I'm saying!" Bellamy groaned and held his head. "Something must have gone horribly awry. The micco is a better man than this."

Micco. Marcus knew that word. "Your inside man is a chief?" *Oh, Lord, not Tall Bull.*

"What does it matter?"

"It matters! Who is your man?"

He told you to keep me alive… Miss McGirth's fear-gouged words came back at him with a stinging wallop. *…isn't through with me yet.*

She'd warned him. And hadn't Tall Bull warned him too? With that slant-eyed threat?

Mimicking pre-battle upsurge, Marcus's heart crashed against his ribs in a flurry of hectic blows.

"What do you plan to do with that?" Bellamy barked the question, pointing. "Put it away."

A glance down found Justice in Marcus's tight fist, her steel a trembling dull gray. It should disturb him that he didn't remember drawing or that he didn't care to sheath or that his muscles swelled in readiness. If it did, he was too inflamed to notice.

"Find your head, Doc." Bellamy stalked past. "Come on. You've got a tide to catch, and I should inform Lieutenant Prieto, so we—"

Marcus snagged his arm and jerked him back. "Who is your man!"

"Blazes, but you chafe a fellow's every nerve!" Bellamy ripped away. "Tall Bull. Satisfied?"

The name was a thrust to the belly, and Marcus had no parry. He clutched his stomach in a defensive maneuver, but he'd already been struck through. Yet not more than she, a nervous creature abandoned in the black, impervious woods with her phobia invading even the air she breathed.

And Marcus? He was worthless to her. Worthless! *God, what are You doing!*

"Little good it'll do you to know the name." Bellamy kept on toward the dugout, spouting excuses as he went. "He's only ever been reliable. I'm certain there's a reasonable explanation for this."

"Reasonable," Marcus scoffed, traipsing after. His boots hit water and sank in the grassy mire, giving him added justification to stomp and storm. They traveled along the bank toward the moored dugout. "Do you find it *reasonable* to put a woman into the care of a man she's terrified of? A true friend would know better!"

Even Marcus, after such short a time in her acquaintance, would never have given an Indian charge of her. Especially Tall Bull! There was sour history between them, Marcus was sure of it.

"I had no other choice!" Bellamy reached the dugout, then put his back into shoving it down the marshy bank to the water.

Unsure whether to keep to his schedule or assail the woods for sign of the brave's trail, Marcus wavered at the dugout's bow.

"He was already in place." Bellamy toiled on, grunting with each push. "Most notably, he was willing."

"Naturally, he was willing, you ox! He's willing to do a great many things for her, *to* her."

At that, Bellamy's spine snapped erect. "Folderol! You don't know him. He's a decent human being. He would never—"

"Oh, this is rich, this witless denial of yours. If you'd taken your eyes off Pretty Wolf for three seconds, you would've seen! The little I witnessed at dinner was plenty to know him by. He was practically salivating. Spinning his web, waiting to get the tasty little fly to himself. Where is she, you wonder? Curled into a ball somewhere in this swamp, shriveled and dying inside. Because your *reliable* chief has sucked the life out of her and tossed her aside without a care!"

"Denial?" Bellamy shot back. "Perhaps it is because I refuse to believe so lowly of him!" He fell back into his work, growling through the effort. "Give me a hand, or we'll never shove off. And why are you still coddling that bedeviled sword!" He tacked on a few more descriptors, these aimed at Marcus. "This is only a crimp in the line. I'll straighten it out."

Boots shuffling in sandy muck, Marcus cast an ardent gaze at the opening in the trees. Logic said blazing a trail to Wakulla would get him nothing but a deserter's noose. Justice brooked a contrary argument, but her rationale couldn't be trusted. Not where Miss McGirth was concerned.

Marcus looked to Bellamy. Back bowed, the man strove to launch the cumbersome vessel alone, still swearing in that grating British quality of his. He might be blind and naive, but he cared. That much was evident in his battle against the sand, in his fiery endeavor to set this right. The craft slipped into the water, and he leapt aboard, jetting the opposite end straight out of the water. Before it slapped back down, he was already in possession of a paddle.

Marcus lifted his eyes to the ruddy moon, now at its peak. The tide. It wouldn't wait. Neither would Bellamy. He sloshed to catch up, seized hold of the dugout's lip, and leaned to put his face in Bellamy's. "Swear to me you'll not rest until you find her."

"I do. Then I'll set her on the path toward home. Mari too. Exactly as planned. I swear it!" Though his eyes were expressionless holes, his solemn timbre conveyed the gravity of his vow.

Myriad doubts plagued, the foremost being the don's imminent return, but trust was Marcus's only true choice. With a lowering of his head that felt more of defeat than humility, he placed Lillian in proper hands.

Justice would happen in the Father's time.

Muscles flexing to hold the dugout in place, he brought his gaze back to Bellamy's shadowy face. "Then I owe you my gratitude."

"She's a friend in dire need. You owe me nothing." He clapped a hand to Marcus's shoulder. "Hear now, mate, either let go or get in. Upon my soul, you're one to try a man!"

Surprised by the smile strumming at his lips, Marcus climbed over him. He exchanged Justice for a paddle and dug into the flow. Once he'd fallen in line with Bellamy's brisk strokes, he raised his voice above the current. "Succeed in getting her home, and at trial, I'll stand witness and speak to your good character."

Rhythm stalling, Bellamy curved back. "What trial would that be?"

"The one where Iron Wood is held accountable for instigating war with the United States." And he would be. No matter Maxwell Bellamy's generous heart.

In the gloom, Bellamy's hearty laughter was a beam of light. "My good man, you have a deal."

Chapter 12

"Tall Bull!" Lillian stamped her foot at the chief's shrinking form. "May your carcass rot on a hangman's noose for leaving me here!" Fists curled at her sides, she watched him disappear into the trees.

An enraged growl shredded her throat, and when it ended, silence and hopelessness enveloped her. The temptation was strong to crumple, but there was no time. The sun was setting, Marcus would be waiting soon, Marisol was leagues away, and Lillian was stuck in the middle of nowhere with only a knife for protection.

Three miles, the distance to San Marcos. She could do this.

Propelled by anger, she gained her bearings and oriented her furious stride to the spring's southward flow. It would guide her.

A half-hour's traipse along a barely discernible trail crushed that idea and nearly did her in. Refusing to give Totka the satisfaction of dissolving into a puddle of tears, she beat her way along the spring's perimeter.

Totka? She'd meant Tall Bull, but what difference did it make? The cousins hated her equally; although, it was Totka who was forever harrying her to mop her eyes.

Night swept in, blinding her, slowing her pace. Heartsick over missing the rendezvous, she shifted her goal to getting back in time to tidy the study before Diego returned. She hadn't cared before when she'd believed she would be long gone by the time he saw it. Now?

Beating through a sticky shrub, she prayed, "This would be an appropriate time for a miracle, God." Did He perform those for weak-kneed doxies?

No, Diego was going to carve her up and serve her to his men.

A drumbeat began to throb through the woods. The Wakulla Red Sticks. Fear scrambled over her flesh, and her aching feet stuck to the path, refusing another step.

Breath hastening, she schooled her frantic mind. "They're not a threat," she susurrated, then repeated it with more confidence.

The beat was strong. They couldn't be far. Might she see the village from where she was? Gripping a tree branch, she edged closer to the embankment and leaned out over the five-foot drop to the water to better see through the foliage. The river was broad before her and shallow, colliding noisily with whatever obstacles lay beneath the surface and shimmering with the moon's lustrous glow.

"Stunning," she murmured.

Almost as stunning as Tall Bull's proposal and prompt abandonment. Hindsight was a heel to the gut. If she'd known *he* was the man to get her out and her great escape would take her only as far as Wakulla Village, she would have considered it. Life as Tall Bull's wife might be preferable to life as the Spaniard's mistress. The absurd quandary made her cackle aloud.

And Marcus, what would he think of this debacle of an escape? A paragon of sensitivity, he never would have paired her with Tall Bull. When she failed to show, he'd be baffled and anxious, as he'd been when he came upon her in the study. He would sail ignorant of her whereabouts, or— Her stomach plunged. Would he defy orders and stay to find her? If he did, Major Ainsworth was zealous enough to hunt him down and string him up from the yardarm. *God, drag him onto the ship if need be!*

For the next hour, the village drums were her guiding light. There was no telling what the Red Stick sentries would do, where they would take her, how long she'd be detained. But the village butted up to the river and going around would add miles.

As expected, the lookouts stopped her. She carried herself with as much poise as she could muster in her ratty slippers and half-soaked gown, but she'd gotten not three words out before Water Moccasin appeared. Solemnly, he escorted her along the deserted bank and past the sentries on the other side.

When they were alone, he left her with a few words. "Do not despair your choice, sweet doe. It was right. You are Beaver, but your future is not with us. Return with courage to the Spaniard. Show him you are not made of grass but of flint."

His challenge raised her spirits and her pace until a black rim formed on the perfect circle of the moon.

The eclipse. She'd forgotten.

It gradually thickened until the world turned dark as soot and obliterated the path. She pressed close against a cypress cone, hugging her knees for warmth as the forest creatures muted their calls. The eerie silence that flooded the forest made way for the incessant pulse floating downriver. Time loitered along, the Natives droned a spine-clenching beat, and the eclipse devoured the night.

At its darkest, the moon came awash in deep, rusty tones redolent of dried blood. An awful dread poured through her, prompting a desperate prayer. During it, there came a premonition, a warning to brace for the worst, but she shook it off, speaking into the unmoving blackness, "You're a coward, Lillian McGirth. Startling at every shadow at every bend!"

The worst was Fort Mims and watching her sister drown in her own blood. That level of atrocity couldn't happen twice to one woman. Even so, her fear persisted. It drove her out of her mind and back onto the trail, rushing headlong through brush that tore her clothes and skin and had her crying for Marisol.

To perdition with the study! She needed her sunshine.

What seemed hours later, torchlight and voices filtered through the thickets.

Señorita…! Señorita Liana…!

Her heart leapt then raced her all the way to Teniente Prieto where she tumbled into his open arms.

"There, there." He stroked her tangles. "You cannot imagine my relief. I have men scouring the country looking for you. *El inglés* the same." The Englishman, Max. "We feared for you!"

And their own hides, to be sure.

With grimy fingers, she whisked tears from her cheeks, at a loss for even a scrap of composure. "I followed the river down from the springs."

"The springs! That's no less than six kilometers of wilderness. No surprise you look as you do."

"When is Diego due back?"

"Midmorning, and by the time he walks through those gates, I want no evidence of this terrible night left on you." He wrapped an arm around her shoulders and guided her to a horse. "Within the hour, you will be bathed and in bed. There's little can be done for the scratches, but I will send up salves with Suni."

When Lillian entered La Conchita, the widow's fierce embrace surprised her. "With each book I straightened in the study, I prayed the salvajes would not roast you for their supper, and look! My prayer is answered. But you are a mud pit! *Arriba.* To the washtub."

Servants carried out her orders, and soon, Lillian was fed, scrubbed clean, and tucked into bed next to Marisol. The baby was warm and smelled of comfort. She soothed away Lillian's worry and made her feel quite the child for having imagined evil in the darksome wood.

Dawn was kissing the windows when Lillian finally closed her eyes.

Noise from the plaza woke her. Still hazy with unmet sleep, she sat up. The place Marisol had occupied was empty and cold, but Lillian heard the baby below, greeting her father with squeals of delight. Diego's voice carried up and invaded the room, its edgy timbre one she recognized all too well.

Groaning with dismay and a dozen aches, she swung her damaged feet over the bed.

Barb stepped into the room, a decanter in one hand, a glass in the other. "I guessed you was awake. That bed's the squeakiest there be. Brought ya some wine to calm those nerves. You gonna need it." Barb's hands trembled as she filled the glass.

"That angry, is he?"

"Oh, you could call it that, but little Mari, she doin' her best to work her magic on 'im." She stood near and watched as Lillian put it to her lips.

"It's soured." Lillian scrunched her nose and tried to give it back.

"I added some a Suni's brew to it, the one she make from herbs."

"Her calming tincture?"

"That's the one. You drink it gone, now. Don't want you flyin' off the handle and getting yo'self in more trouble than what you already is."

Genuinely worried now, she followed her friend's advice.

"Good girl." Barb took the empty glass and picked up the brush. "This mane of yours is wild. Shouldn't have slept on it wet. Let me see what I can do."

With the wine warm in her belly, Lillian let herself be led to the vanity where she sat for Barb's ministrations. Weighted with fatigue, she slumped, elbow on the tabletop, cheek in hand. "I haven't gotten my sleep out."

"It'll be a couple days 'fore you do. That was a mighty long walk. Couldn't have done it myself. I'm proud of ya, Missy Lillian." She hugged Lillian from behind and smiled at her in the mirror. "Just you remember that."

Lillian smiled back, humming a long exhale. Contentment washed over her. Barb's reflection swirled, and Lillian snorted a giggle. "Barb, I think you gave me too much tincture."

"I know." Barb kissed her cheek and spoke softly in her ear. "I's sorry, missy. He made me." When she stepped away, Diego's form filled the mirror's frame.

Lillian startled and whirled to face him, erupting in laughter. "Your hats grow taller every day. Soon, your height will match your ego."

A miasma bloomed over her mind, muffling his reply. "The Americanos, what did you give them?"

She took the brush from Barb, pulled a lock of hair to the front, and indolently swept the bristles down its length. "What are you talking about?"

He nabbed the brush. "I heard what you've done! My eye never leaves this place."

"The Diablo is omniscient after all." Were her words slurring?

Warmth sufficed her in a crashing wave. The lazy serenity she'd enjoyed vanished, replaced by confusion and wariness. She leaned away from his smirk.

"Facetious to the very end."

The very end? She turned back to the vanity, touching her forehead and the sweat dampening it. The tincture. Or was it something more? "I feel ill. Leave. I want to rest."

Hands clamping onto her shoulders, he slanted over her. "Tell me what you gave them."

Her brain scrambled for traction. Gave what to whom? What had he been talking about? "Yes, yes. Right. Marcus." She blundered back into English.

Following Diego's vaulting brow, she pressed on in Castilian. "*Nada.* Nothing. Tall Bull found me searching your records and…" She blinked long and hard. "He took it away."

"Maybe the Indio was worth the trouble after all. I told him to take part of his pay out of you, but I hear you sent him off and came home to me instead." He pulled the body of her hair over one shoulder and laid a warm mouth on her bared neck. "I am flattered."

A metallic taste coated her tongue. Something was dreadfully wrong. She closed blurry eyes and shoved her fingers against his face, pushing him off. "Where is Mari?"

He straightened and stepped away. "How much did you give her? She should be out by now."

"What you told me, señor." Barb's voice was weak. Or was Lillian's hearing growing dim? "Half the vial."

Lillian's lids sprang open. "You poisoned me?" And used Barb to do it. With a curse hot on her tongue, she swiveled and hurled her perfume bottle at him.

The shattering glass and splashing liquid echoed through her sluggish head. Its powerful scent revived her in time to see Diego catch her around the shoulders.

"I should've let you fall, you spiteful minx." The ceiling moved above her as he carried her across the room, the hilt of his sword prodding her back.

"I always thought it would be your blade that killed me." Her head sagged onto the pillow. Above, the canopy gyrated.

"Why does everyone always assume the worst of me, eh?" He flopped her legs onto the mattress. It undulated as he settled down beside her, his hip hugging hers.

"Because you are the diablo...remember?" She tried for a brash glower but knew she missed the mark.

He gave her cheek a set of placating pats. "Liana, I think I might actually miss you. But crush you? Never. Death is a long way off," he said, bending down and taking her by the jaw. "Kiss me, bonita. I am leaving."

"Well, go and be quick." She jabbed the heel of her hand into his shoulder.

He held firm. "Is that what you truly want?" His suave features filled her vision. "Spanish Florida is all but done for. The Americanos left in the night, but they will be back. By the time they return, Marisol and I should be halfway to *España*."

España... He couldn't mean...

Her brain churned with the drug, struggling to order the facts. When they finally fell into place, the truth impaled her like a toro completing a charge.

"No...no, no!" She lurched to rise, but he nudged her back down. "Mari!" she screamed, scanning for Barb who was nowhere to be seen. "Barb, bring me my baby!"

"It is no use to resist." He pinned her with maddeningly little effort and brushed his mouth against hers. "Shhh… Sleep. Let the tonic do its work. And when you wake, consider La Conchita your home. That is, until the Americanos arrive. Then…" He pressed in for a deeper kiss. "*Buenas suerte*, maja." Good luck.

Desperate, teetering on the edge of oblivion, she flung an arm around him and hung on, bowing up to meet his mouth and return the kiss with gusto. He responded as he always had, with abandon, thoughtless of all else.

Including her hand, which slipped down her leg to retrieve her knife.

Begging God for clarity and strength, she fumbled the blade clear of her clothing, gathered her remaining wits, and drove it into his side.

His shout raged in her ear a mere beat before he hauled back and smacked her, accomplishing in an instant what the opiate had failed to do.

Lillian climbed out of slumber to a damp, earthy scent and the endless *scritch-scritch* of a quill nib. She lay blanketless on her back, body chilled and mouth hot. One cold, dead arm dangled off whatever narrow bed supported her. Eyes opening, she worked her tongue over thirsty lips and blinked into the night. Above, barely visible in the flicker of a weak candle, was the underside of a palm-thatched roof. There was one building in San Marcos with such a roof: the friary.

The next beat of her heart brought with it the memory of steel grinding against bone.

Diego!

Had she killed the mongrel? Injured him severely enough to keep him in Florida? She could only pray she had. Whatever the case, he'd been coherent enough—angry enough—to banish her to the friary.

Her gaze honed in on the sound of writing, and not surprisingly, encountered Fray Emilio in the opposite corner, hunched over a desk placed before the room's single window. The candle melting into the tabletop shed a glow over the man, glimmering against his greasy forehead and in the gray of his day-old scruff.

She pushed up with her good arm and, wincing, massaged the tingles out of the other.

The room was small, and she occupied its sole bed. On the ground at its feet sat a stack of her belongings. A spare gown, her mother's Bible, her volume of Santa Teresa's writings, and her rosary bracelet. Either she wasn't staying long, or Barb hadn't been allowed to pack her much. Lillian would hold to the former.

Above the simple headboard hung a wooden cross crudely constructed with twine lashings. On the same wall, a row of pegs held a lantern, a bucket, and a black habit. To her right, a soldado drooped in a chair by the door. Arms crossed, chin on chest, he snored lightly. Then there was Fray Emilio, his trestle table, his neat tower of books, and his repulsive presence.

Lillian's lumbering rise thumped the bed's frame against the wall.

The soldado jumped to attention, but the friar wrote on without a pause.

"I trust you slept well." Fray Emilio bathed his quill's tip in ink and pointed its feathered end at the vacant chair beside him. "Sit. We'll speak of what concerns you."

"I don't want to talk. I want to leave." She needed to find Marisol. No more than half a day could have passed, and the wound she'd inflicted would have at least slowed Diego down.

"Not yet, hija."

"Now." She went to the door and addressed the guard. "Cabo Martín, no? I will thank you to open the door."

"My orders are to hold you here until Fray Emilio says you may leave."

"Whose orders?"

"Don Diego's, señorita."

"I failed to kill him then." It was hard to tell which was more upsetting. The fact she hadn't killed him or her sorrow at the realization of the same.

"Your soul thanks your inept hand," Fray Emilio said.

"Is he at least suffering?"

"He is in pain enough. Does that make you happy?"

"If it keeps him bedridden at La Conchita, yes."

"Then brace for disappointment. His barque sailed an hour ago. He took the child."

"He…he…what?" Her arm flailed, reaching for support and finding nothing. "No, you are the father of wickedness, and I don't believe you!"

"Then take it from Cabo Martín."

She cast pleading eyes on the soldado. "Tell me it isn't true."

"*Lo siento*, señorita. I'm sorry. The ship unfurled her sails with the tide."

Lillian's heart spasmed. It fired off a rush of beats, then seemed to stop altogether. Hands pressed to her breastbone, she sucked air in short, repetitive draws. "Gone? My baby is…gone?" Her voice was a mere squeak.

"Consider the blessings." The friar stood and stroked the rosary looped through his white-cord cincture. "The don is a good father, and Mari has her nurse, *la negrita*."

"The blessings?" Anger sparked and in the next instant became an igneous blast. "The blessings! There is not one good thing can be said of Diego López. Not one! Consider the blessings," she spat, snatching her rosary bracelet off the end of the bed. "What about *me*! How could you allow a baby to be stolen from her own mother?" The beads left her fingers in a flash of rage so acute, they hit the friar square in the face, snapping and scattering in two dozen directions.

She reached next for the saint's memories. "You are a perverse man, Emilio Sanchez!"

"*Basta!* Enough!" Cabo Martín swiped for her, but she was little and quick and dodged him, hurling the book in the same move.

It missed the friar and smashed through the glass behind him. With a shriek and a full set of bared fingernails, she went after the man herself, determined to claw out his eyes. One for each beating he'd inflicted. And for Marisol, she would feed the ants his severed tongue.

Hate billowed so thick and powerful, she saw nothing but the friar's broken body, bloodied by her own hands. It propelled her forward, but her momentum was cut short by the cabo's purchase on the back of her gown. It ripped, and cold air slapped her sweaty skin.

Lillian launched herself again, but Cabo Martín's arm whipped about her waist, latching her down. "You are a horrid, despicable man!" Arms stretched toward the friar, she struggled against her captor, praying for one moment of freedom, just one, in which to dispatch the fraud to Satan's abode where he surely belonged.

The cabo clapped a hand to her forehead and tugged her straining body back against him. "Señorita! This is not how it's done! To attack God's holy servant is to invite His wrath."

"Coward!" She jammed her heel against his shin. "It is my wrath he should fear. Let me have him!"

"For what it is worth." The friar nursed the red spot on his forehead. "I advised the don against returning to court with a misbegotten child, but he was resolved to it."

She forced a mocking laugh. "Satan's stooge absolves himself." Another wrench nearly freed her, but the cabo was catching on. "Not a thing you say has an ounce of worth."

"Be *still*." Cabo Martín grunted.

"His Lordship was in possession of a letter," the friar went on, "that, after perusing, I found to be indisputable. The king's own seal has legitimized the girl as Don Diego's offspring, and his letters patent has made her his heiress."

The shocking statement sapped the life out of Lillian's fight. She went limp, her ribs digging into the cabo's forearm. "He legitimized her? Is that…allowed?" And if so, what did that mean for Marisol, for Lillian? She wanted to feel hopeful, grateful. But dread of the unknown was stronger.

"He is the king. He can do whatever he pleases. Especially for the right price." He shrugged and used a book to begin sweeping glass into a pile on the desktop. "It would seem your daughter is now a titled lady. La Doncella Maria del Sol López Ybarra. And one day, upon her father's death, viscountess of Apalachee. You should be proud."

Lillian's head began a slow, untrusting shake. A child's name always included its mother's surname. Where was McGirth in that title? Nowhere. "And what of *my* name? Was it on the document? Lillian McGirth. Was it written there? Why Ybarra?"

"Not yours, no, and Ybarra comes from la Doña Sofía, naturally. Baseborn or not, the child needs a mother. A proper one." He looked back at her, glass tinkling beneath the sweep of his book, the semi-smile climbing his face a vile creation. "What a muddle you have made of things." At last, the black-robed bane spoke a word of truth.

Hadn't she said as much herself just the previous night? Lillian was exceedingly talented at muddles.

And now Mari was gone, *gone*! Not only had Diego stolen her, he'd legally written her out of Lillian's life. There was no going back from a king's seal.

As pain scored a cavern into her heart, the friar, wearing a smile meant to assuage, dumped glass into a bin. "After consideration, I've chosen to support His Lordship's decision. It is in the girl's best interest to be reared at court under the watchful eye of His Catholic Majesty. And you, my iniquitous child, may return to your father to begin life afresh, as Christ would intend—pure and free of the encumbrance and shame of sin. After your proscribed mortification, of course." The bin he deposited on the stone hearth landed with the finality of a judge's gavel.

"Mortification? From what?"

"Why, attempted murder." He covered himself with a hasty sign of the cross. "Was the deed so slight in your eyes that you have already dispatched it from your conscience?"

"My child was just ripped from arms! I don't care what comes of me!"

"You should. Don Diego most graciously chose not to press the case, so long as you repent and follow reparation through the Holy Church and Her Sacraments. You may choose to forgo it. But that would require I hand you over to Capitán Luengo to be tried and sentenced per the law, which, as you know, would break his gentle heart. On the other hand, *I* am always willing to help bring a stray lamb back into the fold."

Willing and eager. He, his pietistic *question*, and his bloody rod.

And wasn't Lillian the perfect lamb, vulnerable in her weakness, defenseless in her sins with not a man to come to her defense?

"Does the capitán know where I am?" How was it Lillian had been left in the friar's custody for so many hours? Hadn't Max promised to help her? And why was Toño never there for her when she needed him?

"You were brought in discretely under cover of dark. No one is coming to your rescue this time, save for Christ and the redemptive power of his mercy should He choose to extend it."

Should He choose…

Invariably, He turned his holy back. This time, He'd taken Mari with him. Was Lillian so debauched that God believed her child to be better off with…*Diego*? Or perhaps it was a display of his mercy that He provided Mari a valid name, one she could hold her head up to. A gift, really.

But the cost, the cost!

It pounded Lillian's heart and jellified her bones. With her cry of agony, her legs wobbled. Cabo Martín let her wilt to her knees in supplicant's posture.

Diego had won. Fray Emilio, too. He had her at last, flat on her face beneath his sanctimonious sandal. There was no telling what he would require of her, but did it matter? She'd lost everything anyway.

Nose in the dirt, she dug into her hair and gagged on grief.

"*Muy bien*, very good," the friar said. "I believe she is ready for confession. Set her there, if you will."

Cabo Martín hauled Lillian to her feet and dropped her into the chair the friar indicated. He turned when a scratching sound came at the door.

"See who it is," the friar instructed.

The soldado unlatched the door and peered through a two-inch gap. "It is a woman. *India*. She has food."

"Let her in."

The cabo admitted a short woman accompanied by the sweet scent of corn pone. Her face was indistinguishable in the dim light, and her form was lost beneath the wolf fur mantel that draped her shoulders and reached her knees. Her hair was knotted at the base of her head in the fashion of married women, and she was stooped with ailment, carrying the bread before her like an offering. "*Pan*. Bread from clan Beaver."

Sunflower? Hope lightened Lillian's heart and feet. She rose and stepped toward the Indian. Had Beaver come for her? The shadows were too deep to see much, not that she would recognize her clan mother if she saw her.

"It smells delicious," the friar said. "Cabo Martín, give her a coin."

Grumbling, the soldado stuck two fingers into the tiny pocket on his jacket front. The silver piece he withdrew caught Lillian's eye, but the woman, muttering thanks, was bowed deep and couldn't have seen.

Cabo Martín neared, shaking the coin before him. "Here. Take it."

She came up fast, bringing her knee with her, burying it in the man's groin with a sickening *thump*.

He doubled, clutching himself, mouth gaped in a soundless cry.

A tomahawk was suddenly in her hand, the butt of its handle being laid against the cabo's temple. He went down like a side of beef slapped onto a butcher's table.

The woman pivoted to Lillian and the friar, sending her mantle arching wide. In that flash of a glimpse, Lillian saw the woman wore nothing but a breechcloth, a strip of binding about a naked torso, and a belt sagging with the weight of weapons.

"Mink." The name eked from Lillian's gnarling throat.

On a growl, the friar cursed God, Florida, and every Indian in it. He grabbed the nearest chair, swung, and released it on the woman.

Nimbly, she ducked. It crashed into the unconscious soldado behind her. Before it came to rest, she was charging the friar, backing him frantically into the table, over the top of it, against the fractured window pane. Horror warbled his sagging jowls as well as the cry that fled his mouth.

In a single leap, she landed one foot on the table, one on Fray Emilio's rotund belly. The books toppled, snuffing the candle. Darkness shrouded the scene but not the sound of a beating or the terror-stricken wails that accompanied it.

Lillian startled with each blow, and with each, she shrank farther into the blackest corner of the room. By the fourth, the friar was silent, leaving space in the air for Lillian's own whimper.

She clamped her tongue between her teeth and her hand over the accelerating breath that betrayed her location. As if the warrior wouldn't find her anyway.

Alarm shot through Lillian's body, charging her blood. Hadn't Fierce Mink warned her about hurting Tall Bull? Well, the deed was done, and now the crazy Red Stick woman would follow through on her promise.

The softest of thuds followed the woman's silhouette as it sprang off the table. She stood before the window, framed by moonlight, her pose alert.

Lillian's hand flew to her throat, squeezing it to trap her breath within.

"If you make me come for you, I will be angry."

Air burst from Lillian's lungs in a crazed laugh. "And what was *that*? Love's sweet embrace?" she replied in Muskogee.

"That? Nothing. The restoring of balance." She stalked forward at a measured, deliberate pace. "Holy men are not above clan law."

Ah yes, clan. This insane woman was a clan sister. Blessings did indeed abound, Lillian thought wryly.

"I do not understand you, Bitter Eyes. Most would be glad to see vengeance exacted. The Black Robe's debt to Beaver has been settled. Four blows were returned for the four he gave." The dull surface of her tomahawk caught a few beams from the window, giving Lillian an unnecessary reminder of the woman's power. "Why do you cower? Come. You leave now."

"*Rvpvketv*? With you?"

Her laugh was dry as a pipe chamber. "If you hope for Tall Bull, you will be here until Grandfather next veils himself."

That went without saying.

"You are unpredictable," Lillian said. "How do I know you will not harm me? I've not forgotten your threat."

Three full, noisy breaths passed before she responded, more subdued. "Even sisters quarrel. I am sworn to preserve your life, but I would rather you finish it out in Tensaw. I will take you." As far from Tall Bull as possible, no doubt.

Hope flickered in the stygian recesses of Lillian's heart, but she could no longer consider the luxury of going home. "My child is headed the opposite direction. It is *her* I want." Her voice cracked miserably.

Mink's breath came out in a long, flagging stream. She crouched to Lillian's level, the outline of her body relaxing. "I admit, the Spaniard has dealt you a cruel blow," she said, her tone softened, "but you cannot strike back while shrinking in the dark. And Beaver *always* retaliates. Together."

She laid a firm hand on Lillian's shoulder in a gesture of support that was just shy of manly. "I will get you as far as the Gadsden fort. There, you will find allies to help your search. Surely, you will. Whatever the case, you will be a free woman, able to do as you wish. While you're away, the People will be vigilant. Should your child be brought back, we will claim her, for she is our child, as well." Mink's voice came ablaze. "So, take my hand, Sister, get on your feet, and show me the strength of women."

The wind bit at Lillian's throat. To block it, she pinched Mink's fur robe closed and crouched to follow the woman under the shelter of a magnolia. Its low branches and broad, stiff leaves created an interior hollow that provided a screen around the tree's base. It smelled of earth and decaying plant matter, security, and rest.

Might Marcus be inside? For six interminable days, she'd longed for him almost as much as she had her child. How she needed him!

"Look there." Mink used her bow to point through a gap in the foliage.

Fort Gadsden was planted on a distant bluff, its pickets strong and bold in their star-shaped pattern, its flag a proud wave of heartwarming colors—a sight so welcome it doubled the moisture in Lillian's eyes. She opened wide to dry them before Mink noticed, but the warrior's focus was elsewhere.

Mink redirected the bow's tip to the horizon where several blue-coated soldiers stood in foolish contrast to the autumnal shrubs behind them. They were a mere shout away.

She turned back to Lillian and held out a water gourd. "From here, you go alone." As Tall Bull's right-hand warrior, the woman would be a valuable prize.

"I understand." Weary, Lillian propped her backside against the magnolia's trunk and accepted the gourd. "Maddo." She wet her throat and passed it back.

With her forearm, Mink swiped a dribble of water from her chin, corked the gourd, and flung the strap over her head and across tightly bound breasts. "Walk out slowly and stop. Wait to be noticed. I did not bring you so great a distance to have a skittish bluecoat blow a hole through you."

"Yes, Mink." Lillian thanked God again for the warrior who, over the last six days, had orchestrated Lillian's every move. Her own mind was too numb for anything beyond breathing, chewing, and planting one foot before the next.

Mink had challenged her to be strong, and so she had been. The steely war woman, who never indulged in emotions, made it attainable, and Lillian was proud to say she'd remained dry-eyed since they'd left San Marcos. It helped that every step in this rugged land required her full attention. But tears or not, Marisol was always at the forefront of her mind, the questions unceasing.

Had Diego's vessel made it to the open ocean yet? Was the baby seasick? Would she forget Lillian? Would Lillian ever find her; would she survive the crippling ache in her chest?

She staunched the incessant flow. "I will wait to move out until a good while after you have left." To give Mink time to put distance between herself and the soldiers.

Lillian untied the wolf pelt and gave it back with a grateful smile. Mink had insisted she wear it, despite Lillian being more warmly clothed.

The woman had turned out to be exactly as Tall Bull had declared her — a loyal protector. When it came to comforts, she'd put Lillian first every time. First to eat, first to bathe, first to bed down. In dangers, Mink had forged ahead, allowing Lillian to follow only when the way was secure.

It hadn't taken long for Lillian to appreciate then admire her. And now that their paths were splitting, she realized it saddened her to think she might never know what became of her clan sister.

"What about *you*?" Already cold, Lillian rubbed her arms. "Where do you go from here?" Did Mink understand she meant more than the path home?

"To my lodge and…" She lowered her head, kicked a brown leaf with her moccasined toe.

"To Tall Bull."

Her gaze whipped to Lillian and went hard. "To my chief." In one fluid motion, she flung the cloak about her and spun away to survey their surroundings.

The correction was clear, but Lillian wasn't deceived. She knew a woman in love when she saw one; the soft-eyed far away expressions, the subtle curve of the lips, the absentminded twirl of the hair at her nape. War women, Lillian was intrigued to note, were no different. Not even one who'd been labeled a man in all ways but one.

But Tall Bull had said more than that.

"He said he misses you." Lillian approached and laid a tentative hand on Mink's back. "Keenly."

Mink shifted away, giving a little snort of disbelief. "Aloud? I cannot believe it."

"Yes, aloud. I have yet to read a man's mind." Lillian smirked and invaded the woman's space again, bumping shoulders with her. "*Cunning* and *brave* were two other words he used to describe you. After these days under your care, I agree."

Mink shrugged it off. "Every warrior he keeps near is cunning and brave. He will not have them any other way."

"But I wager not every warrior's absence creates a hollow inside him. Also his words."

Mink's evasive glance wasn't quick enough to hide the mixture of hope and pain tightening her features. "Why are you telling me this?"

"Because I owe you a great debt, and the only gift I have is to offer encouragement. Maybe in time he will come to see—" YOLO

"Time!" Her voice broke, followed by another downward swoop of her gaze. A beat later, it sailed back up, firmer than when it sank. "The People are being crushed. The world is closing in on us. Time is fast running short, Bitter Eyes."

Perhaps, but it hadn't yet. Not for Mink.

Careless of the woman's prickles, Lillian gripped her arm. "Then hurry home to him! Cherish every moment no matter the form it takes, for we never know which will be the last."

Marisol's darling face, fringed by abundant, wispy hair, filled Lillian's mind and wrested her heart. If she'd known what their last moments would be, she wouldn't have wasted a wink in sleep.

After a silent beat, Mink squeezed Lillian's hand, removed it, and hooked the sack she carried over the bend of Lillian's elbow. Mama's Bible. Mink had carried it every step of every mile.

Her farewell smile was grim. Three steps away, she paused and swung her gaze back around. Indecision wrote lines in the space between her eyebrows as magnolia leaves moved in the wind *tap-tapping* against one another. At length, she spoke. "Go straight to Tensaw. Do not linger."

Lillian tensed, mashed the book-shaped sack to her chest. "Why? What schemes are the Red Sticks hatching?"

"No questions. Just do as I say." Chagrin wrinkling her forehead,

Mink looked farther on through the branches to the fort. It teemed with men, cannons, power. Security.

But security could be false. Mr. Mims' stockade had been the frontier's most lauded and secure. But it didn't take much to bring a stronghold down—a simple mistake by one in power, a shrewd strategy by the enemy, and five hellish hours.

"Very well. I will leave as soon as—" Lillian looked back and found herself the hollow's sole occupant. "Mink?" She rushed to the opposite side and peeked through the leaf cover, but the forest behind her was barren.

Loneliness was a cold pool, closing over her head, as well as the sudden, unwelcome need to take over directing the course of her life.

Then she thought of Marcus, and her spirits kindled to life. There was a chance their paths would cross here. A teary smile blossomed but dissolved at the recollection of Mink's warning.

If Marcus was here, she would see to it he didn't stay long.

Chapter 13

Big Winter Month (December)

"Do you *have* to pull it, doc?" Private Petit rubbed his swollen jaw and whined like a three-year-old at bath time. He'd been on the examination table fifteen minutes and counting. For a tooth.

The line of needy patients stretched through Fort Gadsden's medical marquee and out into the yard, and Marcus had only himself to make them well. Whatever patience he'd brought into the clinic that morning had evaporated around minute seven of Private Petit's visit.

He pinched the bridge of his nose, wishing he were instead tending to little Marisol and her feisty mother. For three seconds, Marcus escaped Fort Gadsden by letting his mind fill with their lovely images. Soon, it skittered off, frightened away not by Private Petit's bellyaching but by Marcus's own guilt and the inescapable agony in his chest. He pulled a breath through his constricting throat and was treated once again to the specter of Miss McGirth's voice.

Sometimes my heart swells so full of love that it pains me to breathe. Have you ever felt such a thing, Doctor?

Why, yes, miss. Unfortunately, I have, he would say, if ever she were to ask again.

As he had innumerable times over the last days, he shoved her aside and dug deep for bedside manner. "There's always a choice,

Private. You can either give me the tooth now, or come see me later when that festering root turns your brain green. My personal preference would be to wait. Putting you six feet under has *got* to be easier than dealing with the namby-pamby ruckus you're raising now."

The *Gallant Lady* had anchored in Apalachicola Bay the previous day. The fort hadn't had a surgeon in five weeks, so Marcus put himself to work sorting through a line of hangnails and headaches to find patients in more serious need of attention. Unfortunately, Private Petit qualified.

"Since you put it that way..." The private's mouth opened a fraction.

"Open wider. Wider. And if you bite me again, I won't be blamed for extracting the wrong one." He shoved the dental key between Petit's chattering teeth.

"Surgeon! Captain Buck!" His name was shouted from across the parade ground.

Marcus ignored it, having hooked the key over the rotten tooth. "Hold there. Hold, I say!"

Another man stepped up. A seaman, pale and trembling with fever. The grippe was hard at work in the camp. Little to be done for the miserable fellow. "Want me to hold him?"

"That won't be necessary. Get off your feet before you pass out." Marcus used the distraction to turn the key.

"Aaah-aaaah!" Under the instrument's pressure, the tooth broke and split away, leaving a nub.

Invectives took a spin inside the seal of Marcus's lips. "Spit," he ordered, exchanging the dental key for his pliers.

Head between his knees, the soldier gagged and drooled and swore with such alacrity even the seaman winced.

"Captain Buck, I've got one you're gonna want to see right away." The same voice was at his back now.

"Wait." He pushed the private into an upright position and rapped his jaw with the tool's tip. "Let's give it another go."

Eyes watering, the private shook his head. His wide-eyed gaze shifted beyond Marcus, and forthwith, he tipped his head back and dropped his jaw, offering a beautiful view of the offense.

"That's more like it." Ten seconds and two tugs later, he held up the remainder of the smelly, black molar and wrinkled his nose. "Congratulations, Private Petit. You hold the title of most difficult patient of the year. Quite an achievement considering it's the fourth of December."

"Thank you, sir." The soldier shoved a wad of gauze into the cavity, stood, and performed a sloppy bow. "Good morning, miss."

"Same to you, Private."

Marcus pivoted and promptly lost his breath, his speech, the hold on his jaw.

He'd done it. Bellamy had gotten her out. He'd sworn to it, but Marcus, who'd fixated on being God's solution, hadn't let himself believe. There had been too many obstacles, too little faith.

Yet there she stood, just out of reach. Alive, well. Stunning in her roseate, wind-chapped cheeks. As poised as ever but more lovely than the image he'd faithfully revisited. He was pleased to discard the old for the new, and as his eyes fed, his tongue staggered. "Miss... What are—? How...?"

"Hello, Doctor," she supplied and bred a smile that was both reserved and stirringly beautiful.

"You two acquainted?" asked her escort.

"Something of that nature," Marcus said, incapable of taking his eyes from hers.

"Ain't every day we pull a lady from the swamp."

She didn't look like she'd been pulled from anywhere, much less the wetlands. There was a scrap of something in her loose hair, a bruise on her cheek, a shallow scratch on her bare forearm, which, he noted, was covered in chill bumps.

"The swamp, was it?" Marcus worked the buttons on his coatee.

"Yessiree. Found her myself. In case you don't recollect, this here is Miss Lillian McGirth. She's running from the Spanish." So much for anonymity. "Lieutenant Fanning said she comes to you first, the colonel after."

Marcus wrangled the last arm from his jacket and flung it around her.

"Thank you." She shuddered. Helping snug it around her throat, she brushed his knuckles and with a look, passed him a thousand words.

It said she'd missed him, perhaps more than he did her, if that were possible. It said she remembered: his pain, her own, their private engagement in the orchard, and the devotion she'd laid in his palm. And it said one other thing. Something…disturbing.

That *something* set in motion a reflex he harnessed an instant before destroying that hateful twelve-inch abyss separating them. Resolved against impetuous behavior, he increased the gap.

"The doc'll want you on the table, miss," Petit mumbled around the gauze, arm extended. "I'm happy to help you up. Name's Petit, Clive Pe—"

Marcus backhanded his shoulder. "That's enough of your impertinence. Get your cap and move out. All of you. I want the tent cleared! Go on," he said to the groans of those waiting to be seen. "The lady needs privacy, so out with you."

Including her protesting escort, Marcus herded them all out, closing the tent flap behind the last. Almost timidly, he turned back to her, holding himself with restraint, a hundred queries pecking at the backs of his clenching teeth. Arms straight at his sides, he took up a mantra inside his head. *You will not fly to her like a besotted youth. You will not hold her, you will not, you will not…*

Hands clasped at chest level, she held his sight. Long silent seconds passed as Marcus put things in order—God's directive, his desires, her needs—and over the course of them, her composure began to slide.

Lip slipping between her teeth, her frame contracted as though straining to hold itself together. Breath increasing its clip, she blinked rapidly through widening eyes. Or was it the welling of tears that made them so large? "I thought it prudent to use my real name. Only the guilty hide." She sucked her lip again, bumping a tiny shrug.

He nodded, withholding a grimace and wondering if Ainsworth were bruiting his opinion of her at every stop along the Gulf. He'd certainly filled the *Gallant Lady* with it, and now, half his men were at Gadsden. It wouldn't be long before her reputation found her.

Her fingers began a nervous twist, and her arms… They were empty.

Dread wrenched Marcus's gut. "Where is Marisol?"

Shaking her head, she took a quick step toward him, but stopped, lids falling shut. "She's, she's…" Her voice was unusually tight.

His body twitched, an attempt to go to her. He gave it no leave, repeated his mantra.

"Diego, he-he left for Spain." Her chest lurched with a sharp intake. "With Mari. Marcus, she's gone."

Tears cascaded over her lower lashes, but she remained perfectly erect. Not a sob, not a whimper. Just gorgeous, heartrending dignity. It wasn't until she was coming toward him, obliterating his mantra beneath her rushing feet, that he realized his arms were open.

All decorum lost, she plowed into him and encircled his chest with her arms. Fingers digging into the shoulders of his shirt, she riveted to him as though he were hers and it were her right to hold him, demand comfort of him, soak his clothes with her grief.

And wasn't he? Her guardian, her doctor. Her future, if God willed. The man who'd failed her, left her to the vacant mercies of three belligerent nations. But God's mercy had been greater, praise His bountiful name.

And then, there was Marisol… Why, why the baby?

Marcus laid his cheek atop her head and let her cry. The half-healed cut under his eye smarted. An insufficient sacrifice. He should have stayed, fought on, deprived López of life, or laid down his own. Mari was worth it, and this grief her mother suffered… The Spaniard's blade may as well have skewered him, for he felt the pain of it from sternum to spine.

His arms constricted about her before he remembered her

contusions, but she made no show of pain. She was quiet, amazingly so, considering the sobs wracking her. But she felt good. Fuller, healthier.

He rubbed a gentle circle into her back, marveling at how she fitted to him, like a long-lost puzzle piece locking into place. How different this was from their embrace in the grove.

That one had been stilted, reserved; but this… This was *right*. As though God had built Marcus, body and spirit, for this precise moment. So she could empty herself into him and, in so doing, fill those dusty, desolate crevices inside him. He could stand there till day's end and not breathe a word of complaint, but minutes were ticking past, and the line of sick waiting a few yards off wasn't growing any shorter.

Setting aside myriad questions and worries, he homed in on the one nearest her heart. "We'll find her," he said, hating the empty ring in his promise.

She leaned back, reliance peering through her wet lashes.

Good glory, she moved him.

Fingers burying themselves in her hair, he yielded a fraction of his resolve and took her damp face between his hands. "If it takes a year, if it takes a lifetime, we'll find her, and we'll bring her home." His grip tightened with determination. He put the same into his eyes and voice and directed both straight down at her. "We *will*, Miss McGirth. Depend on it."

Slowly, the tiniest of hopes awakened and eased the rigidity in her shoulders. She worked an arm so she might underline the slit of his wound with a cool fingertip. Whatever cord bound her ribs snapped free, allowing her a deep draw of air. She released it through moist lips that begged for more than a caress of his eyes.

For two beats of his heart, he pondered it, told himself she would find his mouth's warmth a comfort, instead of the shameless pilfering it would be. Then, she lifted ever so slightly on her toes, chin mirroring the move, and his blood went hot. It throbbed in his neck, bending it downward against his better judgment.

Her tongue swiped her lips. She wanted this as much as he, and the awareness turned his better judgment into none at all. There was only her and that tempting mouth. Him, and his mindless desire.

Retaining enough sense to give her time to flee—or slap him—he hovered an inch from the mark. Their breath mingled, a frosty white cloud between them, and still, she didn't retreat. No, she came in search of him. Softly, tentatively. As sensually as ever he'd imagined she might. She rose on her toes, brushed lip with lip, then ebbed, as though to test her footing. Only, she knew exactly where she treaded, and it snatched his breath, turned his belly to stone, and blasted his restraint to dust.

At the next rise, he seized her lips. Sank into their heat, consumed the groan rolling from her throat, and delved for more. He hauled her against him, aggravated at his bulky coat, at the very air for standing between them.

"Captain Buck? Doc?" The seaman spoke from outside.

Marcus froze, blown and spent with far too little to show for it, and he was still within aching reach of her mouth. He considered its plump lower rim, the shimmer left there, and the pleasure it would be to clean up. "I asked for privacy."

"But Colonel Stoneham's here, sir."

Marcus jolted, blinked into her startled face. He put a breath of space between them and swallowed hard.

"Is the patient ready for an interview, Captain?" The colonel.

She's your patient, idiot! His ward. The one he'd pledged to send home untouched. But wasn't she more? His ally, his friend? The woman whose child he longed to father? Indeed, she was all these things, but what she would *not* be was his lover. A list of men had misused her. He would not be counted among them. Pledge or no.

"Another minute, sir, if you will." Expanding the space between his body and hers, he said in undertones, "Forgive me, miss. I've overstepped." And all it had taken was one moment of weakness. One!

"No, I wanted—"

"Yes." He applied shushing fingers. "I have." Although he wasn't daft enough to promise he wouldn't do it again.

Hurt refreshed the damp in her eyes, but she kissed his fingertips anyway.

Savoring it, he curled a fist and slanted a sad smile. "A man can take only so much before he stumbles."

An adorable crease marred her forehead. "It was my doing, and you would've stopped. I trust you."

Trust him? Whatever her definition of the word, it did not balance with his own, and he would be wise to remember it. Grudgingly, he released her. "Come in, sir."

Ears full of the river, Marcus kicked hard, hauling air to sprint the last fifty-yard stretch to the shore. At last, Fort Gadsden looked down on him from its lofty bluff, its harsh black angles imposing against the predawn sky. His feet hit the silty river bottom, toes crimping with a spasm.

He'd overexerted himself. Strain did that to a man, drove him to recklessness. But the exercise had pumped tension from him like noxious water from a bilge. He forced weight on the screaming arch of his foot and rose from the water. It streamed over and down him and back into the frigid current.

Just ahead, where the soggy ground turned to grass, Miss McGirth sat hunched into herself, heels pulled to her thighs, arms wrapped around her knees.

Alarm straightened his frame and sharpened his senses. No woman should go unaccompanied in this wilderness where beasts and Indians lurked, and even his own soldiers weren't wholly trustworthy. A thorough scan told Marcus the area was clear. He relaxed and decided to take this as a windfall.

They'd had not one private moment since those he'd stolen in the marquee yesterday morning. As it did every time, the recollection of those few minutes goaded his blood and burned his chest—four parallel grooves directly over his heart.

With the taste of her lips, she had done something to him, something disquieting and bewitchingly delightful. With the orange trees looking on, she'd climbed inside him, taken up residence, but yesterday, in their brief connection, she'd put down roots and entwined them so firmly with his, he wasn't sure he could keep that blunder-pocked vow alive for one more day. But his word to McGirth wasn't wholly ruined. He could renew it, be the gentleman he was reared to be. He could.

He cut an agitated hand across the water's surface and prayed she hadn't figured him out. It wouldn't do for her to know he was so on edge he'd woken two hours before dawn to wear himself out on the Apalachicola, so he wouldn't be tempted to do the same on her. Because, God deliver them both, Marcus knew like he did the signs of a malignancy that, with the slightest encouragement on his part, she would let him.

Thankful the dark obscured his naked back, he trudged up the gently sloping shore. Elsewhere, the bank was a sheer wall of mud and tree roots, unreachable behind thick patches of cane and cypress knees. He should run to them, seek shelter in the maze of their stalks. Instead, he wriggled into his shirt and lowered himself beside her, his trousers sopping and clingy. "Couldn't sleep?"

"When I woke, you weren't there." *And I needed you* — the unspoken remainder of the simple statement.

He understood it. Shared it. But whereas his need stemmed from love — yes, love — hers was grounded in fear. Carrying it in her eyes, she shadowed him everywhere. Through sick call, through the mess line, to his evening debrief and morning revelry. To the river to wash soiled basins, the latrine to dump sloshing bedpans, the kettle to boil tools and rags. And her cot, too far away for his own liking, had been erected in the medical tent three feet from his own.

Her constant presence wasn't an inconvenience. Not in the least. She was welcome company, working as a tireless, steadfast assistant, and the men responded well to her. But her emotional state wasn't a healthy one. Additionally, it was deteriorating.

He'd risen earlier than usual for his morning swim, to get it in before she woke, but it hadn't made any difference. Since arriving, she hadn't relaxed a moment, perking to every odd sound, scanning the pickets and the trees beyond.

For warring Natives.

Colonel Stoneham had listened to her warning, doubled the guard, and told her she was slated to take the next transport out. Marcus had lobbied, nigh pleaded, to accompany her, stating that her mental stability depended on his presence. Since his assignment to Gadsden had always been temporary duty—a cover to get him through San Marcos—the colonel had relented, and good thing because Marcus was done, finished, beyond through letting other men do his job.

She removed the blanket from around her shoulders and tossed it over his head. "You'd make a good Indian. They're crazy enough to swim year round too. But you're tempting death."

The blanket held her heat and her scent, and he smiled into the wool. "Death by swimming." He scrubbed at his dripping hair. "A great way to go."

"You like it that much?"

"It clears my mind, and exercise is good for the heart. Work makes almost anything stronger." He dug through his pile of clothes for his coatee and held it open before her.

She accepted, slipping her arms into the sleeves. "Maybe I should work more."

"You work plenty hard, miss, and you're stronger than you know." He gathered her loose hair to free it from the jacket. Before releasing, he encountered debris lodged in the tresses. She must have been lying down while she waited for him. Good. Maybe she'd caught a little more sleep.

"Did you know you're toting grass?" He picked it out and repositioned himself for a more thorough search. "With your leave, I'll check for more."

"Please do, but I warn you"—she canted her head back at him, voice uneven—"I don't feel strong. Not at all." The breathy admission was a clear deviation from the topic's initial route.

Halting mid-rake, he counseled himself to back off but dug deeper. The task wasn't one he'd expected to find on the day's docket, but it would unequivocally be the most pleasurable. He wasn't about to relinquish it.

"Contrary to a recent performance, I *can* behave." He tugged at a strand. "Tip this way, and I'll get the other side."

She did, smoothly rolling her neck and pouring her hair over his arms, a grave menace to his willpower. It was inviting, thick and heavy with wave enough to create snags and trap bits of this and that. He worked methodically, beginning at the roots and moving down the entire length of her back where the edges curled around her waist.

"I've always been weak. My child is living proof. Precious though she is," she said, deftly returning to their earlier thread. "I'm a poor example of restraint. Just you remember that, Marcus Buck. I'm no good around men. Or for them."

He grinned into her dark, silken depths, having no doubt she was dead wrong. Marcus wouldn't deny it—there was weakness in her. Even so, he couldn't bring himself to hold it against her. Especially not after that speech Barb had given him. And the lady had been mighty good for him.

It could also be argued he was no good for *her*. Barb averred Miss McGirth had sworn off unlicensed intimacy, yet the looks she gave him… Either Barb was mistaken, or Miss McGirth lost her footing in his presence. All the more, he should keep his.

"Maybe one day I'll grow into the woman my mother prayed I'd be. Like my sister. Maybe… If I survive the upcoming assault." There was a tease in her tone, but he skipped past it to address the worry at its center.

"Yesterday's scouts saw no sign of Indian activity within five miles of the fort. Not so much as a toe print. You're safe here."

"I've heard that before."

Unable to argue the point, he worked his fingers under a gnarl, massaging her scalp in the process, and felt her rigidity give way.

Through a sigh, she leaned back on her elbows and looked up at the waning moon, hair cascading and pooling on his thighs, heating him from the inside out. "What did you think of that eclipse?"

"Not much. My mind was elsewhere." On her. "I would like to have appreciated it though. It won't come around again for a while." He ditched his grooming efforts and simply indulged in the feel of her, combing and stroking and praying God's strength into his weakness.

"Twenty years, Mink said." She twisted back to look at him, resting a hand on his knee, driving him to the precipice. "Did you see it turn red?"

"Hmm?" was all he managed.

"It was…disturbing. As if it were a-a premonition, an omen of…evil." She went hoarse. "I can't shake it. Then Mari was taken, and Mink all but said the Red Sticks are on the rise."

Abruptly, she sat forward. Her hair corded through his fingers and fell against her back in a curtain. Tension vibrated the air around her as her posture hardened. She tossed her head, chin angled high, and sniffed. "He legitimized Marisol. Gave her a title of nobility."

Marcus cocked his head, struggling to keep up. "He who? López?"

"Yes, that wretch." She dabbed at her nose with the backs of her fingers.

"Can he do that?"

"No, but King Ferdinand can. And he did. The title is all well and good, except that it comes with a new mother. Diego's wife."

The shocking facts, laid out so precisely, so succinctly, obstructed all thought. Marcus opened his mouth, then closed the useless thing. What did one say to such news? He moved forward so that he sat beside her, knees lifted and splayed, elbows crooked around them.

"They literally wrote me right out of my own child's life. Even if we find her, Marcus, it'll be nearly impossible to get her back."

Legitimized nobility. That changed everything. Absconding with the child would call down wrath from the Spanish royal court. The political ramifications were immense.

"You saw proof of this?" he asked. "Documentation of some sort?"

"No, but…"

"Who told you?"

"The friar."

Ah ha. "And you take his word at face value, the man who beats women?"

"I take your meaning, but it *is* consistent with Diego's behavior. His honor and good name are everything to him. He wouldn't dare enter Spain without the king's blessing on her."

Marcus exhaled his frustration. "And you know for certain he left for Spain?"

A tart, pithy laugh shook her before she buried her face in her hands and mumbled despondently, "She could be in her cradle at La Conchita for all I know."

"Chin up, duchess. This moping doesn't become you." He tilted sideways into her until she looked up and gave a meager nod. "Besides, he hasn't routed us yet. We're fighters, and we have more help on our side than you'd think."

"How so?"

A breeze galloped in off the water, and chills gripped him. The damp blanket was little help, but he wrapped it more tightly about him anyway. "Florida's surrounding waters will be treacherous for a man wanted by the U.S., and there's a good stretch of it to navigate before reaching the open Atlantic. Our outlying frigates are in good number, and they're on alert. The don's name is one of a number we've been watching."

"That's fine news. Very fine indeed." Tone lightening, she straightened and nodded again, this time more emphatically.

"What's better, he's likely aware of it. Is there no other place he might've gone? Some hideaway closer to San Marcos where he might weather the storm?" He shivered and laid a hand on her shoulder. "Think on that. If I don't get into something dry, I'll be the next one down with the grippe." And the sky was lightening.

Achy with cold, he collected his things, found a discrete thicket, and came back to her clothed and with Justice tapping faithfully at his leg.

She'd moved to stand at the water's rippling edge, looking tiny and defenseless inside his jacket.

Securing his hands behind him, he drew alongside her. "Come up with anything?"

"There's Tallahassee Village, but I don't think he has much there apart from a trade partnership with the chiefs. He has a place in St. Augustine though. I've never been, so I can't speak to it, except to say it's in the city center."

"Not good for a man looking to disappear. Ambassador Reynolds would pick him off in a heartbeat."

"*El Retiro* is a possibility, but Mississippi is vying for statehood. I can't see that he'd go deeper into American territory."

Marcus pulled thumb and forefinger down his rough jaw. "That's what he'd want us to think. Where is this…retiro?"

"Pass Christian. It's a smaller plantation house. Family-owned. Leftovers from Spanish rule in the nineties. But it's isolated. About a mile inland."

It sounded ideal, a retreat Marcus himself might use. A smile nudged his mouth. "We'll try there first."

"Do you really think it's a possibility?" She fronted him, head oblique, voice winsome and trusting, and he became irritated at the sluggish sun for denying him a clear view of that exquisite face.

His eyes craved her. As did his mouth. And no denying it—the rest of him did too. But the faith she placed in him was sobering. It was a fragile gift meant to be cherished and treated delicately. Like a glass box whose integrity would be spoiled by a single hairline fracture.

He offered a shallow bow to disguise the backward trek of his heels. "I do."

Lillian squinted to better decipher Marcus's expression, but he was all grays and blacks and ermine-white teeth. Regardless, she cleaved to his certainty, for she *certainly* had none of her own. Not about Mari's location or going home. Even less about their upcoming two-day voyage upriver.

Her heart was another matter. It knew exactly what it wanted. As did her mouth. She sucked her lower lip. The kiss had been decadent and far too short.

One touch, one tender word would suffice, she'd told herself when she'd laid eyes on him. He'd given her both, but they hadn't come within a mile of her need.

Tacking the sail, she'd harnessed the wind and lured the unfortunate man into behaving against his principles. To selfishly soothe her ache. Expecting his usual prim indifference, she'd been astonished when he'd descended like a hawk and answered her question in full. He most certainly did want her.

Not for a lifetime, no. For an hour. Time enough to fill a baser need and destroy his noble soul. If not for the last, she would give him his hour and any others he requested and in so doing, patch her hurt. The man made her forget every contrite minute at the altar. His mouth outdid any calming tonic he could have given her, but he was too wise to fall prey to the eddy of lust that had dragged her down time and again.

He'd kissed her and true to his character, taken the blame and reestablished boundaries. She stood by her trust.

"Either way, we must rule it out," he said, stretching his arms forward and back, voice tight in that now-familiar way she'd come to believe signaled pain. What hurt him? "A voyage to Spain is our very last resort."

She liked that he used words such as *we* and *our*. It made her feel not so alone, but the truth? As soon as he left Tensaw to fulfill army obligations, she *would* be alone.

Papa would back her. He would sell the plantation to find one of his girls. He nearly had to find her. But if Marcus's prognosis was correct, Papa didn't have much longer.

Tear-bitten, she swung her eyes back to the river. For one blink, it wasn't the Apalachicola but the Mobile, and she wasn't a woman grown but a girl, fishing with Papa, poles forgotten, gazes fastened to the treetops in anticipation of the sun's first splashes of gold.

Soon, there would be no sanctuary from grief.

When that awful day came, the plantation would go to Charlie. With Adela in Kossati, Lillian would probably manage the place until her little brother reached his majority. Fifteen years was a long time for such responsibility. It would require wisdom, competence, and a level head. She couldn't bury the family in debt or disappear for half a year on a perilous journey to Spain. All that, assuming their usual associates would even conduct business with Zachariah McGirth's prodigal.

Overwhelmed, she loaded her lungs with air and clung to it.

"One day at a time, miss." Marcus settled a light hand on the back of her shoulder, and her heart knocked insistently, reminding her of its demand.

Him, it said. *Him*.

She shushed the noisome thing, so she could hear him speak.

"There's worry enough in the trip up the Apalachicola to keep us plenty busy."

Though they didn't set out for another few days, the first leg of their overland trip to Tensaw was the flatboat ride to Fort Scott. The stockade had been erected on the border of Georgia and Spanish Florida to give the army easy access to insurgents, and according to Marcus, it was tightly secure, if remote.

"Are you sure you're comfortable venturing inland?" he asked.

The next ship to Mobile wasn't due for another two weeks. The Mobile Road via Fort Scott, however, would have her home in half that time, and if she had to stay in Gadsden one day more than necessary, she might lose her mind.

Mink's warning was vibrant and fresh, and Lillian had already risked too much by ignoring it this long. Not that she'd had a choice.

"This place is a target," she recited, "and I'd sooner slit my own throat than become trapped in another doomed fort." A tremor joggled her. "Besides, I won't risk running into Major Ainsworth. If there is anything to be said of that man, it would not be that he is one to extend the benefit of the doubt."

Marcus audibly exhaled and said nothing. There was risk no matter the route they took. It was tragic that she had to choose which was more dangerous, the Red Sticks or her own government.

"Two days on the river, another in Scott, then the Mobile Road. You're practically home." As though anticipating the day he left her, his hand dropped off, leaving a cold spot on her back.

Disdaining his attempt at disengagement, she turned into him and hugged his arm with both of hers. "I miss you already."

He kept silent, but she felt a shift in him. A softening. An agreeing.

And she knew he would speak if he were not loyally attached to propriety. Whatever else he might think of her—and there was no telling, apart from his glaring attraction—he *would* miss her. They were friends, after all. Having come to that conclusion, she laid her head against the bulge of his arm and let a smile mold her lips.

Together, they watched the first streaks of pink highlight the uppermost needles of a thousand trees and spray the expanse above with God's glory.

"Will you write to me?" she said.

"What is this write nonsense you speak of?" A grin spread his cheeks. "I've accrued a good bit of leave and have only to get it approved. I should have thirty days coming to me."

"That's wonderful." She lifted delighted eyes to him.

Meeting them, he fervidly told her what his mouth would not and pulled her against his side. "It is, duchess, and I intend to spend every one of them with you. Hunting for Mari."

Chapter 14

"Holdin up, Sergeant?" Bracing against the sway of the flat-bottom boat, Lillian leaned over Sergeant Horne's prostrate form and brushed sweaty hair off his forehead.

One of thirteen suffering from the outbreak of influenza, Sergeant Horne lay amidships atop a pod of crates. Above him rose the single mast whose square sails bulged with effort. Despite the icy wind coursing over the vessel, the soldier perspired heavily. "I reckon I'll live," he said through clacking teeth.

She smiled down at him and pressed her cold hand against his cheek; it blazed. "I reckon you will." After she helped him sip from his canteen, she laid his head back down and tucked the blanket tight about him. "You enjoy this fine, lazy day and let us do all the work getting you to post. That's an order now, young man."

"Yes, ma'am." He worked up a shaky smile, splitting chapped lips.

Dabbing the spot of blood with her kerchief, she lifted searching eyes, needy of a glimpse of Marcus. At the stern, he held an experienced stance on the Durham's pitching deck, legs spread, hands clasped at his rear.

His mouth twitched, lids constricted. That nagging pain. His back, he'd said when she'd ask. An old wound. After sharing that, he'd shut down so swiftly, she hadn't ventured for more. Whatever Englishman had inflicted that wound, she hated him for perpetually antagonizing her darling Marcus.

Captain Fanning faced him, hand on the sweep, keeping them on course. Neither looked at the other but at the thick wall of vegetation passing along on both sides of the Apalachicola.

As though sensing her, Marcus swiveled his head. His studious expression found her and, with the small upturn of his lips, lost its edge. She held it, wondered at its message. There had been many such silent exchanges, each more soulful than the last. For her part, she was memorizing every angle and divot of his face.

The chiseled nose. The thin upper lip and the lower one that made up for it. The hair that fell in clusters over his forehead and always looked as though he'd just come from a swim. Usually, because he just had. And the breadth of him…

A sudden rush of blood scalded Lillian's veins. Her depraved mind suffered the same at the rush of imagery she enjoyed too much to quash. Only God knew what was going through the good doctor's head. They'd hardly had a moment to speak since boarding the vessel yesterday morning.

Last night's stay at Mr. Hambly's plantation on Spanish Bluff had held promise of an evening stroll through the herb garden. Marcus had suggested it himself, but dinner had gone late, the officers and their host had retired to Madeira and cigars, and the ladies had cajoled Lillian into a game of euchre that had taken them deep into the ten o'clock hour.

At a quarter to eleven, Elizabeth Lane and Rose Blackburn, wives of officers stationed at Fort Scott and Lillian's travel companions, had yawned and turned in. And still, the men hadn't emerged.

Lillian had sat alone in the parlor at the empty card table, shuffling the deck until it was pliable and warm. All the while, the men's heated dialog penetrated the closed door in muffled, rumbling waves. Disturbed, she'd retired to her room and, arms aching for Marisol, had cried herself to sleep. She hadn't seen Marcus until she'd boarded the vessel before sunrise. He'd been as he was now, a fixture upon the deck, his pose stately and commanding. Midstride, her foot had adhered to the gunwale's walking board where it happened to be the moment she caught sight of him.

"My, my. What a view he creates," Mrs. Lane had murmured, passing her up and tacking on a wink.

Lillian hadn't given a rat's tail that she'd been found out. By Mrs. Lane or by the man himself, who'd lavished her with a smile gorgeous enough to arrest the heart and obliterate last night's breach — and any others he might happen to make between then and eternity.

Fingers combing into her hair, she recalled the intimacy they'd found under the Gadsden moon and longed like an addict for his touch.

His mouth angled, cheek jutting up. Was he remembering too?

Her pulse skipped toward him, and her body quaked with hunger, then sighed in reluctant resignation. Half a boat's length away was simply a half a boat's length too far.

Thirty days of leave, he'd said. For Mari's sake of course. When he returned to duty, she would need to undergo a purging to rid her system of him. Her community's disdainful welcome would help in that regard. Meanwhile, she pined for him like a love-sick girl.

Love… It was a daunting word, unwieldy in her grasp, but she couldn't find another more suited to the condition of her heart. Until she found one, it would have to do.

"Your turn, Miss McGirth. Give us your best story." Private Petit's speech was still garbled due to the knot swelling half his face — ravages of the infection Marcus had predicted. Cradling his jaw in his palm, he slumped in the center of the five benches traversing the stern.

They'd entertained themselves yesterday swapping stories, but Lillian's were in highest demand, and she was happy to accommodate. Whatever made the unfortunate lads a little less miserable. Their lot in the army was a poor one. Remote assignments always were. And these had Red Sticks to contend with.

The boat dipped, and Lillian skipped to rectify her stance. She backed up to the nearest crate and deposited her haunches on its splintery planks. "Hmm… Which would you like to hear? The snake in the privy, or…let me think…the angry mama gator in the dugout."

"The snake," Corporal Horne said from behind, voice weak.

Private Petit scoffed. "Nah, that's boring. Everybody has a snake in the latrine story."

"Watch your manners, young man." Mrs. Lane poked the back of Private Petit's shoulder with the butt of a rifle she wouldn't relinquish.

"Aren't you from Tensaw?" the private asked Lillian, ignoring the matron's admonition. "I bet you could fill a book with tales of Injun raids."

Lillian's insides flipped. Why, yes. Yes, she could. She could fill the day's remaining hours with the telling of a day in history she'd rather never speak of again. Feeling a rise of panic, she flicked her sight to Marcus, but body tight and eyes hard, he was conversing with Captain Fanning at close quarters. Strain rolled off him, soared over the sixteen heads between them, and infiltrated her calm, raising the fine hairs on the back of her neck.

"You want an Indian story now? Out *here*?" Mrs. Lane, face twisting with appall, hugged the weapon closer to her. "Please, anything but Indians."

Lillian quite agreed. There wasn't strength enough in her entire body to pull up those dreadful memories, but she feigned grit. "My stories would turn you inside out, Private Petit, and you're already green." Truth was, if he persisted, she might be the next one hurling over the side.

At least she'd made it out of Gadsden with her scalp still attached.

The men laughed and good-naturedly slapped at Private Petit. He shielded his inflamed jaw and beat them off, but his bravado failed to die. "Green? You kiddin' me? I was at New Orleans with Old Hickory. Faced down four British batteries. Three hours of pounding, but you didn't see me cowering. No, sir! I have stomach aplenty for whatever you got to throw at me."

"Knock it off," Sergeant Garrigus said, sitting taller, emphasizing his ample brawn. Marcus had assigned him Lillian's personal security detail, and he was taking well to his role. "Can't you see the lady don't wanna?"

"But, Sarg, I told my little brother I'd come home with at least one good Indian yarn," Private Petit crossed his arms with a forced slump. "Been in Red Stick territory comin' up on a month and haven't seen a single redskin yet. Franklin's gonna be sore let down."

"Give it time," Lillian said, burrowing through her memory stores for an anecdote to appease him. "You'll have your own yarns soon enough. But if you'd like something to write home about, you can tell Franklin you rode the Apalachicola with a member of Beaver Clan."

"You?" Admiration shone from Sergeant Garrigus's eyes.

"That's right." Warming to the safer topic, she injected strength into her volume. "I, gentleman, am adopted Creek."

Marcus turned then, breaking from whatever had him ruffled with Captain Fanning.

"How'd you manage that?" Private Petit leaned into the question, finally interested.

"During the attack on the fort, an Indian took us captive. Me, my sister, and Mama. We—"

"Wait. What fort?" Petit said. "Were you at Mims' massacre?"

"Shut up, Petit! Do you want to hear the story or not?"

"Thank you, Sergeant," Lillian said and meant it, not keen at all to veer into that bloody account. "As I was saying, we lived with him until the war's end."

"What was that like, living with a savage?" Garrigus propped his bulk on his knees.

"Savage? No, no. Not Nokose." What *was* her captor? Terrifying, yes. But only at first, when he'd been naked and decked with paint and blood. Later, he'd been... She let her mind fill with the sights and sounds of the lodge. The children's laughter. Nokose's.

"He was a good father," she said, surprised at the conviction in the statement. "A fine provider, too. Dedicated, not given to drinking. And he protected us. Even when it was a risk to his own life to do so. He was..."

Melancholy crept over her, took her to a place she'd never been. An uncomfortable one but good and healthy. It felt right to finally put the truth into words.

The men quietly waited. Even Private Petit, though his jaw ruminated. Mrs. Lane lent her a little smile and nod.

Totka was a different story, but Nokose… "He was a good man," Lillian finished, voice firm.

"Imagine that." Petit thumped a fist on his thigh. "Didn't know the heathens had it in 'em."

Lillian touched the corner of her damp eye with the tip of a pinky, gaze drawn to the trees and the wilderness that stretched in a never-ending threat beyond them. "To further protect us, he adopted us into his clan. And that, my fine friends, is how I came to be Beaver."

Nokose was no savage, but there wasn't a Red Stick within a hundred miles, save for maybe Mink, who would do the same—risk his neck for hers. Not even Tall Bull. No, to the rest, she was just another white woman invading their territory and owning a scalp pretty enough to covet. And would they stop in their battle frenzy to ask if she by chance was adopted Creek? Most assuredly not.

"Miss McGirth," Private Petit said, eyes narrowing, "you telling us you got a soft spot for the Red Sticks?"

How had he come to that conclusion? A laugh stormed her throat.

"The interrogation is over, men. Give the lady a rest." This from Marcus, who, even at fifteen feet, could soothe her with a look, a subtle lift of his mouth. Pride, compassion, affection—they were each clearly etched into his eyes and directed singly at her.

Oh, but he made it difficult for her to stay her heart!

Unabashedly, she began moving his direction, shimmying through the ranks, begging pardon, and accepting the numerous offers of assistance with the sweetest of thanks.

When she reached Marcus and lifted a hand to join him on deck, he stared at it a moment, a protest on his pursing mouth. He would refuse her? A beat before she gave up, he grasped her at the wrist. "For a minute, then I want you seated beside Sergeant Garrigus." He hauled her up the three-foot leap to the deck.

The boat's movement was more keenly felt here, so she was

grateful that he kept a light hand at her back. She turned her face into the wind and watched the eddies and foam trailing in their wake, but Marcus studied the shore.

On its western edge, a community of glossy black snakebirds sat on a limb overhanging the water, their long beaks and webbed feet a gorgeous ocher that reflected brightly in the water.

"They're stunning," she said. "Serene."

The boat mounted and dipped in the river's rising swells, setting butterflies loose in her stomach. She pressed a palm against it as a low chuckle filled her throat. "Did you feel that?"

He directed an indecipherable look down at her and fashioned a smile she didn't quite buy.

The butterflies became stinging bees. "What is it, Marcus? Is something wrong?"

Shunning her searching gaze, he dragged a hand along the back of his neck. "How do you find Sergeant Horne?"

If he wanted to shield her from worry, she would let him. "A shade worse, I'm sorry to say."

"This wind, it isn't good for him. I should've chosen Judson instead."

"You couldn't have known Horne would relapse. We did our best with what we were given." That being two hours in which to choose thirteen men from the infirmary to fill the gaps in the Durham's passenger hold. The other seventeen slots had already been filled by the last of those fit for travel.

Fort Scott had requested an immediate increase in manpower, and Gadsden had leapt to provide. It advanced their travel by a day, but Marcus had been on edge ever since, and Lillian had no desire to ask why. She trusted him. It was enough.

"Yes, we did. Our best." Though his attention remained fixed on the shoreline, he took her fingers in a discrete move, crooking them tightly. "When you leave, the men will turn surly on me. Your absence will be sharply felt."

She returned the pressure and raised a coy smile. "By them, or by you?"

It was an unfair question, seeing how it put him in an awkward place, but before she could retract it, a violent lurch nearly sent them off their feet.

Marcus snagged her by the arm and yanked her to him. He whisked them both out of the way of Captain Fanning, who was stalking past, shouting orders. "Get her into the hold, Captain Buck."

The planks beneath her feet vibrated with a series of grinding thuds; the hull was scraping bottom where the hastened current had thrust them around a bend and closer to shore.

"Carr, Higgins, Worley," Captain Fanning shouted men to attention. "To the walking board. Grab spare poles. Help the setters keep the vessel clear of the shallows. We mustn't run aground!"

Marcus shoved Lillian toward the deck's edge. "Garrigus!"

The sergeant was already on his way.

As Marcus took her under the arms to lower her, she looked past the poling soldiers to the shore they pushed against and beyond to the forest looming up a musket's reach away. A flash of red yanked her attention to the left.

Stripped and painted for battle, a warrior braced against the back side of a broad trunk, the muzzle of his raised weapon level with her chest. No, it was higher, and his black eye wasn't on her. On Marcus?

Her throat clenched tight, damming the scream that climbed it. Arms flinging protectively wide and eyes pasted to the Red Stick, she slammed herself against Marcus, knocking his chin with the back of her head and releasing a screech that curdled her own blood.

The Indian bared his teeth; they shone white against his black-and-red mask. He punched the air and shrieked a battle cry. A deafening eruption followed, swallowing the shore in flames and the white smoke of a hundred muskets.

A belting force to the ribs blew her backwards. Through the din, she distinguished Marcus's shout of alarm. As she went down, his fingers grasped, scraped, missed. There came a loud splash an instant before her back hit the deck. Her head smacked wood as it was flung over the rimless stern. Her arm followed, fingers splashing into the river.

Strangely absent of pain, she remained as she was, dangling backwards over the boat's edge, unable to move. The rush of blood in her ears drowned out all other sound.

As darkness crept in, she looked about with a peculiarly unhurried detachment and lighted upon two sights: the horde of Red Sticks pouring from the trees, storming the shallows, jaws gaped in battle cry; and the frothy draught sweeping Marcus out of view.

The current was unexpectedly fierce.

By the time Marcus oriented himself and got his head above water, he was already in the river's center and heading swiftly for the next bend. Violence assaulted his ears. It went dim as he was hauled under again.

Weighed down by boots, woolen clothes, and Justice's encumbering steel, he kicked ferociously to keep his mouth clear of the foam. Spitting water to capture precious air, he fumbled icy fingers over his jacket buttons. Having shed the coatee, he plunged headfirst into the flow, toeing his heels to free his boots.

Lighter now, he found his breath and his stride and the capacity to formulate the semblance of a prayer. God forgive him for not overriding Fanning's irrational drive to forge ahead!

Marcus never saw what had terrified Lillian, driving her backwards into him. Body acting as shield, she'd purposefully taken a ball intended for his gut, then unwittingly sent him stumbling overboard where the next wave of musket shot couldn't reach him.

The audacity of her to act the heroine and toss away her life for his! Biting off a grievous sense of failure and loss, he dug into his strokes. There was no time for guilt or anger. Only for getting back. The river had taken him too far in too short a time.

Minutes. No more than three, maybe four, had passed since the first blast.

Too long, too long!

The Natives were everywhere. In the trees, the beach, the water. Every square foot of the boat.

And Lillian was among them.

Oh, God, why? Of all people, of all places!

Battle lust built within him, heightening his senses and pumping his muscles with energy. How many would he take down before it was over? Before *he* was over? Whatever the number, he would die standing over her, defending her.

The boat lay some ten yards ahead now, beached at the bend, her mast pointing at the treetops and her deck sitting at a sharp tilt. The shallows were tinted red and coursing his direction.

Lillian, where was she!

Red Sticks still swarmed, but the war whoops were dwindling. Was there no battle?

The firepower that had lit up the forest was intense. Maybe even hot enough to take out every man—and woman—on board with a single volley. It seemed that it had. Not one American blue coat remained erect.

But the fight wasn't over. Marcus was coming. Another set of aggressive kicks increased his speed.

A woman's weak cry propelled his watch to the beach. Marching resolutely toward the cover of trees, a warrior carried a nearly senseless woman over his shoulder. Blood drained from some part of her, leaving a crimson trail in the sand.

Her full frame identified her as Mrs. Lane. Marcus's pity went out to her, but there was no helping the poor woman. Marcus wouldn't make it ten steps onto that beach.

He ripped his frenetic gaze from Mrs. Lane. Scanned the boat again. Became ensnared on Lillian's unconscious form draped over the stern, hair streaming into the water. Marcus's heart lost its rhythm, and he floundered for half a stroke. Regrouping, he consoled himself that she'd yet gone unmolested.

There was hope.

Praying the warriors would be blinded to his approach, he dove under and sprinted the last yards, coming up in the shadows of the stern directly below her. Toes grappling with the rocky bed, he held his ground and took her head in a cradled position. It was limp, and a knot was forming on its back.

With unsteady fingers, he checked her carotid pulse. It was slow but strong. Gravity held her lids at half-staff, but she saw nothing. It didn't matter. He would drag her off regardless. Rotating and rising to find a secure purchase on her arms, he came eye-to-eye with a Red Stick.

The warrior was bent over her, one hand gripping the clothes at her belly, the other, a tomahawk. His eyes expanded, cracking the red paint on his forehead. He recovered with admirable speed, employing his weapon in a lateral swing.

Retaining hold of her wrist, Marcus plunged to avoid a braining. His fingers were affixed to Justice's grip before he'd completely submerged. A shout of fury sent him back up with the blade's shiny tip aimed at the Indian.

Hers was one scalp that would *not* be taken.

The warrior dropped her and skipped sideways but earned himself a slicing cut along his ribs. It served only to infuriate him. Shrieking, he reared back for another strike when an angry roar from across the boat caught the attention of every man onboard.

Sergeant Garrigus burst from the captain's roundhouse, a swivel butted against his massive body like an oversized shotgun held at the hip. The small cannon smoked from its rounded end, but Garrigus stood unafraid, grinning like a gator in a catfish pond. "Let's give 'em fire, boys!"

The cannon's *boom* shot Garrigus backward into the air and over the gunwale. Gunshot sprayed the deck, mowing men down in its broad, bloody sweep. The blast pitched the boat, and Marcus's Red Stick took a lifeless, headlong plunge into the water, leaving a pale, pink mist in his wake.

A hasty glance across the vessel revealed a score of Indians writhing in the throes of death. Five, no six, soldiers scrambled to their feet and launched themselves overboard. They shot for the opposite shore as Garrigus floated past, facedown.

Shock dissipating, another surge of Indians splashed into the river to converge on the scene.

Marcus seized the moment, stowed Justice, and heaved against Lillian's weight, thankful for once that she was so slight of frame. When the river took her in its grasp, she woke with a start, arms going into an automatic paddling motion that quickly morphed into a fight. He clapped a hand over her mouth and slipped back under the shelter of the boat's side. "It's me! Marcus," he hissed into her ear.

Instantly, she calmed, but her breath came ragged and panicky from her nose. The current pushed her body flush against his.

A bright red stream swirled around them. His fingers went into an instinctive search of her ribcage, easily finding the tear in her gown and the mangled flesh beneath—a hand's width below her left breast, between the sixth and seventh ribs.

No blood at the mouth or nose. Stomach and lung, clear.

Had the ball lodged between her ribs then? He probed. Nothing. Too deep to feel. But a rib caved slightly under pressure.

She loosed a muffled yelp into his hand and arched away from his prodding, but it was the thudding footfalls directly overhead that halted the examination.

When they moved on, he lowered his hand from her mouth and worked to unbuckle his sword belt. "We're undiscovered for now," he whispered, mouth at the side of her head, "but we can't stay here, or we'll be found. Are you understanding me?"

She jerked a nod, all ten nails digging into his forearm. "How many...are there?"

"Enough." Hundreds. "As soon as you catch your wind, I'm shoving off."

"But I can't—!"

"Shh, Lillian, I'll carry you, and the current will carry us both." He rammed the scabbard tip-first deep into the river bottom, silently swearing to Justice he'd survive to return for her. Feeling more buoyant, he hooked one arm under each of her shoulders and bent them at the elbows. "Do nothing. No splashing, no waves. Relax. Trust me!" He faced upstream and kicked off the bed, casting them into the jet.

Eagerly, it swept them away.

They bobbed on their backs, Lillian's ear at his eye. She was behaving beautifully, making not a sound, letting her legs dangle and her arms fall to the sides. The perfect float. But her chest protruded from the water and was broadly exposed. There was only kick and pray and trust God's mercy wouldn't fail them now.

He kept careful watch on the boat and judged the distance. Ten yards and growing. Twenty, forty. And still, no shout of alarm.

Gaining confidence, he adjusted his hold to free one arm, extend it ahead, and pull in long, scooping strokes. It felt good to labor in the river. Familiar. He made quick work of the bend, and within minutes, they'd traversed it and were sailing into calmer waters. Out of sight now, but assuming Red Sticks were patrolling the length of the waterfront, he struck out for a thick stand of cane that shot up from the river's western edge some three hundred yards distant.

Miraculously, they arrived without bother. Breathing hard, Marcus took Lillian in his arms and slipped his way up a boggy incline. He stole a glimpse of her.

She was shuddering, muscles constricting, and her lips were as gray as the overcast sky. Blood continued to flow from the wound, creating a vibrant puddle in the bowl of her abdomen. The amount, though, wasn't enough to convince him of internal damage.

The knowing allowed him a snatch of optimism, but it wouldn't take much to worsen the situation. Such as that fractured rib puncturing a lung.

She muttered something incoherent, as her white-knuckled fist filled with his shirtfront.

"Stay with me. Lillian!" The order worked a grunt out of her that didn't gratify.

As he crashed through the wall of cane, woody detritus slashed at his bare feet while cane stalks swayed a good five feet overhead. They gave way to him with resounding snaps that surely carried the quarter mile back to the enemy hotbed, but once he was in far enough, there would be no tracking them. A man could lose himself in these forests.

Feet and ankles sinking into the boggy soil, he tugged hard against the suction. Surrounded by enemies with a woman bleeding in his arms, and he could barely take a step for the quagmire he'd gotten them into. Exhausted, he released a strangled cry. "God, help me!"

He needed flat, dry ground and an armload of clean bandages. He had neither. And he could see nothing but endless cane and the uppermost branches of a bald cypress visible off his starboard. He veered that way.

Like a beacon, it led him, shaken and drained and limping, in a trudging path to the brim of the canebrake and blessedly solid earth. The cypress was ancient; its massive buttresses, weathered and hoary with Spanish moss. Its front was sunken deep into the muddy river, but its rear stood proudly on firm land. Within the folds of two of its back-facing pilasters, Marcus found enough room to shelter three grown men.

Once inside, he ushered up hasty gratitude while falling to his knees, utterly spent. It jarred Lillian into full wakefulness and produced a whimper that broke him. "I'm sorry, I'm so sorry! Here." Arms shaking with exertion, he did his best to lay her out as gently as possible. "You can rest now. No more moving."

"Where are we?" She trembled violently, clawed fingers hovering over her stomach.

"Safe."

Affixing those claws to his arm, she ensnared his attention, eyes frantic. "Out here, we're never safe…from *them*."

"We are, miss. I assure you." He panted and gasped. Willing steadiness into his hands and voice, he stroked the wet hair off her forehead until she released him. "We're perfectly…hidden. Let's put you…back together, shall we?"

Taking the slight dip of her chin as response, he ripped her gown open at the wound. He did the same with her petticoats and corset. The clothes would have to go altogether soon, to regulate her dangerously algid body temperature. But first, the hemorrhaging. And that musket ball.

The entry hole was smaller than expected, indicating the ball had traveled a good distance before finding her. Less impact. He slid his hand around her ribs, fingers inquiring at her back. As suspected, no exit wound.

Not good.

He envisioned his forceps digging, ripping flesh and tissue, drowning in a river of blood he couldn't staunch.

"Marcus…" She lifted a hand, face contorting with pain. "My back, it hurts, it hurts…"

Her back? Whatever for? "I'll have a peek. Over you go." He eased her onto her undamaged side, pausing when she inhaled sharply.

She let it out slowly through a clenched jaw.

He cleared hair from her eyes. "That's right. Breathe through it. You'll be fine, just fine," he said, hating himself for what might very well be a lie.

Gritting his molars, he crushed the doubt. He would get her out of this. God will it, he would!

As gently as possible, he wrestled her waterlogged corset off her, tossed it aside, and tore a hole in the back of her gown. Long, straight bruises, faded by time, slanted across her backbone, but it was the bulge at her upper thoracic curve that snagged his eye.

Upon first inspection, it was soft and swollen, deeply purpled. When palpated more thoroughly, it revealed a hard, round center.

The ball.

But here? So high? The entry wound was a good four inches lower. The angle was all wrong.

He stared at the site long and hard until he noticed that one of the bruises along her side wasn't old. And it wasn't straight. In fact, it wasn't a bruise at all, but a trail of damaged flesh, the subcutaneous path the ball had taken as it ricocheted around her ribs to lodge against her backbone.

There would be no burrowing forceps, no exploration of her abdominal cavity.

Danger still loomed—blood loss, hypothermia, infection—but her chances of survival were improved. Excellent compared to two minutes ago.

Relief filled him so rapidly and with such force that it spilled from him in open-mouthed laughter.

Eyes half closed, Lillian cocked her head back to look at him, mouth twisting. "Saint Peter's call is no…laughing matter." The line came out weak and scratchy but with such typical brass that Marcus chortled again.

"Listen to you and your muddle-headed talk of saints and death." Still laughing, he bolstered her head with his hand, fending off the urge to kiss that smirk from her mouth.

Her next inhale robbed him the thought; every movement of her ribs had to be excruciating.

"You're just afraid…" She flinched. "I'll reach sainthood…first."

"Duchess, you've found me out." Chest filling again with laughter, he bowed over her and playfully deposited a noisy kiss under her jaw.

While there, he stumbled upon her pulse. The doctor in him lingered, lips alert and listening. Her heart was fragile but holding, its rhythm speaking to him in such wonderfully regular tones that it wiped the smile straight off his face.

"Truth is…" Her throat vibrated against him, her shaky fingers light against his temple, in his hair. "You achieved it today…premortem."

The full weight of the attack, the escape, of nearly losing her, crashed down upon him. He tipped into her, nestling her head in his elbow and pressing his face into her neck to hide the sob building in his gut. But it was no use. It wrenched him from the inside out, doubling him painfully.

"Now, now, Doctor Buck," she said, stroking his cheek with fingers far too cold to be living. "That's no way…to behave with…a patient."

Her breath came in snatches, between shivers and rattling teeth.

He lifted to look at her and allowed a self-conscious chuckle. "It isn't at all." In the next breath, he regained his bearing, but before he could pull away completely, she latched onto his collar, halting him.

Tentatively, she rotated at the shoulders, face pinching then relaxing, and looked him straight in the eye; her own, large and brown and glistening. "Probably a mistake to admit, but…whatever comes of us, of today or tomorrow… You need to know… I love you, Marcus Buck."

A mistake for sure. The distancing of Marcus's dewy eyes told her it was. Then why couldn't she feel regret?

Maybe it was the shock, the trauma to her mind and pain-wracked body. Maybe the cold had frosted her brain. Or maybe it was that childish dream of spending the rest of her life with a man like him.

Enough with the delusions. It was Marcus himself she wanted. *Him,* her heart insisted — with a clapboard cabin, a dog on the stoop, and little Mari propped on a rounded belly that had only Marcus to blame for its girth.

Delusions upon delusions. And yet, she laid her hand against his warm cheek and topped off her eyes with a love that delved unexplored reaches of her heart.

Tilting out of her caress, he produced the smile that was never far from his lips. The one that held reserve. The smile he gave to all his patients. "Such sentiment should be reserved for when one is lucid."

A little stung for the doubt and for having been left stranded with her affections, though not wholly surprised, she withdrew her hand. "I'm lucid…enough." She braced for the stab in her side and pulled in a fuller breath. It didn't disappoint. A gasp preceded her rush of words. "I'll try not to act on it, but I won't take it back either."

Embedded in his role of surgeon, he slowly released pressure on her wound to check beneath his blood-stained hand. "You might take it back" — he frowned, clearly not pleased with what he saw — "once I start knifing for that ball in your back."

The warrior's hideous streaked face rose up in her memory. "May Creator…strike them all…down," she cursed.

"And you said you were lucid." He clicked his tongue and ripped a strip of fabric from her gown, making her suddenly aware of her exposed flesh. "You know I don't understand Creek."

"I…no… Did I…?" Maybe he was right. Maybe she wasn't quite herself.

"Umm hmm. Bump on the head, remember? You're a little zany but not so far gone you can't lend a hand." He fashioned an impish smile while folding fabric into a thick square, but she was no longer in the mood to match his tease.

Details of the ambush began sifting back. The explosion, the stench of scorched powder, the crack of her skull against the boat's edge. An increasingly oppressive force, those horrifying moments weighed on her, demanded attention.

And answers. How long had she been unconscious? What happened while she was out? Blessedly, she'd seen little. A single warrior. A blur of fire. Then, Marcus.

But in between? She could well imagine.

Shivers convulsed her, wringing her so that she clenched her jaw to keep from biting her tongue. "How many died?" She touched her stomach, fingers seeking the hole that drained warmth over her pimpled skin.

He moved her hand out of the way, laid the wadding against the wound, and bore down.

A firebrand lit up her side. White flecks danced in her eyes, and the world dissolved into nothing but pain and the need to flee it. But every movement only made it worse. She glared at him over top a pursed mouth. "I take it" —she gasped—"back."

His grin was taut. "The doctor always knows best." He positioned her balled hand over the bandage. "Can you keep it there? Half a minute. Until I wrap your ribs. It'll make you feel better. Promise."

Eyes and lips crammed shut, she groaned and half listened to him ramble as he manipulated her body to wrap strips of muslin about it.

"The ball went around the track of your ribs. Wedged itself against your backbone. Didn't I say you had one? 'Stronger than you think' were my exact words, I believe. And now we know the truth of it. Your limbs are functional, I see. What about your toes? Can you move them?"

Cracking an eyelid, she scowled at him but tried anyway. She grunted a reply, not caring whether he took it for a *no* or the *yes* that it was.

"Good." He pulled, tightening the binding to secure it. "Extraction should be simple once I get hands on my bag. I'll be returning for it."

Returning? Her eyes flew open. "No! The Indians—"

"Will be long gone by then."

Her head went into a lateral wag that had to have looked as pathetically weak as it felt. "They're never…long gone." Not in these parts. Didn't he know that?

"Besides, a courier was sent by land ahead of the boat as a precaution. Troops will have already been deployed from Scott. I'll likely run into them."

Assuming the courier was still alive.

Having finished binding her, he began removing what remained of her gown, ripping her sleeve at the shoulder.

When her arms crossed modestly over her chest, he paused. "You can keep one layer. It'll dry quick enough on its own, but the rest must go. Your temperature is plummeting, and these wet clothes are no help at all. I'll scout out a few palm fronds and pine boughs. They'll do far better by way of warming you up."

She arched her back to assist in removal of a sleeve, but he coaxed her back down. "I'll do it. Until that ball is removed, I want you as still as possible."

He worked rapidly, professionally, avoiding contact with her skin and maintaining a stoic mien. Either the sight of her in a damp chemise did nothing for him, or he had the ability to winnow the man from the doctor.

She, on the other hand, waffled between a self-conscious hankering to smack him away and the desire to pull him in and steal his heat. She chose the safest route, that of trusting him, and became a ragdoll until he finished, set the scraps aside, and rose, not once having settled his eyes where he shouldn't.

"I won't be long."

Where was he going? Her mind battled to function beyond the sear of her chest. Wherever it was, it was away from her. "*Espere!*" She grabbed the wet cuff of his trousers.

Leg extended in a curtailed stride, he looked back, a question lowering his brows. "English, Lillian."

She blinked up at him. "What are you doing?"

"The pine boughs. Remember?"

Ah, yes. She nodded. That didn't mean she approved of being left alone on her half-naked back in the middle of Red Stick territory.

Icy water squeezed from his trousers, through her fingers, and over his bare foot. He had to be as cold and distraught as she, but apart from the pallor tinting his lips, he was the same self-assured, unshakeable Marcus. His resistance to cold and strain was remarkable. As was his steadfastness in the face of turmoil. It buoyed her.

"Moss." She released him and straightened the backbone he was adamant she possessed. "The Indians use Spanish moss in a pinch. To keep warm."

Wearing an approving smile, he touched his temple in a two-finger salute. "Moss it is."

Chapter 15

From the folds of the giant cypress, Marcus stood watch, leaning against a buttress that at its thickest reached shoulder height before merging with the trunk. Only his head was visible above it. Arms crossed to retain warmth, he tucked into the shaggy bark to avoid the wind. It had kicked up in the afternoon, drying his hair and disturbing the treetops. They chattered above him and disguised the rustling noises Lillian created with her shivering beneath the dead fronds.

But no afternoon breeze was strong enough to mask her whimpering. She'd controlled it admirably while awake, but when sleep claimed her, she'd begun a heart-stabbing, tearless mewling that reminded him of nothing so much as little Marisol at the fever's worst. The last hour had taught him the mother had the same effect on him as the daughter. And then some.

"Marcus," she mumbled.

His shoulders jolted, as they had every other time she'd called out for him. The first time, he'd rushed over and accidentally woken her. The second, he'd gone to her, lifted away the frond and made sure it wasn't a legitimate call. The third and fourth, he'd closed his eyes and willed her to speak any name but his.

"Marcus…" The plea ended with a tail of disjointed babblings.

He gripped his forehead, pressing fingers and thumb into his temples, and begged God for intervention. For nightfall.

The woman needed warmth and food. And a stiff serving of the laudanum in his kit. The one stored in the captain's roundhouse—unless a despoiling Red Stick had absconded with it. Marcus intended to find out as soon as darkness joined them.

The sun, though not visible through the hazy atmosphere, was at least two hours from relinquishing its control. In the meantime, he'd continue to guard against stripping out of his damp clothes and plastering his warmer body against hers.

From the moment he'd begun peeling off her layers, he'd been in a perpetual battle with propriety, professionalism, and passion. So much so that he could no longer distinguish between them.

At what point did propriety give way to necessity? Was it unprofessional of him to let a woman suffer because he was inexorably attracted to her? And what of passion? Was it his passion for healing that urged him to her side or his passion for *her*? It had all become a muddy soup in his head, made worse by the deliciously roving images he'd spent the day chasing. Sometimes, chasing away and sometimes, chasing after.

God forgive him, but she was beautiful. Every curvaceous inch of her.

She gave a frightfully violent shudder and moaned, converting his prayer into a curse directed straight at himself for his helplessness as a physician, his weakness as a man, his ineptitude as a guardian. The self-loathing might have gone on the entire evening if not for the sound of voices.

Male. Indian. Alarmingly close.

His heart slammed into his ribs, springing him into action. In seconds, he was at her back, burrowing under the foliage, hand seeking her mouth. He found it, sealed it off.

From head to foot, she lurched into consciousness. Her eyes rolled toward him, the whites prominent.

"Hush now," he whispered, "hush, hush."

Warm air gushed from her nose. It came in a long stream of relief but cut off at the next wave of dialog from the Natives. She went deathly still. Until a tremor began. It showed first in the hand that had hooked onto his. It traveled up and over her, accompanied by a chaotic breathing pattern that bordered on panic.

The voices increased in volume.

Had he not covered his tracks well enough? He wasn't a complete idiot when it came to these things, but he knew from his experience with Totka Hadjo that trained warriors had an eye for a disturbed leaf or nudged stone.

Tracks aside, Lillian herself would give them away, if she didn't get control of her anxiety.

"Shh, shh. They'll go away," Marcus consoled. They'd go, but perhaps not before discovering two of the massacre's last survivors.

Cautiously, he released her mouth and dragged her close until she was smooth against him. Pinning her with a strong, two-arm embrace, he threw a leg over hers, locking them down. He froze, and prayed they were sufficiently concealed.

Interminable minutes passed as the voices neared, went quiet. Began again.

Their steps were silent, but the direction the occasional comments came from — south, north and south again — told him they were circling or… Or maybe it wasn't a handful circling but a large body moving en masse.

"Can you understand them?" he whispered. "Are they friendly?"

Her gaze went to the opening of their pocket, which was blocked from view by the drab green of dead foliage. Lashes fluttering, nostrils flaring, she held her study. Finally, she looked back at him, confusion tugging at her forehead. *I don't know*, she mouthed through stuttering breaths.

Whoever they were, friend or foe, they were confident enough in their control of the land to travel casually. Indians on the warpath never spoke. That much Marcus knew.

"It's all right." His hand nestled the side of her head; his thumb stroked at the worry lines. They eased away, and minutes later, her eyes drifted shut.

Another warrior spoke, so close Marcus was sure he could throw a stone and nail the man. But he had no stone. No anything. He resisted the urge to curl tighter and longed for Justice.

The passing of warriors was never-ending. Over the course of it, Marcus caressed Lillian's forehead and breathed into her ear—slow, steady, deep—to transmit a fortitude that, should it be given a tongue, would name itself a falsehood.

Whether she bought the lie or chose to release her fear wasn't as important as the fact that she calmed, breath regulating, body relaxing. His body followed her example, loosening what had to be a painful hold on her. To be safe, he stayed as he was, waiting a good hour before daring to consider a more appropriate position.

Lillian had hardly moved in all that time, and about the moment he deemed it safe to question her about comfort, he realized she was asleep. He brushed aside the hair that had fallen over her eyes and found her lashes resting and her mouth ajar.

He smiled.

How long she'd been that way, he hadn't a clue since none of the usual signs were present. No groaning, no whimpering. Not so much as a twitch or shudder.

And she hadn't once cried his name.

Did his physical presence regulate her so completely? Though he was glad for a tonic to ease her distress, he recognized its detrimental qualities. Especially to a woman as unstable as she. It also did nothing positive for his miserly ego and tenuous control.

The ground was ice against his side, but his chest was warm and heating. If she were awake, she'd no doubt feel the pound of his heart against her ribs.

This was why he'd let her shiver, why he'd stood sentry and ignored her pleading. He'd known he could warm her, comfort her, enjoy the feel of her far more than their relationship dictated.

He'd known right.

But night wasn't afar. Already, he strained to see the details of her face. It wouldn't be long before he left for the Durham and his supplies.

He mentally rehearsed the steps to administer anesthesia, extract the ball, and suture the wound. It was a good exercise, calming. It carried him safely into the darkest hour of night, when he caressed Lillian's cheek, temple to chin, to gentle her from slumber. He took his time drawing her out, promising himself that one day, when they'd left this misery behind, he would wake her just so and give her a dose of the man inside the surgeon. Until then, he was her doctor. Her very dedicated doctor.

She sighed, licked her lips, and angled her face back to him. The movement snapped her from her drowsy state; she went rigid with pain. It spoke to him in the bite of her nails against the bones of his hand.

"Have they gone?" Her voice was strained.

"We're alone. I haven't heard a sound in hours." He let her absorb that important fact before pressing on. "It's time I leave. If everything goes smoothly, I'll be back within the hour."

Her head was shaking before he'd finished speaking. Short, tight denials.

He stopped it with pressure to her hand, unwound her fingers from his arm and himself from her body. "Yes, miss. I'm going. You're well covered. Stay quiet, and you'll be fine. I'll see what I can do about dry clothes and something to eat." Before she could raise another protest, he laid his lips at her temple and slipped into the misty night.

An hour had passed. Surely.

And still, Lillian huddled beneath her crackling leafy blanket, shivering and combating a crippling duo of temper and terror. Coiling into herself, she indulged in an angry pound of her fist against the frozen earth and regretted it.

Pain was a constant. The worst was her ribcage, but the cold did its bit too. It cramped every muscle and burned her bare feet. Marcus had taken precious heat with him, as well as her control. She had yet to find it again. Whenever she came close, she remembered the warriors.

How many had walked past? A hundred? Two? Easily.

Not that numbers mattered. One would suffice. Marcus was

unarmed, yet he'd chosen to leave her so he could tiptoe around them, and for what? A dry shirt and full belly were hardly worth his life. Did he expect to find survivors? The surgeon in him was a force, but if he wasn't careful, he'd be counted among the dead. The thought strangled her.

Her breathing went wild, as did her imagination as it pasted his face onto any number of butchered corpses she'd stumbled over in her flight from Fort Mims. The memory morphed into Beth sputtering her last words through a mouthful of blood. Marcus Buck deserved better than such an end. Any Red Stick who knew his heart, his strength, would hold him in high esteem. Hadn't Tall Bull? But tonight, there would be no pause to study one another's character. There would be only slice and hack and sever.

A noxious bilge formed in her gut. Knuckles ramming her lips into her teeth, she held it in and lifted her eyes to Heaven on the chance God cared to extend a little more mercy. "For Marcus, God. For him."

When Marcus told her he was leaving, she'd taken a stab at bravery as he'd wanted. But she should have raised a ruckus, hobbled along behind him until he gave up and came back to wrap his arms around her. She hadn't even asked him what to do should he, God forbid, not return.

They were out in numbers those Indians. Hunting up another fight. Making their will known. Going about it the entirely wrong way. They were sore that American soldiers were here, enforcing the treaty and poking their bayonets into the Red Stick's last refuge. Lillian could almost understand their plight, but hadn't they learned anything at all in the last war? Didn't they know it was futile to stand against the U.S. government? Or did they simply not care?

Totka and thousands more had figured it out. Why couldn't these? No, they had to fight on. Violently, fanatically. And Lillian suffered for it. Again.

But as she lay in her pathetic little den too frightened to remove even a single palm frond for a clean breath of air, one thought faithfully returned. It first appeared as a simple observation, but with each visit, it grew until it became powerful. So powerful, it was beginning to overshadow all other thoughts.

It was the one thing that kept the tears behind her lids and the scream in her throat. It made her cling to hope and the notion that God loved her yet. That maybe, just maybe, His plan wasn't so faulty after all.

The rapid crunch of footfalls against dead leaves perked her ears. It was slight but too noisy to be an Indian.

Marcus!

Lillian burst from concealment, sitting up with barely a care for the knife in her side. She took hold of a pilaster and lugged herself upright. Sparse moonlight outlined the form of a man carrying a sword on his hip and a bundle over his broad, unmistakable shoulder. He strode straight for her.

"Oh, thank God!" she exclaimed, frightening herself with her own volume. It surely carried clear to whatever lair the Indians had made for the night.

And Marcus so exposed.

"Hurry, Marcus!" she shouted a whisper.

"Miss?" His tread became a jog. The bundle fell behind him. "You shouldn't be up! That wound won't stand for it."

What a beautiful welcomed sight he was! Heedless of his warning and her own paranoia, she flew to him, each step an agony.

"Stop, stop this instant!"

Reaching him, she flung an arm around about his chest, piqued that the one bolstering her ribs stood between them. She'd meant to drag him back, but the robust feel of him brought her short, quelled her fear.

"Miss McGirth!" he protested, hands planted on her shoulders. "Have you any idea the risk you take? That ball is abutting your spine! If it shifts—"

"Shut up and hold me." She crammed her face into his bristly neck and filled herself with the scent of man and damp wool. His uniform, it was new, and he was divinely warm.

"Hold me, she says." He plucked her off the ground and went directly back to their tree where he gingerly set her on her feet. "I'll hold you, all right. Straight over my knee."

Unable to distinguish his expression, she searched his tone for humor, but found little. Whatever he'd seen had rattled him.

A caress to his cheek would never suffice, but she tried anyway.

He ignored the gesture and slid a hand through the hole he'd torn into her chemise. "If you're bleeding again, I'll birch your hind end for that little stunt." The tease in his voice was weak.

He clapped onto her arm and felt along her bandage, his hand not its usual steady self. What had he seen out there? Never mind, she didn't want to know.

His lungs drained themselves in a lengthy, petering tide. "I cannot tell you what a darling sight you are."

"You're rather darling yourself. And a sight more handsome than the back of that moldy palm leaf."

His chuckle went through her like sweet medicine, but it may as well be an alarm. She covered his mouth. "Shh, they'll hear."

"The area is clear," he said but shushed his voice anyway. "You should lie down." Instead of moving her along that way, he cupped her jaw in both hands, lowered his forehead to hers, and shared her breath.

The urge to steal his straight from his lips was a force to be reckoned with, but reckon she did, though it nearly killed her. She settled for a handful of the hair at his nape and held on, listening to his ragged breath until it wrung her heart. "I understand. All too well, and I'd take those awful pictures from your head if I could."

"Never. You're still carrying the last thing you took for me. It's more than enough." He pecked her nose and pulled away. "We were transporting regimentals. I brought a set for you. No promises it'll fit, but it'll be warm. Wait here and I'll get it."

He left and returned shortly with a bulging pack. The contents spilled at her feet. He draped a blanket over her head and squatted to dig through the pile.

Lillian sighed at the instant warmth. "I've had a thought, Marcus." She kept her voice at a hush and was relieved when he did the same.

"Tell me while you put these trousers on. I need to get you warm. No bending that back. Right foot first."

She lifted it, using his shoulder as a prop, and let him wriggle the wool over her foot. "It's about Mari. What if—" A lance pierced her middle. She snatched a pained breath. "What if she'd been here?"

He paused and looked up at her. "She'd probably be dead."

A somber nod preceded Lillian's next mind-churning thought. "What if God took her away to protect her?" Being with Diego wasn't ideal, but if being with Lillian would have been fatal…

"I'd say it fits His character." A smile made his timbre glow.

"Does it make me a bad mother to say I'm…thankful?"

"Far from it." He tapped her left ankle, so she gave it to him. "I'd say it's perceptive, wise even, to find beauty in the ugly. There's scripture about it. Not an easy one to follow. I should know." He whisked the trousers under her chemise and up her legs but gave a grunt of annoyance when he reached her waist. "Two of you could fit in here. These are all wrong."

"They're heaven." She took the enormous waistband from him, pulling the front clear up to her chest where she clutched the blanket.

"Yes, well, *heaven* is going to end up at your ankles when you let go to put on this jacket."

She stifled a painful laugh and let him help her juggle the task.

"I found my bag." He straightened her collar to better cover her neck.

"Oh?"

"Everything's inside. Laudanum included. As soon as the sun is up, I plan to remove that ball."

Sunset of the same day, sounds of activity floated downstream: the chopping of wood and the unmistakable snap of a sail catching the wind. Marcus gave Lillian a calming dose of tincture of opium and alcohol—which she'd very much needed—hid her beneath the moss and fronds and set out again for the site of the attack.

It had been gory enough in the dark. He didn't relish returning.

On the brighter side, the surgery had been a simple procedure with no complications. The ball had come away without struggle, and the wound had sutured neatly. A model for bravery, Lillian had faced his scalpel without flinching. The same hadn't been true of his announcement that help had arrived and he was leaving to retrieve it.

She'd quaked like a stalk of grass weathering a gale until he'd topped her off with that tincture. Now, she slept soundly and would for another two hours or so. All the time he needed to get there and back.

He traveled by land, shocking the first soldiers he came upon. They were scouring the landscape a full quarter mile from the scene. Not slowing, he brushed off their questions and sought out their commanding officer.

Marcus found him inside the tight perimeter that had been established in the trees ringing the bend. The guards displayed worriment—faces pale, eyes roving, muskets poised for rapid shouldering. Their superior, Major Ralph Cooley, was equally edgy, maintaining a piercing gaze on the tree line even as he and Marcus exchanged known facts.

Through the major, Marcus learned that the other two women were missing and six soldiers had survived. The men had fled to a nearby peaceful Indian village for refuge.

"All were wounded," Major Cooley said, "but they should pull through. Tell me how it is you got away with your life, Captain Buck. I'll be sending a dispatch to General Jackson before the day's through, so be as thorough as you can."

Marcus recapitulated the event with enough detail to satisfy the man and aid the general in deciding his countermove. All the while, he wrestled fidgeting feet that nagged him to turn back for Lillian.

"Couldn't tell you how many marched past," he concluded, "but I wouldn't put the number at less than a hundred."

"God help us." Major Cooley removed his bicorn and swiped a

handkerchief over hair dampened by sweat. "They're on their way to Scott, I'll warrant. Doubtless, they'll arrive before we do. Mrs. Lane in tow. Until we hear otherwise, I'll presume Lieutenant Blackburn's wife is captured as well." He crammed the hat back on his head and swore richly. "Devilry is what this is! Positively abominable!"

"Cunning, sir. They are cunning. It was a clever ambush. Efficiently executed." With a sweep of his arm, Marcus indicated the grisly arena.

Friendly Indians worked with soldiers to lay out corpses in bloody rows that stretched the length of the beach. Beside the boat was anchored another army Durham identical to the first except for the crippled sail and blood-washed decks.

Marcus had experienced his share of bloodshed, but this scene was a true test of grit. In great part, because he and Lillian should be among the dead. A shiver climbed his spine. "Our foe was taken too lightly."

"Hmm," Major Cooley grudged.

"Sir, might you spare a few men to help transport Miss McGirth? She should be moved with care."

"Yes, yes." The major flapped a hand toward a pod of men building a raft. "You'll find Sergeant Hedley there. He'll have access to the dinghy."

On the way, Marcus passed several stacks of articles being collected on the sand—supplies, arms, and personal effects recovered from the boat. Among them, Marcus found Lillian's Bible and his own haversack, untouched down to the last sheet of correspondence: a letter from his mother, the ripped halves of Lillian's note, and McGirth's transfer of authority.

A boon that the Indians hadn't been of a plundering disposition.

He stored the Bible and stationed the sack over his shoulders before looking down the long row of dead. One unpleasant task remained before he could return for Lillian and begin classifying this tragedy as a disturbing memory. On leaden feet, head hanging, he walked the line of boots, paying the men his respects.

Higgins, Wayford, Garrigus that steadfast sergeant…

He'd laid down his life for the six who'd escaped. Marcus and Lillian besides.

Combating the swell of emotion, he moved on. At Fanning's still form, he lowered to a squat and laid a burdened hand on the toe of his friend's boot. By the blood saturating Fanning's trouser leg, Marcus deduced a ball had likely destroyed the femoral artery. A swift end, God be thanked.

The same couldn't be said of most others occupying that tract. The Red Sticks had been true to their characteristic warfare, sparing no stroke of their blades. Worse yet—none there needed to have died. Fanning's decision to complete the journey despite advice against it would undoubtedly come under investigation.

Mr. Hambly had warned them both. Heatedly. Long into the night, he'd provided report after report of heavy Red Stick activity. While *they* had only twenty muskets between thirty-four men, half of which were ailing. A pittance compared to the number of their enemy.

Mr. Hambly and Marcus had pled with Fanning to delay the voyage until support could be sent down from Fort Scott, but Fanning had been confident they would be safe if they maintained course at the river's midline. No Indian war party would cross open water to assail them. But why should they when they could use the currents to do the work for them…?

A disturbance at the trees catapulted Marcus to his feet and Justice to her ready.

An Indian emerged from the cover of the forest. He carried a woman whose head lolled awkwardly over his arm.

Mrs. Blackburn. The green and purple calico gave her away; the red slash at the juncture of her neck left no doubt as to her state.

The sword sank to Marcus's side; his heart followed. He'd so hoped the woman would be brought back alive. His mind leapt to Lillian, alone and vulnerable, and he was suddenly more than done with this place. Having sheathed Justice, he moved toward the raft builders and Sergeant Hedley. He'd nearly arrived when his name was called.

"Buck! Marcus Buck!"

He looked back.

The warrior who'd found Mrs. Blackburn hailed him. He'd left her with the other men and was now jogging around a set of soldiers who skipped to avoid his massive, lumbering frame. The man's height and brawn were misleading, for he was young, not yet marked by sun, tattoos, or battle scars. He came alongside Marcus and stopped, hands on hips, a lopsided grin distorting his whiskerless cheek. "Have I changed so much that you don't know me?"

Marcus should know him?

The Indian's deeply graveled voice wasn't the least familiar. He handled English like an American, but he was fully Creek in his russet skin and black, plumb-line hair. The reed choker with silver cross pendant blended cultures and spoke of shared faith, but it was the crooked nose that turned the key.

"Why, if it isn't True Seeker," Marcus said, at last reciprocating that stout grin.

Their paths had collided at Negro Fort and carried on a short while at Fort Scott, which had then been called Camp Crawford. Shortly after, life had split their ways, but the young man had left an admirable impression. It was right good to see the boy again, fully grown and making his own way.

In greeting, he jutted out his arm, but True Seeker bypassed it for an embrace that crushed the wind in Marcus's chest. He coughed and beat the man off him with a teasing punch. "You rascal, you've grown a yard both ways."

"So I have, and I'm no longer True Seeker but Strong Bear."

"No question why. What have you been doing?" He smacked the fat muscle of Strong Bear's arm. "Working a dock?"

"The forge. With my brother, Totka Hadjo."

Totka Hadjo. Now *there* was a name that warmed Marcus's heart. "That explains it. What brings you to Spanish Florida?"

"A woman." The new voice came from behind.

Marcus turned.

Totka, the man himself, was two hobbled strides away and grinning every bit as widely as Strong Bear.

"Totka Hadjo in the flesh." Laughing, Marcus pumped the entirety of his arm, happy to note the man might soon be his brother. "The sight of you has brightened my day. Considerably." Thoughtful of decorum, he squelched his laughter. "It's been rather…dark."

The statement sobered them all. Silenced them for a respectful moment.

Totka broke it, gesturing to the desecrated vessel moored in the sand. "The mind of Hillis Hadjo is in this. It is said he spends much time in the river in talks with the Water Spirits. The river is a weapon to him."

"If that's true, he used it well," Marcus said with a fierce distaste for the topic. He reapplied a modest smile. "How long since I saw you? A year and a half? Closer to two?" Totka had been instrumental in undoing the stew Marcus had created at Negro Fort. Marcus's gratitude was undiminished, unending.

"Too many sleeps. Your face makes my eyes glad." Totka's smile was fuller than Marcus remembered, warmer, and it reached his eyes, proving their gladness.

He looked distinguished, standing there erect and proud, the butt of his handsome rifle on the ground at his feet, its barrel held before him with one ringed hand. His clothing was of quality weave, his shin-high moccasins were of new leather, and his silver ornaments were buffed and plentiful. He was doing well for himself. Rising in the nation, no doubt, and it doubled Marcus's smile.

"Same to you, my fine friend. This army keeps me moving. I'm fresh off an assignment in San Marcos. Red Stick territory, if you can believe it."

"Red Stick territory you say?" Strong Bear leaned in, trimming his volume. "Maybe you've seen my woman. She is Polly of Alabama Town."

"Polly of *Francis*," Totka muttered, looking at Marcus from the sides of his irascible eyes.

"*The* Francis?" Marcus said, mimicking Totka's volume. "As in, Hillis Hadjo…?"

Totka looked as grim as Marcus felt.

But Strong Bear, apart from being cautious not to be heard, remained as blithe as before, eyes round with hope. "His younger daughter."

Polly and Pretty Wolf, then, were the same. "You've set your heart after Pretty Wolf?" Marcus blinked at him incredulously. He'd had no idea he was dining with the daughter of the infamous prophet. Probably a good thing. "What exactly are you carrying around in that skull of yours?"

"Nothing," Totka supplied, as Strong Bear practically glowed.

"She goes by Pretty Wolf now? Good name. Strong. How do you know this?"

"I shared a meal with her not two weeks ago. She's in Wakulla Village, three miles upriver from San Marcos." The memory lit up Marcus's mind with a vision of Lillian enveloped in silk. It was promptly overthrown by a more current version that tugged his desires toward her hideaway.

Ripping his gaze from that direction, he turned back to Strong Bear in time to see him wallop Totka with the backs of his fingers.

"Did you hear? She is well; she is well!"

"I have ears." Totka's peevish scowl failed to mask his pleasure at the news. "The question you should ask is if she's bound to a man."

Marcus had never seen an Indian go pale until Strong Bear, who turned back to him, lips draining of color. "Tell me she is not wed."

"No husband, no, but not exactly unattached either."

Hurt flashed through Strong Bear's eyes. He looked off briefly and came back a different man. Afire, determined, not a hint of breezy youth about him. "Who is he?"

"A former navy man. English. The name is Maxwell Bellamy. Also known as Iron Wood, if my suspicions are correct."

"Iron Wood!" Totka spat the name like a curse. "He is the prophet's choicest ally. You cannot stand against such a man, little brother. Her father will insist she wed him to strengthen ties with the English. And she will do as he asks."

"She will not! I told her I would find her. She's waiting for me. I know it." To the dubious quirk of Totka's brow, Strong Bear raised his voice. "I *know* it."

Pity swelled within Marcus, but fact was fact. "Unfortunately, I agree with Totka. It isn't promising at all. Besides, only a cast-iron Red Stick would get within twenty miles of her."

Taking that in, Strong Bear angled a smug bearing to Totka. "A Red Stick? Why did I not think of it?"

Totka dispensed a backhanded smack and rattled off a spate of Creek, but Strong Bear, ignoring him, wrangled a white feather from the bundle in his hair and pointed it at Marcus. "You, Marcus Buck, are a wise man. My full admiration is yours if you can convince Totka." He backed up at a trot.

"Convince him of what?" Apprehension tightened Marcus's chest. "What are your plans for that feather? Don't even *think* about painting it red. True Seeker!"

"It's Strong Bear," he replied, grinning again and still moving. "And we need a man in their camp anyway. Maddo, Doctor. I am in your debt!" He was off, running for who knew what parts.

Judging from Totka's disgruntled mumblings, he had a good idea.

The young man might be difficult to corral now, thanks to Marcus. He scratched at his scalp and raised an apologetic quasi-smile. "I'm afraid that's all my doing."

"No, he is a stag in rut. The scent of a doe makes him careless of the hunter."

"At least you can sympathize with his predicament."

Air left Totka's nostrils in an impertinent rush. "Copper Woman is different."

Chuckling, Marcus rolled his eyes. When it came to that woman, there was no arguing with the man. "How is she, this Copper Woman of yours?" He'd be thrilled to take word to Lillian.

As predicted, the question brought the smile back up Totka's cheek. "I will be a father. In two moons."

"Congratulations!" News to put a little spirit back into Lillian's outlook. "I'll pray for a safe delivery. Her sister will be pleased to know. I assume you're aware your father-in-law asked me to fetch Miss McGirth home?"

When Totka shook his head, frowning, Marcus assumed he also didn't know Zachariah was dying. McGirth had asked Marcus for confidentiality. It would appear he meant from his family as well. "Pardon me if I've spoken out of turn. Whatever the case, I found her in San Marcos. She's with me now. Or *will* be. Actually, I should—"

"The Bitter Eyes? *Here?*" Totka's gaze skipped about and came back to Marcus, having gone hard. "Where?"

Based on that look, Marcus wasn't sure he should tell him. "Don't call her that." He snapped his syllables. "It's a cruel name, and I won't stand for it."

Totka's head pitched back, but he stuck to his guns. "She is called what she is."

"What she *is* is God's child. You have something against her?" It was uncharacteristic of Totka to be spiteful, but Marcus wouldn't abide it, not as it pertained to Lillian.

"Ask her." He jerked his chin. "Ask her what she did. Why she left."

"You mean the Spaniard? I know already."

Totka simply stared at him, face morphing into a mask of nothingness. "How is my wife's sister? Wounded in battle?"

So, then. The man wouldn't divulge anything. Admirable, but it left Marcus uneasy and wondering. He'd been so certain McGirth had laid out every detail. Had he held something back? To protect her?

"She was shot in the ribs, but I won't let her die." Marcus's smile was tight. "I've hidden her in a cypress downstream a ways. I'm returning for her now. The polite thing would be to offer to bring you along, but I'm not sure it wouldn't do more harm than good."

"You do not want me near her. The woman's head is sick, and I am the disease."

What in the name of decency had happened between them? At least he seemed to have Lillian's welfare in mind. And might he have further insight into her volatility? "And the cure?"

"Only Creator knows." He looked about, from the mangled Durham to the string of dead men. "She will weather this poorly, and you will be unprepared." The warning came attached to a tone of genuine concern. For Marcus? For Lillian?

Either way, Marcus couldn't be angry at the disparagement. Only grateful for the foresight, though he'd already figured the same.

Totka threaded an arm through his rifle strap and settled it on his back. "I leave soon as runner for Cooley."

He was the courier? "You're on your way to General Jackson?"

"With Strong Bear."

At last, a blooming, fragrant wind. A new smile found its way to Marcus's mouth. "Then I need a favor of you."

Chapter 16

*M*arcus boarded their new transport vessel, displeased to find Lillian standing on the opposite side, staring blank-eyed across the river at an abandoned rookery and swaying with the boat in drunken fashion. One wrong move and she'd be overboard.

"Please, miss, you shouldn't be up." Arm about her waist, he tugged her toward the pallet he'd laid out for her on the deck. "That wound is more distended than I'd like, and because of its proximity to your spine—" He cut the medical jargon. She was too groggy to capture any of it anyway, thanks to the drops of laudanum he'd served with breakfast. "I want you down and immobile for the duration."

She stumbled along, bungling to circumvent a bench in the passenger hold. Face puckering, she looked up at him as though finally registering his statement. "No. No lying down."

Wincing, she spurned his help and lowered to the bench behind her, eyes averting from the bloody beach to the keel-plank. Despite the swelling, she was functioning more fluidly this morning, breathing more efficiently through the pain. "I leave like I came. Sitting up."

He didn't like it. Not one bit. But he had to admire her spunk. As well as the adorable figure she cut in her oversized regimentals. The coattee hung off her shoulders and swallowed her hands whole, and the trousers were tenuous at best. Twine held them up, cinching half a yard of fabric into a wad at her waist that, under the shirt hanging to her knees, made her look pregnant. Adorable, indeed.

He stepped to block her view of the slaughter behind him. "You have no back support there. Give it five minutes, and you'll be changing your mind."

"I won't be found on my back, defeated and vulnerable." Her insinuation that they would be attacked again was disheartening. He agreed with her hunch, as did Major Cooley, but he'd hoped to spare her the worry.

Little doubt her experience with the Natives far surpassed that of every man on board. To think he could hide this stark reality from her had been a fool's notion.

Last night had proven long and sleepless, permeated by the stench of death and the awareness of what lay nearby. There were good odds that any number of those attempting rest on the beach and boat might join the dead before they saw this venture through. Countless times in the night as Marcus had watched Lillian's pain-infested body shudder with misery, he'd reproached himself for not having kept her in the cypress. They would have been safer, slept better, and instead of a chaste and frigid five feet away, she would've been in his arms.

The boat was still in irons, its sails luffing noisily overhead. Each soldier went about his task with grim determination: arranging the last of the crates, retrieving the setting poles from beneath the benches, and storing blankets and haversacks. Their expressions said they wanted to be done and gone.

Marcus's sole obligation, however, was to his patient, the only one he had at present. He tossed etiquette over the gunwale and straddled her bench, facing her. "Fine, but you'll lean against me and no argument."

He needn't have been so firm. She became clay in his hands, letting him carefully arrange her so that her uninjured side rested against his chest and her legs hung over his thigh, stockinged feet dangling. As men scurried about the shoreline, transferring the last of the cargo onto the raft, his thumb worked covert circles into her knee. Slowly, she fell into him, releasing her weight and the tension that hardened her body.

Regrettably, there was no time for burial—the sun was climbing, and Fort Scott wasn't getting any closer. Major Cooley threw torches onto their despoiled vessel, then climbed the last raft to leave the riverbank.

Once on board the Durham, he announced a moment of silence, which he ended with a prayer. The roar of flames devoured his final *amen* as the boat transformed into a pyre of massive proportions.

When all was in order, the iron-shod setting poles were taken in hand, and the sails were backed. Favorable winds kept the sheets taut. Even so, the poles were employed without rest. Sets of soldiers, one on each side, took turns on the walking boards, tramping from bow to stern and driving the Durham at a reckless speed.

It was a blessedly warm day, made more comfortable by Lillian's body heat and the mantle of her hair over his arm.

She napped away the morning hours and woke with a start. Instantly alert to the dark forest lining the river, she pushed off him. "They're watching us," she hissed.

Marcus scraped strands of hair from her sweat-dampened cheek and temple. "You were dreaming."

"Not a dream. They're there. I feel their eyes." The fragility of her mental faculties was concerning. A side effect of the opiate? That ill weather portended by Totka?

"Then look at mine." His finger guided her chin.

It took her some time to unhook her gaze from the passing landscape, and when she did, placing her brunette eyes on him, Marcus felt genuine fear.

Yesterday, he'd barely kept her alive and that by Divine grace. He was hard put to imagine it holding out another day with the river narrowing, leading them into the farthest reaches of Red Stick country. Fort Scott was situated at the border of the United States, but it was still desolate land. Untouched by civilization for many miles. Treacherous, inaccessible.

He should have left her at Mr. Hambly's, no at Gadsden. Surely, Major Ainsworth would be more sensible about her fate than a band of inflamed warriors.

Marcus battled to keep the disturbing thoughts from marring his expression while searching for a change of subject. "I ran into your brother-in-law yesterday. He's been in the area, fighting under McIntosh."

Head to foot, she went rigid and began scanning the boat. "He's here?"

Wrong subject, you dolt. "Was. He left," Marcus rushed on. "He's anxious to get home to your sister. She's expecting."

As hoped, the news quieted her body. She softened, smiled even. "A baby. Mari has a cousin. They'll play together one day."

"I believe so too. And your brother. That boy is all mischief one minute, all charm the next."

"Charlie?" Her smile doubled. "Yes, that's him to a tee. Creating trouble at every turn, but he's usually out of it again just as quickly. It's those blue eyes, you see. They get him anything." Her own were dilated and lethargic; her voice, the slightest bit slurred, but she navigated the drug's effects remarkably well. "I miss the little rascal."

"I imagine you do. Why did you leave?"

Lillian blinked sluggish lids, boggled by the question. "You know why."

"I don't think I do. Will you share it with me?" He took her hand in an inspiriting squeeze.

No! She wouldn't bare her soul to this saint, at least not its blackest regions.

"Miss McGirth?"

Seeing no recourse but to give him something, she plunged her gaze to his eagle-embossed buttons and moistened dry lips. "I met the don in Mobile in the winter of fifteen. I found him struggling to pay a liveryman who didn't speak Spanish. After I stepped in to translate, he offered me employment."

Her eyes returned to the bosky tangle; it could house a legion of murderous Red Sticks with the Americans none the wiser. Heart stampeding, she sheltered back into him, grinding his button into her shoulder bone.

That hypnotic thumb of his resumed its work, bringing her back to the telling. "I turned him down at first, but the idea of getting away and seeing new places was attractive, and well…he was too. The following spring, he sought me out and convinced me to leave with him for Pass Christian."

Marcus laid off his caress. Even in her dulled condition, she caught his sudden rigidity, and her tongue stuck to her teeth.

Did he sense she wasn't telling the complete truth? If so she was too far gone, too proud to enlighten him about the full weight of her cowardly nature and supreme bitterness.

She delved ahead, committed now. "San Marcos was never part of the deal. Not until much later. By then, I had Mari and was dependent on him. He promised marriage, so I was baptized into the Church. Another way to control me. As a Catholic, I fell under the friar's authority, and" — she flipped a clumsy wrist — "you know the rest."

After a pause, he said, "But not all of the beginning, I think."

How could he know that he didn't know? Confusion fogged her already numb head.

He arched his back in a stretch, and tenderness commanding him once again, he began re-rolling her coat sleeves into neat cuffs above her wrists. "It's true, though, that no man is without his sins and secrets. In time, perhaps we'll develop enough of a confidence to divulge them to one another. How fine a thing it must be to unburden oneself."

The man had sins and secrets? Hardly plausible.

"In time…perhaps." Or perhaps not.

The sun reached its peak, then gave way to an endless afternoon, torturous in its spine-clenching monotony. With the dimming of day, a jetty came into sight. Soldiers began a murmur and solemnly readied their weapons.

Marcus set her away and did the same, repositioning his sword belt so that the scabbard hung straight down. Mouth set in a grim line, he took up his musket and, while checking its priming, jolted with the

Durham's thud against the dock.

Men leapt the gunwale and began streaming down the landing, weapons cradled for quick action.

"Between that dock and the fort"—Marcus pointed—"there's a twenty-yard stretch of woods to traverse and another thirty of cleared land. Do you see it?"

"I see it," Lillian said.

A wagon path led through dark, foreboding trees, but at its end was a bright, stump-studded field surrounding a picketed structure. Men lined the walls' upper walkways, their heads and torsos frightfully exposed. Except for the river's soft-footed running and the babble of canvas sail being furled, all was quiet.

The presence of hostility burrowed into the back of Lillian's neck. "They're here." To finish what they'd started.

Eyes on the bank, Marcus flung his haversack into position. "I won't lie. There's a strong chance they're lying in wait. I'll carry you so—"

"I'll be fine on my own feet." She popped up to prove it but wavered with pain and dizziness. Blast that laudanum!

He clamped onto her elbow. "You can hardly *stand* on your own feet."

"I've been through worse. But give me a knife. I'll feel better if—"

The fort's gates flew open and spilled soldiers by the dozens. A shot rang out. Then another.

"Down!" Marcus shoved her by the back of the neck flat to the planks, stationed a leg on either side of her.

Gunfire erupted from all directions like kettle corn gone mad, and arching above it all, an unremitting savage battle cry. The screech tunneled under Lillian's skin and clawed at her mind, promising butchery and death.

Hunkering against the boat's frame, she shrieked along with them.

"Prepare to engage!" someone bellowed. "Affix bayonets!"

Lead pelted the arena in a barrage of deadly hail. A paltry display compared to the previous attack but effective enough to splinter the railing and spray Lillian with a stranger's blood. She clapped her ears against the man's shout of pain.

"Abandon ship," came the charge. "Make like the devil for the fort! Leave no man behind!"

Without warning, Marcus snagged her under the arm and dragged her up and straight over the side. A score of others jumped with them.

Her back slapped the surface with a flash of agony. Mouth opening to scream, she swallowed the river. Her vision turned a murky green, and the muted *glug-glug* of the current swamped her ears. Before her feet could find purchase, Marcus had her about the ribs and was hauling her at a beleaguered pace through the hip-deep water.

She coughed and scratched at the hair clinging to her eyes. A jostling glimpse of the fort revealed a semicircle of men stationed before the gate. Others coursed across the field toward them. The punch of musket fire and the scorch of its powder pervaded her senses, injecting her veins with a familiar terror.

She wanted to scream and swim the other way, but her slumberous body refused commands.

Marcus was in control anyway, and his trajectory placed them at the battle's dead center. He reached a two-foot embankment and, still clutching her, dismissed it with a leap. He thrust her behind a tree and drew his sword. "Stay close at my back!" he ordered, but her focus had already abandoned his haversack to consume her surroundings.

Half-naked men, their bronzed bodies splashed with garish tones, streaked through the woods, shouting their warbled rallying cries and seeking flesh for their blades. Clusters of men engaged in close combat, faces flushed and contorted with battle heat.

The fighting was intense, each side fresh and holding its own. But a hasty glance said the Red Sticks outnumbered them three to one, reinforcements included. The soldiers wouldn't last long.

Before Lillian could catch her next frantic breath, Marcus was off, slashing at a maze of winter-stripped vines, making a way to the wagon path and the fort's reinforcements. His blade was efficient, laying open a trail.

Lillian rushed to follow but her overlong, waterlogged trousers twisted about her feet. She tripped, nails gouging tree bark to keep herself erect. Tooth and nail? She couldn't even walk! Her uncooperative fingers worked to untie the twine belt. The trousers had to go. She would run half naked herself before dying in a helpless pile of sopping wool.

Realizing he was alone, Marcus twisted, heart spluttering, eyes raking the landscape for Lillian. Before he found her, an Indian darted at him wildly from the right, followed closely by another.

Anticipation shot through him.

Marcus had held little hope that skirting the melee would get them around it unseen, so he was ready for a fight. Eager, even.

Except for Lillian…

Gracious God, protect her where I cannot!

Certain she was somewhere in the narrow strip of land between his back and the river, he determined to hold this ground. Digging in a heel, he transferred his weight, effecting a swift half-turn that brought his face around and put Justice into position. A single upward stroke should end the warrior, if he obliged.

He did, bounding at Marcus with a disorderly toss of his body.

The swordsman in him triumphed before he'd even begun an arching slice of his blade. As predicted, it scraped bone and dispatched the man to a writhing heap. Embracing the moment, Marcus swung his leg around and back to confront the next head-on.

But this warrior, having witnessed the diagonal furrowing of his companion's chest, came on more warily. Wielding both knife and tomahawk, he held outside of Marcus's five-foot reach.

To lure him into a false confidence, Marcus assumed a lazy middle-guard—right foot forward, pommel at his naval, sword angled slightly south. "What's the matter, Red Stick?" he applied a practiced grin that belied his malice. "Afraid of a little Justice?"

"Marcus!" Lillian called from behind, frenetic.

Relief hastened his pulse, then alarm, but he dared not turn for a glimpse to learn what tragedy was befalling her, and it gouged him deep, nearly drove him into a thoughtless assault. Instead, he firmed his grip on the sword and sought an opening.

At the second shout of his name, his foe glanced toward her, one brow spiking with curiosity.

There, the opening.

Marcus charged over the fallen warrior and engaged, driving the startled Indian back with a flurry of cleaving blows that sprayed fluid and sent him to the dirt. A grunted thrust of steel made certain he stayed there.

Anger broiling, Marcus heaved for wind, spat out the Indian's blood, and spun for Lillian. He caught sight of her, rear end propped against a trunk and yanking at her clothes.

He broke into a run, slashing his blade in the direction of the fort. "Lillian, go, go!"

"Help me!" Grappling with her trouser legs, she stumbled forward several paces, encumbered and disoriented.

He harangued himself for the laudanum, for the clothes, for having lost track of her. The thought was still rolling through his brain when an unengaged warrior turned, having been alerted by Marcus's shout. Two more joined him.

And a third bypassed them all for Lillian.

At the first strike of Marcus's blade, breath caged in Lillian's burning chest. She didn't doubt his abilities, but even the most skilled swordsman couldn't defeat three warriors in the time it would take the one to reach her, even if that one did approach at a trudging, contemplative pace.

The Red Stick's face was painted solid red; his eyes, fastened purposefully upon her.

A humiliating whimper emerged as her legs churned into a reverse stride that toppled her. The ground met her backside with a jarring thud. It stole her breath and washed her world in flickering white. In agony, she scooted backwards and gasped for air.

"Lillian, get up!" Marcus's command sounded a mile off. "Run!"

A deep, forced breath and a rapid succession of blinks brought her vision back. Her first view, caught through the veil of her hair, was that of a warrior's beaded leggings following her snail's flight. He was an arm's reach away and holding his distance. The blade of his tomahawk hung at eye level, swinging slowly with each stride.

Hadn't she always known a Red Stick would end her? Still scrambling, she prayed for a swift, effective strike.

It didn't come.

The Indian held his distance, letting her thrash in her useless attempts to escape him. What was he waiting for? If it was a plea for mercy he wanted, she would not oblige.

To the sound of Marcus's enraged shouts and his rivals' answering whoops, the Indian swatted her hair aside and grinned down at her, displaying a chipped tooth. "Hello, sweet doe."

Panting through a lock of hair, Lillian scowled. "Water Moccasin?"

"At last, she knows me." Chuckling, he squatted and gave her cheek a brotherly pat. "Tell the Bluecoats they have to a count of five hundred to get themselves and their wounded inside the stockade. Then the fight resumes. They may thank you and your blankets for the reprieve." The muscles of his bare thighs rippled as he rose. Hooking her under the arm, he pulled her up beside him and yanked the hair from her mouth. "It is good to see you alive, little sister."

Before she could voice one of the half-dozen questions forming on her tongue, he shoved two fingers between his teeth and rent the air with a sharp, battle-halting whistle.

Chapter 17

*F*atigued from a long day of work and worry, Marcus stepped away from Lillian and Private Petit, who was using his need for a transcribed letter to distract her from the gunfire encircling Fort Scott.

Over the three-day siege, the Indians had nipped at any man unwise enough to show his head. The Fourth had given back as much as it had taken, its sharpshooters kept at the walls around the clock. Though paltry, the fight had been continuous, and it had shredded Lillian's nerves.

Scott was proving itself a sealed vault, and the hospital, built at its center, was the most secure location in the garrison. The ideal place for a Fort Mims survivor to ride out another Indian attack.

And still, she maintained precarious hold on self-possession.

Marcus tossed his jacket onto a chair in the rugged six-cot infirmary and moved to the open doorway to lean against its post. The evening breeze was brisk and laden with the stench of burnt gunpowder. It invaded his shirt and cooled the day's sweat.

To the *pop* of random musket fire, he worked a strip of cotton into a tight roll. Lillian was due a bandage change. Her wounds were healing at the peak of his expectations. To watch her move about, one would hardly know she was covered in bruises; her tolerance for discomfort was admirable.

Marcus, however, internally winced with every step she took. The purple and black striated bands ringing her abdomen were enough to make him deliberate violence.

Justice hung by her belt on the hook beside the door. He glimpsed her longingly and wrenched at the roll's tail. It popped from his grasp and unwound down the front of him. Agitated, he began reeling again, tuning into Lillian's low voice to mollify his temper.

"Your socks? Oh certainly, any mother would be pleased to know."

Marcus smiled, breathing deeply to release his own anxiety.

She was alive. She was here. She was mostly healthy. As her guardian, he should be grateful, considering she'd had a Red Stick chief stalking her, but the only emotion he could conjure was agitation. At the warrior who'd shot her, at the one who'd terrified her. At himself for being unable to get to her. It burned his innards and soaked his clothes and kept him tossing on his cot at night.

He hadn't felt this level of angst since he'd gone insane on the *Scourge* and slashed his way to freedom. The perpetual pecking at the fort fueled it. Soon though, the Red Sticks would tire or deplete their ammunition. In the meantime, he would continue to exude false calm. For Lillian.

Several soldiers worked near the breech-loading swivel gun that was stationed before a firing port cut into the palisade's corner. A row of chambers lay on the ground before the men, each being packed with its measure of grapeshot and powder.

Up to now, there had been no need for the swivels, their largest pieces of artillery. That the chambers were being prepared and lined up for rapid fire led Marcus to suspect an enemy assault to be eminent. A last-ditch effort, perhaps.

The three-man crew began the final stages of firing. A chamber was loaded; the swivel, ranged; the matchstick, lit.

Casually, Marcus stepped back over the threshold and closed the door. Lillian sat at the table, writing. Private Petit watched over her shoulder.

At the click of the door's latch, her gaze flashed to it and back to Marcus.

He explained. "The artillerymen are about to fire a round."

The cannon erupted, punctuating his warning. Petit grinned,

Lillian jumped, and Marcus donned a relaxed smile.

In a noble attempt to respond, the corners of her mouth twitched upward but washed away along with the blood draining from her face. Distress permeated her. It was in the death grip on her quill, the perspiration on her upper lip, the perpetual jounce of her knee.

Marcus expanded his smile, but in the squalid recesses of his mind, he sent to the devil every Red Stick within a five-mile radius. Suggestively, he rested his forefinger on the bottle of opium powder that sat on the table. Her reply was a dainty curl of her lip.

If she'd take the stuff, she would feel better. A full day since her last dose and Marcus was sorely regretting giving her the choice to go without. He'd been thinking more along the lines of pain management and foolishly hadn't anticipated this level of angst.

Totka hadn't spoken idly. Marcus was wholly unprepared.

"And the cure?"

"Only Creator knows."

Perhaps Creator would share the knowledge with her inept doctor...

Fortunately, the hospital was empty, quiet. Nightfall, only minutes away, would bring respite from the sporadic fire, and Lillian would unwind. Hopefully.

"Is there room for scripture there after my name? Ma'd like that," Petit said. The soldier seemed oblivious to her declining poise. Two more minutes, and Marcus would be piloting him toward the door.

Stiffly, she turned back to the letter, dabbing at her face with her sleeve and re-inking the nib with half a dozen rapid dips. "I-uh... I believe so. Which shall I include?"

"There's the one about the valley of death. Will that work?"

"Certainly. If you're trying to make your mother cry."

Marcus opened the door, went back to his post, and grinned into the parade ground.

"Yeah, better not," Petit said. "How about the one with flyin' arrows?"

"I don't recall that one. Is it at all encouraging? What's the reference? I'll look it up."

"Shoot, miss. Couldn't tell ya."

"David's psalm. Ninety-one," Marcus said without turning, the homey scent of boiled beans competing with that of cannon fire. Scripture pages rustled at the table, but he beat her to it, having memorized the verse early on in his venture into Indian country. "Thou shalt not be afraid for the terror by night; nor for the arrow that flieth by day."

"That's it!" Petit enthused.

Lillian cleared her throat. "Again, arrows and terror…"

"Try the same passage, verse two," Marcus offered. "I will say of the Lord, He is my refuge and my fortress: my God; in him will I trust."

"I like it," Petit said.

"It's definitely applicable." The tremor in her voice suggested she had yet to actually apply it. "Thank you, Doctor Buck. You're handy to have around."

Private Petit grinned. "Not as handy as you, Miss Lillian, getting us out of such a pickle, like you did."

From outside the walls, a macabre chorus of Indian war whoops preceded an explosion of rapid gunfire. Marcus ducked inside.

Lillian hunched in her chair, eyes flared and hands flat to her ears.

In two strides, he was behind her, bumping Petit out of the way.

While their men shouted and returned the volleys with equal and lengthy enthusiasm, Marcus remained at her back, hands on her quaking shoulders and speaking as calmly as possible. A chore, considering the cacophony and her own wailing. "Give them another minute, and it'll be over. One minute more, one more."

The battle defied him, dragging out interminably, increasing with ear-pounding, rapid-fire booms that failed to completely mask the Natives' squalling.

"They're coming in!" Fingers digging into her hair, she doubled over.

He followed, maintaining a firm hold, lest she crawl under the table. "They won't! They can't. We're too well fortified."

She rocked over her knees, eyes crammed shut until finally, blessedly, the noisy exchange died to its usual *tat-tat, tat-tat.*

"There. Done." He squeezed her shoulder, straightening slowly with a careful eye to her response.

Unfolding herself halfway, she peered up at him through wet eyes and threads of dangling hair. "Are the gates closed?"

At the jut of Marcus's chin, Petit stuck his head out the door and came back, bearing his teeth in a triumphant smile. "Closed and barred."

"Are you s-sure?"

Lips bunching, Petit studied her. "I see 'em from here, miss. Walls are clear. Post is secure. The boys wouldn't let those savages get you."

"Thank you, Private." Marcus gave him a pointed look and returned his focus to Lillian. "It's almost sunset. They won't try again." Marcus smiled at her, stepped out of her view, and let a frown have its way. Tugging at his lower lip, he stared at her profile and the tremor that vibrated her tatty braid.

Her enlarged eyes remained fixed on the open door; her respiration not decelerating as he would like. They couldn't go on like this.

"She all right, sir?" Petit's raspy voice yanked Marcus from his examination.

"Miss McGirth has overexerted herself." He reached over her to cap the inkwell. "You may try back tomorrow."

Petit collected his shako from the hook by the door. "Much obliged, miss. Feel better soon."

She sniffled, unhearing.

Marcus ushered him out and closed the door. He stood before it and conducted a close-range study of the bird's-eye figure in the maple, debating whether to force a sedative to ensure a solid night's sleep or pray she could calm and find rest on her own.

"Don't forget the bolt," she said with a frantic look toward the supply closet.

She'd spent half the day inside its dark, narrow interior, organizing shelves. Hiding.

Petit's arrival had been heaven-sent. While Marcus had cleared him for duty, he'd discreetly suggested Lillian's letter-writing services, then he'd coaxed her out with a slip of parchment and the notion of a mother in dire need of news from her son.

Now, she wanted back in.

"The bolt," he said. "Of course. For a short while." Catering to her fears enabled them, but it was easy enough to bar the door, and a man would have to be a hard-boiled soul not to be overpowered by pity. He retrieved the beam from where it stood in the corner and dropped it into the staples.

Another barrage of artillery sent her to her feet, chair skidding. "You said they were done!" Her parted mouth moved air too quickly. Sweat ran a trail down her neck.

"Deep breaths, Lillian," he said from where he was, needing her to cope without his touch. "Slower, deeper yet. You're perfectly safe in here."

With a concentrated look, hands twisting her overly long sleeves, she adjusted somewhat per his instructions. Not enough. At this rate, she would lose her wind and fly into a real panic.

"A little help, I think." He went for the bottle.

She backed away. "No more. It-it makes my head fuzzy. I need to be able to run, and-and I need… I need to see to that bin of bandages," she said on her way to the closet, gripping her ribs.

As she passed, Marcus clenched to keep from snatching at her. "Bring them out here." He spoke in her wake. "We'll roll them together."

"All right."

Dubious, Marcus struck a match and brought the flame to a nubby candle. He waited, hands flat on the table, head dangling over the brown-glass bottle of opiate, willing her to find the strength to come back out. Behind him, the door thumped closed. He took the candlestick in hand, sighed, and picked up the bottle, too.

It killed him to drug her.

He was still five steps from the closet when her panting reached him, stabbed his gut. Schooling himself about his exact role, he opened the door. The entry was narrow, slightly wider than his shoulders, which he angled to step through.

His candle filled the small space with a flickering amber glow, illuminating floor-to-ceiling shelves lining both sides. Bed pans, blankets, bowls, tubs of gauze and bandages, trays of tools, and at the end of the recess, a pitiful sight.

Lillian stood some eight feet away, holding herself yet shaking so badly the bottles rattled on the shelf she slumped against. Her next forceful intake became a loud, drawn-out wheeze. "I c-c-can't breathe!"

Marcus shoved the bottle and candlestick onto the nearest shelf and, begging Creator for that cure, went to her.

The little room tilted and swirled. Contending for breath, Lillian tried to right it but couldn't find up. She flailed for something to hold on to, but her numb hands refused to grip.

Stop, stop, stop! The word hammered her brain. Why wouldn't they stop!

The door opened, obliterated the dark, let in the incessant war cries.

Marcus! Help, help. "I c-c-can't breathe!"

Legs becoming gelatin, she propped against a shelf and began a sliding descent.

Marcus was too far away and coming far too slowly, but his calm voice reached her well enough. "You're overbreathing. You need to slow it down."

Unable, she shook her head, flinging her braid into something that crashed to the ground beside her.

"Then stop breathing altogether." He was beside her then, grabbing her by the elbow, halting her wilt. "Hold your breath. To a count of five."

She tried, but her pounding heart demanded her lungs expand. "Make it st-stop. M-Marcus!" Though she called for him, she swiveled away in search of fresh air.

"I'm here!" In the dim of her frantic mind, she lost track of him until he was suddenly behind her, arms binding her heaving chest.

"It's all right, Lillian. I'm here now." His gentle tones warmed her ear and soothed the most ragged edges of her fright. "Breathe into this for me." A pad of gauze covered her nose and mouth.

Her instinct was to swat it away, but Marcus was speaking again. "It'll help. Just breathe. Slower, if you can. In… Now, out. In…" He demonstrated the tempo, coating her neck with his breath, bowing her twinging back with the flow of his lungs.

Still quaking uncontrollably, she replicated the pattern until her air returned and the world steadied itself. Strength came back to her legs. She straightened them, took back her weight.

"Well done." The gauze came away. "Now, relax. You're all a-jitter." Lazily, his fingers combed into the hair at her temple, withdrew, and went back again for the same but deeper, firmer, persuading her head to fall back against him.

"They won't find you in here. And if they do, they'll have to go through every man on post, including me." His self-assurance made the idea of the Indians plowing through every soldier into an impossibility, but she'd seen it done before.

A stack of woolen blankets stared her down as she tuned her ears to the outside. After a time, the blasts dwindled, then nothing, save a cricket in the corner. Quiet overtook them. And blessed peace.

Blocking the nagging fact that it was temporary, she concentrated on the faithful knocking of Marcus's heart and the hypnotic repetitive twining of his fingers in her hair. Tension fled her, relaxing her muscles and leaving her exhausted.

Senses returning in full, she suddenly became aware of their intimate posture and her embarrassing behavior. She lifted her head, and his hand fell away. "Forgive me, Marcus. I don't know what happened to me." Somehow, she'd gone from afraid to terrified to disintegrating. What must he think of her? Maybe now he would stop insisting she was strong.

"An attack of anxiety. Fear took over your breathing. You *can* control it though, given the right tool."

She reached back and laid bold, if unsteady, fingers against his jaw. "That would be you," she stated.

His cheek bunched. "I'm a temporary fix. The binding on a wound that requires sutures. You'll have to see a physician far greater than me for that. Fortunately, he's only a prayer away. His fees are reasonable too."

Her hand dropped. "God? He and I have spoken plenty on the matter, and I find His fees to be rather steep."

"Then they haven't come from Him. His mercy is abundant, and His grace is free. Always. Anything else is a fraud."

Such as Fray Emilio. But the penance he taught, the fasting and prayer, it *seemed* right. Justice required she work off her sins with suffering, didn't it? She'd earned it. "I can see that applying to you, Saint Marcus."

His tongue clicked. "Enough with the saint nonsense. No saint can have the distasteful past I do."

"Oh? Do you have an illegitimate child tucked away somewhere?"

He spun her for a straight-on view of his grave face. "Stop hiding behind Mari. Whatever shame it is you carry has little to do with that precious child."

Reproach scored a groove between his brows and enhanced his rugged beauty. Or maybe it was his firm use of authority that made him beautiful or his familiar use of her child's name or his loyal protection. A great part of it was his insight into her past.

There was also the strength in his muscled neck and shoulders—strength enough to carry her through any trial, as well as the way his reproving mouth puckered. He couldn't know what that expression did to her, or he'd use another. Marcus Buck was too much the cavalier to intentionally wile her, but he'd accomplished it anyway.

Of its own doing, her tongue slipped over her lips.

His head thrust back, the groove between his eyes vanishing in the upswing of his hairline. "Miss McGirth..." His dutiful hands set her away and let go.

She hadn't intended for her musings to be so transparent, but since they were, she wouldn't mind if he explored the faithless side of commitment.

By the way his nostrils flared for his quickening breath, she knew he was reading *these* thoughts as well. His body tensed and shifted toward her, a mere half-step, but it awoke something in the recesses of his eyes. Hunger fit him handsomely. It coursed the length of her, from her parted mouth, over her riotous heart, to her steaming middle. And back again.

The clench of his jaw revealed his struggle, but like she knew every plane of her own body, she knew that with the lightest of touches, she'd unravel him. And stars above, she wanted him unraveled.

Pulse loud in her ears, she was reaching for him, aiming for that solid arc of his chest, when his eyes flicked to the exit. The near panic in them snapped the buzz right out of her.

Her hand withdrew, and while every fiber of her shivered unfulfilled, he, with a few blinks and barely perceptible nod, put himself back in order. Incredible, his control. But she would have been woefully disappointed had her rock floundered.

Clearing her throat, she scrambled to pick up the tail of their conversation, hoping to end it before he induced her to bear her ugly soul. "You're right. It's more than Mari, but you said yourself we're each entitled to our secrets. I'm content to keep mine. Aren't you?"

Hurt clouded over him. He angled his face from her, gaze scraping the ground, and made a fist of the shirt fabric at his waist, and then he became very still, indecision beaming from restless eyes.

"Marcus, what is it?"

Air surged from him. "I'm unsure. Of…"

"Of what?"

"You." His lashes lifted to allow a scrutiny so intense, she felt bare and for the first time, judged. Little wonder, after her conduct.

Shrinking a little, she tucked her chin. "You have good reason not to trust me, but if you worry that I cannot keep a confidence—"

"Lillian." Her name left his tongue on a tender sigh. It drew her eyes to his and the mellow reprimand etched there. "That's not it at all. I do trust you." A couple of tugs freed his shirt from his belt. "Give me your hand."

Eyes widening, she did.

He flattened it low against the hot skin at his side. Holding it fast, he heaved a sturdy exhale and propped himself with an arm on a shelf above, leaning over her. His waist was slick and lean, allowing the detection of every quivering muscle, but there was nothing seductive about his posturing. The plunge of his head to his forearm more closely resembled the bearing of a great burden, and it discomfited her.

Seconds ticked and sweat dripped, and when Lillian was opening her mouth to question, he collected a slow, full breath and pressed into her, simultaneously guiding her hand around his side and up to the center of his back. Her first thought was to his nearness: the abundance of muscle shuddering with some unknown dread, the breath stirring her hair, the heat spilling off him.

A strange sensation at her fingertips obliterated all that.

His skin… It was tough, puckered into a line. A long, thick scar. No, a patch of scars the width of her hand, crisscrossing and extending out and—

She gasped, mind recoiling. "What is this?" But she knew. He'd told her that first day, but was it so severe? "Marcus, no!"

He stayed her hand from its scramble to escape his shirt and tilted away enough to level their faces. "Look at me. My eyes. Please, Lillian, I need to know."

She did, though it taxed, and all the more when she detected a gloss of, of what? Vulnerability? Indeed, and that was fearful expectation bating his breath. "To know what?"

His gaze was fixed on her, probing, a contrast to his hesitant replacement of her hand, lower this time. But there, too, the flesh was mangled. How far did it go? The suffering, oh, the suffering he'd endured! A man would have to be a beast to have done this, an oak to have survived it.

Flooding with the effort, her eyes fought to break free of his, but she chastened them and held. She flexed her fingers into a ball, narrowly shushing a rising sob. His pain was too much. Far greater than her own. Here she'd thought them equals, when in truth, their experiences didn't even belong on the same scale.

"No more secrets, duchess." He cradled her head, placing his thick-throated plea against her temple. "If we hold them too long, they wound us. Am I content to leave them, you ask? No, I am not. Finish." The last was solidly spoken, no compromise.

Employing both hands, she muted another sob and did as told.

The horror stretched from shoulder to shoulder, neck to tailbone, even wrapping partway around his sides in tangled threads that left her ill. She swallowed bile and eased away from him, keeping contact with the least offensive flaws, caressing them in a futile effort to wipe away the hurt; such an ache was never removed.

"Tell me," she croaked through repressed tears.

He stayed as he was, pitched over her, seeming concentrated on her touch as he spoke. "There were four. Lieutenant Long tied me to the mainmast. Bosun Perry applied the lash, but it was the first mate who left me hanging for a day. Captain Hillary tossed me in the brig to tend my own wounds."

The tip of her middle finger tracked a thick welt around his ribs; his muscles contracted to escape her.

"Did I hurt you?"

"No." He pulled the front of his shirt down, cutting into her forearms and forcing her to withdraw. He was ashamed, then?

Molars grinding, she bedamned the bosun and his lash. "What were you accused of to earn such cruelty?"

"Striking an officer while trying to escape."

How could he speak of such things and display not a hint of emotion? "Are you not angry, bitter?"

A snort blasted from his nose. "Bitter enough to kill them all before leaping the rail."

That explained it. He'd already had his say. "I'm glad for it. The devils had it coming."

The slow shake of his head brushed his hair across her ear. "Not a one was armed."

He felt guilty? "It was war. It was justice."

"It was revenge! Don't excuse it." He pushed off and opened a wide, wintry gap between them. "I, a physician sworn to preserve life, killed *four* unarmed men. What's worse—I enjoyed it. That is my shame to bear" — he rapped at his chest—"and only Christ can take it from me." Broken, he stood before her, shirt rumpled, hair hanging over one eye. Drinking air in lessening gulps, he regarded her, waiting, at length saying, "And yourself?"

"Me?" In light of his past, her grievances became pathetic. She would rather pretend to have misunderstood than speak of them. "I had no idea. You hide it well. Has that been hard to do?"

For an eternal five seconds, he studied her impassively, then tipped his head toward the door. "Are you ready to leave?"

"Leave? Why? No." At the stiffening of his expression, she stammered on. "I mean, I-I asked you a question."

A wistful smile accompanied the dip of his chin. "Yes, it's been difficult. Until now, only Phillip knew of the floggings. Of the rest, only you," he murmured, neatly establishing that he trusted her with his pain as he'd trusted no other.

Empowered by that, she clutched her baggy cuffs and sighed resignation. "You asked once why I left Tensaw."

"And you said it was the Spaniard's doing."

"Partly true. I left out of fear."

"Of what?"

"My sister's husband. I thought he might kill me. Or-or hurt me. I don't know…"

His head slanted. "Why would Totka—?"

"He was a Red Stick, you know, at the massacre," she rushed on, twisting her sleeves, latching her gaze to a wrinkle on his shirtfront. "He's a frightful man. Always scowling. He hated me from the start. Just as I hated him. But he wanted Adela, and I, well, I was convinced she was about to ruin her life with him, so I stepped in to" — she popped a self-conscious shrug — "to protect her."

"What did you do?"

"I led each to believe the other was…dead. They believed it. For a year." A putrid lump of regret clogged her throat and refused to be dispatched. Lifting her eyes to receive his censure, she found only a neutral consideration of her and a small nod for her to continue.

"It was miserable. For everyone. Myself included." Could he see the remorse staining her cheeks? By the burn of them, they were crimson. "Naturally, Totka found her, and he knew I was to blame. He's not a man to release vengeance, especially where she's concerned. His Copper Woman, as he insists on calling her."

"So you left."

She nodded and loosed a dry chuckle. "Tragically, I now realize they truly are a fitting match."

"When you see Totka next, make sure you tell him."

"I might do that." She glanced toward the pitch-black hospital. "If we get out of here with our scalps."

"Duchess, darling," he said, nudging her chin back around and pegging her with an ardent look. "No one's touching this hair but me."

Spoken like a man who'd overlooked her trespasses.

A sated trough under a primed pump, Lillian's chest filled to overflowing. It swelled with love and splashed over, wetting her lashes and cheeks. If she didn't drain some of it into him soon, now, she would rupture, and with every inch of her skin crying out for him, those two fingertips on her chin were but agony.

She crawled her hands beneath his shirt, and the ridges of his abdomen hardened with his crisp intake.

"Lillian…I can't."

"Then walk away. Or be quiet and let me love you."

Though his ribcage crashed and refilled in the same dramatic manner, he stood rooted and made a noise like pain in his throat.

A gratifying response, but she wasn't aiming for the perfect granite of his chest. Her fingers rounded his torso and sought that labyrinth of scars.

He flinched, grabbed onto the shelf on either side of her.

Lips against his neck, she hummed a soothing note that discharged his lungs and tipped his head into hers.

Skin-prickling silence followed as she explored and kneaded, and the tension drained from his body. After some minutes, when she was satisfied she'd laid a solid foundation for her claim, she spoke, quiet yet sure. "I love you, Marcus." Her palms pushed upward over rugged flesh. "Even here. Especially here."

His arms fell in a heavy, encompassing arc that drew her up on her toes and reminded her she'd taken lead for him. She would take it again if ever the need arose. Lead, arrows, a knife to the heart. Any of those would top a life without him.

She trailed her mouth along his jaw, pouring tears and love and gratitude all over the man, not caring one jot he wasn't reciprocating. Her heart thundered over a blurry space of time. He broke in by bending to lift her beneath the knees. Next, he was moving, leaving the safe confines of the closet.

The candle went out, drenching them in darkness. Cool, fresh air bathed her. For three panted breaths, her body starched, her nails embedded in his collar until his mouth brushed hers with a whispered, "You're safe."

Was she? For the moment, yes. Because of him. When she fitted their mouths together, he relaxed for her, but her mind, however, warned that this was neither love nor consent but a diversion.

Even so, she pressed in, familiarized herself with his lips, their breadth and form, cherishing him more for his sterling character and liking herself less for exploiting it. Then, her back met a cold mattress, jarring her with compunction. She broke from his mouth. "Oh, Marcus. I'm sorry. As I said, I'm no good for —"

"Hush that." Down on one knee, he reached with trembling hands for her blanket and tucked it about her. "Sleep," he said, settling onto the ground at her pillow, gathered her hair, and began a finger-comb that outshone the Orient's finest opiate, and like an opiate, he lulled her heart from its mad race into a sluggish rhythm that carried her into a beautiful, fearless sleep.

Chapter *18*

Three hundred and twelve... Marcus languidly raked Lillian's hair and clung to his meticulous count, tossing out any censure he'd had for the men who'd fallen under her spell. Even Diego rose a notch higher in Marcus's estimation. A wonder, that.

But then, so was the woman.

Marcus would allow himself thirty-seven more. He couldn't stay, or he'd ruin the half hour he'd devoted to putting her to sleep, then he'd ruin her perfectly ordered, knot-free hair.

Bedlam still burned a path through his body, his mind. Sitting a measly foot from that tempting mouth, he was in dire need of a set of wedding vows. Or a mile's worth of breaststrokes. Against current. Denied both, he'd make do with a head dunk in a horse trough.

Except he couldn't find the willpower to do more than watch her breathe with the cadence of slumber and gnaw at his lip. She'd owed him that apology.

He owed her one, as well, for using seduction to distract her. Only his fixation on her anxiety and need to sleep had locked it within him. There was also the little matter of the pledge he'd fractured. The thing was a mean encumbrance he intended to rectify posthaste. Give him a straight shot to Tensaw or a reply from her father, and he'd be kissing back.

He propped an elbow on his upturned knee and leaned his head into his palm, weary beyond exhausted. But his diversion, though questionable, had worked. She was out of the closet and sleeping peacefully, sans laudanum.

However, tomorrow was coming…

Three hundred and twenty-seven. Lids heavy, body sore, mind numb, he judged the available space in her cot and decided he'd fit nicely. And that was the end of that.

Creaking like a rheumatic, he climbed off the ground, brushed her forehead with a feather-light kiss, and went to the supply closet for a bundle of blankets. Toting them under his arm, he eased the bar off the door and entered the night. He made a bed on the patch of grass before the hospital door and blinked up at the sky. It was clear for once, flaunting a bevy of crystals embedded in a sea of indigo velvet.

The thought of velvet carried Marcus back to Lillian's caresses—specifically, those applied to his scars, which had never been touched until her. Not that his destroyed flesh had sensed much, but the act alone had been a mending salve. More so than two years of telling himself a hideous back didn't matter.

When he'd spoken of unburdening the soul, he'd meant it for her. His own guilt he'd given to God a thousand times, if one. At each occasion, he'd been reassured of God's love, but with Lillian's touch, he'd been shown a woman's. Told as much. Again.

His ears still tingled with pleasure, but that was the last time she would say it before he did. It tweaked his pride, this reversal of roles, and made him into a hoggish sponge. Not merely in appearance but in fact. A decent fellow would have walked away, but he'd fed hungry eyes, curled into her, and soaked up every stroke like a famished stray come home.

The doctor in him said it was insane to believe his heart now beat stronger, steadier, that it had grown in his chest and learned to speak her name. The man in him said it was insane to deny it. And the soldier in him… Well, the soldier would fight for the man and leave the doctor in a ditch; there was no denying her touch had healing power.

Her own journey toward healing was newly begun, but it was a strong start and showed promise of a woman bound for a noble purpose. If she would but recognize Christ's mercy and accept His unconditional grace!

Admonishing himself, he shed the thought. Only Christ could question the state of another's soul. Marcus understood Totka's anger—would likely feel the same in the man's place—but as far as Marcus's opinion on her, the confession changed nothing. It would take far more than that to alter his feelings for the woman whose heart paralleled his own, the one who'd placed herself in the path of his death, and as soon as he was able, he intended her to know it.

Succumbing to sleep, he closed his eyes to the repose of God's approval and opened them to dawn's chill and the report of a squad of muskets.

Heart firing in response, he launched to his feet, rotating to find the source. Having gone full circle, he concluded the fighting had resumed on the opposite side of the fort. He huffed and scrubbed his face and scalp until he'd scraped away the sleep.

And so, another day began, the first thought of which he dedicated to Lillian.

He peeked through the crack in the door's seam. She lay on her belly, lids lowered peacefully, hair in absolute chaos. Smiling, he snuck inside for his bag. He'd make a couple of rounds and go for victuals. Lillian would wake hungry, having skipped dinner. Marcus's mouth excluded.

In the supply room, he plucked a few roles of bandaging from their container and shoved them into his bag. An unusual swatch of bright blue peeked at him from behind the box—the lady's dress Sergeant Lane had brought by their first day on post. One of Mrs. Lane's.

Lillian had thanked the sergeant sweetly, seen him out, and cried on Marcus's shoulder, insisting she couldn't bring herself to wear it. He'd not stressed the matter. If it helped to wear unshapely regimentals instead of a captive's frock, he was for it.

As he ran his fingers over it now, he took her name before the Lord, praying down the Holy Spirit's peace and a supernatural moving in this place, in her soul.

A gurgle from his middle reminded him the morning was sneaking past, so he pulled the folded garment out to the front and instructed himself to march quick-time through the infirmary.

Halfway to the barracks, he stopped at the shout of his name.

"Doc Buck!" A soldier he couldn't identify hailed him, running helter-skelter across the compound. "Come quick! There's an Indian, sir!"

Marcus was already trotting. "Where?"

"Outside, sir!" The man pivoted and began back the way he'd come.

"What does he need?"

"They wanna trade, sir. Their war chief for you."

Lillian bolted upright, rocking her cot and punishing her ribs.

Where was Marisol? She blinked groggily.

The hospital.

It was barren of all but brilliant morning sun streaming through the cracked-open door and the muffled buzz of a crowd outside. That dose of reality sat bitterly with her, made worse by Marcus's glaring absence.

For no good reason at all, her heart took a frightened sprint up her throat, clogging it. She was a mess. Genuine trouble.

At least she'd slept hard, as though she'd guzzled half of that foul tincture. Turned out, sampling the doctor had been equally potent to sampling his physique, yet far sweeter. The night had been a solid span of nothingness, but as morning had neared, reveille had played through the fog of slumber, and musket fire had resumed. It had taken the shouts of a quarrel to yank her upright.

She tossed off the blanket, re-rolled the hems of her manly trousers, and skittered barefoot to the door to squint into the new day. A few yards off, Private Petit craned for a view of whatever was taking place before the gate. The *closed* gate, thank God.

Presently, its stout crossbar was being secured.

The wind rustled her hair, blew it across her eyes. She gathered it in a fist but still saw nothing beyond a throng of men moving as a body across the compound. Their path would lead them past her. "What's going on?"

Private Petit whirled about, eyes bugging. "'Mornin', Miss Lillian. Can I bring you some grub? Fresh biscuits today."

"Maybe later. Where's Captain Buck?" She moved out from under the covered entry, but Private Petite whipped around her to block her progress.

"He, uh… There was an emergency, miss. He'll be back in a wink. Why don't you—?"

"Why the ruckus?" She sidestepped him to see.

The throng shifted, opening its center to reveal a blood-drenched Indian being prodded at gunpoint, arms at his back. Indignation stiffened his carriage and etched his face with indomitable pride.

Lillian shaded her eyes. "Is that—?" The snake twining up his arm readily identified him. "Water Moccasin!"

His hard eyes swung from their fixture on the pickets, encountered her, and amplified.

Having no purpose, she broke into a smarting jog that Private Petit halted with a clamp on her wrist. "That Indian's dangerous! Stay away!"

As they marched Water Moccasin past, he strained toward her, desperation swamping his features. "Sweet doe, you must take my talk to Tall Bull. Tell him, 'for my brother, my chief, and for the People. No fences, no fetters!'"

"Tall Bull? No fences, no what?"

"Get moving." A soldier jabbed a rifle butt between Water Moccasin's shoulders.

He stumbled but retained purchase on her eyes and with his own begged a promise of her.

"Stop that!" she demanded of the soldier, while stretching the length of her tether, following their progress, wrenching at Private Petit's hold. "Can't you see he's wounded?"

"That ain't his blood, miss."

Then whose? And where was Marcus!

"Fetters!" Water Moccasin shouted, twisting back. "Will you tell him?"

Another blue coat blocked her, and the squad moved on. "Get the lady out of here, soldier."

Private Petit reeled her in. "Come on, Miss Lillian. This show ain't for delicate eyes. The doc'll have my hide for what you've seen."

"What show?" Were they going to kill him? But he was the one who'd halted the attack!

"Tell him!" Water Moccasin's voice was faint now but no less urgent.

"I-I will!" she shouted back, half hoping he didn't hear, for it was an empty assurance. She had no intention of seeing Tall Bull again.

The private tugged her back into the infirmary.

She tore free, came toe-to-toe with him, fists forming at her thighs. "Where's Marcus?" He backed toward the table, heel bumping the chair. "Don't you worry yourself about the captain. He's got a troop of our best men with him."

"With him *where*? The truth, Private! Where is he?"

"The doc's gone...out."

"Out where exactly?" He couldn't mean... "Out *there*?"

"Yes ma'am, but like I said—"

"Why? Why would he do that?" A vision of him bracing to receive three warriors choked her mind: lunging, skewering, commanding their corner of the battlefield. He'd been stunning, but in this vision, there was no victory. Not against the hundreds swarming him.

"Didn't say. I only got orders to see you're cared for. But he'll be back. Wanna sit?" He pulled out the chair and patted its back.

"No, no he won't! Water Moccasin was the only decent Red Stick in the lot, and now he's in irons!" Air struggled through her cinching throat. She heaved for more. "How do you think the war party is going to take that, Private Petit? Badly. Very badly!"

"Now, don't go get yourself all riled up. Everything's going to work out. How 'bout we finish that letter?"

"Forget the letter! Where's your musket?" Spying it on the table, she slammed the door shut. Marcus's sword jostled on its belt where it hung on the wall. He didn't even have Justice with him? A sob tore at her.

She drove the bolt into place, ignoring the rip of pain in her side. "Give it an hour and every Red Stick within two miles is going to be storming these walls."

The man stared at her, mouth agape, completely useless. She knew his type. During the massacre, more than one man had wet himself, unlike Marcus who would brave any number of opponents. Who *had*.

And was probably dead as payment.

"Take it!" She shoved Petit's weapon against his chest, but he put it right back down.

"You've got no call to be jumping to concl—"

"Do your superiors have any idea who they've caught?" Shaking powerfully, she snatched up the musket herself and wrangled the powder horn off his belt. If he wasn't going to use them, she would. "Water Moccasin is no nameless brave. They won't stand for his capture. They'll take their revenge out on Marcus, then they'll come for us. And, God have mercy, they won't stop until this ground is wet with blood!"

A spectral of Beth's sightless eyes surmounted every thought. Fleeing it, she plucked Justice from its peg and, battling for wind, hauled everything into the closet, the buckle of the sword belt rattling along behind her. Having bumped through the narrow entry, she spun and kicked the door closed. She was backing into the cell's recess when it occurred to her she hadn't grabbed the man's shot bag.

Too late to return for it.

Her back collided with a shelf, and pain overran her, collapsed her knees. She went down in a pile of iron, steel, and baggy wool, keeling over so low that her mouth scraped the ground and her gulping lungs dragged in dust.

An attack of anxiety. Fear took over your breathing. Marcus's voice was so vivid, he might have been there, leaning over her. Except he wasn't.

And she couldn't bring herself to think of where he *was*. Not without dripping cold sweat.

You can control it though, given the right tool.

No, she needed *him*. Him!

The whole of her throbbed; the ache caused by her wounds and that of Marcus's absence melded into one disorienting agony. A disturbing wheeze grated her ears. Her own racket.

She was losing her wits. As sure as the Red Sticks were plotting her destruction, she was going insane. But more pressing than her sanity was the want of air.

God...God...mercy! Was all the prayer she accomplished.

The gauze Marcus had used — where was it? Gasping, she fumbled in the dark, ransacking the shelves until she detected a folded bedsheet and buried her face in it.

A timid knock came at the door, followed by the private's muted voice. "Miss Lillian, you don't gotta hole up in there. Everything's dandy. You'll see."

In... Now, out. In... She breathed as Marcus taught her. *Out... In...* By degrees, she regained control of her breathing, if not her wild thoughts: Marcus was gone. Mari was gone. The Red Sticks were coming, and there was no Mama or Adela to huddle with this time.

She rocked over the bundled sheet and released long, deplorable wails into it.

God spare him! I beg you! Spare him! The prayer cycloned throughout her, intensifying with each pass.

"Miss? Miss?" There came another rap. The door creaked open.

She lifted her head and hiccupped three times fast.

By his aghast expression, he was more frightened of her than the impending assault. "I brought you somethin'." He crouched, set her Bible on the threshold. Its hardened-leather cover scraped dirt as he scooted it toward her. "Ma likes to keep hers near when she's in a sweat. Um... awful dark in here. I'll leave the door ajar."

Her eyes leached to the Bible.

Clinging to the blanket, she crawled over the pile of weapons and pulled the book to her chest. Breathing in its dusty scent, she was whisked away to Tensaw and Mama's knee. The Book had often been there, and except for the year of the war and the one following when Adela had loaned it to Totka, it had always been a part of Lillian's life. She'd left Tensaw with nothing but a change of clothes, but when Papa found her in Pass Christian, he'd come bearing the Bible and the request she bring it home.

She opened to the title page. The blank sheet facing it displayed her mother's beautiful script: a Proverb. Adela's was below it, listing Mama's death, Charlie's birth, her marriage. Beside her Indian name was Totka's signature, written in his own hand.

Boldly, neatly.

She traced it, struggling to associate the immaculate, elegant letters with the warrior who'd terrified her for so long.

And the way his name flowed seamlessly from the end of Adela's… No doubt he'd done it intentionally. The man could scarcely breathe without expanding Adela's own lungs.

It was a provocative position for a woman to own. Lillian coveted it. Wanted the same of Marcus. Instead, she was hiding in a musty cell, awaiting her doom and fearing he might have already met his. A cavern yawned in her heart and echoed his name with an empty ring.

Sniffling, she used her sleeve to mop her face but missed a tear. It plopped onto the Bible still open in her arm. A swipe of her finger removed the drop but made Totka's perfectly scribed name into a black smudge.

Lillian groaned. Wasn't it like her to aggravate the man, ruin his name?

She was a perpetual bur in his side, and he in hers, but—she riveted her gaze to the threatening space beyond the door—at present, there were any number of things she'd give to know that Totka and his tomahawk were standing out there. Because the grievous truth was, he'd fight every Red Stick beyond those pickets to save her. Not for *her* but for his wife. To shield her from grief.

But did the motivation matter? The fact that he would, despite hating her, spoke volumes of the man. She dabbed at the smudge in a futile effort to salvage it.

Just as everything else she touched, it was spoiled.

Heartache and loneliness consumed her. She was utterly raw. Stripped bare of every loved one, every security. She had only herself, a worthless musket, and a sword that should be in the hand of her strongest defender.

Private Petit's form blackened the gap. "Looks like Ma was right about that Bible. She'll wanna know. We got room in the letter for that?"

Lillian couldn't help her wobbly smile, which strengthened as she realized she had one other thing apart from weapons she couldn't wield—she had Mama's Bible. Following that line of thought, she reasoned she also had the belief that God's protective hand was on Mari.

Lovingly, she stroked the names Zachariah and Galena McGirth, then dragged her finger to the untouched space beneath Adela and Totka's marriage. Two new names belonged there. Adela's little bundle and… Vision blurring, Lillian sketched with a finger: Maria del Sol López McGirth.

The barren Doña Sofía Ybarra de López would have to steal another child. Mari was Lillian's, and as soon as Lillian broke free of this fort, she intended to hunt her baby down. If she had to move three nations to do it, God avail, she would. But before she could conquer the fort, she had to conquer this stuffy little room and the fear that chained her to it.

Determined, she flipped to the Bible's center, the Psalms. "Do you remember the verse about the arrows? Where was it found? What passage?"

"Don't recall, miss, but it was about not being afraid of 'em because the Almighty is all the stockade we need."

In him will I trust, it had ended. That part she remembered.

It was a simple statement. A simple trust. Too simple.

But the idea of it was attractive, and she was curious to try it. Not because she was convinced He could truly love her black heart, but because she had no one left. Nothing else to lean on.

Nothing but a family Bible and a God her mother and sister had adored through every flame, every tragedy. A God Marcus believed capable of healing her broken mind. Not just capable, but willing. For a good price too, so he'd said.

A smile bloomed through her tears. *"His mercy is abundant, and His grace is free. Always."*

Marcus applied that to himself even after having taken lives in anger. To hear him tell, he equated his actions to murder, yet he believed God's mercy extended to him. If that was true, what of Lillian? Her sins were abundant, but she'd never killed four unarmed men.

If mercy was given to Marcus, why not her...? Hunched over the Book, clinging to its binding, Lillian absorbed that revelation and decided it was worth pursuing.

The door hinges squawked as Private Petit buttressed himself against the frame and pointed at Lillian's lap. "That a lady's frock you found there?"

Setting aside the Bible, she discovered the bedsheet she'd cried into was in fact Elizabeth Lane's cobalt blue gown. With a little squeak of anguish, she fingered the intricate lacework on the sleeve and considered poor Mrs. Lane, who must that very minute be suffering the trials of captivity. If such was the case, she might find comfort in knowing Lillian had escaped and was making good use of her clothing. During her own captivity, Lillian would like to have known such a thing...

"It is," she replied, smoothing wrinkles from the muslin. "Mrs. Lane's. Her husband dropped it by. Shall I wear it?"

"You do that." Private Petit nodded enthusiastically and reached for the door latch. "If you're up to it, I had biscuits brought for ya. Coffee too."

Now that he mentioned it, she did detect the aroma of coffee. It sprouted moisture in her mouth. "Tempting but...the Red Sticks." Was it already time to employ that trust?

"Hasn't been one shot fired since that chief was brought in. I reckon you'll be all right if you come out for a swig of coffee."

She angled her ear to the outside and found it to be true—no gunfire, no whoops, no orders being shouted and relayed, no…anything. Only eerie quiet.

Pulse quickening, her mind rushed to concoct all manner of reasons for it: a false calm before a storming attack, a gathering of warriors to witness Marcus's violent end, a council to—

She snipped it off, replaced it with a hasty muttering. "In Him will I trust."

"You mean God? That's the way, miss." Private Petit grinned and extended a hand to her. "Ma'd be proud. You should tell her."

Offering him a tremulous smile, she braced her burning torso and gratefully accepted his help up. "Maybe I should." First, she would seek out Major Cooley and information about Marcus's whereabouts.

Feeling incapable and weak but determined to test God with her next hours, minutes, she slipped into Mrs. Lane's gown. After she'd ordered and braided her wild hair, she fortified her lungs with a deep inhale, placed her life—or death—in God's hands, and emerged from the closet.

Having partaken of a few bites and downed that swig of cold coffee, she removed the door's bolt and stepped into a world she'd never known.

The same splintery pickets greeted her; the same bedraggled soldiers camped on its upper walk. The same hazy sky stretched overhead with the same rusty hue staining its breadth. The same odors permeated the air: munitions and beans and, when the wind was right, a whiff of corn from the granary.

But above it all, a fresh, acute awareness of God's presence and with it, the sense that He was watching and waiting. For her.

None too soon, the gates shuttered closed behind Marcus and the twelve heavily armed soldiers that surrounded him. To a man, they slumped with relief. They were the best the Fourth had to offer, but outnumbered twenty to one, they wouldn't have stood a chance had the Red Sticks decided to renege on the deal.

The deal being the life of a war chief in exchange for the attempt to save the life of one of their senior warriors. A strange arrangement. Very strange, considering their inverted ranks. But it wasn't Marcus's job to question, only to follow orders.

The circle parted for Major Cooley, affording Marcus a view of the hospital, Private Petit, and… was that Lillian?

She was barely recognizable in Mrs. Lane's dress and leaning serenely against the porch stake, cheek resting on the back of her hand. Watching him.

Was she not aware of what had transpired and where he'd been? He'd be sure to thank Petit later for sheltering her from it. When he'd sent the private to look after her, his expectations for proper care had been low, but Petit was the only one who had a little insight into her emotional state. Besides, there hadn't been time to find anyone else in the twelve breaths he'd been allowed before being ushered into the hands of the enemy.

As the major shook hands all around, the crowd shuffled and obstructed Marcus's view. "Does my heart good to see you, men," Major Cooley exclaimed. "The army thanks you for your service and your outstanding bravery. Head to the kitchen for an extra ration. You've earned it. Dismissed." He whipped a kerchief from his pocket and passed it to Marcus. "What's the verdict? Are we to release the chief?"

"I think not." Marcus set down his bag to scrub dried blood from his knuckles.

"Excellent! Capitol work, Surgeon." Cooley clapped Marcus on the shoulder. "Get cleaned up and see me for a full report."

Marcus saluted his dismissal and gathered himself to greet Lillian. Hair to hips, he was speckled and sprayed in blood. She wouldn't take well to the sight of him, but no argument, if the need arose, he would administer laudanum. Unless Petit already had…

With Marcus's first stride, his boot thumped a soft object. It was a palm-sized, twine-enwrapped bundle attached to a leather thong. A warrior's medicine. The prisoner's. Marcus collected it from the dirt and slipped it into his pocket.

Lillian and Private Petit walked out to meet him, and unless Marcus was blinded by wishful thinking, she'd found her poise again. Apart from the careful way in which she held her ribs, she looked like her old elegant self, the one who'd enraptured him at the soiree. No, better.

This rendition had a more robust figure, as outlined through the wind-swept homespun that enveloped her, and there was something about her manner…

Somewhere in the scant hour he'd been away, she'd found a measure of peace.

Smiling, he shoved the notion of a sedative deep into his bag and stopped before them. "Thank you, Private. We'll speak later."

"Yes, sir. Later, sir."

Marcus vaguely noticed his departure. Breath seizing with apprehension, he stood silent for Lillian as she perused his soiled clothes and he conducted a cursory examination.

Her lashes were clumped with wet and a thick sheen of moisture covered her bloodshot eyes, negating the idea she'd come through the ordeal completely unscathed. A tremor commanded her, and her knuckles whitened about her clasped hands, but he sensed it wasn't from fear but from the effort to hold herself in check.

The Lillian he'd come to know would have her arms about his neck by now. Sadly, she refrained and instead stretched out her hands. When he put his in them, she ground his joints.

"You, my dear sir, are a darling sight," she said, thick-throated, reusing his own words. "I would kiss you right here if I had less respect for Mrs. Lane's clothing."

From the looks of that bold smile, he believed her. Odious gown.

"It would wash," he tried on a rising smirk.

She rubbed a stain from the back of his hand, brow pinched. "Did you leave any blood for the poor man?"

He gave a full exhale, satisfied with his morning's labor. "Plenty."

"Will he live?"

"Yes. At least, that's the answer I gave the chief. He was satisfied I'd deflected death, but" — he lifted a shoulder — "God will decide."

"It must have been someone of consequence to give up Water Moccasin for him."

"Not as much as I would have thought, but there's no accounting for Indian loyalty."

"They'll try harder now to break through. To free him."

"I don't think so. We had an agreement. His life for that of the other. They'll stick by it. Whatever the case, you'll be fine."

"You might be right." Her fingers tightened again, pulling. "Come in. Hand over that uniform. I'll wash it."

"In a minute. There's something I need to do first."

When Marcus was admitted to the holding cell, the Indian was on his knees, hands restrained behind him. Here was yet another man who'd saved Lillian when Marcus could not.

An hour ago, they'd passed each other in no-man's land. Marcus had snagged little more than a profile glimpse, but that tattoo… He'd known the warrior in an instant — the one who owned the masked face that for days had epitomized Marcus's anger. For a full minute that evening, he'd been the one responsible for Lillian's death. He'd held her life in his hand, and Marcus had struggled to forgive him that, despite the warrior having halted the inevitable slaughter.

But now? Who could hate a man willing to sacrifice himself for an inferior?

At the sight of Marcus, the chief's eyes lit with expectancy, then — after noticing Marcus's filthy state — with horror; he shot off a few lines in Muskogee.

Not waiting for the translation, Marcus stalked across the small space. "Where has the Spaniard Diego López taken his daughter?"

The chief listened to the interpreter, then spoke a single crisp word. "España."

Marcus flinched. He'd been so certain the don would have chosen to stick closer to home. López was a close-fisted son of a boar and too controlling to wander far from his holdings. Unless the Red Stick was lying?

Marcus stepped closer, eyes slitting in menace.

The chief responded in an instant, and the interpreter supplied, "López told him España, but your woman should know that double-tongued wasp could be anywhere."

Confirmation of Marcus's own theory. Eyes closing, he nodded and decided to try the man for one last question. "How did the war woman know to free Miss McGirth from the friar?"

"Iron Wood." The chief answered promptly in English.

"Do you mean Maxwell Bellamy?"

"Iron Wood," he maintained, giving a firm nod that jostled his feathers.

Did he not know Iron Wood's English name, or was he being obstinate? Either way, there was only one man who would go out of his way to help her. The only one who knew Marcus would be disembarking at Gadsden instead of traveling on to Mobile with Major Ainsworth.

Bellamy. Iron Wood. One and the same.

Marcus was doubly indebted to that mooncalf. It irked, but gratitude snuffed the sting out of it.

He dug the bundle from his pocket and dangled it by its thong. The surprise and light coming over the warrior's face spoke of the object's value. Marcus placed it around his neck, working respectfully around the feathers in his hair.

The chief responded with a lowered head and beseeching speech.

"He thanks you," the interpreter said, "and asks if the warrior has begun the spirit's journey."

Marcus took a long look into the warrior's desperate eyes but knew at once that he wouldn't tell him there was a chance he'd lose his life, or that it might be for nothing. He found a meager smile. "Only God knows."

Chapter 19

*S*leep was carting Marcus away when the sound of his name snatched him back. His lids opened to a lanky cloud traveling across the moon, then blinked lazily toward the voice.

Lillian occupied the infirmary's doorway, lower legs exposed beneath the shirt she used as bed shift. His shirt. Wind billowed the garment and swept both her hair and his blood into a tizzy.

"Marcus!" Her whisper was hardly that. "I need you!"

His pulse sprinted, nearly beating him to her side where the sound of her labored breath struck an alarm within him. "What's wrong? Is that new suture bothering you? Too tight?" Conditioning sent his hand behind her to feel for seepage.

"The suture's fine."

Before bed, while changing her dressing, he'd found the incision on her back had broken open—likely, during her latest nervous eclipse. They'd spent the next half hour under candlelight and needle, repairing it. Never a pleasant affair. But she'd braved it well enough. Better than he, since she'd refused to dull the pain.

The opiate could have ferried her through the procedure and into the night. Perhaps she was of a different persuasion now?

"Having more than average discomfort?" He skimmed the width of her back. All seemed in order, near as he could tell from outside the shirt.

"No, Doctor, but you're welcome to keep checking." She tapped his chin. "Or you can help me with this." She ducked under his arm to reveal a shadowy mound near the door.

He moved inside and, fists on hips, stood over a heaped mattress. "Lillian McGirth, what have you done?"

"As you can see, not much. I hadn't the strength to haul it very far."

"It's *plenty* far. Why are you moving it at all?" There was no curbing the remonstrance. The mattress was little more than straw, but it was unwieldy, and that wound was tenuous enough on its own.

"I intend to join you outdoors."

"Do you now?" So, she was still attached to him at the ribs. No surprise, considering only that morning she'd believed him butchered and left for the buzzards. This dependency wasn't desirable, but it was vast improvement from yesterday's episode.

Although, to listen to her, she didn't sound dependent. Merely…companionable.

"Indeed, I do. A forfeiture of comforts to be sure, but every vow of loyalty has its sacrifices, and, sir, *someone* must attend to your well-being." Her face was a gray, indecipherable mask, but that syrupy intonation, while inviting, was a sure forgery.

Air stuttered as it left his nose. "*My* well-being?"

"Naturally. I'm sparing you the heartache of enduring that magnificent night sky all alone."

"Naturally."

"Hmm." Her body tipped his way, wrecking his pulse. "Well?"

Defenseless against her, he chuckled and hefted the mattress. "You win. I'll give you half an hour, then it's back inside with you."

"No, I'll give *you* half an hour," she purred, scooting past. "And you'll thank me for it."

He likely would.

Once outside, Marcus made sure she was wrapped to her chin inside a blanket and stretched out beside her, keeping a more-than-modest distance. The grounds were vacant, but the patrol would be by soon, and while he doubted there was a man in the Fourth who didn't know her reputation, he didn't care to initiate its downward slide.

At present, they admired her—for having survived the two massacres, for staying the slaughter, for assisting Marcus on his rounds and doling out smiles by the dozens. The last, having started only that day. She'd been too distraught previously to even consider leaving the infirmary.

It was good to have her back at his side, but he had yet to hear from her mouth what had cued the positive change. In all honesty, he was terrified to ask on the chance it ignited another bout of anxiety.

He did have Private Petit's report, which had been full and exuberantly delivered. The account would have sounded outrageous two days ago, but this afternoon, Marcus merely frowned, thanked the soldier for bearing up, and ordered discretion.

Marcus trusted he would obey. The young man seemed wiser than at first believed. Wiser than Marcus for having utilized the one thing that could give her unshakeable security. Private Petit had accomplished what Marcus had failed to do—persuade her to come out on her own. God's methods were more varied than Marcus would like, but far be it from him to disapprove. In fact, he folded his arms beneath his head, peered beyond the stars toward the Unseen, and ushered up gratitude for this blessed shift in the wind.

"Clear skies since this afternoon," she said. "Dare we hope the miserable haze is gone for good?"

"We do."

"Then we shall." Hope strengthened her delivery.

Inspired by it, Marcus let his head fall to the side and splurged in the study of her silhouette: the lashes that in a few blinks could sweep away prudence, the lips that looked like glory and tasted it too, the jaw whose hollow had nestled his mouth so perfectly. How tempting to put it there again...

She chose that moment of debility to tip her head to him. Cheek bunching with a smile, she tenderly raked through the hair falling over his forehead. "I cannot imagine another man outside of my father to whom I could entrust myself in the dark. You are strong where I am weak."

In truth, as he relished the feel of her fingers furrowing his hair, he feared that somewhere along the road to Tensaw, indiscretion would have its way with him, mauling integrity into a shameful pulp.

If she but knew his wrestling heart! But she mustn't, for if there were ever a woman who required an unshakeable pillar, it was Lillian McGirth, now, in this imperiled stockade. Conscience pricked, he retreated from her. "If any strength is to be found in me, any integrity at all, it isn't my own but the Father's. That, I can assure you."

"I predicted you would say that. This only affirms my conviction, you understand."

Footfalls sounded behind them. The patrol. The man veered wide, passing near the wall but close enough to reset Lillian's proper distance.

"My sisters and I were wont to do this. Stretch out on a cloudless night, count shooting stars." Her tenor deepened with nostalgia and a shade of grief.

It cracked Marcus's bones that hardly a thing could be said or done, but Lillian wasn't painfully reminded of the war.

"We'd have competitions," she continued, "to see who could compose the strangest picture in the stars. Most nights, I couldn't be beat."

"Now you've done it, put my pride in a bind, obliged me to defeat the champion," he quipped, gunning to lighten her mood. A merry heart couldn't be bottled, but it was fine medicine nevertheless.

"Sounds delightful." The smile in her voice concurred. "I accept the challenge."

"I do hope you take losing in good stride."

"That confident in your abilities, are you?"

"There's no topping a manatee with a pirate hook. Look, it's there." He pointed to a random patch of stars. "Start with that dim one. Follow it up and around for, oh, eleven more. Give or take. That's its head. Three out to the right from that bluish one would be the point of its fin, and—"

"Manatees don't have fins, Marcus."

"This one does. Why are you laughing?" He executed a playful harrumph. "This is my star picture. I can make it however I please."

She cleared her throat, snorting in the process, dispensing that medicine with liberality. "Pardon *me*, sir. Do finish. What of the flippers?"

"No flippers, remember."

"Ah, yes, the pirate hook. And where exactly would that be located?"

"It isn't visible. The fin is in the way."

Her responding laughter was full and scarcely dampened, an efficacious tonic that healed fissures of strain and worry clear to Marcus's marrow.

"I concede!" she said, still laughing. "Here, my white flag."

"Captain Buck, is that you down there?" a voice called from the elevated walk.

Marcus popped upright. "It is."

"Is, uh, Miss McGirth with you, sir?"

"Er, well—"

"I'm here," she said, sweetly. "The captain and I are playing a star-gazing game."

"Can I play?"

Marcus scowled. "Aren't you supposed to be looking the other direction? Something to do with picket duty."

"Yes, sir. Sorry, sir. Good luck to you."

"The cheater doesn't need it," Lillian mumbled and jabbed a finger into his ribs.

Chuckling, Marcus volted a second poke, then captured her hand and lay back down. Even once settled, head flat on the ground, he kept hold, rubbing the cool from her fingers, integrity quite secure beneath the watchful eye of the patrol.

Surrendering without protest, she edged closer, easing the stretch of her arm. She sighed, long and doleful. "This hour might be perfect, except for…" She could have been talking about the nip in the wind or the hostile Natives encompassing them, but Marcus knew better.

"Except for Mari."

Silence settled in for an aching stint. At last, she interrupted it with a snuffle. "It hurts. Here." She knocked her sternum, voice thickening. "Every day. Every infernal minute! Like a thorn I cannot pull out."

The one pain no laughter would touch. "I would pluck it from you this second, if I could. But make no mistake, I *will*. It might take some doing, but I'll find her, duchess. I swear it."

She squeezed his hand. "If it comes from your mouth, I trust it."

"Even if it's a hook-finned manatee?"

"Even that. See?" She indicated. "Its eye is the North Star, steady and true."

He looked off, to the guard who stuttered sleepily along the wall walk in much the way Marcus's mind did at her trust in him. Where did she get such faith? He'd failed her again and again.

"Marcus?" Volume crumbling in that disturbingly fearful way of hers, she tightened her hold.

He set to work massaging away the worriment. "Hmm?"

"We'll see our way beyond these pickets…won't we?"

There it was, the reason she needed so desperately to believe in him. Certain of this one thing, he gave firm delivery. "We will." Though he couldn't say when or how.

"We *will*," she repeated quietly, as though to herself. "In Him will I trust."

Was she quoting scripture? Did she mean it? Sensing there was more to come, Marcus lifted on his elbow to better see her.

A black cloud billowed about her head, fell across her neck, and spread onto the strip of dirt between their pallets. Admonishing himself not to be greedy, he twirled his finger through a single lock, withheld a half-dozen questions, and waited.

"God met me," she said, rewarding his patience. "In the supply closet while you were away. At first, I didn't quite see it, but as I've thought on it, I've become quite certain it was Him."

"What did He say?"

"He spoke to me of trust, which I gave Him. But stepping from a closet in an infirmary is a simple matter compared to that of the soul. To entrust Him with my own, I must believe in absolute mercy." Replicating his posture, she came up on her elbow, and though it wrung from her an abrupt, throaty inhalation, she forged ahead, determined and intense. "My heart longs for such a thing, Marcus, with a yearning I cannot even express. My soul, though... It demands justice be wrought against it, and I cannot free myself of the thought!"

Angst was a crushing thing; the guilt, a load she needn't bear.

Desperate for her to listen, to embrace Truth, he gripped her hand with a fierceness not his own. "Your soul isn't mistaken. Its demand is more than reasonable. But, dear woman, justice has already been wrought! Against the Son. Your scourging was already endured. This suffering of yours—the fasting, the fear, the self-recrimination—it's a crippling, wasted effort. Let it go! Cling to His abundant mercy instead."

He inclined her way, adding stress to his message. "You were taught this from a child, Lillian, I know it. Now, *believe*."

As though caught in his flame, she drew toward him. "And you believe it for yourself, despite your...offenses? Without doubt?"

"Without a shred of it. I'm too proud a man to worship a God who hasn't the power to atone for every wrong, no matter the weight, no matter the number."

Marcus spoke with such utter conviction Lillian almost believed. Almost. "Your faith is persuading."

"Believe for His sake. And your own. Can you do that?"

He was right, of course. As he most always was. Such a profession was too grave to make without absolute certainty. There was no loss to be had by embracing complete mercy. It was the arrogance of the matter that disturbed her. Who was *she* to think God might care for her enough to erase her past, even if only in His eyes? It was unfathomable.

Now, if instead of trouble at every turn she had evidence, some sign that He'd forgiven her, wished her to start anew with a fresh soul...

She broke from Marcus's silent, head-tilting inquiry to peer skyward.

Evidence, Lord. What evidence is there?

She was ever on the hunt for it. For justice, for innocence, and now, for Truth.

Though she took thorough stock of her circumstances, she saw no further than the mountain of consequences that forever cast a pall over her: the loss of her virtue, her dignity, her child. And when she arrived in Tensaw, there would certainly be no clean slate to welcome her.

The fact she continued to draw breath might be proof enough, if she weren't convinced God hadn't spared her to complete her earthly purgatory. Did He love her enough to forgive it all? Could He possibly? Scripture claimed He did, but...

Biting back a groan of pain, Lillian lowered herself to the mattress. The bruises to her heart and body had done more than slow her down. They'd blurred her spiritual vision so that she couldn't see past her own miserable situation.

If the Almighty wished her to believe, to trust, He would have to wave the proof beneath her nose, shove it into her arms, pour it throughout her parched spirit.

Could she believe for His sake? Eyes burning with fatigue, she let her lids fall shut. "I don't think so, Marcus. I just don't think so."

"Ask Him for faith. He won't deny you," he said, climbing to his feet. "But ask Him in the infirmary. I'm too tired to amputate frostbitten toes tonight. Up you go." Shades of playfulness brightened his tone; it wasn't catching.

The last thing she wanted was to part from him, but too soul-sick to gripe, she rose and followed him into the dark building and watched his indistinct form rearrange her bedding. At the prospect of being alone, her body convulsed with a shiver, but wordlessly, she crawled under the covers, throat rattling with a sigh.

Marcus stilled, looking down at her, then stepped away and returned with the *tink-scrape* of iron against flint. A candlewick caught and washed his face in warbling golds that snagged on his scruff and made his eyes into pools of liquid charcoal. Their touch was gentle yet struck oddly. Something was different about them. They held a trace of…what? Not tenderness, per se—he was focused, jelled in that studious expression she'd come to love. Then…what?

He brought the candle nearer to her, making her squint and weakening the clarity of his features but not so much that she missed the downward curve of his mouth. What did he see on her that caused it? There was no telling. The man was forever concerned about something or other. It was in his nature to worry and—

He loves you.

She blinked into the brilliance, and to the sound of the closet cricket chirping a weary tune, she worked the idea over.

From the first, she'd known he desired her, respected her. Later, he'd made it apparent he appreciated her, trusted her. She'd capitalized on the first, and it was hard enough to believe he managed any of the rest, but *love* her…? Was that what she was seeing?

On herself, love was commitment, sacrifice, protection. But what exactly did genuine love look like on a man not her father? On Marcus? Curious now, she reconsidered his expression. It was intense, probing, narrowed with query. Nothing sensual about it, nothing particularly adoring. Yet the plunge of those brows… It told her he wouldn't rest until she did. Diego had never looked deeply enough to detect weariness much less worry over it.

Marcus bumped a fingertip over the knuckles she used to clutch her blanket. "Do you need anything?"

A simple offer. One of a thousand such he'd made over the weeks. Combined, they constructed a picture not of duty or desire but of prolific dedication. Was that the evidence of love?

Perhaps so. But there was more. His passion to see her healed— without, within. And his restraint, that beautiful, cursed restraint! Every time he stayed his hands, he loved her.

It came again, firmer—*he loves you.*

The power and beauty of the notion beclouded her vision and jostled her smile.

When he sank to a crouch, eyebrows crashing inward, her theory was proven correct. Only love responded to so little with such great fervor.

Oh, Marcus... Did he know his heart? If so, he was heeding her warning to guard it, for he'd verbalized no interest beyond help of a practical nature. But then, she'd already concluded he was a wise man...

"What's wrong, duchess?"

"Nothing. Can't a woman love a man to tears?"

Those two liquid orbs solidified into blood-scorching coals that set the flame in his hand to dancing, and it had nothing to do with airflow. "She may, so long as her conscience can bear the cruelty she inflicts." The twitch playing at his mouth bloomed a cheeky smile on hers.

"I should stop then?"

He blew out the candle, swaddling them in darkness and the incense of burnt cotton. The cot squeaked as he used it to rise, a grunt pushing softly from him. Admit it or not, that back of his pained him. When she'd given up an answer for lost, he sank and linked the corners of their mouths in a motionless almost-kiss.

A miss? No, every pump of the man's heart was deliberate, every blink a well-thought-out plan. She closed her eyes and savored him, filling her lungs with his sudsy scent.

"Stop," he said, voice husky, "and I'll never forgive you."

Under the curious eye of the black-capped chickadee garnishing the clothesline pole, Lillian balanced laundry in her arm and groped several drying rags. Satisfied, she crammed them between her chin and the top of the pile.

Hey-sweetie, hey-sweetie! The bird cocked its adorably oversized head at her, its feathered throat undulating with song.

"Hey to you too, sweetie." She smiled, delighted to hear birdsong versus that of the musket. Not a one had been fired since yesterday right before Water Moccasin had been marched across this very ground.

When she reached for the last stiff rag, the sleeve of Marcus' uniform jacket flopped out of the pile, threatening to unravel everything. She snatched it up and hugged the mound to prevent any more escape attempts. If only the man were as easily contained.

Before the thought could settle, she banished it. Would she want him any way other than endlessly sacrificial? Not for a moment. That was the quality she most admired, and to constrain it would be to ruin the man.

One thing she *could* control—his regimentals. Her knuckles had given skin for that filthy jacket, having scrubbed until the bucket water no longer pinkened. Even so, if the fabric were anything but black, it would surely reveal a world of stains.

Red Stick blood.

Another banished thought. She was a fractured eggshell and didn't trust herself in the hands of even the mildest fear.

She crossed over the patch of flattened grass where only hours earlier she'd lain under the stars and heard the faintest of Divine traces. How lovely it would be to believe it had been God's call to pull her out of the dirt.

"Men approaching!" a soldier called, running along the wall walk toward the gate. "Prepare to open. They're ours!"

Americans? And they'd made it through? The toe of Lillian's oversized shoe caught on grass as she stammered to a halt. "Doctor Buck!" she called toward the hospital. They would surely need him.

He appeared in the open doorway and tracked her gaze.

The smaller, single-door gate gave way to three soldiers and slammed shut again, rattling the picket clear to where she stood. All were travel-worn, but there wasn't a scalp missing among them: two dusty Americans and one sandy-haired, crimson-trimmed Spaniard.

Lillian's arms went slack. The laundry hit her feet. She leapt over it, jarring her wounds, and darted past Marcus. "It's Prieto! Teniente," she shouted en route, skirt in hand. "*Soy yo.* Liana!"

Sighting her, the soldado grinned and, breaking from those gathering about, accepted her enthusiastic set of kisses. Juniper eyes all a twinkle, he stepped back and scoped her form. "By the blessed saints, I do believe that is fat on your bones again. The medico has done well by you. But señorita…" He scowled, gaze falling to where she cradled her grumpy ribs. "You are hurt?"

"A token to remember the ambush by."

"I heard of it. A tragedy, and I am deeply sorry." He removed his shako, lashes sinking.

Marcus strolled into Lillian's periphery and stopped, body frozen in an arrested turn. The other two arrivals were nearby, looking from him to the flag-topped headquarters building and back, seeming dependent on Marcus and eager to be off to whatever business had brought them.

His gaze went to Prieto and swifted back to her. The inquisitive arch of his brows told her he would delay his task if she but asked. Further confirmation of his love.

She smiled a thank you and raised her chin to usher him on his way, then refocused on Prieto, sensing Marcus leave.

"It must have been dreadful," he was saying, "and now, a siege. The commander of Fuerte Gadsden is not aware."

"We barely got in with our lives. No courier would make it past that wall of hostiles. How did you get through?"

"The chief and I have an understanding."

"The prophet Francis?"

"*El Toro*." The Bull. "He let us pass."

Tall Bull was out there? She'd not seen him in that terrifying race from the riverbank to the fort, but her wits *had* been negligible. Whatever the case, he was there now, and no doubt, he was aware of her as well.

What glorious pleasure it would be to give that Red Stick a piece of her livid mind! Then again, every grain of powder in his horn likely had a prayer whispered over it—a curse on her name. Her stomach gave a nauseating flip.

In the next instant, sweat cooled her upper lip. She swiped at it, gathered composure. "What brings you this way, Teniente? I take it that cockroach of a don sacked you." Otherwise, the teniente would be with him now. "It was on account of helping me, wasn't it?"

"Nothing of the sort. *Escuche*. Listen." He donned his cap and took both her hands, the gravity in his tone sending her belly into another roll. "Our ship was boarded off the coast of *Pasa Cristiana*. An American warship overtook us in the night."

Blood rushed Lillian's head, pounded her cracked rib, and set her off balance. She stiffened, gripped the teniente hard. Dare she hope, dare she speak Mari's name? No, she hadn't the strength. "And Diego? What of him?"

Sunlight vivified the green in Teniente Prieto's steady eyes, as well as the gratification wrinkling their corners. "In irons."

"Madre santisima, the Americanos have him? Was there a battle?" An image came to her of his sword flashing in the moonlight, defending his precious honor. He wouldn't have been easily subdued.

"Sí, señorita, but he fought poorly thanks to your dagger." His fingers compressed hers as an admiring smirk disturbed his lips.

A laugh burst open her mouth. "Is it evil to rejoice at this small victory? No, I refuse to have an attack of conscience. Where is he now? Tell me he is in a dank cell being fed flavorless mush."

"Moldy crusts and maggoty water, no?" The teniente's bubble of laughter merged with hers. "Sorry to say he is only under house arrest, secluded to his cabin but eating as sumptuously as ever." He segued into an account of the short-lived battle, but Lillian's train of thought persisted in another direction.

If Diego was in custody and Teniente Prieto was here, then... "Where is she?" Lillian interrupted, leaning to see beyond him, as if Barb might appear at the gate, babe in arms. "Where is my Mari!"

He beamed an understanding smile. "The vessel is moored in the bay of Apalachicola and is under control of Fuerte Gadsden. La doncella waits for you there."

Shock snatched her breath. Mari, so close!

He continued relaying instructions. "...leave immediately...two days' travel..." but his voice was overcome by that of the Divine—a single word she could not refute.

Evidence.

Palms flat on Major Cooley's desk, Marcus stared at the parchment laid out before him. A bold, black signature decorated the bottom right corner. General Jackson's.

No getting around this one. Even so, he glared at it, wished it voided.

The new assignment was disruptive enough, but the postscript from Major Ainsworth... It stirred turbulent eddies within him.

...her dutiful assistance is requested...she would be wise to...

Lopez's confiscated vessel was sure to store a handsome cache of condemning evidence, but to expect Lillian to return and dig it up—because his useless soldiers couldn't—and facing the don in the process, was brutish. So typically Ainsworth!

Requested? Rubbish! This was an indisputable summons, and they would be fools to ignore it. The next week or more would see Lillian plundering the ship and stationing herself behind a desk to tediously translate her former lover's files, and every day she spent at that glum task was one less with her father. Her pay? A cleared name.

"This is happy news, Doctor," Major Cooley said above the indignant throb of Marcus's heart. "Even an ailing father will recognize its import. McGirth will forgive the delay, even if you do not. Frankly, this offer of Ainsworth's astounds me. He isn't a man to extend an olive branch."

Marcus straightened, dragging the orders off the tabletop. "Indeed, he is not." And Major Ainsworth was the least of their worries. Jackson was the true hurdle. "Miss McGirth is astute. She'll be grateful, but I won't have her know of it until I deem it appropriate," he declared as though he were senior officer among the four in the room. "She should have this time to cherish news of her child."

Mari, that beautiful baby—his own precious child, he dared hope—not one hundred miles south of this very spot. Healthy and safe. The best of tidings, and contrary to Marcus's multiple vows, he'd had absolutely nothing to do with the intricate details required to see it accomplished. Though he exulted in the clever God he served, he again questioned his own purpose.

Bellamy had brought her from the brink of starvation. The war woman had seen her clear of López's stranglehold. God's own miracle had saved her on the boat; Water Moccasin, in the ambush. Even Private Petit had succeeded where Marcus had not—he'd gotten her to walk out of the closet on her own. Now, Lieutenant Prieto brought news of Mari…

Thank you, Father, but have I displeased you, missed a turn in the road? I pledged to protect them, but You continue to choose others. I ask you, Lord Jesus, let me! If I am too weak, be my strength. Be the marrow in my bones, the healing in my touch, the power in my blade.

His blade, indeed. How he would have thrilled to be the man to bring López to heel!

Lieutenant Prieto would have told Lillian by now the don was captured and the baby awaited. Marcus should be with her, rejoicing. Instead, he was at headquarters, scratching his head over his uselessness and orchestrating her fate to the best of his limited ability.

Not of a mood to quibble overlapping authority, he faced Major Cooley with an imposing air and concluded with, "As her surgeon, I exert the right to dictate this matter and all others pertaining to her. Are we agreed?"

By the strict line of Cooley's lips, they were not. Even so, he nodded. "Very well, I will defer to you. Sergeant Sutherland, you now fall under Major Buck's command."

"Understood, sir," the sergeant said. "My orders are to report back immediately, no delays. Since we have a full day of travel available to us, I put to you, Major, we start out at once. Major?"

Marcus blinked, jolted. He was being addressed. "Granted. Swing by the commissary for rations for the lot of us, and—"

The door banged open.

Lillian burst inside, eyes radiant, braid whipping sideways with her abrupt halt. Her eyes bolted to his. "It's Mari! She's in Gadsden!"

"Miss McGirth, won't you join us?" Major Cooley said with an impatient sweep of his arm that went wholly unnoticed by her.

She was already flying to Marcus, then clinging to his sash, blind to her audience. "Don't speak to me of Ainsworth. I know he might be there, but I don't care. If they release Diego on a lack of evidence, and he disappears with her again—Marcus, I've *got* to go back. And Prieto assures he can get me through the siege. He'll take me today. This very hour!"

Constructing a smile, Marcus smoothed the wild hair from her face. "Of course, you must. I'll take you."

"You will? The major will allow it?" She looked to Major Cooley.

"It, uh… With pleasure. Captain—er *Major* Buck has been assigned your escort. Lieutenant Lynch here is his replacement." He gestured to the surgeon, another of the three arrivals.

Drawing a breath of surprise, Lillian smiled broadly at Marcus. "You've been promoted. Marcus, that's wonderful!"

It would be more so if it were up for trade. His rank for her good name. Taming an irascible curl of his lip, he held up the half-crumpled ordinance. "Promoted and…reassigned. I'll soon be working directly under General Jackson."

"That's"—her lashes fluttered in her pause to take it in—"quite complimentary. Going back might give you another shot at justice. Will you work as his personal physician?"

Since the Red Sticks raised the war club, he'd given barely a thought to justice, Maxwell Bellamy, or any British infraction. It had become insignificant. Still was. He'd rather be with Lillian than pursuing satisfaction for wrongs against him. "No specifics stated. Only that I'm to await further instruction at Gadsden."

She flinched at this, countenance declining, and Marcus readied for a breakdown. "And your thirty days? No chance of it?"

"I'm afraid not, but Mari has been found," he hurried to add.

As hoped, the reminder rallied that breath-catching smile of hers. It was slow in coming but worth the wait. "So she has." The woman purely glittered. Misting over with emotion, she spoke for him alone.

"God is indeed merciful."

Mouth parted, as close to excruciatingly speechless as ever he'd been, Marcus gazed at her perfect serenity. *May Your mercies be abundant, Father; may they see the week through.*

Fortunately, she didn't wait for a reply but sniffed to clear her tears, dignified her spine, and strode queenly to Major Cooley. "Major, your hospitality has been gracious and gratefully received." She offered her hand, which he took and bent over. "That said," she went on, her smile glutted with charm, "you must excuse me. I am quitting this dreadful place."

Cooley laughed. "I don't blame you in the least. My prayers for safe travels, miss."

"Thank you, sir, for we shall certainly need them."

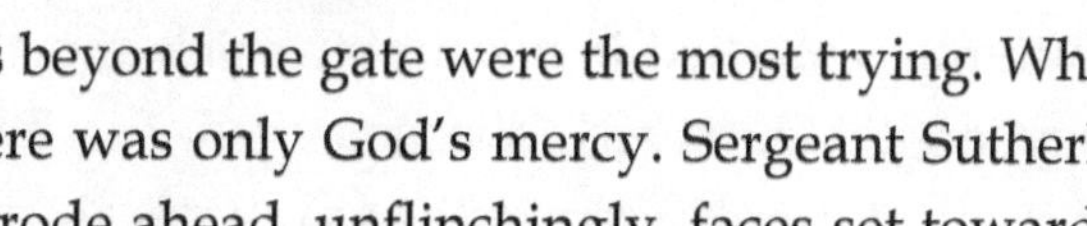

Lillian's first paces beyond the gate were the most trying. When it closed behind her, there was only God's mercy. Sergeant Sutherland and Teniente Prieto strode ahead, unflinchingly, faces set toward the river. Then there was Marcus, his able sword, and his willingness to die. But for all their manly courage, this hour belonged only to the Red Sticks and whatever power God allowed them.

Lillian focused on that, on Him. There was no sinister forest, no lurking Indians, no pillaged, half-sunken flatboat at the end of a dismembered dock. There was only God above, Marcus alongside her, and Mari at river's end.

The men pressed into their march, leading her swiftly through the stump-speckled field and onto the broad trail bisecting that wicked plat of brushwood and trees. Quiet rustlings and murmuring met her ears as their enemy emerged from the shadows to casually line the lane on both sides, observing.

Lillian kept her eyes and feet on the wagon-wheel rut that reached toward the water. Mrs. Lane's shoes created an obscene *clomp-clomp,* drawing attention to Lillian and the fact these very Indians were responsible for the shoes being on *her* feet instead of those of their unfortunate owner.

You're adopted Creek, she reassured herself. *Beaver.* Water Moccasin would have made it known.

Marcus's hand covered hers, its warmth an instant salve.

Her gaze lifted to him. It registered his loving smile a beat before entangling with movement beyond him.

A familiar figure waded through the thickets, his shaded face directed at her. He stopped before reaching the sunlight and propped himself on the trunk of a palm. The lofty height and unshaven hair ordained him Tall Bull.

That scoundrel, he'd abandoned her! The echo of his cruel laughter reverberated between her ears, bringing to sharp memory every furious heartbeat, every insult she'd shot into his receding back, every foul word she'd ever attributed to the Red Sticks and their savage cause.

Bitterness swelled in her throat, thick and choking. "Tall Bull, you mangy dog!" Outraged, she snatched her hand from Marcus and barreled past him, then past the four, five, six warriors who snarled at him to halt.

"Lillian? Lillian! What are you —?" Marcus's voice was tight with exertion. "Hands off me! Lillian, darling, don't be rash. Think!"

His plea reinstated her good judgement; it killed her charge as she was coming up under the nose of a warrior who sidestepped to barricade his chief. "That is not peace you bring, little sister."

"Let her come." Tall Bull's strangely frail voice broke on the last word. "There is talk in her, and I will hear it."

The guard moved aside, revealing a man who leaned not out of casual repose but out of necessity. The vibrant copper of Tall Bull's skin had yielded to an unhealthy sandy hue; his lips, to the pallor of some grievous malady. Remnants of blood stained his poorly washed shirt and suggested the cause of his affliction.

Had Tall Bull been the one Marcus saved? Had *his* blood stained the bucket water? Lillian's fingers twitched, their knuckles still riotous over her abuse. If so, Marcus hadn't breathed a word, but then, he knew the limits of her feeble mind...

Arms languishing at his sides, Tall Bull kept silent. Fatigue lined his wan features with age he didn't possess. Slouched and vulnerable, he was an altogether different man. His eyes, however, were the same swaggering globes she'd encountered at the pillory when he'd tied the cape about her neck and advised her to salvage dignity.

The crack of cane against bone came rushing to her in a memory as stingingly fresh as five seconds past. Her lungs lurched in want of air, capturing a whiff of holly in their efforts. Tall Bull's scent. What might have become of her that day if not for him, his disgust and defiance?

Liana, the friar is determined. Barros spoke anew into her ear. *You will not survive the question!*

But she had. Because of the man flagging before her.

Every recrimination she might've spouted evaporated in the blazing knowledge that the debt she owed him outweighed his presumptuous kiss and spiteful neglect. And in the end, hadn't God worked His good will? She was all but free; Mari, all but restored to her.

Everything between that frightful night and now was a blur of war and violence and held no bearing on *this*, on them and their uncommon connection.

Her shoulders deflated, and Tall Bull's brow perked.

"Well, Bitter Eyes? Speak your thoughts. My ears will hear."

Was that humility or ailment lowering his tone? Not that it mattered, Lillian no longer had a sour lecture with which to bless those willing ears of his. She'd rather be scudding down the Apalachicola toward Mari. As her heels began a backtrack, she cast an eye about for her clan sister. Mink's glaring absence brought to mind another person missing from this scene.

Lillian's remembered promise interrupted her retreat. "Water Moccasin spoke to me."

Eyes flaring wide, Tall Bull shoved off the tree and stood erect, limbs quivering. With weakness, hopeful expectation, wrath? Whatever the cause, he pridefully hardened his lips and waited.

"His message to you was, 'for my brother, my chief, and for the

People. No fences, no fetters.'"

Tall Bull's knee collapsed. He flailed. A warrior leapt to assist, but Tall Bull shunned it. Though his breath was shallow and irregular and his strength nearing spent, he rectified himself and made indignant fists at his sides. "What else of my brother?"

"His fate is yet undecided." But it wasn't good, judging by the fort's injurious sentiment.

Water Moccasin, of all Red Sticks...

A film coated Lillian's vision. She lowered her lids to disguise it. "The commander hesitates. I pled for his life, but..." A meager shrug finished the despairing thought.

"Then we will wait and hope."

"Have you said your piece?" Marcus called. "Come back to me, duchess. Mari awaits."

Gripped by a sudden, fierce longing for them both, Lillian glimpsed behind her.

"Go to your man." Canting again toward the palm, Tall Bull dismissed her with a jerk of his head. "Two of my braves will see you safely through to Hambly's lodge. From there, you will encounter no trouble."

"Maddo and...farewell." Breaking from his lethargic eyes, she turned.

"Liana."

She paused, looked back.

Tall Bull remained as he'd been, but softness had come into his face, erasing an element of the ravages of war and refreshing his masculine beauty. "May your journey be swift, guided by Master of Breath," he said on a wistful smile. "May your heart sing and your belly laugh, and may our beloved Grandmother Sun shine her gift of life upon you. Until we meet again, Sister."

Chapter 20

The dory's transom was still several yards from sliding onto Gadsden's bank when Marcus froze mid-row to glance behind and grin. "Nearly there, duchess."

Craning for an impossible view of the fort, Lillian huffed. "Not nearly enough." A sparkle leapt into her eyes an instant before she quitted her seat at the sternsheets and scampered over every obstacle that lay between her and the bow, including Marcus's legs and Sutherland's dripping oar.

The man raised an outcry that was cleaved short by the boat's violent pitch. Lillian gained purchase on the mast, but Prieto, the unlucky fellow, was chucked headfirst into the water.

Balanced imperially on the forward thwart, she graced the sputtering soldier with a downward glance, tacking on two Spanish words that might have been an apology but for the brazenly delighted chortle that pursued them.

Laughing, Marcus tossed aside his oar and, predicting an abrupt introduction with the shore, rose to brace her. "Have a care, Lillian. You'll tumble when we—"

Her merry squeal cut him short. Skirt hiked to her thighs, she leapt the gunwale, sank to her knees, and was sloshing inland before he'd gathered his loose jaw.

Having shouldered his haversack and weapons, he left the other men with the boat and set out after her. By the time he tramped upon solid ground, she'd kicked off her shoes and was halfway up the wooded rise that led to the fort. Bare feet a blur, hair a tattered banner struggling to keep up, she pressed hard. Her stride met with some minor obstruction, and she lurched.

Marcus hissed a wince. Before the day was done, his suture thread was sure to be recommissioned, but he didn't have the heart to shout her to a halt. As if she would listen. Indeed, even now, she clutched her ribcage but carried on, gaining speed and lighting Marcus's face with a grin.

The woman was uncontainable.

He bent for her shoes—Mrs. Lane's actually, for Lillian maintained she would return every borrowed item to the woman's own hands. Said with such hope, too. Hope, confidence, trust in the Almighty's mercy—a thing she'd begun claiming on Mrs. Lane's behalf.

The Lillian McGirth who'd uttered that darling prayer during their private moments at dawn was a far different creature from the one who'd leaned into him on this very bank, scorched his blood with a simple roll of her head, and trembled with premonitions of evil and talk of losing her child forever.

Had it been only twenty days since that early morning chat? Not possible. It was a month, a year! A mere tick of the heart in light of the lifetime he intended for them.

At Gadsden's picket, a chirpy soldier waved Marcus through the gate. "Welcome back, Doc."

Marcus arrested his march long enough to reciprocate a smart salute. "Thank you, soldier."

"If you're lookin' for Miss McGirth, she took off for the parade grounds. Told her I saw the little miss there, takin' the air not five minutes ago."

The man needn't have said; Lillian's cry was beacon enough.

"Mari, Mari!" It was the voice of agony, the wail of a mother whose deprived heart would spare not one beat more unless given to her child.

Ripped clean through by it, Marcus rounded the guard shack,

putting in his sights the expansive, soldier-strewn grounds and Lillian's hunched form limping a sprint across it.

Beyond her, Barbury performed a speedy about-face, black shawl slipping off her slender shoulders. She matched Lillian's shout of joy and broke into a jog; Mari jostled against her bosom.

Lillian flew into her embrace but swiftly came away with the baby, laughing and crying, spinning and kissing a giggling Mari in every conceivable spot.

The picture drew Marcus up soundly. It felled the shoes from his grasp and the musket from his shoulder. The loss of their weight was no counterbalance to the relief and gratitude that bowed him, forced propping hands to his knees. Head hanging, he resisted the nip behind his lids, then gave in and let it water the dead grass between his feet.

They were out; they were safe; they were together.

"They're yours," he said to himself. The whisper, though hoarse, was firm and set his mind to plotting.

He straightened, blinked away the sheen, and topped off the swell of his heart with a greedy look at his two loves. Mari held her mother's face between her hands and gnawed her cheek with open-mouthed kisses. Lillian's laughter was full and bright, but her eyes were not on her child. They were focused long. On him.

She shifted the baby to free an arm and extended it toward him with a luscious smile.

His heart stammered; his body stirred. Before God, he would marry that woman. Today.

Lillian lay on her side, head pillowed on the crook of her folded arm, growing drowsy on Barbury's humming and Marisol's rhythmic, soppy noises. Dead to all but her lash-fluttering dreams, Mari snuggled face-in against Lillian's chest, mouth working her forefinger like a milkmaid.

Barbury tidied Lillian's gown, tugging it over exposed ankles. "You go on and sleep now, Missy Lillian. Been a hard stretch a days. Reckon you done earned a siesta or two."

Two hours after being reunited, Lillian had joined Mari for a nap in Barb's room, a windowless chamber in a row of six. Officer's quarters, if Lillian had a guess, but still barely challenging a deck of cards for size.

"Barb," she whispered, nabbing the woman's hand as she was pulling away. "What do they know? About you."

Head lowering, Barbury relaxed her grip, but Lillian held fast. "Told 'em I's yours."

"And you are. Mine and Mari's. Our true friend."

"Ain't so, missy. I done you wrong by—"

"No call for that. You were powerless and used. Threatened, too, I'm sure. A hateful situation for any woman. I know its bitter taste, and I hold no ill will. You'll come home as my slave, and no one will be the wiser until we've arranged your freedom—whatever form that may take. Now, let me hug you, then see if you can work your magic on those torn stockings."

Once Barbury had settled in with her needle, the bed grew snug, sleep locked horns with her, but she dug in her heels, unwilling to lose sight of her baby for the span of even a wink.

Her present world consisted of Mari, her innocence and vulnerability; her flawless skin, plush satin against Lillian's fingertips; the tiny puffs of air fluttering her nostrils and disturbing the ribbon at her throat. Every part of the child became a mind-consuming miracle. Even Marcus, her heart's desire, was dim in Lillian's thoughts.

But beyond their door, life did continue.

Teniente Prieto, who oddly hadn't left her side since returning, had stationed himself outside the door as sentinel, dropping Marcus's shoulders by a full inch before he'd excused himself to report to the commander. He'd promised to return with grub and more commodious sleeping arrangements.

She'd expressed her appreciation, but really, she could manage where she was. Besides, if she played it right, they would be leaving in a day, two at most. She was a smart woman; she could find the documents and ransack them in nothing flat.

Mari—as well as Marcus's justice—depended on her. If Diego were to be extradited from their coasts, she might find a way to sleep at night without the fear that he and his nobleman's army would show up on her porch step red-faced and shaking a fabricated birth certificate before her nose. If he wasn't, well… According to Diego's handsome documentation, Lillian had no rights to her own child. Without condemning evidence to hold the don, the major would be obligated to apologize and let him go, putting Mari into his arms to aid in restoring marred relations.

She would fight herself bloody before that happened.

Fingers skimming the back of Mari's flossy head, Lillian delivered another worshipful prayer of thanks and pledged on spiritual hands and knees she'd become a mother worthy of this second chance. If God could be gracious a little longer…

A tap sounded at the door. At a nod from Lillian, Barbury set aside her darning and rose. She opened to a blast of white afternoon light that squeezed around Marcus's broad shoulders to forge inside ahead of him. It outlined the chaos of his hair and shadow-blackened his face and pierced Lillian's eyes.

She sealed her lids against it, listened, and waited in delicious anticipation of the sight of him. Whispers were exchanged; the door was clicked shut; footfalls neared, muted but sure. The clean scent of lye reached her ahead of him, and she smiled. When her lids came apart, Barb was gone, and he was roosted low before her, knees splayed, bicorn hanging from the hand that hovered between them, looking not at her but at Mari.

Rising slightly, he leaned in to brush his lips against the baby's crown, eyes tightening in discomfort. Then, he claimed Lillian with a burdened gaze. "From the hour you fell into my arms," he said on a wisp, a strange desperation hurrying his words, "every choice I've made, succeed or fail, has been with your welfare in mind."

What was this? Fear? Of what? Losing her respect, her love? Impossible. "I know that, Marcus." She skimmed the pinkened, pencil-straight line of his scar. "I trust you with my life. And Mari's."

"I plead God that never changes." Wearing doubt-riddled eyes, he showed her a sedate smile. "I love you, Lillian." He lifted over Mari and sank to Lillian's mouth.

Before she could savor the word *love* or the tingle curling through her womb, he pulled back to stare dismally at a distant point over her head.

What could possibly be dampening his spirits at this, of all moments?

A squall gathered in his gray eyes. "My mind is in a veritable spin over how to manage that weasel of a don."

As was hers at his fluctuation. She traced the worry lines marring his brow. "Try not to fret. I have a good idea of where to look."

He blinked away the storm, pressed her fingers to his mouth, and smiling, spilled moist breath between them. "All right, duchess. No fretting." Taking on a sudden twinkle, he blessed her with an enchanting smile that was skewed with mischief. "I've decided you were right about—"

Marisol stirred, peeped a complaint, and redoubled her suckling.

Copying his scant volume, Lillian rubbed Mari's little back and prompted, "Right about what?"

"Your need to assume a new identity. Start afresh."

One of her brows launched upward. "Oh?"

"Best for all involved, chiefly myself." He gave her a coltish grin and settled a hand on the valley of her waist, a bold requisition. "I want it squared away as soon as possible. This afternoon."

Heart storming the walls of her chest, she delivered a few dim-witted blinks.

If this wasn't a proposal of marriage, she didn't know the man at all. A flattering, spirit-soothing notion, that of marriage, but dismaying for the counsel she would be compelled to give—wedding a kept woman would bring trouble. Regardless, she dared not presume. "Great day, what a rush you're in."

"You leave in, what? Three, four days? Too few, and I want them all. So, tell me, duchess—any particular name you'd like to take?"

She bunched her lips thoughtfully. "I've always been partial to Brown."

He chuckled, a breathy thing that bathed her belly in warmth. "It's overdone."

"Baker?"

"Too...yeasty."

"What of Bell?"

"Lillian Bell? I hate it."

"But it has such a nice *ring* to it. I think I'll keep—"

The swift, hard press of his mouth shut her up, but she laughed through it, full and uninhibited.

The baby startled awake, her wide, confused eyes lighting upon Marcus. In one delighted burble, she absconded with him. Straightening, he swooped her out of the bed and devoured the rolls of her giggling throat. "Your mother is very bad at picking names," he said, laughing along with her. "Shall we help her along?"

Enjoying the sight of them, Lillian swung her feet to the ground. "What would *you* suggest?"

He lifted a blasé shoulder. "Myself, I'm partial to Buck."

"Buck..." She sucked her canine as though mulling the name over. "Would it make me a saint?"

"It would make you mine." The oblique eye he cast down at her peeled away her clothes, her skin, her every encumbering trespass, leaving only her parched spirit and prurient need.

"Tempting, but..." She tore from his eyes to study his boots. Their leather was sodden and their soles rimmed with dried muck and shreds of grass, testaments to the hardships he'd faced because of her. "Haven't you had enough trouble on my account? Once you tie your life to mine, you will see no end of disgrace and contempt and—"

"Stop it." The boots shifted, shedding clods of dirt, crushing them. "I have the facts, and I know my mind." Sporting light shades of irascibility, he regarded her, unflinching. "We've covered this. I won't have you debase yourself. Or God, for that matter, by thinking Him too weak or unconcerned to redeem your future. Our future. I love you, and I need you. We need each other."

Indeed, she did, but she wouldn't tie him to a scandalous life he wasn't certain he could choke down every single day for as long as they both might live.

She chose a different tack. "What of my father? Should you speak with him?"

"Already done." He shifted Mari to his other hip and withdrew an envelope from inside his coatee. "I've had a letter from him. Not an hour ago. Major Ainsworth carried one for me to Mobile. The reply was waiting here. Read it if you'd like. There's a line in there for you."

A little stunned, she took and unfolded it, her father's unkempt script exacting mist of her eyes.

> Sir,
>
> You cannot know the joy you bring an old man. I would fill a sheet with sentimental flummery if your superior's man were not standing at my elbow, hand extended to carry away my answer.
>
> In brief, dear boy, she is yours, the child as well, with all my heart and blessing. I would urge you to love them as you do your own body, if you had not already thoroughly convinced me that you do. Instead, I will beg, in broad light of day, for you to bring them home with all haste.
>
> To Lillian, my darling girl, none here condemn. Come back to us.

Marcus and Mari strolled the room, trading babbling nonsense, while Lillian's eyes skipped about the letter in search of a place to land. On Papa's blessing? His portending urgency? His pardon? They chose the word *love*, tarried, and skipped to the date in the upper corner.

She strode to Marcus, pointing to the sentence. "Explain this. You had to have written Papa before I arrived with Mink, yet he says you convinced him you love me. Marcus, you didn't even know whether you'd see me again."

He scanned where she indicated, set his palm at her jaw, and curled his fingers into her, branding her with resolution. "I told you, I know my mind. All we lack is for you to know yours. What do you want, duchess? Truly want."

So many things! She drooped with the weight of them. Recent days had overflowed with wishes and wants. Some, she would never have—another lifetime with Papa; some, she already did.

Mari gaped at her, forefinger hooked on her lower lip. Saliva hung from it in a long, shiny thread. An abrupt laugh made Lillian snort, drawing Marcus's attention to the sight.

He collected the drool so that it hung from the finger he held up between them. "Would you look at that. I knew our girl here had a natural bent for leaking, but this is proper talent." Face a comical contortion, he flung it off and finished the cleanup, using his knuckles to wipe at her chin.

Our girl. A common enough endearment, but it resonated with goodness. For Mari, for them. And she loved him. Lord knew how she loved him!

"You. I want you." She stole his slimy hand and encased it in a double-grip that plastered Papa's letter between them.

Gentleness swathed his mouth—a most becoming contrast to the tummy-tightening fire banked in his eyes. He returned her squeeze and spoke with voice-roughing promise. "I'm already yours."

Not a quarter-hour later, they were ten strides from Major Ainsworth's billet when Lillian glanced back at Teniente Prieto. "Teniente, do you need something of me?"

"Not you, Señorita Liana. Don Diego transferred my commission to the doncella. I am to guard her at all times."

And perhaps prohibit Lillian from leaving Gadsden with her? Surely not. It pained her to think he might try.

"I see. Well, she is quite safe." She gestured to Marcus who'd stopped beside her. Mari perched on his arm; only her face and bootied foot showed outside her blanket, its white angora fleece radiant in the full sun—clear skies for three days, a sign of better things to come?

The teniente's back went rigid. "*Igual*, I will do my duty."

"Bueno. For now." She frowned. "You may wait outside."

"Sí, señorita."

Major Ainsworth's sentry admitted them. Marcus stepped into the facility ahead of her, but at the threshold, he came to such a curt halt she kicked his heel. Rotating, he cupped her elbow and glanced beyond her. For two blinks, she was certain he would take flight, hauling her behind.

Then, the grooves smoothed from his forehead; the upward slope of his shoulders reversed. He gave several rapid jerks of his chin. "This is best. Yes, I prefer it. Remember what we spoke of, what you decided to tell him."

"Tell what to whom? Marcus, you've lost me."

When he moved to slant an arm across her back, he cleared her view of the well-lit room.

Major Ainsworth, arms straight at his sides, was a pillar beside a trestle table stacked with orderly piles of papers, folders, account books. As staid and imposing as ever, he became insubstantial when set against the backdrop of the Indian presiding over the farthest corner.

Totka Hadjo.

Lillian choked on a swallow, gaze fleeing the warrior then sprinting back in disbelief, but it *was* Totka. All six-plus feet of him.

His silver armbands glittered in the light of two lanterns; his eyes the same, their whites stark against those dark, dark irises. No mistaking their faint war cry.

It raised the hair on her scalp. Throat squeaking shut, she lurched backwards but went nowhere for the rail of muscle behind her.

"Better to have it done, duchess." Marcus breathed the incentive into her ear, releasing her to remove his hat and salute the major. "Sir. Miss McGirth, as requested." The men swapped affable greetings, even pausing to include her.

Unable to think past Totka's confusing presence, she heard none of it. What was he doing here! He belonged in Kossati, in Tensaw, in the farthest reaches of Cathay for all she cared. Anywhere but here, sucking the air from her body and the command from her knees.

Her brisk inhales dried her throat in moments and drew a sidelong squint from Marcus; her deliberate exhale erased the crinkles around his eyes and sent them back to the men's conversation, giving her space to think. Or try to.

She wasn't ready for this, hadn't prepared, hadn't crafted the apology that would make everything right, for after all she'd done, there was no other way to come at the warrior but with complete humility.

Brain a-swirl, she closed her eyes and scrambled for her wits, scraping their shattered bits into a semblance of confidence. A speech should be forming in her mind, a neat catalog of wrongs, followed by vows to make it up to him, but she produced nothing better than the impulse to cling to his clothes and plead forgiveness.

When her eyelids lifted, Marcus was speaking with him—something about his journey home the following day—then Totka was reaching for Lillian's baby. "And this pretty kitten?"

Marcus released her to him. "Your niece, Marisol. With a baby on the way, you're probably wanting a little practice."

The protest dashing up Lillian's throat mired at the image of Adela large with child. She would make an exceptional parent, and to be fair, so would Totka. His nieces proved it. Wherever children were, his heart thrived—a fine place to reach him now.

Lillian stepped toward him, her reluctant feet hissing at the ground. Despite her best efforts at persuasion, her gaze refused to lift above the copper gorget centered at his chest. "I hear the latest addition to the McGirths is due in February. Happy news."

"Yes, during the windy moon." At the glow raising Totka's inflection, Lillian braved a look.

He was smiling for Mari, jangling his glass-bead bracelet before her clumsy grasp. "Another child for the *tribe*"—he tossed Lillian a meaningful, albeit unheated, glance—"and a cousin for this little

Beaver."

Message received. With it, a prickle of annoyance. Would he argue his child and Lillian's shouldn't receive the McGirth name? Insufferable. Chin notching up a degree, she said, "My daughter has quite—"

Marcus cleared his throat, applying pressure to her hand.

Air snorted from her nose. Fine. She could roll over, play opossum in the interest of peace. "She has…quite the concoction of blood. Spanish, American, even Creek. Our children, yours and mine, are blessed to have a home wherever their feet may land."

Approval molded Totka's mouth into a partial smile. "Fine talk, woman."

"Surgeon, if you would," Ainsworth broke in, directing Marcus toward the table. "Before I lay out Miss McGirth's instructions, a couple of details. Lieutenant Lynch asked that you look in on these patients while you wait for transport out." He tossed a sheet of paper onto the table and rapped its creased surface. "This one, your official orders. You will now report directly to General Jackson. Read and sign on the mark."

"Certainly." Marcus squeezed her hand and left her with a reassuring smile and an Indian who whisked her pulse into a lather. With Major Ainsworth hovering near, he bent over the table to read. Though on occasion his lashes lifted her direction, Lillian was alone.

Not so. She had God and His mercy—everything she truly needed.

And there was Mari.

Letting her blanket puddle on the ground, Totka swung her high above him and plummeted her to hip level, producing a chortle as any treasured uncle might. Mari, slumped against him, fat cheek crammed to his chest, seeming to agree with the qualifier. The little traitor. Or…emissary of goodwill?

Feeling foolish for her leery gait, Lillian retrieved the blanket and, reaching up to account for the man's intimidating height, wrapped it about her baby's back. "Take care," she said, shifting to his language, "or she will steal your heart."

Lips curving, he covered Mari's back with his large, brown hand. "She is a skilled thief and holds my heart already."

"For good reason. Creator blessed her with your Copper Woman's sweet disposition."

He paused mid-pat, eyes amplifying. The statement was simple enough to the average listener, but she and Totka both knew her use of the Indian name was a long overdue admission.

"Totka, if I—" Heart quivering, she winced through a moistureless swallow. "If I were a man, I would assemble my pipe and invite you to ceremony. Since I am but a bitter-eyed woman, I can only pray you to listen and consider."

Silent and vacant, his appraisal nudged her heels backwards in the tiniest of cowardly steps. Expecting encouragement from Marcus, she stole a glimpse his way, but at that moment, he turned to speak with Major Ainsworth. Fisting the gown at her thigh, she proceeded on a prayer. What was it Marcus had encouraged her to say? "I am...I was mistaken to-to think you are wrong for my sister. You are her perfect match, and... and..." Water rushed to her eyes; she beat her lids to eradicate it, concerned for his dislike of tears. "I abused you gravely. Copper Woman besides. Since those days, I have lived in constant, miserable regret. Creator has forgiven me, and though I deserve no quarter, I beg it of you and ask peace between us."

Nursing her finger, Mari gazed adoringly at Lillian. Training her hopes onto her little bundle of answered prayer, Lillian left the matter with God. *Grant him a merciful spirit, I pray you.*

While Totka's inspection of her continued unaltered, Marcus laid down his writing implement and, too slow for her liking, applied the blotter. The sounds of fort life filled the space: the faint calls of a marching drill, the *crack* of musket practice, the shouted command of a disgruntled superior. She'd prefer any of those to Totka's conscience-debriding stare.

At last, when her nerves could take no more, humanity entered his eyes; it softened his stance. That half-smile returned, though it spared her the usual air of victory. "If you were a man, I would share your pipe." He pulled an envelope from his pouch and held it up so she could read the front and the name traversing its center. Her own, in a hand she didn't recognize. "Accept this as our white feather of peace. I have borne it a hundred sights, asking Creator at each step that He might bind the cords our sharp words have shredded."

Rendered voiceless, she nodded and pressed the letter to her heart, as deep within her personal underworld, something burst. The rattle and clank of chains hitting the ground was an audible force that freed her spirit of that dark place. "Maddo," she squeaked.

Marcus joined them and stole Mari back, a question in the lift of his brow.

"I leave you with it," Totka said. "Sleep well, Sister. Or"—he offered Marcus the shake of his arm, eyes cutting back to her with a sly glint—"perhaps not."

Word had wasted no time getting around. Sleep would most assuredly be shunned tonight—after their audience with the chaplain—but for all her shameless experience, Totka's mention of it still brought on an instant flush.

He chuckled, and she shoved at him, helping him out the door. "Oh, be gone! Incorrigible man." She mumbled the good-natured slight and shifted attention to the post.

The crimson seal beneath it bore the imprint of an open-winged eagle. She broke it and skipped to the signature line: *G. A. Jackson.*

Her eyes shot to Marcus. "General Andrew Jackson?"

"What's this you say?" Major Ainsworth deposited the blotter onto the table with an unceremonious *thunk.* "The general?"

Baby on hip, Marcus came with a bouncing stride and looked over her shoulder. "Appears to be." Their gazes connected, hers growing hot with fear, Marcus's a steady beam of calm. "Lillian, if he wanted you in stocks, he wouldn't send an invitation. Not to you, at any rate. Read it. You might be surprised."

She did in silence and handed it to Marcus, dazed. On unsure legs, she sought the room's only chair and dropped into it, mentally rehearsing such words as *loyal citizen, grateful country, continued alliance.*

"Dear me, Miss McGirth. So grievous? I do hope not." The major made a sympathetic clicking sound that she didn't believe for a moment.

"This is not the face of grief, Major." She rectified her posture. "The general kindly thanks me for the intelligence I provided. He intends to act on it immediately with every confidence for success. There followed a request for me to travel with Major Buck and stay on as temporary advisor in matters pertaining to San Marcos and its Red Sticks. Not that I will." She cocked her head at Major Ainsworth. "This must be a result of the information I passed along about the Prophet Francis."

"No, in fact, I never sent it. I have no idea how —" He paused, then whipped about to Marcus, brows dipping.

"I might have had a certain Indian carry it to him." With a smug bend to his mouth, Marcus sent her a wink that probed her belly with a welcome ache. To the Red Sticks with Major Ainsworth and his incurable choler! Where was that chaplain?

"You were instructed to destroy that, Captain!"

Marcus set Mari in Lillian's lap and faced the major with a staunch bearing that brandished the power in those fine shoulders. "It's *major*, thank you, sir. And I admit I stepped out of line. I apologize and humbly submit to whatever repercussions my chain of command deems appropriate." Marcus's command being Jackson himself, as of five minutes ago.

To stanch a snigger, Lillian pressed her mouth to the back of Mari's head and spoke in her ear. "That papa of yours is a bright fellow. We're lucky girls, you and I."

Major Ainsworth tramped to his desk to right the tipped blotter, straighten the pen box, dust it of drying sand. "That won't be necessary. If the general is grateful, your country is too. Well done, Miss McGirth. I was mistaken to believe you had anything but our nation's best interest at heart."

Before Lillian could respond, Marcus stepped between her and the other man's hard, implacable smile. "Naturally, this development excuses Miss McGirth from any suspicion, though I don't doubt she's still eager to blacken López's name. As am I."

His eye, too. "I'm more than eager, Major Buck. I am determined."

"On that count, we're agreed," Major Ainsworth said, plucking his bicorn from a shelf behind the desk. "Several hours remain in the day. If we're lucky, we'll have what we need before sundown. Come then, I'll escort you to his ship myself."

"Thank you, Major." Marcus wove his fingers through Lillian's and tightened. "But first, I think, a visit with the chaplain."

Chapter 21

After a brief ceremony in which Marcus and Lillian swore unending love, comfort, and honor, she boarded Diego's barque as Mrs. Marcus Buck, angry mother to a stolen child and waspish former lover to the devil himself.

The skirt of Mrs. Lane's unfortunate gown received the brunt of her long, increasingly furious strides. The heels of her shoes flopped and hammered the barque's weather deck, a clarion broadcast of her approach. Good. Let Diego hear her coming.

Up to a short while ago, she'd done well to contain her rage. When her view filled with his ship—that ruinous vessel of sin, polished, agleam in turquoise waters, lazily lifting and sinking at its leisure—her gut had become a smoldering pit. Mounting, its smoke billowed off her so thickly, she'd begun a slow choke.

Thank the good God, she wasn't alone in her fury.

Behind her, in the forms of her husband, Major Ainsworth, and four infantrymen, came the might of the U.S. Army, plus one indignant Indian. Totka, at his off-beat trot, had run the length of the beach to make the launch before it shoved off. Folding his long legs into the narrow bow, he'd grumbled briefly about thieving Spaniards, then complimented the gurgle and splash of the sea with the grating noise of whetting stone against tomahawk blade.

Indian vengeance. For Mari, had to be. The Creeks were fierce about their children and brought a new level of meaning to the Hebraic axiom "an eye for an eye." Well, Totka could have the Spanish diablo. Right after Lillian scraped her shoes on his impaired body.

The soldiers quick-timed around her to arrive at the great cabin first and file through.

"¡Bienvenidos, amigos!" Diego's greasy charm slithered through the opening and coated her in the brine of repugnance.

God above, let me get my hands on that infernal man!

Five strides yet remained of the passageway when Marcus took a pace-slowing grasp on the back of her gown. "Hold your fire, soldier. Let our boys secure the place. Catch your breath."

She nodded, grateful for the interruption. Gaining the upper hand required a cool head. Nostrils flaring with her lungs' drag, she shook out her friend's crimped, sea-dampened gown and, remembering the personal items she'd stored in the cabin, shocked herself with a little burble of laughter. Gathering it to herself like a treasure, she flung back her shoulders, lengthened her neck, and, imbuing herself with grace, entered the opulent rooms she'd once shared with the devil.

Little was visible beyond the alley of rigid blue coats that reached from the door to the cabin's center. At its end, Diego stood reclining beside his captain's desk, forearm on the back of its carved, throne-style chair. The stretch of his cheeks flaunted every alabaster tooth, but her experience picked out the slight sideways cock of his jaw, a flag of irritation that struck a jubilant chord within her.

Beholding her, he popped upright. "Liana, is that you?"

"Call me Señora Buck. I have wed."

"A chivalrous gesture on his part. Or perhaps brainless." Leering, he stepped forward and abruptly stopped, facing her straight on, feet planted shoulder-width apart in a pose that exploded that single glad chord into a triumphal opus. "Holy Mother, Liana, you look dreadful! What hideous thing are you wearing?"

Certainly not his prick-me-dainty attire: impeccable linen shirt tied at the throat with a ribbon whose canary yellow carried throughout his outfit in his shoe strings and silk waist sash, emerald-green breeches and waistcoat parading a profusion of silver buttons and clasps, white leather gaiters, and that ridiculous hair net…

She snatched a titter before it found freedom and tucked it behind a demure smile.

Mrs. Lane's gown suffered a poverty of fashion and shape, neither of which hampered Diego's imagination or memory or whichever of the two was responsible for slashing color across his cheekbones and jerking his lecherous gaze from her to the bed.

He wagged a brisk, abolishing hand before him. "It matters not what you wear. Your armoire is as you left it. We are sure to find something more befitting that splendid figure. But why do you stand there?" In a characteristically exaggerated gesture, he scooped armfuls of air toward him. "Venga, come to me!"

In apparent obedience, she glided down the aisle, heart a thunderous wreck, Marcus's brittle tread ticking close at her right ear. Before the don, she lowered her eyes and bent a knee, sliding her right foot behind her left in a deep, courteous genuflection that angled her torso sharply forward. "Mi señor."

"Ay, maja. Rise. Leave that puppy of a medico and give me my kisses. We will forget our grievances and your blunder in marriage. We will toast to better times. You, me, our little sunshine."

A contemptuous guffaw rang through Lillian's mind. Scum, the man was, and comically desperate. Remaining abject, she fisted both sides of her skirt. "I have been wondering, Señor…"

"*Dígame*, bonita. Tell me."

"How is your back?"

While he replied — some nonsense about the wound being nothing but a prick — she summoned Mink's strength of women. What would the war woman do? Strike him where it counted most. How satisfying that would be!

Marcus clamped onto Lillian's shoulder. His lips moved against her ear. "Whatever that pretty brain of yours is scheming, forget it. I'll take him from here. You focus on what we came for."

Her lungs emptied in an explosive breath. "Will you make him hurt?"

"If I can help it" — he grinned — "yes."

Conceding to her husband with not a little reluctance, she straightened, then breezed past Diego on her way to the armoire, veering into Spanish. "Your Lordship is right. I should change."

Marcus shoved a chair into the backs of Diego's legs, forcing him to sit, and while Diego smacked him away and retched curses, Lillian burrowed through yard upon yard of lustering and gold muslin to reach the armoire's recesses.

Her fingers closed around the last item on the rack, a simple blue calico, faded by Tensaw's intense sun. Its prim collar buttoned to the hollow of the neck, its only embellishments, five mother-of-pearl buttons and the mud stains on its hem. Cramming the fabric to her nose, she drank of its scent: cedar, dust, and — in the wishful regions of her heart — home.

Using the cabin's private dressing area, she shed Mrs. Lane's garb and donned her own. The old frock, stitched by her own needle, greeted her with the exuberance of a parted friend, hugging her curves with loose modesty. Not permitting herself sentimentality over it, yet feeling a new person nonetheless, she swept around the partition, placed Mrs. Lane's folded things onto a trunk, and, brushing off a cabin full of cheek-burning stares, went direct to the desk.

"What will you give me, sweetheart?" she asked of its map cabinet.

Cubbies bearing rolls of parchment occupied most of the cupboard's space, but a row of glass-knobbed drawers lined the right side. She unlatched the third from the top and whisked it from its home. Peering into the dim enclosure, she reached inside to pull a small lever that, with a jarring clatter, released the bottom two drawers straight down into the desktop.

She swept her arm into the new opening and far into the wall behind, grinned, and brought out a stack of thin books, six or seven high. The very ones that had eluded her in Diego's study were in her possession at last. "There you are, gentlemen" — she smacked the topmost ledger — "account books for your reading pleasure. Or mine, as it were."

"Duchess, you're brilliant! I'll keep you." Marcus plucked her off her feet and wet her cheek with a solid, vocalized mash of his lips.

"Not much choice anymore." She laughed and shoved him off, heels landing with a merry *clack*. "And it's a bit early for thanks. Wait until I've presented proof enough to keep our girl out of that mongrel's hands."

The next hour saw the soldiers drooping at their posts; Marcus pacing the width of the Persian rug; Major Ainsworth snoozing on the bed, soiling its satin coverlet with his dusty boots; Totka keeping the shadows company; Diego sitting silent and smug; Lillian poring uselessly over the books, sweat gradually accumulating in the pits of her sleeves.

So far, she'd found scant evidence of intrigues, if any at all. Trade with the Indians filled the rows, but the gunpowder was measured by the handful and the balls of shot were tabulated individually in amounts a man might use for a winter hunt, not a war. Not even a decent, dag-blamed skirmish.

While she desponded of success, Diego hounded her from his seated position before the wall of large, mullioned windows. "Ala! What are you doing, mujer? I am viscount of Apalache and your daughter's sire. Have you no respect?"

Forehead pinching with a scowl, she flipped another page, tearing it in her haste, and scanned the columns of numbers for something substantial.

"Go on then if you must," he said. "Stab a man in the back. You have done it before!"

On the brink of despair, she sent Marcus a pleading look.

"Ignore him." He came and lifted the hair off the back of her neck, letting out the heat. "Anything? Anything at all?"

Sagging, she closed the last book and shoved it away from her. "Nothing. These are decoys. He has others. I'd swear to it. Trouble is, I don't know where else to look." She sent a discreet glance to Major Ainsworth, still snoring gape-jawed, and whispered in a hoarsening voice, "He's going to give her away. We'll lose her!"

Marcus straightened, distancing himself, hard by to being affronted. "Never again on *my* watch," he said, mouth a determined slash. "Tell the worm I challenge him at swords."

"No. When I said hurt him, I didn't mean meet him on the dueling field."

"Not a duel. A gamble. Should I win, I'll receive Mari and a full confession. He may—"

"Are you insane? I say *no*. Absolutely not." Huffing, she snatched up a ledger. Maybe she'd missed something. It was worth another look. "We'll tear the ship apart before I allow you to fight him again."

"Allow me?" Barking a laugh, Marcus spun and addressed the room. "Is there no one else who can translate?"

Major Ainsworth sat up, groggily smacking his lips. "What's this about?"

An infantryman, round of face and newly whiskered, raised a hesitant hand. "I manage all right with the Spaniards, sir."

Marcus clapped his hands together. "Excellent."

She gained her feet in an instant. "No!"

"Private...Chase, is it?" Marcus pushed on, not even glancing her way.

"It is, sir."

"Good, tell the don I put to him a rematch. As before, first to draw blood wins. The stakes—"

"First blood, ha! Drained straight from your heart." Fear plowed up Lillian's spine. "Marcus, he's a cheat without a conscience!"

He rounded on her. "Precisely!" Was that elation making his voice shine?

Astounded, she blinked crazily. "Where is your good judgement?"

"Where is your trust?" he shot back.

Tall Bull had accused her of having no faith in Marcus. He'd been right, and Marcus had lived, but he'd also lost. Dearly.

A subtle beseeching inside Marcus's eyes yanked a toggle in her head, and it was as if he spoke aloud. *Every choice I've made, succeed or fail, has been with your welfare in mind.*

I trust you with my life. And Mari's, she'd declared.

I plead God that never changes.

Had it changed so soon? No, that needn't happen. She *did* trust him. What's more, she trusted the Eternal plan. Still frightened for him, for them all, she moved woodenly to rest her lips against his cheek and the outcome of his last gamble. "I misplaced it, but it's been found."

After a clipped nod, her ever-sedulous husband went straight back to business. "As I was saying, Private, the stakes will be the baby and the ledgers still in hiding, and for the don…" he rolled his hand "…whatever he'd like. He may name the specific terms, so long as they fall within the scope of a gentleman's scrimmage. Can you repeat that verbatim?"

Lillian confirmed that he did.

Diego listened, mouth slowly twisting with ugly delight, then a chuckle presented itself, low and wicked, the same he'd used moments before abandoning her to Varela's games. He rose smoothly. "I accept your generous challenge. These are my terms: I draw first blood, I leave with my child, my ship, my honor, and letters of passage through to España. You cut me first, I give you every ledger, including those my beautiful lover has not found. I will also concede my child and give my word on the Holy Church to never pursue her."

"What a fool you are!" Lillian spat. "Risking your child, willing to exchange her for such a trifle as your honor." Whereas Marcus, who had nothing to lose but a last chance at justice, fought to regain a treasure he'd lost.

"But, maja," Diego said, lengthening the last syllable. "It is no risk at all."

The taunt had its desired effect, lancing her with alarm. She would scream indecencies at him if it weren't imperative she seal her lips to quell rising gorge.

Private Chase translated.

Focused on nothing, Marcus touched his scar. "He's right. My risk is greater." His eyes sharpened and swung to Diego. "I want more. Her legal parentage."

Diego clucked regret. "Alas, the only man with that power is His Illustrious Majesty."

Lillian sank her head into her palm, sick that this was even a topic of discussion, but Marcus shrugged it off. "Ah well. Regardless, I accept your terms. To the deck then!"

Diego grinned his wide devil's grin. "To the deck."

Lillian posted herself with the men lining the rails of the main deck, the majority being Diego's sailors and soldiers who'd been brought out of holding for the event. Excitement rode through the ranks in great murmuring waves crested by flowing *cañas* of flaxen rum.

Lillian, whose stomach was a cataclysm of acid, took no part in it but braided her fingers beneath her chin and reminded the Father of all the things Diego was and had done and could do. No matter His answer, she was certain He listened.

Ship hands cleared the deck of encumbrances, while Diego disrobed of trimmings and glared intimidation Marcus's direction. In somber conference with Totka at the base of the mainmast, Marcus had granted his opponent no more than a casual glance.

Bedecked with weapons, complete with strung bow, Totka split off and came her way, his stalking gait and concentrated, illegible features depicting her worst nightmares. Today, he was a welcome sight.

"Join me above," he said in Muskogee. A yank of his head indicated the forecastle deck.

Her chin cut upward. "I will not seek high ground while my husband faces that trickster Spaniard on my behalf."

Lids tapering, he regarded her, stance uncertain in the vessel's lean. The wind billowed his full sleeves, made knots in the tail of his roached hair, and dried every speck of moisture from her expanding eyes. Finally, he looked to Marcus, who'd stripped to his shirt, trousers, and sword belt and was now sauntering to the water barrel like a soldier with a solid battle plan, eager to clog the air with the stench of gunpowder.

"Have you seen him fight?" Countenance grim, Totka distractedly plucked a dull note from his taut bowstring. He was worried?

"He is magnificent with the long knife. Your cousin called him a formidable enemy." She dried her voice. "To my thinking, Tall Bull enjoyed the previous match far too much. I scarcely drew breath, but he was a boy at a stickball game cheering his favorite shooter." With a thoughtful touch to her chin, she added, "Who, come to think of it, was probably himself."

Totka opened his mouth and let a laugh come full and free. "You know my kin better than I would have thought. Very well. Since you assure me your Buck can handle his weapon, I will climb to that quiet loft there, light my pipe, and enjoy the contest." He pointed to a nook behind two barrels. "Put yourself there, out of harm's way. Your man will fight better without the distraction of your safety."

Heeding his advice, she found a more secluded place along the rail but stayed within clear view of the arena.

Minutes later, they met in the center, Diego taking up the typical profile stance associated with the Spanish style: feet close, sword high and parallel to the ground, its tip aimed at Marcus's face. A menacing posture, it daunted Lillian from ten feet away. She couldn't conceive of any move Marcus might make that wouldn't threaten his own flesh.

Of seemingly the same mind, Marcus remained outside the range of Diego's extended sword. Demeanor cool, sword provokingly low, he strolled a cross-stepped circle about his rival.

Tracking with him, Diego maintained his pose and the tether of Marcus's steadfast gaze. Except for the seagulls cawing from the rigging, silence held the ship captive as it waited for that first ringing clash of steel that snubbed them all.

A lion on a hill, Diego stood his ground, challenging the contender to try for a piece of his domain. "Come and ply your sword, you overgrown piece of dog offal. If you dare."

Indifferent, Marcus hooked a semi-smile and let him snarl. Time stretched unmeasured, noticeable only in the gleam accumulating on Diego's forehead and the slight tremor of his sword's tip. All the while, Marcus rotated the deck, Justice slicing the air before him in elegant figure eights that were as mesmerizing as the ship's lullaby sway.

Lillian stepped over a limp towline to lean against the rail, the muscles of her rigid back cramping and screaming for one of them to strike and put a start to this awful matter. The next pulse of her heart got its wish.

In a blurring flash, Diego thrust and Marcus blocked—a single, pure note high on the scale that rushed out to sea and returned the men to their previous positions. But shortly, Diego broke form again, another darting probe that Marcus effortlessly deflected.

Thrice more, Diego tested and teased, and each time, Marcus sent him back. As the minutes dragged and Diego struck repeatedly without either driving Marcus back or luring him in, he lost the image of king of the plain and became a caged predator teetering on the brink of insanity.

"Fight me, *cobarde*! Or throw down your sword and admit to the lesser man!" With his next lurching pass, a hank of black hair lashed free of the net and plastered to his neck. Starting high, his steel cut down and across, on target for the shoulder.

Deftly, Marcus swung upward. Justice twanged and hissed as she slapped Diego's attack back the way it came, then carried through in a powerful arc that brought her full circle for a slash across Diego's gut.

Diego skipped back, shirt parted in a bloodless slice, and back again as Marcus advanced, no *flew*, into a vicious battering.

Justice took to the air in a whooshing, zipping assault so thickly laid, Diego had no recourse but to retreat, heels blundering. Stunned, he parried sloppily, to Lillian's untaught thinking, but efficiently enough to keep Justice off his skin, if not his shirt. Marcus opened it at the elbow and the breast, each miss wresting uproar from the onlookers.

Raising on her toes, Lillian gripped her throat. Through it, blood buffeted her fingers in its mad, heady race. A startling clang jerked her gaze to the planks and the sword wobbling between the men's tramping feet. Diego's.

"Marcus, you beast," she said on a winded laugh.

"*Alto, alto!*" The ship's captain, their designated arbitrator, interjected himself between them, but Marcus had already halted, arms swung wide.

Chest heaving, Diego swooped to collect his weapon, so the captain announced, "Caballeros, ¡resumen!" The words had no more been spoken than Diego was charging, devilment writ in his eyes.

Though swift to deflect the flurry of swings, Marcus was forced back, made to eat the ground he'd gained. Their resounding blows came more furiously than before, and as they fought, Marcus's backward scamper drew a line directly to her.

At the rail to either side of her, men scattered and opened a gap. Lillian, too, flung herself out of the way. Marcus was practically upon her now, but his boots entangled in the towline. He tumbled the last steps, back slamming the rail, curving over it. To his growled bellow, his sword arm pitched out over the water.

The actions that followed were rapid-fire but as clear to Lillian as the warm blood strafing her cheek like musket shot. The clamor that arose from the rushing masses, however, was a chaos of sordid opinions that made Marcus the victim, the victor, and the bravest of losers.

Victor. He is victor, you half-wits!

She carried his blood on her cheek, but he carried the day, and Mari was hers. *Theirs.* Thank God, theirs! Peace descended over her, while the rest of the ship hollered its various verdicts to the unfortunate arbitrator.

"The don cut him first," a man shouted at her ear, jostling to be nearer the heated center and driving her away from Marcus. "He did it before the blade fell. Before, I tell you! The don is champion!"

"Bah! Your old eyes are a ruin," a swabbie replied, his stockinged hat flopping with his energetic protest. "The drop was first! The cut, second. Don Diego has fouled the court."

"Yes, just so!" she added to the hubbub.

Diego cursed her, then cursed the sailor, sword brandished high. "Who are you to judge me? Show that fetid tongue again, Sanchez, and

I'll have it from your body!"

Straining to see Marcus, Lillian shut it all out. They could shout about swords until their throats gave up, but eventually someone would figure out where the true fault lie.

"Marcus!" Lillian battled the crowd to reach him three strides distant.

He'd given them all his broad back. Hands relaxed on the guardrail's beam, he squinted down at the waning day's rippling reflection, as though to catch sight of Justice being laid to rest on the sea floor.

All Lillian saw as she sidled up was the half-inch, horizontal slit intersecting the upper quadrant of his old wound. A perfect cross. Another beautiful sacrifice.

Blessed soul, but she loved him. Her heart, a throbbing, swelling knot, ached with it, stifling her wind. Cheerfully breathless, she crooked her arm through his and nestled close, the scent of hot sweat never so endearing as now.

At her touch, he blinked as from a trance, and smiling, freed his arm and pulled her flush to his side, exactly as he'd done at the riverside sunrise. Now at eventide, the plump sphere was burying itself in the bay, spreading its marmalade rays over water, coast, fort, and Marcus's handsome profile.

"What are they saying?" He spoke over the debate behind them.

"Nothing yet. And everything. The captain can't get a word in sideways."

"He seems a capable fellow. He'll wrangle them down." Marcus returned his study to the water that smacked at the barque's hull.

She stroked the rutted flesh discernible beneath his damp shirt back. "I'm sorry about Justice."

His smile rose a shade above wistful. "It's only a sword. Standard issue."

"Maybe." Not at all, actually. "You dropped her on purpose."

He lobbed an ironfisted gaze over his shoulder. To Diego? Roguery gathered at the juncture of his screwing lips. "Maybe."

Maybe nothing. His fingers had sprung open a solid two seconds after his jarring encounter with the ship's side; though, she doubted any but she had been in the right position to notice. Another two ticks had strolled past before Diego's sword ripped skin. At his cyclonic speed, those ticks were the span of an eternity. Plenty of time to notice Marcus was unarmed. Plenty more to divert a lunge.

"That was quite a risk you took," she said.

"Not really. Odds were high he'd strike and strike small. The man is predictable."

She quirked her mouth. "Predictably treacherous."

Even now, Diego ranted. "Death to any who questions my honor, starting with that slut and her unholy swordsman!"

She closed her eyes against a shudder. How easy it was to imagine the straining cords of his neck. Cold tentacles of apprehension wended up her body.

"Let's go, duchess. I miss our girl." He nudged her toward the accommodation ladder and the jolly boat hung from the stern.

She balked. "Go without hearing the ruling?"

"Silence!" the ship's captain screeched, quelling the madness. "The sword is irrelevant! A cut to the face is an undisputed offense in any gentleman's contest. Don Diego forfeits the win, his account books, and, God be merciful, his child."

The announcement spawned a dissonant roar. Most appeared to agree with the arbitrator, but the handful of Diego's faithful were heatedly vocal. Diego himself, now eerily mute.

She kept her back to it all, eyes latched to the rope ladder trailing the ship's edge. "There, you've officially been named victor."

"To the ladder. Go." He took her arm and began rotating her toward the stern.

At her rear, pounding footsteps merged with startled outcries.

"No!" Hand darting to a barren scabbard, Marcus swore, wrenching her away, blindly tossing her off and over the unforgiving belly of an iron swing-gun.

Disoriented, she climbed off it, righted herself, and pirouetted back to the scene.

Two men lay at Marcus's feet. One, hunched and groaning. The other, immobile in a telling crimson pool.

All that was visible of the latter was his arm, extended fully before him. His jeweled fingers still clutched his sword, its tip resting not two yards from the hem of her gown. Diego, the accursed fool, he'd come for them! Fool for ruining his honor in the heat of anger, and then, rather than live without it, risking an American noose and earning a Creek arrow instead.

The injured man clawed at a scarlet line that slashed his chest on the diagonal. "*¡Ayudeme!*" The sea captain.

To reach him, Marcus leapt over Diego, filling Lillian's eyes with the tragic length of him.

His corpse lay belly down, eyes open and dull, lower cheek vanishing in a red tide that stemmed from the hollow of his throat where an arrowhead had made its home.

Lillian's benumbed brain registered the vibrating cane that protruded from the base of his skull, then lifted her eyes to its owner on the forecastle.

Grave and circumspect, Totka's face glowed a beautifully vibrant copper in the day's lingering wilt.

Unannounced, her knees buckled and met the planked deck with a biting crack. All the better for thanking the holy name of Christ for Marcus's love and sacrifice, for his smart sword and sharp mind, for Mari and the unimpeded liberty to take her home, and for her sister's husband, the warrior she had the honor of calling brother.

Chapter 22

A solitary chime interrupted the muted waves lapping against the barque's hull.

Lillian thumbed burning eyes, then lifted them from the open bookkeeping register to glimpse the mantle clock atop the map cabinet. Three hours earlier, when Marcus had boarded the launch with the wounded captain, Diego's shrouded corpse, and the promise to return with Mari and Barb, she would hardly have guessed that by the smallest hour of the night, she'd be seated at Diego's—no, *Mari's* desk, in the vessel's great cabin, wearing nothing but Marcus's shirt and nigh to tears for want of him.

A candle burned next to the inkwell; it cast ripples of marigold light over the nautical painting that hung on the paneled wall before her. A lighthouse burning brightly in the midst of a turbulent sea, it brought Christ to mind as well as the husband He'd given her. Her absentee husband…

The idea to stay on and search for the missing files had been hers. A day, she'd said. No more. If they'd uncovered nothing in twenty-four hours, she would pack their few belongings, beg provisions of the army, and, under Totka's care, turn their faces toward home. Marcus would continue on to…wherever it was the general made camp. In vicinity of the Spanish-American border, Lillian deduced; Marcus wouldn't say.

When the launch returned, it bore Teniente Prieto in her husband's stead, as well as the message that the captain's wound was extensive, so Marcus would remain unknown hours at surgery. Her consolations to loneliness had been Mari's wee body curled against her and two items of interest brought by Prieto himself, who upon learning of Diego's death, had declared himself Mari's vested sentinel, hoisted her little trunk from its alcove, and divulged its false bottom.

Lining the compartment were three ledgers. Laid atop them, a leather document holder embossed with the arms of the house of López de Aragon. The folder's contents included the deeds to every López holding in the Americas, Diego's royal commission as a supplier for the king's Realista Army, and Mari's official legitimization. True to Fray Emilio's report and per King Ferdinand VII's seal, the baby had been christened Doncella Maria del Sol López Ybarra.

Spontaneously ill, Lillian had emptied her stomach into the nearest receptacle, vowing to burn the document and spit on its ash. Teniente Prieto had talked her down, using a thick, sealed envelope as leverage. It contained Diego's last will and testament, he'd said, as well as Mari's letters patent giving her all López estates: La Conchita and El Retiro, Diego's possessions and coffers, his vessels and trade—all hers when she wed, to be managed until then by the gentleman of her mother's choosing, her listed mother being Doña Sofía Ybarra de López.

Unwilling to destroy her daughter's staggering legacy, Lillian had returned the certificate to its place and sworn that if Mari's "mother" wanted her, she would have to come pry her from Lillian's vicious fingers. Teniente Prieto had patted her hand and assured her that Doña Sofía would care nothing for the child, only the profits stood to be gained from López holdings.

Appeased, Lillian had put Mari and Barb to bed in another berth, bathed, and begun rifling through the ledgers. If she must wait for her husband, she may well use the time to scratch around for his long-sought-after justice. What a wedding gift it would be to offer him redress! Something substantial to elevate him before General Jackson.

The task, however, had devolved into less satisfying labor than she'd reckoned for. Every scratch of the pen cried Diego's name. And this room! She could scarcely stand to be in it, surrounded by his things, and there was no ridding herself of his repulsive voice.

Venga, come to me…give me my kisses…

His fluid Castilian rang so vividly in her mind, if she turned, she might see him stretched out on the bed, born up by his ego and a hill of cushions, his chest a golden vee between laid-open folds of a bleached-white shirt.

In reality, he lay stiff and gray, sewn in canvas and awaiting burial on the morrow. She would attend, toss soil onto his body, and try like mad to move on with her life—a trial of shame and shoulder-rippling regret that would be made less burdensome once Marcus became a permanent fixture in their lives. When that might be, only God in His Heaven knew.

Tonight, though, he was hers. Or, *would* be once he unstrapped himself from duty. Of all nights to be indispensable! At least she had Diego's books to plunder in the interim. Halfway through the first, she'd found disappointingly little more than in the others.

Grunting, she stretched her arms high, careful of her churlish wounds, and bent at the elbows to rake hair that at one point had been brushed to a neat blanket of waves. Now, it cascaded down her back in gnarly confusion.

Behind her, the bed's blush-red sheets seduced her weary body in vain. She would bed down with Marcus or not at all, but it would not be in *that* bed. A new creature made clean before God, she would not sully the holy sacrament of marriage by touching so much as a pillow from this cabin. A hammock in the hold would be preferable.

For now, Diego's spacious desk afforded more room to spread out and work, but fortunately for her wedding night, the captain's cabin, one door over, was available, its porcelain heater set to a slow burn. She too simmered, a sensual flutter tickling her ribs at the memory of the last words Marcus had brushed against her cheek.

Turn down the bedding, Mrs. Buck.

"Mrs. Buck," she repeated on a soft sigh, as dreamily as any girl in short skirts.

Obeying an impulse, she jumped up, teetering with the floor's sudden pitch, and retrieved Mama's Bible from Marcus's haversack. Back at the desk, she flipped the cover and rummaged through a tin of dip pens for a fine-tipped nib. Leaving a wide gap under Totka's smudged name, she scribed her own, Mrs. Lillian McGirth Buck, followed lovingly by that of her husband. She hesitated at Mari's, then set her jaw and wrote in bold script: Maria del Sol López Ybarra.

Denying her child's legal name might one day jeopardize her inheritance. Personally, Lillian would curse it all to the four winds, but Mari — grown and seeking a spouse — might feel differently. It was her choice to make. Many, many years from now. Until then, Lillian intended her to have a halcyon childhood on the Mobile, sinking toes in mud and skipping rocks with siblings.

Smiling, she dusted the crow-black ink with pounce, blew it away, and examined her work. "Welcome to your new life, Lillian Buck. New life, new woman."

Brimful, she prayed endless blessings on Marcus for giving her his good name. A perpetuity of favor and kisses and every conceivable form of affection. If only she could begin this very minute…

Surrendering to an extended wait, she set aside the Bible, chose a new register, and pulled the candle closer. This latest book logged copious transactions with Wakulla Village: corn, beans, yards of duffel, a dozen kegs of tafia, several ponies, and — Lillian's stomach roiled — in a column all its own, Marcus's undeniable evidence.

On trusty sea legs, Marcus toweled dripping hair and clomped barefoot down the companionway, taking the steep treads two at a time. In lieu of a bath to remove vestiges of a trying surgery, he'd stripped and swum the last hundred yards to the ship. Clean and limbered, he'd scaled the accommodation ladder and put on the fresh clothes his thoughtful wife had left out for him: white summer-weight trousers and linen shirt, untucked, unbuttoned at the throat and clinging to the ocean on his skin.

Two of the clock was a shameful hour for a man to make an

appearance at his marriage bed. Offerings of regret would never suffice; he would have to make it up to her another way. Not an entirely unpleasant dilemma.

The captain's berth, where she'd instructed they meet, was heated but dark and empty; however, light spilled out from under the great cabin's door. A change of heart about their sleeping arrangements? He'd have none of the sort. López's rooms—blast, López's *anything* would forever reside next door to Hades.

Satisfaction over the scoundrel's death was running roughshod over every Christ-like character Marcus should be exhibiting after such a tragic development. Worse, he had yet to feel much more than a twinge of remorse; relief and gratitude had monopolized him.

On that deck, for one ghastly swordless second, Lillian had been dead. In the next, Marcus himself. The captain's intervention, though costly, had given Totka's arrow time enough to find its mark. Marcus would be a long time hunting words adequate enough to express his gratitude to both men.

López was dead, and Mari was free. Justice at its purest.

This time, Marcus would not be found whining about God employing another to accomplish His purpose. To the best of his imperfect ability, he'd obeyed the Spirit's prompt, used the don's arrogance against him, and drawn Justice as a last resort, instead of the second he laid eyes on the man, as he'd itched to do.

Though cutting López would have gladdened Marcus, he had never intended to win that fight, and in the end, he concluded, he'd been utilized plenty; the slaying of Mari's father was a burden he gratefully bequeathed to her uncle.

And if all else had failed, he would proudly, most delightedly, own this: just as Christ had covered Lillian with the shelter of His name, so had Marcus.

She had his name, his life, his love—the last, however, he doubted she fully grasped. In light of the times and ways he'd *wanted* to demonstrate it, his actions had been vague, his words vaguer. Earlier, after he'd marched them to their appointment with Ainsworth, he'd realized what a shameful botch he'd made while expressing his sentiments. Before the night was through, he would mend it.

Pausing outside the great cabin, he fully expected Lillian to rush him with either contention, kisses, or both. He laid a quiet fist to the wood, waited, and turned the knob. A serene chamber lay the other side. No rushing of any sort.

Unease settled about him.

The wool runner pushing up between his toes led his eye to where she sat with her feet flat on the seat of the chair, legs folded beneath a shirt, arms wrapped about them.

Cheek resting on upraised knees, she smiled softly. "How fares the captain?"

Was her voice somewhat breakable, or was that water clogging his ears? To drain them, he tipped his head to each side. "In considerable pain, but with rest, he should recover."

"Bless his dear heart. At least, he has the army's best tending him." Yes, breakable. "And the swim?"

He gave his head one last rub, then balled the towel and lobbed it into a corner. "Good. Cold."

"We'll right that soon enough." The sultry reply allayed his worry and allowed his husband's eye to rove her form.

Every night since the ambush, she'd used his shirt as a bed shift, driving him into the wintry elements, to the opposite side of the campfire, up a tree, anywhere he couldn't get to her without effort. Every imagining of this night had seen her wearing only her sumptuous honey skin, but the teasing concealment of his own shirt was oh-so-much sweeter.

Tucked as her legs were, the garment's fabric stretched thin over her sides, hugging the inlet of her waist, the same curve that had often lain beneath his doctorly care, bared yet achingly untouchable. Now, it was his to have and to hold. The fact flushed his skin, and begged that he storm the cabin and crush her to him. Logic subdued the urge.

A man laid unchecked eyes on his new bride but once in a lifetime. He would prolong it, record the vision for future parsing, delight in every dark, wild strand that twined about her face and arm and over the chair's rail.

Behind her, a tall, porcelain furnace emitted waves of heat visible in the few tendrils that rose off her back in a sensuous dance. Spellbound, he approached, adjusting for the ship's fluid roll and pondering how it was such a creature had pledged herself to his army life and broken body.

A dim ache awoke in his chest's center. He recognized it at once, it being a recent acquaintance. The day he'd sailed from San Marcos it had introduced itself as Love and declared itself a permanent fixture. They would live together, it said, laugh together, cry together, and when their days had been accomplished, they would die together.

He pressed a fist to the ache, and though his heart knew every cleft and knoll of her face, his eyes strained against the dimness to see it. The tongue of her candle lent little by way of assistance, highlighting the tip of her nose and chin and twinkling in the set of tears freckling her cheekbone.

A groan spawned in his soul and crawled from him in the shape of her name. "Lillian, duchess…I'm sorry."

Senses primed to her, he bent and tenderly braced her head in the basin of his hands. Swabbing her salty skin with his lips, he teased his airways with a full draught of her crisp, lemony scent and rested his forehead against hers, ready with a lengthy, self-effacing apology.

"Forgiven." The word caressed his ear an instant before her fingers, bound for his hair, did the same, furrowed deep, and sowed the seeds of desire.

He disrobed his tone. "So easily? I'm indebted to you, wife of mine, but I'll atone with interest accrued. How would you like payment?" He pinpointed her glossy lower lip and was journeying there to suggest a method when she slipped arresting fingers over his chin.

"I'll be collecting in short order, but first, look." As she sat forward, her legs, more richly honeyed than he recalled, emerged from the shirt. "No, darling. Here." She turned his head to the desktop and a mood-spoiling heap of books. One lay open, exhibiting columns of figures and rows of Spanish script.

"López accounts?" Marcus straightened with a snap of his spine. "Are these new?"

"Yes. They were in Mari's trunk. Lieutenant Prieto opened a false bottom." Her hand flattened over the gutter of the open register and dragged it nearer him. "Look." The command, though weak, fissured her voice.

Apprehensive of her nerves, he complied but shook his head at the Spanish. "Tell me what I'm seeing."

"These columns list items given to the Indians." Her finger traced a wobbly line down the page. He'd like to blame her tremble on excitement over a discovery, but her eyes weren't shining, and tense brackets had formed around her mouth. "Most of it is food, utensils, sundry supplies, but this one here and here" — she pointed out several words, breath accelerating — "muskets, shot, powder."

Why was this distressing? He listened to her respirations and, fighting off a frown, took up the book and followed each line item to its corresponding column and numbers. Large numbers. Startlingly large. "These figures, are they monetary or quantities traded?"

"Quantities."

"Impressive. Enough for a small army."

"Mmm. Or two ambushes." Girding her old wound, she shoved up from the chair, forcing him back a step. "This room, I cannot breathe in it!" Tramping footfalls carried her to the windows. She unlatched two and flung them out over the water. Clutching the casement, she stared into the black beyond. An arctic blast agitated her hair and twisted the garment about her meager frame — a keen reminder of her too-recent fast, her fragility, and that propensity of hers to break.

The exaggerated movement of air through her lungs triggered Marcus to action, but he gripped the chairback to stay the drive, to allow her a chance to steady herself. She had the right Tool, if she would but reach for Him. As Marcus waited and watched her body take on a gradual slump, he absentmindedly thumbed through the ledger, only partly interested in learning more.

That one page was gavel aplenty, all the backing for invasion the general would need, as if the Scott Massacre, as it had been coined, weren't backing enough.

"Mission complete." The murmuration was devoid the expected thrill. This find represented betrayal and deceit, Lillian's pain and, likely, the deaths of good soldiers. No joy could be found in that.

Wind spiraled through the cabin, sucking away warmth and rustling the ledger's pages. They fanned closed, exposing the title page and a name that robbed Marcus of coherent thought.

Bellamy and Co., West Florida.

Owner: Mr. Robert Maxwell Bellamy, licensed trader.

What was it doing here, among López's things? Being held ransom? Or maybe Bellamy, suspecting American invasion, had simply asked López to get it out of San Marcos.

Whatever the case, Marcus stared at it, heart mushrooming with delicious vindication and the aroma of justice, then shriveling in dread. If Lillian knew her friend was responsible, she would be devastated. Impulsively, Marcus smacked the cover closed, drawing her around.

Sorrow swelled her eyes and streaked her face.

She knows.

Gnawed by the sight, he began toward her, arm extended, ready to carry the grief she buried in her hands.

"I suspected Max was involved," she said, cry muffled, "but I stopped my ears to it. I created a fantasy in which he was a simple trader, and I was truly his friend!"

"You were, Lillian. Are!" One stride more and he had her against him, the cool of her skin penetrating the layers between them. She was still drinking the wind, so he left the window open, pulled her close, and gave her his heat. "The friendship you share is rare but genuine. I'm witness to it. The man was in fits of worry when you went missing, and I've never seen a fellow row so hard to reach a place as when Maxwell Bellamy got it into his head to set up a search party for you."

That infernal Englishman was as mired in machinations as ever Marcus believed him to be. More so. Without his trading post, the Red

Sticks might be nigh to powerless, instead of terrorizing the countryside with full shot bags. But it had been Bellamy who'd put food in Lillian's mouth; Bellamy who'd talked Marcus out of desertion; Bellamy who'd called the war woman into action.

Marcus fisted the ledger in one hand and Lillian's hair in the other, acutely aware that she would not be in his arms but for Mr. Maxwell Bellamy. Confound that maddeningly likeable deviant!

"Really?" Bowing back over the brace of his arms, she peered up at him, hopeful.

"Really. For all his sins, Mr. Bellamy cannot be named a faithless friend." Friend or not, he was a gallows bird once General Jackson came into possession of this book.

"If all that's true, then..." Breaking from his embrace, she took a step back, pinning the book with an accusatory glare. "Marcus, I can have nothing to do with bringing him down. Take the book. Complete your mission. Bring him to justice. He deserves it, and you deserve to be the one to exact it, but if I must look at that thing again or-or even think of what might become of him..." She crammed a fist to her mouth and, eyes squeezing shut, turned away from it.

From him.

Marcus held the book loosely at waist level, hating it for coming between them. It burned his palm, sent fiery waves up the hardening muscles of his arm and across a dozen jagged scars. Each one cried out for long-anticipated, much-deserved justice. It lay here, in his hand, ripe for wielding, but how much would it cost his wife and his fledgling marriage?

She hadn't asked him to choose. Nevertheless, it was a choice.

There was justice and the mission. Then there was her, them.

As for the mission... Earlier that day, with the touch of nib to parchment, he'd removed himself from the assignment and all obligation to it. That responsibility now, thankfully, belonged to another man.

And what of justice? Securing it only required he drive a knife through his wife's heart. On second thought, there really was no choice.

The flick of his wrist sailed the book, pages fluttering, into the black chasm of space. A count of two, then a dim *plash* that spun Lillian back to him.

Her enlarging eyes skipped from his empty hands to his face, out the window, and back to him. Gripping the casement, she doubled over it, pushing her torso into the night to look down. "Marcus, what have you done? What of justice?"

"I'm done with it." He pulled her away and closed the panes. "If God wants the man brought to justice, He'll use someone else to achieve it." The window fasteners clicked into place with a finality that brought unexpected release.

Beyond the glass's glare, there was only blinding midnight, but Marcus imagined he spotted the pale sheets of a book floating out to sea carrying away his life's purpose.

Not true.

His purpose stood behind him. He shifted his focus to his wife's reflection: dark, lawless hair streaming over white cotton. Even blurred in warped glass, she stripped him of breath, made every nook of his body stamp its feet in demand.

Bating it, he watched her steal close, flinched at the frigid hands she slid up the skin of his back. His shirt rose with them, chilling him waist to shoulders. Jittery over his scars, he shuddered but wanting it done, yanked the garment over his head and stood unstrung for examination.

None came. Leastways, none that stilled her hands and mouth, both of which she applied liberally with her usual bold charge. Unable to sense much beyond a numb burn, he relaxed into her command, greedily soaking up her love without condition. Then her caress moved to his front in a dizzying, nail-traipsing dance. Undone, he effected a swift turnabout, hoisting her into his arms and ending her reign.

Somehow, through the distraction of her deep-throated chuckle, he snuffed the candle and ran the bumping, stumbling gauntlet to the next cabin where the ship's sudden pitch flopped them with a comical *umph* onto the captain's turned-down bed.

Too late, he thought of her ribs, but he needn't have worried. Beneath him, she shook with laughter, which he stifled with a kiss intended to leave her breathless, an undertaking he tackled with every diligence. He knew he'd succeeded when she broke free and gasped for air.

Doing the same, he lifted on an elbow to hobble their sprint; he was resolved to speak his heart first. No easy task, and harder yet since the darkness had endeared itself somewhat to his eyes, allowing him to distinguish the curving black lines of her silhouette.

"Come back, tease. No one gave you permission to stop." Clinging to his nape, she pulled up to him, but he grinned, and with a finger to her sternum, he pushed her back down.

"The duchess has been dethroned," he said.

"I have a throne?"

Concerned for her low body heat, he flung the covers over them and drew her close. "You *had* a throne. It belongs to me now."

"And how shall you rule, my lord husband? With justice?"

"With munificence."

"A fine word." She shivered and, arms tucked, snuggled into his embrace. "When applied to me, I quite approve. I bet Harvard taught you that." She placed her smiling mouth against his, inviting him to explore but hindering his attempt with her chitchat. "Did they also teach you finance? Debt? Interest accrued?"

"Maybe." Voice lowering, he traced a tickling finger over her back in a patternless swirl. "Are you calling in my bill?"

"Indeed, Your Grace. But I'm open to discussing installments. Might you consider, say, a fifty-year plan?" Great day, but he would miss this woman!

He chuckled. "Where do I sign?"

"Anywhere you'd like." She laid the maddening whisper against his ear. "I'm all yours."

He would survey the canvas to choose a place but for the blasted dark. "A thousand curses on that cold candle," he grumbled.

Rich laughter sprang from her. "Put your eyes into your fingers, and for mercy's sake, love me." She flattened his hand to her belly and let a long sigh carry her over to her back.

Desire flared, but he checked it. Love was a great deal more than rapturous caresses. She knew that, didn't she? Taking into consideration her abusive past, he wondered if she was able to recognize love as God defined it. To Marcus, it was that pang behind his ribs and its unceasing whisper: *be patient, be kind, honor, forgive, protect, trust, hope, persevere!*

How strange to have fallen so swiftly, so completely, and for a woman whose life had contradicted his core values. No longer. Lillian McGirth was dead. In her place lay a woman whose life now exemplified God's transforming power. That same gracious God had given her to Marcus, of all men.

The knot in his center burgeoned into a breath-snuffing mass. He forced air into his body, voice becoming unsteady with the drive to make her understand. "Love you, duchess? Done. A thousand time, done."

"How you can love me… I'm bewildered."

"What is there to be confused about?" His spreading hand spanned her width, registering her quivering warmth a beat before it did the evidence of her having borne a child. "I love you here, where you gave Mari life." Traveling north, he made a bumpy trail up her ribs to that circular patch of new flesh that had worried him so. "And here. Where you saved mine." Next, he laid an ear to her chest. "And especially here," he murmured. Where Christ gave *her* life.

"You love me," she stated, chest buzzing against his cheek.

"Never doubt it." He harked back to their first stirring exchanges. "Sometimes, when I think of you, love grows so large inside of me it hurts to breathe." Like now.

After a whist pause, she stroked the tract of his deadened back. "Wealth comes in all shapes."

Wealthy… Yes, he was. Abundantly so.

Smiling, he closed his eyes and riveted to her touch and the wholesome tap of her heart. The organ's rhythm—so dissimilar to the one that spoke to him those first trying days—was stable and strong. A beautiful sound he could listen to forever. Fifty years, at minimum.

She curtailed it with the drum of her fingers against his ribs. "So then… All in proper order, Doctor?"

Putting sentimentality aside, were they? He could sail that ship.

"By no means. Your heart is sluggish and suffering from a dreadful lack of exercise." Its stout kick and trip was a contagion that spread to his and brought on a wicked grin.

"A saint once told me exercise makes everything stronger. I'm keen." In contention for the throne, she stretched to reach his chuckling mouth.

"I'm ever so glad. Roll up your sleeves, duchess," he said, rising to give her what she strove for. "We've got a health regimen to begin, and I've got a contract to sign."

Chapter 23

Leaned over one of the beds in their rented room, Lillian tied off Mari's clean napkin and, fending off peddling kicks, pulled the wool pilcher over her chunky bottom. She gave it a pat for good measure, and when Mari giggled, Lillian stoppered her wet mouth. "Shh! Uncle T is sleeping," she whispered through her own stifled laugh, glancing behind to the room's other bed.

The morning was two hours gone, yet Totka still slept. Fully clothed, an arm slung over his eyes, he lay as he'd fallen at dawn when he'd come in to rouse them for travel. Ten minutes on his feet had sent him crashing to Barbury's tidied bed.

The three-day voyage to Mobile had done him in. Lillian hadn't known a body could be so averse to choppy seas: dizziness, vomiting, cold sweats. By day two, he was so far gone, he'd lost the will to protest the cloth she dabbed to his forehead or the liquid she fretfully urged down his throat.

What would Marcus do? The ever-present question.

Longing for him surged highest the night she tended Totka straight through to sunup and returned to her cabin to lament a furnace gone cold. Never had covers been lonelier.

Heartache over his absence was a stymying force, but Totka kept her engaged. Yesterday afternoon, it had taken both she and Teniente Prieto to help him down the shifty gangplank. At her insistence, they'd delayed the last leg of their journey—half a day's row upriver—so he could find his feet again. The coin purse Marcus left her had rented them a room and funded a visit to the shops to include the unassuming gown and mobcap she tugged over Mari's feathery hair, as well as the satchel at the foot of the bed. It bulged with flannels, linens, muslins: the ingredients of a frontierswoman's wardrobe.

Lillian collected Mari's crushed-silk gown and pearl-trimmed stockings and shoved them to the bottom of the satchel along with her angora blanket and the title *viscountess*. For whoever asked, Marisol López was a commonplace girl whose birth father died and who was, in every practical sense, a Buck. No one need know any different, least of all Mari.

Lillian wanted San Marcos dead and buried with its don.

A light knock at the door admitted Barbury and a steaming bowl. Without a word, she exchanged it for the baby and left for a mid-morning feeding. Totka stirred, stretched, and blinked up at the ceiling.

"Forgive us for breaking your sleep." Lillian took the gruel to his bedside. "But since you are woken, you should eat."

"My stomach will not like it."

"Copper Woman will not like the sight of your ribs."

Croaky morning noises escorted the swing of his legs over the bed. He sat up and accepted the dish, peering at her from the tops of his eyes. "You know where to pinch a man."

"The only thing I am pinching is my nose. Hot bath or the river?"

He sniffed his shirt and recoiled. "Bath."

"Good choice." The less the public saw of him, the better.

Native antagonism ran at flood levels. As did the cost of a room. It had doubled when the proprietor learned one of his guests was Indian. *For added risk,* he'd snipped.

For added spite, more like.

Totka's woozy glower had taken Lillian some fast talking to excuse. In the end, another coin had earned him a cot and the blanket she'd thrown over him.

Forgive me, Sister, he'd rasped, pulling the quilt to his chin.

Ack, the man is a money-grubbing beetle and deserved your censure.

He'd eased open an eyelid and managed a tender smile.

The last days had been backward, surreal. They still were, she thought, as she strode to the bureau for a stack of folded clothes. "A few things for you." She set the pile beside him. "Consider it payment. Not every man would take on the enemy to carry a letter a hundred sights for a bitter-eyed sister."

Porridge forgotten, he buried his fingers in the fox-fur vest and took an appreciative gander at the length of breechcloth strouding. "They are very fine."

She smiled. "Another day of rest for you?"

"No. I am well enough."

"If you are certain, Prieto will hire a boat, and I will bring a tub." She turned to leave, but Totka touched her wrist, stopping her.

"Sister, you are…much changed. For the better." An unexpected observation.

She tipped her head. "You see it? I *feel* changed. As Creator says, made a new creature."

"Yes, it is in your eyes. They are bitter no more."

A vicious cramp seized her throat; hope, her spirit. "Any chance I have shed that dreadful name?"

After a thoughtful pause, he gave an unhurried nod. "As a butterfly sheds its old life and old ways, perhaps so have you. I will speak of it with Beaver. Butterfly seems fitting."

Lillian's lungs hitched as she cherished not only the new name but the fact God had sloughed the old. The notion razed the dam on her tears; they ran and dripped from her jaw, each one a prayer of gratitude. "Maddo, Brother. I pray to be truly worthy of it."

Frowning, he waved the spoon between them. "Dry that river. There is no call for tears. It is only a name, and the clan mothers have yet to agree."

"I have earned my tears!" Fist jammed to her waist, she took him to task with a look. "Though I am some changed, my bent toward weeping is forever fixed. If it disturbs you, look away."

The piqued backward jut of his chin slipped the fist from her hip. How tragic it would be for her reprobate tongue to stamp out their peace pipe before they'd barely taken a draw from it.

She softened. "And it is much more than a name. It is a gift from a forgiving brother and evidence of Creator's healing mercy."

Totka chuffed an exhale, demeanor mellowing. "It is not the weeping that disturbs me, woman. It is my own...weakness at the sight of it." Of a sudden, he became fastidious with his porridge, scraping it all to one side of the dish then back again.

Totka? Weak? What a concession! Battling a smile, she cleared the gruff from her throat. "I see..." In deference to his discomfort, she trod for the door. "Eat. Let me know if you want more."

"Butterfly."

Hand on the knob, she halted. Busily eradicating the joyous prick behind her lids, she stayed as she was while Totka spoke.

"You are worthy of it."

Apart from the cutting wind, the ride up the Mobile passed agreeably. Teniente Prieto kept them in songs, rowing to the beat of the ditties he belled across the water, and Totka, after passing Mobile's limits, gave over scowling, the fresh air seeming to brighten him. The prospect of seeing his Copper Woman, whom he'd taken to Tensaw for the duration of his travels, likely had nothing at *all* to do with his improvement.

Mari, in Barb's arms, found both men endlessly amusing, but Lillian was simply glad for the distraction from her rampant nerves. Her stomach had been out of sorts, growing crotchetier as they neared home.

The last bend in the river washed every last anxiety into the bay.

Papa stood on the bank by the dock, the butt of a fishing pole propped on his too-lean belly. Silver had overtaken his auburn hair, and his cheekbones were startlingly prominent, but those broad shoulders, so like Marcus's, still delivered their promise of shelter and protection; they turned toward her now and rose sharply with the cry that ripped from him in a semblance of agony. The pole jerked free, swept away by the current. He clapped a fist over his gaping mouth, garbling her shouted name. "Lilly!"

"Papa!" She leaned over the dugout's side, nearly spilling out. "I'm coming!"

Totka doubled his clip at the paddle, but all his efforts combined would never make the grade. Matching Papa's lament, she rose to a wobbly stance, eager for the landing, unable to recall a single reason she'd left.

Gaze pasted to her, he took several hesitant steps along the water's edge, and then, he stuttered to his knees with a wail that could crumble the stoutest of granite hearts. Sorrow flipped Lillian's insides; dismay flipped them back. Was he so bad off already?

The shore's curt greeting hurtled her from her perch. She tripped out and sloshed through murky puddles until she was falling down beside him, and he was hugging her sobbing body against his own.

"I'm sorry, Papa. I'm sorry, I'm sorry!" She adhered to his neck and drenched him in apologies until his soft shushing noises penetrated the fog of her shame.

"You're home, sweet girl," he said against her hair. "It's all that matters now."

Minutes passed in that manner with Papa consoling and forgiveness suturing her self-inflicted wounds. At length, she sniffled and realized they were alone with the empty dugout and the woodpecker that violated the cypress above them.

Papa set her away to cup her face and to look at her, long and deep. "Beautiful. So like your mother." The gray rimming his sunken eyes said the two would soon be reunited.

No thoughts of death! Not now. She strong-armed a clogged swallow. "I've come home a redeemed woman, Papa. God has forgiven me."

Joy stretched his gaunt cheeks. "We serve a good God."

"And Marcus gave me his name."

"No surprise there." Humor vibrated his chest. "Why do you think

I sent him to you?"

"Oh, Papa. You couldn't have known he would love me."

"I most certainly did know. What man, taking half a minute to see your beautiful heart, wouldn't jump at the chance?"

"Plenty!" Pure laughter rolled through her. "That's a prejudiced father speaking."

His chuckle broadened. "All right, a little prejudiced. Maybe I'm recalling my wishful thinking. My *expertly concealed* wishful thinking. Did he tell you how I made him swear to keep his distance?"

"No!"

"Ask him." Knavery flickered in his beaming eyes. "Love that overcomes that degree of a father's discouragement is a love worth having." Wincing, he rose, aided by her arm. "What of you? Do you love him? Tell me you do."

She nodded long, breath crippled by a swift, brutal ache. "So much my heart hurts with it."

"As it should." Smiling, he hooked an arm behind her.

Basking in the beauty of restoration, she molded to his spare frame. Though his body waned, the strength of his love remained as firm as ever. "My heart hurts with love for you, too, Papa. Thank you for not giving up on me. For sending Marcus and loving me home. I won't leave you again. Not for one miniscule second." Not until his spirit sprung into his Savior's arms.

Water suffused his eyes. He opened his mouth to speak, but unable to make more than a choked sob, he shut it again and merely nodded.

Throat an agonizing knot, she kissed his trembling sandpaper chin and angled their path homeward. "Now then, let's find that sweetie granddaughter of yours, shall we?"

Epilogue

Windy Month (February) 1818, two months later

Another clod of dirt crumbled beneath Lillian's slicing hoe. February was early to be turning over the garden, yet this was her second round since returning home. Whenever grief or worry got the better of her, the earth obligingly received the brunt of it.

Yesterday, it was Marcus and his silence—not a letter, not a solitary note.

Today: Adela, her distended belly, and the child occupying it. Anticipation had Totka at a near fast; Adela made up for it, not worried in the least; and Lillian pummeled the earth.

A week ago, surrounded by family, Papa passed into the Lord's presence. His and Lillian's time together had been sweet, favored. As promised, she'd stayed by his side round the clock until the last grains of soil had been smoothed over his grave. Better he didn't suffer, but how she longed for him! His genial laugh, his worn-out stories, his calloused hand covering hers.

If Marcus were here, the pain would surely lessen. Where *was* that man? On a ship at sea, taken captive? Dead in a Florida bog? If he would but write, her lungs might learn to expand again.

She hauled back and cut the ground once more, throwing dirt over her shoes and relishing her muscles' wearying burn. Hopefully, sleep would come easier tonight.

"You'd better have the finest of excuses, Marcus Buck." She swung the hoe high, muscles bunching for another strike.

"Or what, duchess?"

Lillian yipped, tool tumbling behind her, and twirled about.

Not ten feet away, Marcus stood, hip propped against the plot's split-rail fence. He wore ill-fitting civilian garb, suffered the recent absence of a razor, and beneath the shade of a dusty tri-corned hat, he flashed an adorably boyish grin. Without Justice, his thigh looked forlorn, and those bedraggled boots! He was nigh on unrecognizable.

"Marcus?" she said, stupidly. Unbelieving.

"Has another man taken to calling you *duchess*?" He shoved off and began toward her with that self-assured saunter that made her silly heart flutter.

The cogwheels of her brain meshed and lurched.

"Marcus!" She charged him, spurting peals of joy and contrasting his sure stride with her skirt-raising, ankle-wobbling traipse over the rutted parcel.

Arms wide, he laughingly received her bounding leap, but her bungled launch slammed her chest off-center with him, wrecking his stability.

Yielding a cheep of alarm, she strangled him with all four limbs, and though he flailed nobly for balance, the horizon flipped, taking her stomach with it. In the next instant, his body flattened hers to the lumpy ground. Shocked, her lungs skipped a draw—meager fee for lying in her husband's arms thirty seconds after setting eyes on him.

One of his elbows snapped straight, thrusting him half off her. "Have I crushed you?" His eyes, too serious for the blunder *she* had caused, performed an evaluating sweep, his hand going, as though by force of habit, to her ribs and that old wound.

She chuckled through recuperating breaths. "Hardly."

"Duchess, you've married a lummox." Brow corrugating, he put the bumper of his hand behind her head, then dusted her cheek and nose, swept vagrant strands from her face, and fretted, seemingly, for the sake of fretting.

While he did, she devoured the dear sight of him, relished every glancing touch. He was thin and weather-beaten, but the semi-beard was a striking addition. A dreamy sigh slipped from her. What a comely, lovesome man she'd been given. "I'm the lummox, Marcus, throwing myself at you like a riotous pup, but I couldn't have plotted a more convenient how-do-you-do if I'd tried." Arms twining about his neck, she made herself an anchor and winked a suggestion.

He vaulted a brow and conducted a skimming survey of their surroundings. Blessedly barren. Coming back, his gaze went potent. "A most valid observation, Wife." His tidying strokes became spine-shimmying caresses and migrated to her lips. "Shall I improve on it?"

One corner of her mouth drifted upward. "If you don't, I will."

Embracing her with the confidence of a husband and the desperate temporality of a soldier, he kissed her to a tingling pant. Soul-sore and deprived, she soldered to him, knowing she'd never be satisfied until she was under his clothes, inside his blood, one with his very bones — a crazy, nonsensical desire that she clung to as desperately as she did the man. Thirty days of leave were but candied torture.

Too soon, he broke away for a long, close-up study that ended on a sigh. "I missed you."

"Did you?" she teased naughtily, itching to reprimand the lack of correspondence. "Exactly how much?"

"As much as I miss breathing on a long dive," he popped off, as if it were a well-rehearsed thought. But it was shrouded in subtle pain and…what?

She perused his austere features and determined he'd lost something. A certain spark, perhaps? In his eyes? Yes, they'd dulled. Disquiet stirred within and plaited her fingers with his shirt ruffle.

"In the first minute underwater," he continued, "the need for air is an annoying discomfort, something I can work through. In the second, my chest burns, followed by every muscle in my body, and my heart, it-it—" Emotion hacked his words; it reddened his eyes and moistened his lashes.

She cupped his prickly cheeks and was speared through by the tremble in his jaw. "I know; I missed you too," she breathed, disposing of every prepared remonstrance.

The earth's moisture seeped through the back of her gown, while his gaze fell unseeing and traveled to parts unknown. "It became so that I could think of nothing but my need for you. As a man needs his wife, yes, but more so as a man needs his-his…his humanity!"

Great Father, what had he witnessed?

He went on, his voice a splintered, soul-weeping sound. "There were times I couldn't see beyond the day — or even the hour! — and I would *long* for you. Like a man drowning. One clean breath would have seen me through the assignment. *One*." He hauled her against him and buried his damp face in the crook of her shoulder. Air cooled her skin as it skidded past en route to his burgeoning chest.

Of all the homecomings she'd dreamt up, none shared even the color pallet of this one: a drab gray. Tacking her wide-eyed gaze to a cracked slat in the barn wall across the lot, she harrowed his hair with loving fingers until he withdrew, his usual sturdiness coming back into him. "Lillian, I left the army." The flat statement rippled a muscle in his jaw.

Relief engulfed her — he wouldn't be leaving! Heartbreak overtook it. His shining career was over?

"Darling, why? What sort of assignment could provoke such a change? Can you speak of it?" Whatever it was, she hated it for having morphed her blithesome Marcus into this injured variant.

Head shaking, he sat up, arm about her, bringing her with him. "Enough about me. How's our little sunshine?" His lips curved tightly.

Disappointed but conscious of his raw state, she accepted the digression with a happy mien. "Perfectly sunny."

"Is she sitting up yet?"

"Sitting? Pft! She's pulling up!"

Light reentered his eyes, substantiating his smile. "Already?"

"Already." Lillian glowed with pride and stood, anxious for their reunion. "And two days ago, I promise you, she said *mama*."

"Did she, now?" Belatedly, he concealed a disbelieving simper.

"It *might* have been silly babble, but you won't convince me she's anything less than *una genia*. A child genius."

"That I can believe. She was bound to get *something* from me."

"Take care with the fibs, Mr. Buck. You risk sainthood." Jaw lifting a degree in fabricated offense, she offered her hand to help him up.

He accepted and blended their laughter, seeming much the old Marcus.

The slap of running feet veered them around. Four-year-old Charlie dashed from behind the barn, blond curls slicked back by his own wind. "Sissy! Sissy, Uncle T is dead!"

"What!" Her stomach tumbled. "Where is he?"

"The kitchen," Charlie wailed, bright red patching his cheeks. He sped, howling, into her skirt.

Marcus darted for his kit by the barn; speechless, she plucked up her little brother and patted his heaving back. *God, no. Please, no!*

"Charlie!" Barbury rounded the same corner at the same speed and came to a dust-disturbing halt. She burst out a grin. "Why, Doc! Ain't you a sight for sore—"

He gripped her arm. "What's wrong with Totka?"

"Nothin' a good smack won't fix." She snorted a giggle. "Missy Adela broke her waters, and next ya know, that big, tough-as-leather Indian, he seen it and passed out cold. Felled like a tree, he was. 'Fore I could stop her, the missy went down to help 'im, and now she stuck like a upturned turtle." Barb held her stomach and cackled until she wept.

"That's it? He swooned?" Marcus wagged his head and laughed shakily. "In that case, he won't want me around until he's off his back. How is Adela? Contractions?"

"Ain't had a twinge."

"It'll be a long day then. Barb, you go on ahead. Get her off the floor. I'll be there soon."

"All right, suh, but don't dawdle," Barb said, jogging back the way she'd come. "The woman's big as a barrel, and I ain't got but these two scrawny arms."

Pulse descending, Lillian gave Charlie a squeezing hug. "Hear that, baby boy? Uncle T isn't dead!"

He released her neck to swipe his forearm across his drippy nose. "Not dead?"

"Just sleeping."

Charlie squirmed down Lillian's front and to the company of a little stomp dance, screeched an ear-drilling whoop. She winced, grateful when his churning legs bore him away.

Squinting one eye, Marcus twisted a forefinger inside his ear. "Can we thank Totka for that?"

She rolled her eyes. "We can." Falling in with his languid stride, she pointed across the yard to the mound of settling dirt and the carved cross at its head. "But we can thank him for that, too."

Marcus hooked an arm about her waist. "Lillian, I'm sorry. I wish I'd been here for—"

"Please, darling, no self-reproach. You weren't given a choice, and it unfolded precisely as God intended." Grief surfaced, robust and florid.

His hold tightened. "When you're ready to talk, I'm here."

He was indeed. Here. To stay.

From the paddock fence, Wind Chaser, Adela's mare, waggled her lips and whinnied a soft greeting, then pranced to a cat sunning on a nearby post and nose-butted it off. It hit the ground with a hiss and yowl, the racket of which couldn't compete with Marcus and Lillian's hysterics.

When she'd calmed, Lillian couldn't distinguish tears of hilarity from tears of pure joy at being home and sharing her blissfully simple life with Marcus: the clapboard cabin Papa built, the stubbled tobacco fields stretching out behind it, even the crumbling, defunct servants' quarters that housed so many precious childhood memories.

The cabin door opened, and Totka stumbled out, driven by Adela herself. He tried to reenter, but she beat him back with a wooden spoon and closed the door in his face. Arms crossed, not budging, he stared at it like the mule he was.

"Rough day for daddies," Lillian sing-songed.

"The roughest, but a gorgeous day to be born." Marcus slowed to a stop and tipped his head back. "Would you look at that stunning sky." The vibrant lapis expanse sported not a trace of haze, not a wisp of fluff. "No sign of ash since December. Safe to say our clear days are back for keeps."

"That's the hope." She'd had eighteen months of gloom, marked by rebellion and suffering, a man's loathing, another's love, and the limitless mercy of Christ that covered it all. And ahead? An unblemished future with a good man and a wise Father. She arranged her back against Marcus's chest and pulled his arms around her. "What shall we do with our beautiful days?"

"What do you say we open a clinic. Here, in Tensaw." Skies abandoned, he planted rows of kisses down her neck.

Angling it to better receive him, she pondered the shape of that new world: no exacting commanders, no separation, no fear of losing Marcus in the next engagement. Their life would include the children, the medical practice, and his perpetually accessible help administering the plantation. Contentment overflowed and spilled out on a hum. "Sounds lovely, and I say we'd be daft not to. Doctor Holmes retired last year, and the old Bailey house isn't in use. We could ask Phillip to sell or let."

"Maybe Mari got her brains from you, after all." Voice husky, he nuzzled the back of her ear, thieving her breath.

Once retrieved, it went into a throaty chuckle. "Here's another bright idea. Hester's old cabin isn't in use either, and it's right there."

Without so much as a "grab on," he snatched her up, evoking a yelp of delight, and turned for the servants' quarters. "How are those sleeves looking, duchess?" A saucy smile climbed his lips, throwing her heart into conniptions.

"As ever they are, darling. Rolled and ready." Baffled as to how this fine man had become hers, she swung her feet to miss the door post, laid her lips against the crossbar of his scar, and inhaled the fragrance of sanctioned love.

The End

Thank you for reading!
If you enjoyed Marcus and Lillian's story,
please consider leaving a review at an online venue.

Turn the page to learn more about *Bitter Eyes No More*
and to see what to expect in Creek Country Saga book 5,
Love the War Woman

Meet Totka and his Copper Woman in

Beneath the Blackberry Moon

Boxed Set

AVAILABLE NOW
(digital format)

April W. Gardner

is an indie author whose great passion is historical romance with themes of Native American and Southeastern U.S. culture. Copyeditor, mother of two grown children, and non-trad college student, April lives in South Texas with her husband and two German Shepherds.

Enjoy these other books by April

HISTORICAL ROMANCE
Beneath the Blueberry Moon Series (Native American)
Drawn by the Frost Moon Series (Native American)
Beautiful in His Sight (WW1, standalone)
Better than Fiction (WW1 era, dual-timeline)

BIBLICAL STUDY/FICTION
A Fire and a Flame Series

CHILDREN'S MIDDLE GRADE HISTORICAL
Lizzie and the Guernsey Gang (WW2 standalone)

WRITING CRAFT
Body Beats to Build On

Facebook: April.Gardner1
Website: AprilGardner.com
Email: info@aprilgardner.com
Visit author's website and subscribe for a free novel.

Author's Notes

Nerd confession: the author's notes section is one of my favorite parts of both reading and writing historical novels. This is where I get to tell you how much of the story is based on fact. It's also where you get to put a pretty bow on this fun little history lesson you've sat through.

There's so much I'd like to tell you about this book, its creation, and the great joy (despite the struggles) I had putting it together, but let's start with the history.

Spain ruled Florida for a whopping three hundred years. The *Drawn by the Frost Moon* trilogy will take you on a three-layer journey through the events that kicked off the First Seminole War and whisked Spanish Florida toward its inevitable doom.

By three-layer, I mean that all the characters you've come to know (and hopefully love!) in *Bitter Eyes* will be reappearing in the follow-on book and skipping backwards in time to show you this period from other angles. Tall Bull and Mink will give you the Red Stick perspective in *Love the War Woman* (2018). Through entirely fresh eyes, you'll learn where Mink went after she left Neamathla's lodge, what transpired while Marcus was outside Fort Scott, what becomes of Water Moccasin, why Tall Bull cannot see past Bitter Eyes to the war woman who adores him, and so much more.

War Woman will take you deeper into the historical events surrounding San Marcos and leave you excited to dig into Strong Bear and Pretty Wolf's adventures. Their romance will be told in *Finding Pretty Wolf* (TBA), which will carry you through to the closing of this period in history. In case you were wondering, although the three layers will be enjoyed best as a whole, each will stand on its own.

Why have I chosen to lay out the story this way? Because the setting is so rich and full I couldn't bear to do away with any part of it. It's tricky as all get out to braid these three plots together without revealing too much too soon, but I trust the finished product will be worth the effort.

Now for the actual history, my random trivia list, and the behind-the-scenes tidbits you may or may not find as fascinating as I…

--Fuerte San Marcos de Apalache was established in 1679, but the stone fort in *Bitter Eyes* was built in 1759. In 1817, it was under the command of Captain Francisco Casa y Luengo and suffering from Spain's inability to keep her outposts properly manned and supplied. Today, only remnants of the wall can be seen in what is now a state park.

--The setting of *Bitter Eyes* follows what is the known as the "year without a summer," which was part of a three-year (1815-1818), worldwide span of harsh climactic changes brought on by a volcanic eruption in Indonesia. As a result, the winter of 1817-18 was devastatingly cold. The number of deaths resulting from this eruption is incalculable.

--Wakulla Village was located three miles north of the fort and a few miles south of the beautiful Wakulla Springs. Josiah Francis, the prophet and chief, established the village, then traveled to England to seek help from the king for the Red Stick cause, which is where we find him returning from in *Bitter Eyes No More*.

-- The inspiration for Marcus is based on an actual historical figure. Surgeon Marcus C. Buck of the Fourth Infantry is best known for his role in the Negro Fort tragedy, which is portrayed in book 3, *The Ebony Cloak*. My version of him began there. His historical record (at least what's available online) is reduced to only a few phrases. In an obscure 1845 Boston medical journal (thank you Google books!), I found a tidbit about Surgeon Buck. At the time of the Negro Fort, he was a major on Colonel Clinch's staff. Dr. Buck (as he later became known) was at some point "Military Storekeeper at the Washington Arsenal," and at the time of his death at age 56 was Secretary of the Medical Department of the National Institute. He died of apoplexy in 1845.

--Polly Francis/Pretty Wolf was actually named Milly Francis, but because my series already has a Milly (*The Ebony Cloak*), I chose to name my character after her mother, Polly.

--Maxwell Bellamy is based on the figure Robert Ambrister, also a former member of the Royal Navy who traded with the Red Sticks from a post on the Wakulla River. He and Polly had a close friendship.

--The pseudo-battle at Fowltown (Nov. 20, 1817) portrayed here is true to history; however, for the benefit of the story, I took creative license with the Scott Massacre (Nov. 30, 1817). Ten days passed between Fowltown and the massacre. I expanded that gap considerably to allow for plot development. To reduce the violence (for Lillian's sake), I lowered the number of soldiers on the boat (actual number, fifty) and removed the children altogether.

--A few facts about the attack: The boat was under the command of Lieutenant Richard Scott whose death gave the massacre its name. A total of seven survived, including a Mrs. Elizabeth Stewart who was taken captive and has a remarkable tale of her own. During the short engagement, a Sergeant McIntosh fired a cannon from his arms to clear the deck so others could escape. He died in the manner described.

--Fort Scott was previously known as Camp Crawford (as portrayed in *The Ebony Cloak*), and Fort Gadsden was located on the site of the old Negro Fort (also in *Ebony*). You'll need to forgive another of my liberties, that of preempting Fort Gadsden's existence. The American army did not establish itself in Prospect Bluff until March of 1818, five months after Lillian and Marcus arrived.

--There was no additional ambush outside Fort Scott; however, there was a siege. It began on December 2, 1817, but extreme cold kept the belligerents close to their campfires. Starvation was a very real concern for both parties.

--For better understanding of Lillian and Marisol's relationship to their Creek clan, here's a little about the clan system. A clan is a category of people who believe themselves to be blood relatives, even if untraceable. Bloodlines pass through the mothers. At least at that time, this included adopted members, so that Marisol was automatically Creek even though (per Anglo standards) she doesn't have a drop of Native blood. According to Native bloodlines, Totka (Wolf Clan) has no familial relationship with either Lillian or Marisol. When Lillian refers to Totka as Marisol's uncle, she is using Anglo mentality, and when they call each other "brother/sister," they are simply using terms of endearment used by all Native peoples.

Mink, however *is* related to them, since both women are Beaver.

Clan structure and responsibility extended across the confederacy so that a member of Deer would expect to be received as family in any Deer Clan home in any town, even if they'd never met before. Clan protection was often called upon, with blood law and vengeance falling on clan shoulders. This explains Mink's rescue and revenge on the friar. The Muscogee familial system is used by almost every Native tribe in North America.

--The Spanish Inquisition, that 356-year scourge, was in decline when "the felon king," Ferdinand VII, stoked its fires for one last terrible hurrah. Its active presence in San Marcos is an unsubstantiated guess on my part.

--Spain and her people took a hit for this book. It is the country of my childhood and holds a substantial portion of my heart. All negativity toward it and my Spanish characters is purely for effect and is not a reflection of my personal feelings.

--Majo/maja are words used in modern Spain to mean "nice" or "good-looking." The terms derive from society's lower classes. Common laborers known as "majos" or "manolos" wore elaborate outfits and were boldly coquettish and disrespectful. This behavior was considered attractive by the upper classes who began imitating their manner of dress but with luxurious fabrics. The majo style of dress, which was an exaggeration of traditional styles, was also a blatant anti-French movement. During this time (Napoleonic Era), the country was politically divided, a fact that was displayed in dress by the majos (nationalists/anti-French) and the *afrancesados* or "Frenchified." You'll probably best understand the attire of afrancesados as that worn by Jane Austin's characters, which also happens to be Lillian's style—a convenient contradiction to Diego's. And now, you know. :)

--Speaking of clothing, my talented mother sewed the historically accurate gown and spencer shown on Karina, my lovely cover model. To up the oh-my-goodness factor, she did this from her home in Spain. I mailed the fabric and pattern, and after a few fittings via Facetime, she sent me what you see on the cover. Are you as wowed as I am? My mom is The Best.

--The Spanish version of Lillian's name is actually "Liliana," but I chose the variation, "Liana," in honor of my darling, precocious niece, Lianna.

Thank you, faithful reader, for journeying with me through Lillian and Marcus's search for mercy and justice. Join me later this year in *Love the War Woman*! To be notified of its release, follow me on **Facebook** or sign up to my **newsletter**.

He loveth righteousness and judgment: the earth is full of the goodness of the LORD. (Ps. 33:5) *Let us therefore come boldly unto the throne of grace, that we may obtain mercy, and find grace to help in time of need.* (Heb. 4:16)

Acknowledgements

As always, God gets first kudos. His hand has been present in every book I've written, guiding when I'm lost, comforting when I'm discouraged, but my seven-month journey through *Bitter Eyes* was unique. The full account is that Lillian's story took me five years and three attempts to complete. Finally, the series requirements compelled me to *make* it work, and even then, I fought for every single, come-kicking-and-screaming word.

Those that did land on the page (all 136,000 of them) got there only by God's grace. Over the first months of the writing process, my constant, desperate prayer was, "God, my words are gone! Please, *please* give them back." Ever faithful, He did—one painstaking sentence at a time. In addition, He gave me an army of dear friends who each came alongside me to fill a specific need in a specific time.

Paula and Jennifer, you saw me through those initial months as you read my sloppy scenes for workability. My apologies, girls. You are a special kind of wonderful for enduring that mess. In those first fearful steps, you gave my feet solid direction and encouraged me to find my stride.

Becky, that's where our paths crossed, and boy, am I blessed for it. You were (are!) the I-know-you-can for this little engine who wasn't sure she could. This might have earned you sainthood. We'll ask Lillian. ;-)

Michelle and Tanya, my darling friends and invaluable critique partners, your generous instruction cannot be over-appreciated. Because of your eyes and diligent red pens, my writing is stronger, shinier, worth publishing. Thank you!

Elvira, as far as readers go, you're in a class all your own. You simply blow my mind. As far as friends go, you're of the sweetest. I've officially soldered you into my life. You're going nowhere. Never stop pursuing your dream, *moy talantlivyy drug*. (Did Google get it right??)

Mom, I'm convinced it was *your* faithful prayers that touched God's heart most and saw me through the toughest days of this project.

Can one ever thank a mother enough? Plus, what a trooper you are by always being a text away, ready to answer my 1,001 questions about all things Spain. Then there's your seamstress skills. They are a wonder to behold. I love you and am so proud all your many talents!

Karina, my gorgeous friend, thank you for being my Lillian. You were a great sport through the entire cover-image progress, and it was a long one… I'm so in love with the results!

To my street team, my Inspiration Illuminati, and all my book-loving friends and fans: you are my second set of eyes, my extra brains, and a good portion of my heart. I love and appreciate each one of you!

Edna and Ghost Dancer, once again, you've shared your expertise with boundless kindness. I'm *so* looking forward to our journey through Tall Bull and Mink's story.

Jennifer, research trips are always better with you along. We always have a blast! But you've *got* to be glad all my "I have a medical question for you" texts have come to an end. Doctor Buck and I thank you for your knowledge and your endless patience.

A España (y a todos mis amigos españoles): gracias por moldear mi vida y por jugar tan gentilmente el papel de antagonista. De veras que os quiero de todo corazón.

Jim, Seth, Morgan, let's face it: writers be cray-cray. That you so lovingly support my insanity is a testament to your amazingness. I love you all and would be next to nothing without you.

He giveth power to the faint; and to them that have no might he increaseth strength. (Isaiah 40:29)

The LORD'S loving kindnesses indeed never cease, For His compassions never fail. They are new every morning; Great is Your faithfulness. (Lamentations 3:22-23)

Because of Him,

April W Gardner

9 781945 831034